'Then there's Theroux's very considerable body of fiction. Over the course of a long and productive career, he has set his stories in many and various locations, never losing a travel writer's eye for the hard, clear, material detail of the world around him. *The Lower River* is no exception'
Patrick McGrath, *The New York Times Book Review*

'A deeply engrossing narrative about the horrors of personal change and social transformation. No heart of darkness here. In the impoverished Africa Paul Theroux depicts, it's more heartlessness that becomes so oppressive in a novel that sheds light on timeless subjects' NPR

'A beautifully taut portrait of a man at the end of his tether. One of the many admirable things about this novel is that Theroux's affection for the country never slackens. A savage, sometimes shocking story of love lost and won' *Guardian*

'In this hypnotically compelling fiction, he [Theroux] wrestles with questions of good intentions and harsh realities, addressing what may be the central conundrum of Africa: our own influence is the very thing that makes it impossible for us to "save" it. And what does saving it mean, anyway? A gripping and vital novel that reads like Conrad or Greene – in short, a classic' *Booklist*

'A joyful return to Africa turns into a nightmare for the elderly American protagonist of Theroux's extraordinary novel . . . The suspense is enriched by Theroux's loving attention to local customs and his subversive insights . . . Theroux has recaptured the sweep and density of his 1981 masterpiece *The Mosquito Coast*. That's some achievement' *Kirkus Reviews*

'Theroux successfully grafts keen observations about the efficacy of international aid and the nature of nostalgia to a swift-moving narrative through a beautifully described landscape' *Publishers Weekly*

'[Theroux] invests this very twenty-first-century journey into the heart of ennui with a distinctive caustic bite, like the snakes that pop up throughout' Ben Felsenburg, *Metro*

'As you'd expect, there is some terrific writing here. Theroux's senses are always on full alert' John Preston, *Evening Standard*

'The way Theroux heightens the sense of menace is masterful . . . Theroux has never written a better novel than *The Lower River*'
Mark Sanderson, *Sunday Telegraph*

ABOUT THE AUTHOR

Paul Theroux's books include *Dark Star Safari*, *Ghost Train to the Eastern Star*, *Riding the Iron Rooster*, *The Great Railway Bazaar*, *The Elephanta Suite*, *A Dead Hand* and *The Tao of Travel*. *The Mosquito Coast* and *Dr Slaughter* have both been made into successful films. Paul Theroux divides his time between Cape Cod and the Hawaiian islands.

PAUL THEROUX

The Lower River

PENGUIN BOOKS

PENGUIN BOOKS

Published by the Penguin Group
Penguin Books Ltd, 80 Strand, London WC2R ORL, England
Penguin Group (USA) Inc., 375 Hudson Street, New York, New York 10014, USA
Penguin Group (Canada), 90 Eglinton Avenue East, Suite 700, Toronto, Ontario, Canada M4P 2Y3
(a division of Pearson Penguin Canada Inc.)
Penguin Ireland, 25 St Stephen's Green, Dublin 2, Ireland (a division of Penguin Books Ltd)
Penguin Group (Australia), 707 Collins Street, Melbourne, Victoria 3008, Australia
(a division of Pearson Australia Group Pty Ltd)
Penguin Books India Pvt Ltd, 11 Community Centre, Panchsheel Park, New Delhi – 110 017, India
Penguin Group (NZ), 67 Apollo Drive, Rosedale, Auckland 0632, New Zealand
(a division of Pearson New Zealand Ltd)
Penguin Books (South Africa) (Pty) Ltd, Block D, Rosebank Office Park,
181 Jan Smuts Avenue, Parktown North, Gauteng 2193, South Africa

Penguin Books Ltd, Registered Offices: 80 Strand, London WC2R ORL, England

www.penguin.com

First published in the United States of America by Houghton Mifflin Harcourt 2012
First published in Great Britain by Hamish Hamilton 2012
Published in Penguin Books 2013
001

Copyright © Paul Theroux, 2012
All rights reserved

The moral right of the author has been asserted

Printed in Great Britain by Clays Ltd, St Ives plc

ISBN: 978-0-241-95774-5

www.greenpenguin.co.uk

Penguin Books is committed to a sustainable
future for our business, our readers and our planet.
This book is made from Forest Stewardship
Council™ certified paper.

ALWAYS LEARNING   **PEARSON**

I said to him: "I've come—but not for keeps.
But who are you, become so horrible?"
He answers: "Look. I am the one who weeps."

Dante, *The Inferno*, Canto 8 (ll. 34–36)

PART I

Searching for Someone to Miss Me

1

ELLIS HOCK'S WIFE gave him a new phone for his birthday. A smart phone, she said. "And guess what?" She had a coy, ham-actress way of offering presents, often pausing with a needy wink to get his full attention. "It's going to change your life." Hock smiled because he was turning sixty-two, not an age of life-altering shocks but only of subtle diminishments. "It's got a whole bunch of functions," Deena said. It looked frivolous to him, like a costly fragile toy. "And it'll be useful at the store"—Hock's Menswear in Medford Square. His own phone was fine, he said. It was an efficient little fist, with a flip-up lid and one function. "You're going to thank me." He thanked her, but weighed his old phone in his hand, as a contradiction, showing her that his life wasn't changing.

To make her point (her gift-giving could be hostile at times, and this seemed like one of them), Deena kept the new phone but registered it in his name, using his personal email account. After she was signed up, she received his entire year's mail up to that day, all the messages that Hock had received and sent, thousands of them, even the ones he had thought he'd deleted, many of them from women, many of those affectionate, so complete a revelation of his private life that he felt he'd been scalped—worse than scalped, subjected to the dark magic of the sort of *mganga* he had known long ago in Africa, a witch doctor–diviner turning him inside out, the slippery spilled mess of his entrails stinking on the floor. Now he was a man with no secrets, or rather, all his secrets exposed to a woman he'd been married to for thirty-three years, for whom his secrets were painful news.

"Who *are* you?" Deena asked him, a ready-made question she must have heard somewhere—which movie? But it was she who seemed like a stranger, with mad gelatinous eyes, and furious clutching hands holding the new phone like a weapon, her bulgy features fixed on him in a purplish putty-like face of rage. "I'm hurt!" And she did look wounded. Her recklessness roused his pity and made him afraid, as though she'd been drinking.

Hock hesitated, the angry woman demanded to know everything, but really she already knew everything, his most intimate thoughts were all on that phone. She didn't know why, but neither did he. She screamed for details and explanations. "Who is Tina? Who is Janey?" How could he deny what was plainly shown on the screen of his new phone, covert messages, sent and received, that she'd known nothing about? "You snake! You signed them 'love'!"

He saw, first with relief, almost hilarity, then horror, and finally sadness, that nothing in his life was certain now except that his marriage was ending.

He put it down to solitude. He did not want to say loneliness. He owned a men's clothing store, and business had been—you said slow, not bad—for years. The store was failing. The history of the store was the history of his family in Medford, their insertion in the town, their wish to belong. Ellis's grandfather, an Italian immigrant, had been apprenticed to a tailor on his arrival in New York. His first paying job was with the man's cousin, also a tailor, in rural Williamstown, Massachusetts, where he arrived on the train, knowing no English. He helped to make suits for the wealthy college students there. Though he was no older than they were, he knelt beside them, unspooling the tape against their bodies, and shyly spoke their measurements in Italian. Three years of this and then a job as a cutter in a tailor shop in Boston's North End. On his marriage, striking out on his own, he borrowed money from his widowed mother-in-law (who was to live with them until she died) and rented space in Medford Square, opening his own tailor shop.

4

The move to Medford involved another move, more tidying: he became a new man, changing his name from Francesco Falcone to Frank Hock. He had asked a tailor in the North End to translate *falcone,* and the man had said "hawk," in the local way, and the scarcely literate man had written it in tailor's chalk on a remnant of cloth, spelling it as he heard it. This was announced on a sign: *Hock's Tailors.* Frank became known as a master tailor, with bolts of fine-quality woolen cloth, and linen, and silk, and Egyptian cotton, stacked on his shelves. He smoked cigars as he sewed and, still only in his thirties, employed two assistants as cutters and for basting. His wife, Angelina, bore him three sons, the eldest baptized Andrea, called Andrew, whom he designated as his apprentice. Business was good, and Frank Hock so frugal he saved enough to buy his shop and eventually the whole building. He had income from the tenants on the upper floors and from the other shops, including a Chinese laundry, Yee's, next door. Joe Yee pressed the finished suits and gave him a red box of dried lychees every Christmas.

When Andrew Hock returned from the Second World War, Medford Square began to modernize. Old Frank turned the business over to Andrew, who had worked alongside his father. But Andrew had no interest in the fussy drudgery of tailoring. Plagued with arthritis in his hands, the old man retired. Andrew sold the building and bought a premises in a newly built row of stores on Riverside Avenue—the Mystic River ran just behind it—and started Hock's Menswear, as an improvement on Frank's tailor shop on Salem Street.

Ellis was born the year after Hock's Menswear opened, and later he, too, worked in the store throughout high school most afternoons, tramping the foot pedal and bringing down the lid of the pressing machine in the basement tailor shop, with the tailor Jack Azanow, a Russian immigrant. Ellis also buffed shoes and folded shirts and rearranged the jackets after customers fingered them, milking the sleeves—his father's expression. Now and then he made a sale. Christmases were busy, and festive with the frantic pleasure of people looking for presents, spending more money than usual, asking for the item to be gift-wrapped, another of Ellis's jobs. The activity of the store at this season, and Easter, and

Father's Day—the vitality of it, the obvious profit—almost convinced him that he might make a career of the business. But the certainty of it alarmed him like a life sentence. He hated the notion of confinement in the store, but what was the alternative?

On graduation from Boston University, a biology major, facing the draft—Vietnam—he applied to join the Peace Corps and was accepted. He was sent to a country he'd never heard of, Nyasaland, soon to be the independent Republic of Malawi, and became a teacher at a bush school in a district known as the Lower River. There was something mystical in the name, as though it was an underworld tributary of the River Styx—distant and dark. But "lower" meant only south, and the river was obscured by two great swamps, one called the Elephant Marsh, the other one the Dinde.

He was happy in the Lower River, utterly disconnected from home, and even from the country's capital, on this unknown and unregarded riverbank, where he lived in the village of Malabo on his own as a schoolteacher, the only foreigner; supremely happy.

After two years, he re-upped for another two years, and one afternoon toward the end of his fourth year, a message was delivered to him by a consular driver in a Land Rover, a telegram that had been received by the U.S. consulate: *For Ellis Hock at Malabo. Dad very ill. Please call.* There was no phone in the village, and the trunk line at the boma, the district's headquarters, was not working. Hock rode back to Blantyre in the Land Rover, and there, on the consul's own phone, he spoke to his tearful mother.

He had been so content he had never grappled with the detail of leaving the Lower River, and yet, two days after receiving the message he was on a plane to Rhodesia, and by separate laborious legs, to Nairobi, London, New York, and Boston. Finally back in Medford, he was seated at his father's hospital bedside.

His father beamed with surprise when he saw him, as though Ellis's return was a coincidence, nothing to do with his failing health. They kissed, they held hands, and less than two weeks later, struggling to breathe, Ellis hugging the old man's limp body, his father died. It was three in the morning; his mother had gone home to sleep.

"Are you all right?" the night nurse asked, after she confirmed that his father had drawn his last breath.

"Yes," Ellis said, and mocked himself for the lie. But he was too fearful of telling the truth, because he was himself dying from misery.

He went home, and when she woke at seven he told his mother, who wailed. He could not stop weeping. An old friend, Roy Junkins, hearing that he was home from Africa, called the next day. Ellis sobbed as he spoke to him, unable to control himself, but finding no more shame in his tears than if he had been bleeding. And something about that moment—the phone call, the tears—made a greater bond between the two men.

After the funeral, the reading of the will: Hock's Menswear was his. His mother was apportioned a sum of money and the family house.

"Papa wanted you to have the store."

He'd left Africa suddenly—so suddenly it was as if he'd abandoned an irretrievable part of himself there. He'd actually left a whole household: his cook and all his belongings, clothes, binoculars, shortwave radio, his pet snakes in baskets and cages. What he'd brought home was what had fitted in one suitcase.

He was now, aged twenty-six, the sole owner of Hock's Menswear. He had employees—salesmen, the tailor Azanow, a woman who kept the books—and loyal customers. Within a few years he married Deena, and not much more than a year later Deena gave birth to a daughter, Claudia, whom they called Chicky.

The life sentence he had once feared, he was now serving: the family business, his wife, his child, his house in the Lawrence Estates, inherited from his mother after she died. Every day except Sunday he drove to the store at eight, parked behind it, facing the Mystic River, checked the inventory and deliveries with Les Armstrong and Mike Corbett, and opened at nine. At noon, a sandwich at Savage's, the deli across Riverside Avenue; after lunch, the store. Sometimes Les or Mike reminisced about their years in the army, in dreamy voices, but they were always talking about war. Ellis knew how they felt, but didn't mention Africa except to his friend Roy, who sometimes dropped in. At five-thirty, when Les and the others left, he locked the front door and went home to dinner.

It was the life that many people led, and luckier than most. Having a men's store in Medford Square made his work also social, and selling expensive clothes meant he dressed well.

Over thirty years of this. He rarely took a vacation, though Deena rented a cottage at the Cape in the summer. He drove down on Saturday evenings to spend Sunday with her and Chicky. And after her parents moved to Florida, Deena spent weeks with them. Chicky grew up, graduated from Emerson College, got married, and bought a condo in Belmont.

Nothing would ever change, he felt. Yet changes came, first as whispers, then as facts. Business slackened, Medford Square changed, its texture fraying, a Vietnamese restaurant displacing Savage's Deli, then the closing of Woolworth's and Thom McAn. The shoe menders and the laundry and the TV repairers vanished, and the worst sign of all, some storefronts were empty, some windows broken. The old bakery that had sold fresh bread was now a donut shop, another chain. A new mall at Wellington Circle with large department stores and many smaller stores was now the place to shop. Hock's Menswear was quieter, but still dignified, which made it seem sadder, like the relic the tailor shop had been—a men's clothing store in a city center that was shrunken and obsolete.

But the building—the real estate—was his equity. Ellis saw a time, not far off, when he would sell the premises and live in retirement on the proceeds. In the meantime, he kept to his hours, eight to five-thirty. He waited on customers himself, as he had always done, to set an example, simply to talk, to listen, to hear about other people's lives, their experiences in the world beyond the front door of Hock's. With only one other salesman these days he did this more often, and liked it, in fact looked forward to talking with customers, whose experiences became his.

He knew the business was doomed, but talk kept it alive, as conversation with a bedridden invalid offers the illusion of hope. The malls and the big chain stores, blessed with space and inventory, prospered because they employed few clerks, or sales associates as they were now called. Hock's was the sort of store where clerk and customer discussed the color of a tie, the style of a suit, the drape of a coat, the fit of a sweater. "It's meant to be a bit roomy" and "This topcoat isn't as dressy as that one." Nor did the newer stores offer Hock's quality—Scottish tweeds, English shirts, argyle socks, Irish knitwear, Italian leather goods, even Italian fedoras, and shoes from the last great shoemakers in the United States. Hock's still sold vests, cravats, and Tyrolean hats in velour, with a twist of feathers in the hatband. Quality was suggested in the very words for the merchandise—the apparel, rather: hosiery, slacks, knitwear; a vest was a weskit.

Every transaction was a conversation, sometimes lengthy, about the finish of the fabric, the weather, the state of the world. This human touch, the talk, relieved the gloom of the empty store and took the curse off it. The customer was usually an older man in search of a tie or a good shirt or a sport coat. But often a woman was looking for a present for her husband, or her father or brother. Ellis detained them with his talk, explaining the possible choices. "These socks wear like iron" and "This shirt is Sea Island cotton—the best" and "This camel's hair will actually get more comfortable with age, softer with each dry cleaning."

In the past eight or ten years he'd asked the likelier ones, women mostly, "Do we have your email address on file?" As a result he found himself in occasional touch, clarifying, offering suggestions for a new purchase, describing sale items, often adding a personal note, a line or two, mildly flirtatious. They had bought clothes for trips; he asked about those trips. This was his early-morning activity, on his office computer, when he was alone, feeling small in his solitude, to lift his spirits, so he could face the banality of the day. The harmless whispers soothed him, eased some hunger in his heart, not sex but an obscure yearning. Many women responded in the same spirit: a cheerful word was welcome to them.

Over the past few years these email messages had come to represent a constant in his life, a narrative of friendships, glowing in warmth, inspiring confidences, private allusions, requests for help or advice. But since he met the women only when they came into the store, which was rare, these were safe, no more than inconclusive whispers in the dark, though compared to the monotony of his storekeeper's day, they were like the breath of rapture.

There were about twenty or thirty such women whom he'd befriended this way, various ages, near and far, and these included old friends, his high school sweetheart and senior prom date. Still living in the town where he'd been born, he was saturated with the place. He'd been away for only those four years in Africa, as a young teacher in the district of the Lower River.

When Deena showed him the full year of his email he was more shocked by its density than by the warmth of his confidences—though he was taken aback by glimpses of what he'd written. Writing was a way of forgetting, yet now it was all returned to him and he was reminded of everything he'd said. He did not know that a phone, even a high-tech computer-like device like that, could access so many messages, ones that he'd sent and received, twelve months of them, including ones that he'd deleted (which was most of them), that he'd believed, having dragged them to the trash-basket icon, were gone forever.

But they reappeared, arriving in a long unsorted list, a chronicle of his unerasable past, much of which he'd forgotten. And so the interrogation began, Deena saying, "I want to know everything"—another movie line? She held his entire memory in her hand, his secret history of the past year, and so, "Who is Rosie?" and "Tell me about Vickie."

He was mute with embarrassment and anger. Ashamed, appalled, he could not account for the number of messages or explain his tone of flirtatious encouragement, his intimacies to strangers, all the irrelevant detail. He talked to them about his day, about their travel, about books, about his childhood; and they did the same, relating their own stories.

"What is your problem, Ellis!"

He didn't know. He bowed his head, more to protect himself from her hitting him than in atonement. From the moment he got home from work, for a month or more, he and Deena argued. Her last words to him in bed at night were hisses of recrimination. And when he woke, yawning, slipping from a precarious farcical dream, but before he could recall the email crisis, she began again, clanging at him, her tongue like the clapper of a bell, her finger in his face, shrieking that she'd been betrayed. Some mornings, after a night of furious arguing, the back-and-forth of pleading and abuse, he woke half demented, his head hurting as though with an acute alcoholic hangover, and couldn't work.

Deena demanded detail, but the few scraps he offered only angered her more; and she was unforgiving, so what was the point? It all seemed useless, a howl of pain. She was a yelling policeman who'd caught him red-handed in a crime, not yelling for the truth—she knew it all—but because she was in the right, wishing only to hurt and humiliate him, to see him squirm, to make him suffer.

He did suffer, and he saw that she was suffering too, in greater pain than he was, because she was the injured party. But he knew what was at the end of it. It really was like theater; she needed to inhabit every aspect of her role, to weary herself and him with the sorting of this trash heap of teasing confidences, and when he was sufficiently punished, the ending was inevitable.

They began sessions with a marriage counselor, who called himself Doctor Bob, a pleasant middle-aged man with a psychology degree, a professorial manner, and conventional college clothes—tweed jacket, button-down shirt, khaki pants, and loafers, probably bought at one of the mall outlets, Ellis thought. What bothered Ellis and Deena as much as the actual sessions were the chance encounters with one or another of Doctor Bob's clients, someone troubled—drugs? alcohol?—leaving the office as they arrived, or someone similarly anguished, head bowed, on the couch in the waiting room as they left.

Doctor Bob listened carefully in the first session and said that such a discovery of compromising emails was not unusual. "I'm seeing three other couples in your position. In each case, the man is the collector." He didn't assign blame, he was sympathetic to both Ellis and Deena, and at one point near the end of the first hour, as Deena sat tearful with her hands on her lap and Ellis wondered why he had sent so many emails, Doctor Bob could be heard puzzling, saying softly, "How does it go? That old song, 'strumming my pain with his fingers'—something about being flushed with fever, something-something by the crowd," then raising his voice, but still in a confiding, lounge-singer croon, "'I felt he found my letters, and read each one out loud . . .'"

"Please," Deena said, "this isn't funny."

"I'm trying to put your situation into context," Doctor Bob said. "There are other precedents. After his wife poked into his private letters, Tolstoy ran away from home. And died in a railway station. He was eighty-two."

In the next session Doctor Bob asked blunt questions and acted, it seemed to Ellis, like a referee. He did not sing again. They returned for more sessions.

But instead of repairing the marriage or calming Deena, the counseling made matters worse by offering an occasion to air old grievances, conflicts that, before starting the sessions, Ellis had decided to live with. But why not mention them, the disappointments, the lapses, the rough patches that had remained unresolved? Long-buried resentments were disinterred and argued over. With a referee, a witness, they could be blunt.

Doctor Bob nodded and smiled gently, like the friendly old-fashioned priest at Saint Ray's, Father Furty—reformed drinker, always sympathetic. He let Deena talk, then Ellis, both of them pleading with him to see their point of view, the validity of their claim, as though deciding "whose ball?" in a significant fumble.

He said, "What I'm hearing is . . ."

Letdowns they'd never mentioned were now mentioned, and the sessions became acrimonious: Deena's friends, her absences; Ellis's coldness, his absences.

"You've been leading separate lives . . ."

Ellis thought, Yes, maybe that's why my life has been bearable. It was not a pleasure but a relief to go to work in the morning. Monotony was a harmless friend. He dreaded Sundays at home; most of all he hated vacations. Ellis had never met anyone who hated vacations, so he kept this feeling to himself.

Though Deena had that one issue on her mind—the business about the numerous and overfond emails—this dispute stirred Ellis into defending himself with memories of other disputes.

"I want to know why you were emailing those women," Deena said.

Doctor Bob smiled at Ellis, who said, "I'd like to know that myself."

"My name is nowhere in those emails. You never mention you're married. I don't exist. *Why?*"

Ellis said in a wondering tone that he didn't know.

Pleading with Doctor Bob, Deena said, "He tells them what he's reading! He tells them what he has for lunch!"

By then, about a month into counseling (and the store suffered by his absences), all contact with the women in the emails had been broken off. Deena still had possession of the phone, monitoring it every day. She clutched it in disgust, as though it was Ellis himself she was holding, her hatred apparent; and Ellis hated the sight of the thing too.

Ellis, at Deena's insistence, got a new email address, and used it only for business. Without his contact with those women, he was numb, mute, friendless, but still could not explain the emails he'd sent, his befriending the many women, the strange amorous inquiring tone. To one he had said, "You are the sort of woman I'd take into the African bush," and squirmed at the memory.

"I guess I was interested in their lives," he said. "I was curious. There was a story line to the way they lived, an unfolding narrative. I've always liked hearing people's stories."

With a pocket-stuffing gesture, Doctor Bob asked, "But were you keeping them in your back pocket for later, something to act on?"

Ellis said no, but he was not sure. The solitude of the store, the uncertainty of the business, had set him dreaming. He did not know how to say that to his wife—no longer grief-stricken but enraged—and the nodding counselor. Doctor Bob would have said, "Dreaming of what?" And Ellis had no answer.

"Is there something you want to tell your wife?" Doctor Bob said.

Ellis fixed his eyes on Deena's furious face. He said, "You're overplaying your hand."

Shushing her—Deena had begun to object—Doctor Bob spoke to Ellis. "I see you as untethered," and he explained what he meant.

Ellis nodded. The word was perfect for how he felt, unattached, not belonging, drifting in a job he'd taken as a dying wish of his father's, maintaining the family business. But his heart wasn't in it—had never been in it.

When, Doctor Bob asked, had he been happy?

Ellis said, "I used to live in Africa."

"Oh, God," Deena said.

"I meant in your marriage," Doctor Bob said.

Hands together under his chin, prayer-like, Ellis became thoughtful, and tried to recall a distinct time, an event, something joyous, a little glowing tableau of pride and pleasure. But nothing came. It was thirty-three years of ups and downs, too much time to summarize. They were married: years to share, to endure, to negotiate, to overcome. Yes, plenty of happiness—he just could not think of anything specific. Marriage was a journey without an arrival.

Seeing Deena slumped in her chair, waiting out his silence, Ellis grew sad again. Just the way they were sitting apart, burdened by a kind of grief, with the doctor between them, made him miserable. It was as though they were in the presence of a terminal patient, their marriage dying, and it seemed that these last few weeks had been like that, either a deathwatch—this gloom—or a danse macabre, the hysteria at the prospect of the thing ending.

Nor could they hold any kind of coherent conversation without Doctor Bob being present. Ellis saw himself at sixty-two, Deena at sixty, as two old people who'd now, with the death of their marriage, be going their separate ways, pitiable figures bent against a headwind, or worse, with ghastly jollity, talking about "new challenges" and starting again, joining support groups, taking up yoga, gardening, volunteering, charity work, or worse, golf.

The counseling sessions continued, more rancorous, provoking new grievances, driving them further apart. But along with that melancholy vision of separation Ellis saw relief, too, the peacefulness of being alone. He guessed that Deena was feeling the same, because one day after a session, driving home, she seemed to come awake and said, "I want the house. I'm not giving up that house. My kitchen, my closets."

"I could get a condo," Ellis said. "But the business is mine."

"I'll need some money," Deena said, and noticing that Ellis did not react, she added, "A lot of it."

And like that, snatching, each staked a claim. At the suggestion of Doctor Bob they saw a lawyer and divided their assets.

Hearing of this, Chicky said, "What about me?"

"You'll be all right," Ellis said.

"But what if you guys remarry?"

Deena looked at Ellis and laughed, and he responded, laughing too, the first time in months they had shared such a moment of mirth. They stopped, not because they were saddened by the outburst but because the love in their laughter shamed them, reminding them that in their marriage they had known many happy moments like this.

Chicky, bewildered, and made stern by her bewilderment, said, "Dougie's probably going to get laid off. We could use the money. I want my cut now."

"'Cut,'" Ellis said, echoing her word, "of what?"

"Your will," Chicky said.

"I am alive," Ellis said, wide-eyed in indignation.

"But what about when you pass? If you remarry, your new family will get it and I won't get diddly. If I don't get it now, I'll never see it. And look at Ma. She got hers."

Had this conversation not taken place in a sushi bar in Medford Square—another example of the changes in the town—Ellis would have screamed at his daughter and hammered the table with his fist. Later, he was glad that he had remained calm and had only shaken his head at the sullen young woman chewing disgustedly at him. He replayed the conversation that night, at first bitterly, then in a mood of resignation. Let it all end, he thought; let a great whirlwind drive it all away. Then he offered Chicky a lump sum. She asked for more, as he guessed she would, and he gave her the amount he had already decided upon.

Chicky's husband was with her when he handed over the check. Dougie was merely a spectator to the family negotiation—Chicky had always been annoyed that Ellis, refusing to hire him at the store, had said, "What is he good at?"

"I doubt that I'll be seeing much of you from now on," Ellis said, with the solemn resignation of his new role. "I don't think I want to."

"Okay by me," Chicky said.

With her share of the will in her hand, and her back turned, he felt that he was already dead. He was sorry to think that she did not see the pity in this.

Although he moved into a condo on Forest Street—the old high school—he and Deena still saw each other. Formally, sometimes shyly, they went on dates. They were not quite ready to see other people, and even the sessions with Doctor Bob had not affected their fundamental liking for each other. The dates ended with a chaste and usually fumbled kiss, and Ellis was always sad afterward, lonely in his car. He knew that he had caused Deena pain, destroyed her love for him, made her untrusting—perhaps untrusting of all other men. In the secrecy and confidences of his messages, he had betrayed her. He could be kind to her now, but there was no way to amend the past. On some of their dates she sat numb and silent, suffering like a wounded, bewildered animal. He could not think of himself, because he knew the hurt he'd inflicted on her would never heal.

Ellis dreaded the day when Deena would say to him, "I'm seeing someone." He told her how bad business was, and she tried to console him, urging him to sell the building, that the real estate was worth something, that it was an ideal location.

On one of these dates, she gave him the phone—the instrument of their undoing, which now seemed to him like something diabolical. Or had it been a great purifying instrument? Anyway, it had uncovered his entire private life, shown him as sentimental, flirtatious, dreamy, romantic, unfulfilled, yearning. But for what? What did all those emails mean? What in all this emotion was the thing he wanted?

He did not know. He might never know. He was too old to hope for anything more. No momentous thing would ever happen to him. No passion, no great love, no new landscape, no more children, no risk, no drama. The rest of his life would be a withdrawal, a growing smaller, until finally he would be forgotten. The name on his store would be replaced by another. His marriage was over, his daughter was gone. He could not remember much of the marriage, and yet he missed the eventlessness of it, his old routines, the monotony that had seemed like a friend. There was a certainty in routine; the torpor it induced in him was a comfort.

The day after Hock got the phone back he went to the store, keeping the thing in his pocket the whole day. After he locked up for the night (he observed himself doing this, as if in a ritual), he walked to the edge of the parking lot, where beyond a fence the Mystic River brimmed, and flung the phone and watched it plop and sink and drown in the water that was moody under the dark sky.

2

T O RELIEVE HIS EYES, to clear his head, Hock was standing
in the open doorway at the back of his store, facing the Mystic River flowing past the parking lot, the water dark under
the drizzly clouds, lumpy with debris from upstream. A week
of heavy rain had filled the lakes and sent a torrent down—the
river swelled at its banks, rippling like the muscles of a hungry
snake. The river that had always consoled him with its movement
was a special comfort now that he was in greater need of consolation; the water and that debris swept past the back of the store and
poured into the harbor, into the ocean, into the world, reminding
him that his phone was gone, the corpse of it, sluiced into the sea.

Today he saw Jerry Frezza sidling between parked cars, wiping
droplets from his face. Jerry had a tight smile and a jaunty upright
stride; even in the rain Hock could tell that his friend had something on his mind.

Jerry saw him and said, "I've been trying to call you on your
cell. What's with your phone?"

"I don't have one anymore."

"How do you keep in touch?"

"I don't," Hock said. "You can call the store number, though."
He was going to tell him that in another month the store would be
closing, but he resisted. He didn't want to discuss it, he didn't want
sympathy, he hated the thought of the obvious question, What will
you do now? So he smiled and said, "What's up?"

Jerry said, "You know snakes, right? From when you were in
Africa?"

On the Lower River, at Malabo, Hock had been the *mzungu* from America; in the Medford store, he was the man who'd lived in Africa. The sunny word "Africa," spoken on a wet November day in Medford Square, seemed almost blasphemous and made him rueful again.

The Lower River in his time had been a nest of snakes. He was known for not fearing them; he was feared for daring to catch them. One of Hock's long-ago names in the village was Mwamuna wa Njoka, Snake Man. So he said, "What's the problem?"

"This crazy mama I know, Teya, over in Somerville, has a humongous snake she keeps as a pet, python or something. Get this, she actually sleeps with it."

Hock considered the stupidity of this, and then said, "They like the warmth. How big?"

"Yay big," Jerry said, flinging out his arms. "Almost as big as she is. What do you think?"

"I think, don't be cute. Put it into a cage. But it should really be in an equatorial forest. Ask her if it makes any noise—like a blowing sound."

Not long after that, nearer Thanksgiving, Jerry stopped in again and said to Hock, "You were right. It sucks in air and goofs it out."

"If it's vocalizing, it's a python. Other snakes don't make any sounds."

"Whatever. I told her what you said, but she feels sorry for the snake. The thing's not eating. She gave it food, but it won't touch it."

"Probably it would eat if it was left alone. But they can go months without eating." Hock was folding sweaters that a man had decided not to buy. "She still sleeping with the snake?"

Jerry nodded. "Whack job, right?"

But standing at the store counter on this November day of denuded trees under a brown sky, Hock thought of Malabo, of the snakes he'd collected: green mambas, black mambas, spitting cobras, the swimming sun snake, the egg-eating wolf snake, the boomslang *mbobo*, the puff adder, and the *nsato*, the rock python, which could have been the woman's pet snake. The villagers feared them and would kill a snake on sight. If a traveler encoun-

19

tered a snake at the start of a journey, he would return home. Because of these fears Hock developed an interest and made a study, to set himself apart, so he would be known as something more than a *mzungu*. One of the derivations of *mzungu* was "spirit," but the word meant "white man." He kept some snakes in baskets, and fed them lizards and grasshoppers and mice, and he released them in places where they'd be safe to breed.

Jerry called the store the next day. He did not offer a preamble because their only subject lately had been the woman with the pet snake. He said, "She wants to know why the snake is acting weird. It still isn't eating. It lies beside her, flattening itself."

"Did you say flattening itself?" Hock said. "Listen, get her on the phone. Tell her to put the snake in a cage immediately."

"Why are you shouting?"

Only then had Hock realized that his voice had risen almost to a scream. In this same shrill pitch he said, "The snake is *measuring* her. It's getting ready to eat her!"

He knew snakes. Jerry's story of the woman made him miss Africa—not the continent, which was vast and unfinished and unfathomable, but his hut in Malabo, on the Lower River in Malawi.

After he hung up, he called Jerry back and said, "Where is she? That woman's in trouble."

The house was a wood-frame three-decker on a side street in Somerville, from the outside like every other house on the block, from the inside a tangle of drapes and silken gold-fringed banners, highly colored, smelling of a sickly fragrance, perhaps incense, or from the candles flickering like vigil lights, their fumes the pulpy flavor of fruit, the plush bite of spices. The place was shadowy, as though furnished for some sort of ritual, a séance or spiritual exercise. A small cluttered bulb-lit shrine was fixed to one wall—a dark idol, a dish of grapes and plums before it. The rooms were warm with the aroma of sweet cake crumbs on this raw day.

A white-faced woman opened the door, holding it ajar just a few inches, looking afraid, until she recognized Jerry, and then she smiled and let them in. Her dark hair was uncombed and looked clawed and nagged at.

"Where is it?" Hock asked.

"Is this your friend?" the woman said, peering with her flat smile.

"Teya—this is Ellis," Jerry said.

She spelled her name and said, "American Indian. I wish I would have known you were coming."

Hock said, "The snake—did you secure it?"

"Mind taking your shoes off?" the woman said.

She herself was wearing sandals, with silver rings on her toes, and over her shoulders a robe that Hock knew to be polyester and not silk. She was older and slightly plumper than he expected. "Spaced out" and "hippie" had made him imagine someone girl-ish, but the woman was perhaps fifty. Her left wrist (upright, she was clutching a hank of her hair) was tattooed with a pattern of small dots.

When Hock put his mesh box down, she said, "Like I need an-other pet." But she was pleased and smiled at the small sniffing guinea pig.

Stepping inside, barefoot, his foot-sole cushioned by carpets, he could not see much in the candlelit room. Yet through the furry fruitiness of incense and hot wax he could smell the snake—a dis-tinct tang of flaking scales, the sourness of urine and smashed egg-shells, a rank odor of earth and warmth.

"I've been doing a ton of washing," the woman said. "Just back from Vermont."

"The snake's in a cage, right?"

"Witch Camp," the woman said. She bent down and put her face against the mesh of the box and clucked loudly at the guinea pig.

"Witch Camp. What did I tell you?" Jerry said, pleased with himself.

"Am I wasting my time?" Hock said. "Where is this bad boy?"

"I was just going to say, the Mud Ritual," the woman said. "It was insane."

She had turned and was shuffling in her sandals across the room, to an adjoining room, where parasols hung upside down from the ceiling, the walls draped with scarves and gilt-edged ban-ners and more votive lights.

"In here," she said.

He saw a glass-sided fish tank against a wall, some sawdust and wood shavings heaped against one end, and a snake inside that he immediately recognized as a rock python. A heavy board served as the lid of the tank. And because this room was not as warm as the first one, the snake lay coiled like a rope on the deck of a ship, its head tucked under its thickest coil.

"*Nsato — Python sebae*," Hock said.

Jerry said to the woman, "What did I tell you?"

"Jerry told me about him being dangerous. I put him in here just before I went to Vermont."

"You didn't leave him any food?"

"He wasn't interested." She had taken possession of the mesh box, and now she lifted it and smiled at the guinea pig. "But this little guy looks hungry."

Hock unhooked the small door of the box and reached in. He held the squirming guinea pig, which was kicking its short legs. In one motion he lifted the lid of the fish tank and dropped in the guinea pig. The small creature scampered to a corner, darting against the glass, skidding in the thickness of wood shavings, awkwardly tugging its body as though too fat and top-heavy for its short legs.

The snake did not move — that is, it remained coiled. But then its pear-shaped head tilted, its yellow eyes flickered and widened, and it seemed almost imperceptibly to swell, like an inner tube inflated by a hand pump, fattening, tightening, filling its scaly thickness, as though it was visibly thinking.

"I had him drinking milk," the woman said, looking closer at the panicky guinea pig, the enlarging snake.

"They like their food a little more animated than that," Hock said.

She was peering in, blinking, her nose almost touching the glass. "Maybe they'll be friends."

"How long have you had him?"

"Couple of months."

"They can go months without eating."

"After the milk, he wasn't interested. He let me hold him. He's bigger than he looks."

"They can grow to twenty-four feet."

"He just—like Jerry told you—flattened himself next to me."

"Because he was planning to eat you," Hock said. "Seeing if you'd fit."

"Me?" The woman laughed, moving her body heavily, as if to show her plumpness, to emphasize the absurdity of what Hock had just said.

"You'd be surprised at what a snake like that can fit into its mouth."

The woman was smiling anxiously at the twitching guinea pig, the staring snake. She said, "You actually think they're going to get along together in that cage?"

Hock frowned and said, "Let's leave them to make friends. Okay?"

"Want some herbal tea?"

"Tell us about Witch Camp," Jerry said.

She led them through the room with the incense and the drapes and the shrine to a small kitchen, and they sat at a table while she heated a kettle of water and made tea, crumbling some tiny black twigs into the pot.

"This is very cleansing. It sort of scours the toxins out of your system and heals your linings."

And as she went on describing the purifying powers of the tea, Hock reflected on the untidiness of the room, the pots and dishes in the sink, the crumbs on the table, the dull gleam of the sticky toaster imprinted with a film of grease. And the woman herself, dark hair, pale skin, her heavily made-up eyes—blue eye shadow—squinting from her puffy face. She smiled wearily and shook her head.

"The Mud Ritual, like I was saying—insane. People were copulating. I got mud in my hair and my clothes were filthy. I've been doing laundry for two days."

"Copulating?" Jerry was beaming at her.

"In the mud," she said. "Big turn-on. But not for me. Some of these people just take advantage. The things they put in their bodies! One of them tosses a beer can onto the ground and I goes, 'This is the earth. It's your mother!'"

"Maybe a little chilly up in Vermont for getting tagged in the mud?" Jerry said, and he nodded at Hock.

23

"We'd just done a sweat," she said. "Sweat lodge?"

"That's some crazy stuff."

"A few got wacky-vaced."

Jerry said, "Excuse me?"

"Like medevaced. But they were toasted, I think on mushrooms."

Hock was thinking of the snake, the poor thing captive in her apartment, just another artifact, part of the scene. Yet it was a great coiled cable of muscle, glittering, black and yellowish on its dorsum, with a glossy iridescent bluey sheen all over its upper scales, the pupil of its eye vertically elliptical. It simply did not belong here in a suburb of Boston.

The woman was telling Jerry about the Mud Ritual—Jerry giggling. Hock said, "I want to have another look."

"At Naga?"

"That what you call him?"

"It's Hindu. Naga the snake."

"Naga's the cobra," Hock said. "This is *nsato*. That's what he's called in the Lower River."

"Your friend's kind of interesting," the woman was saying, as Hock left the kitchen and walked through the shrine room to the back room where the snake lay coiled in the fish tank. Now the python was only partly coiled. Its sculpted head was upraised, its neck looped in a tight and thickened *S*.

In a whisper behind him, the woman said, "How's my baby?"

Hock lifted his hand to quiet her. He knew that the snake's posture, the drawn-back *S*, meant it was preparing to strike. The small guinea pig had flattened itself into a corner, where it was twitching miserably.

"Are you sure you want to see this?" Hock said in a low voice.

Before the woman could reply, the snake flung its head forward, jaws agape, and crushed the guinea pig against the glass wall of the tank. The jaws closed, but only slightly, and a pale froth brimmed at the edges of its mouth.

The woman was whimpering, Jerry behind her, softly cursing in awe.

"Can you get him out?"

"It's caught, like a fish on a hook—the teeth are recurved,

slanted back. The more the thing struggles, the more he's pinned. Shall we give them a little privacy?"

"I didn't need to see that," the woman said.

"That was awesome," Jerry said. "Snake was hungry."

"Do you mind if I come back sometime?" Hock asked.

"Give me your cell-phone number. I might be doing my puja. Like praying."

"No cell phone," Jerry said.

The woman said, "That's nice. That's righteous."

Back at the store, Hock thought only of the snake, especially its uncoiling and lengthening across the fish tank to strike at the guinea pig—the woman's gasp, Jerry's curses.

He called her a few days later. When he visited again he brought a mouse in a small box, which he kept in his pocket. The rooms were tidier, even neat in places, more candles had been lit. Teya—he remembered the name—was dressed in a dark smock-like dress, her hair drawn back, fixed with an ornate comb, gold hoops on her ears, bangles on her wrists.

Hock wanted to see the snake, but she insisted on serving him tea first. She was more relaxed, kinder-seeming, and yet was watching him closely.

"Hock—like the store?"

"You know the place?"

"I used to get the bus from there," she said. "My father wore clothes like that. Overcoats with velvet collars."

"Chesterfield."

"Yeah. And always a hat. He'd wear a cravat sometimes. I mean, lace-curtain Irish, but he knew how to dress. He was a comptroller over at Raytheon, terrific with figures. He's retired but he still does consulting. Maybe you could use him."

Hock said, "I'm selling the business."

"Bummer."

"It's served its purpose. It's over now. It's dated, like chester-fields and cravats." When the woman said nothing, he went on, "Things change, things end, things die. Even love."

"What are you going to do with all that money?"

"Ask my ex-wife."

"Money is trouble," she said. "Are you dating?"

The word had always made him smile. "My ex-wife and I go out now and then."

"You should consider massages, maybe detoxing."

"I might take a trip," Hock said, but until he spoke the words, the whole thought had never entered his head. He was giving voice to the shred of a feeling he had, a buried sense that he should go away. "You notice the snake's been sleeping more?"

"Definitely. No funny business."

"Digesting," Hock said. "You like it here?"

"*Comme çi, comme ça.* All the colleges in the area. Kids everywhere — Tufts, Harvard, MIT, kids, grad students, foreigners."

"It makes for variety."

"Know what? I really don't think so."

Hock gestured, turning his hands, encouraging her to explain.

"Whenever you're near a college, there's always this smell of pizza. It's the students. And coffee shops with kids and their laptops. And their bad skin. And the way they walk. There's a typical student walk, because their parents give them money to let them go on being kids and having bad posture. I should move. Maybe move to Medford."

Hock visited more frequently, and the woman who seemed at first so easy to mock, so easy to dismiss for her robe and her rings and her New Age jargon, became a whole person. It turned out that she had an ex-husband, and a daughter of twenty-something. "She doesn't want to be my friend," Teya said, smiling sadly.

"I've got one of those," Hock said.

"I was giving her money and she used it to self-medicate. For drugs."

Teya worked part-time as a massage therapist — she gently corrected Hock when he used the term "masseuse" — and she was a volunteer at a hospice near Davis Square, doing physiotherapy, "to remind them that they're alive."

Hock, alert for decades to the way people dressed, sizing up customers who wandered into the store, guessing at what they might buy — always attentive to details of clothing — noticed that Teya was making an effort for him. And it was odd, because he couldn't tell her that he was visiting not to see her and listen to her stories of her daughter, or the hospice, or her plans to travel, but only because he wanted to see the rock python.

He always brought something the python might eat, a pale pop-eyed mouse, a wobbly frog, a pair of baby guinea pigs—hairless, pink, mottled skin. Sometimes the snake pounced, its jaws wide open, but one mouse survived in the glass tank for a week or more, burrowing in the wood shavings, believing it was hidden.

Teya cooked meals for Hock, always vegetarian, dishes of lentils, curried cauliflower, a stir-fry, and she used these meals as an occasion to tell stories, speaking softly in a monotone, deaf to any interruption, oblivious to his reaction or any comment. Hock would have found her maddening, except the stories were unusual.

In one she'd broken her toe ("I hit it on the stone lingam in the puja room") and was prescribed Vicodin as a painkiller. She found that her daughter was secretly stealing her pills—so many that Teya still had pain but no medicine, and the added pain of her daughter's betrayal. Hock mentioned his daughter again, but Teya spoke over him, not hearing, changing the subject to folk dancing—Thai dancing—saying she had learned to bend her fingers back, Siamese-style. And there was an African student down the street who wore a skullcap and blue shawl and was stalking her. He was from Sudan, with teeth missing and ornamental scars on his face, and one day he left a pair of red shoes for her at her doorway upstairs—how had he gotten in? The police didn't take it seriously, though the African was tall and very scary. She grew herbs, she grew marijuana plants, and explained that some weed was male and some female.

Hock was grateful; her stories were a helpful distraction to him in the last weeks of his business, which would close after Christmas. He even mentioned that. She didn't listen. Jerry didn't listen either. But Teya wanted to see him; she smiled gratefully when he showed up. She needed him as a listener. Customers at the store needed him as a listener. All you had to do to be a friend was show up and listen. He found that Teya could go on and on, and the more he listened and said nothing, the more she depended on him. She said he was a good conversationalist and that she liked talking with him, and he said nothing.

Her stories could be alarming. The Sudanese boy who brought her the red shoes was eventually arrested and charged with harassment. "I took out a restraining order on him." But all her sadness was apparent in the stories, and since Hock remained silent, just nodded and encouraged her to continue, he seemed powerful to her, and supportive, not sad at all. He was touched by her telling him how she gave money to charities that worked with orphans in Africa.

Now and then he excused himself and went to the ripe-smelling back room that held the tank with the python. He sat before it in silence, waiting for its eye to open, its tongue to flick, admiring the gleam on its body, its complex coloring, the patterns straggling down its dorsum. And he reflected again on how the poor creature was trapped in a small space—this six-foot python that could move with such sinuous grace across stony ground could not stretch to even half its length in the tank, but lay coiled, half asleep in the wood shavings.

One Saturday morning Hock brought a kitten with him. He had not intended to feed it to the python, though seeing it, Teya said, "Oh, God, no," and snatched the kitten from him and cuddled it, pressing it to her cheek. "Please don't."

He had guessed what her reaction might be, as he watched her nuzzling the small mewling creature.

He said, "I think our friend needs a new home."

Holding the kitten, Teya watched as he shifted the heavy lid of the tank, and he lifted the long tangled snake, one hand pressed behind its head. Then he shook its thick coils into a burlap bag that he'd brought.

That same day he took the python to the Stoneham Zoo, on the far side of Spot Pond from Medford, where he had often gone as a child to see the caged bear and the mountain goat and the coatimundi. He had called in advance to say that he had a python, and he was told that one of the resident pythons had recently died, so this one was welcome.

"Regular meals, a nice clean cage, plenty of water and light," the zookeeper said. "It's why their life span is so short in captivity."

"*Python sebae*," Hock said.

"You're a herpetologist?"

"I know a little. I'm in the clothing business, but before that I was in Africa."

"That's where this guy belongs. Out of his element here."

From that day, instead of visiting Teya, Hock visited the zoo. Teya called the store a few times, and reminded him that she was a licensed massage therapist. But by then the sale of it was final, the new buyer a computer chain. When the Christmas blowout was over, the unsold clothing and all the fixtures were warehoused, the phone disconnected. Now no one could find him, not even Deena.

He spent much of his time at the zoo's Snake House, always on weekdays so he could be alone—no families, no schoolchildren, no one tapping the glass of the snake cages.

The Snake House also contained some loud screeching birds; it was warm, damp most days, the air ripe with the scaly stink of snake and the tang of their piss, of the fat coiled bodies of the snakes in the cages, and the ancient reptilian odors that seemed like the emanations from an old tomb. On these December days in the overheated Snake House, the sun shining through the sky-lights, seeing a thick snake slipping from beneath a boulder to bask on the heated gravel of its cage, Hock would often close his eyes and listen to the birds and inhale the snakes' sharp odors and imagine he was back in Malabo.

3

O N THOSE DAYS at the zoo, in his reverie, Hock remembered the Lower River, the southernmost part of the southern province, the poorest part of a poor country, home of the Sena people. The Sena, a neglected tribe, despised by those who didn't know them, were associated with squalor, cruelty, and incompetence. And his village, Malabo, was so small, just a cluster of huts, a tiny chapel, and a primary school that he'd helped build, that on the rare occasions when he was buying supplies in Zomba or Blantyre, he'd say, "I live in Port Herald," because no one would know his village. In his time, Port Herald was renamed Nsanje, but Malabo remained Malabo, unknown to anyone outside the district.

From Blantyre to Chikwawa, the road south, below the escarpment, was a sliding surface of loose rocks and deep sand, slow in any season and sometimes impassable in the rains. And bypassing Malabo it narrowed to a dead end, at the pinched-off frontier of Mozambique, then known as Portuguese East. Beyond the frontier lay the Zambezi, one of its obscurest reaches, wide and shallow: no bridge, hardly any villages, only dugout canoes piled with contraband that bumped among the sandbanks. The Shire River at Port Herald was a feeder to the Zambezi, thick with goggling hippos and the snouts of crocodiles, and not navigable higher up except by canoe, because of the Elephant Marsh. The marsh had defeated David Livingstone, who famously dismantled his steamer on the riverbank and sent it north in pieces on the heads of his porters.

The floods in the wet season isolated the villages on the Lower

River; the hot season brought temperatures of well over a hundred in the shade. Records were so dire they weren't worth keeping. October the settlers at the boma called the Suicide Month, because of the heat, but November could be even hotter. The land was low-lying and malarial, the Sena people mocked for holding to their traditions of child marriage, polygamy, and witchcraft. The boma at Port Herald had a generator, the district commissioner's house was lit; but two hundred yards away the light faltered against a wall of darkness. One school served the district, yet the fees kept most students away, and the children were needed in the fields. Cotton was one of the crops, rice another, and maize and vegetables were tended in the low-lying *dimbas*, which were always full of snakes. Small girls looked after infants, and small boys helped their fathers fish from the canoes.

Mud huts, thatched roofs, the hot dust holding footprints in powder on narrow paths; and the silence of the solemn sun-baked bush was broken only by the wolf whistles of certain birds and the screech of insects like the howl of one untuned violin string under a dragging bow. In the mornings he was woken by the shapely notes of birdsong.

One of the first sights he'd beheld as a young teacher was a pair of naked children, the smaller one with his head bowed, the girl child delousing his hair, picking through his scalp, an elemental image of intimacy.

The heat meant that the Sena people wore few clothes, the men tattered trousers rolled to their knees, and a ragged shirt was more symbolic than useful. The women, bare-breasted, wore a wrap-around, an *nsalu* or a *chitenje* cloth. Showing your legs was considered immodest; even the men unrolled their trousers whenever they were away from the river. But they wore only scraps of clothing in the Nyau dance, sometimes a monthly event, which went on all night, the *mganga* wearing a grotesque mask, the drumming growing more frenzied as dawn approached. That ceremony was a way of easing bewitchments. Initiations were another thing. The Sena men initiated the young girls, and in a hyena's pelt, a man would engage in an elaborate defloration. When a man died, his earthly goods were dispersed—plucked from his hut by neighbors—and within a day or two the widow had sex with her brother-in-law beside her husband's corpse, and thus became his junior wife. Women were forbidden from whistling, from drinking beer, from eating eggs, from owning a dugout. The Lower River was populous, but beyond the boma no building was more than six feet high, and so the bush seemed uninhabited, or just more mud; many of the termite mounds were taller and more symmetrical. A shoe was a novelty; even the word for shoe, *nsopato,* came from the Portuguese, as *nsalu* was derived from sari.

The Sena people were small, slender, delicate, and violent only when they were bingeing. They did not seem strong, yet they could paddle all day against the current of the river, especially when they were fortified by puffs of *chamba,* the local form of marijuana.

Most meals were the same: porridge of *nsima,* steamed white corn flour, or rice; greens stewed to a sliminess; and sometimes a small river fish or a segment of roasted eel. Chicken was served on feast days, but there were few feasts.

The Sena lived in a web of beliefs. The Lower River was thick with spirits, *mfiti,* most of them vindictive specters of the dead, restless in their malevolence. Nothing happened without a reason. A tree fell because someone wished it down, a thatched roof caught fire because someone prayed for the flames. Disease, disfigurement, a bad harvest, a broken bone, a stillborn infant—all were caused by human agency, the witch in the next hut or the next village, or the *mfiti* representing an avenging soul. Now and then a Belgian priest visited, a White Father from the mission at Thyolo, and said Mass in starched magnificence. He had a little medical skill and jars of pills that he distributed as though giving communion. "*L'Afrique profonde,*" he once confided to Hock, then left on his motorcycle.

The year turned on two parallel activities: for the men, the rising of the river and their opportunities to fish; for the women, the sequence of planting the garden *dimbas,* rice and maize and cotton—preparing the land in October, putting the seeds in before the rains, weeding for months, and the harvest in June. Then the grinding of the maize in the hand-cranked mills, and later the slashing and burning of the fields, so dramatic inland, the low hills alight, the snakes of flame thrashing on the slopes.

In his first year, village life had seemed a struggle to Hock. But the effort had a point; and for periods, sometimes a month or more, especially after the harvest, there was nothing for the men to do but drink the yeasty village beer they called *mowa,* or *nipa,* the gin distilled from sprouted maize or banana peels. In those quieter months, the women brought their corn to be milled into flour and gathered firewood. The children looked after each other, and older girls carried the babies.

Bhagat's General Store at the boma stocked Sunlight soap, Koo ketchup, cooking oil, bottles of Lion Lager, cigarettes sold singly, and loose tobacco and tea. But few people had more than a few tickeys, the thin gray threepence pieces that bought two cigarettes. The market stalls sold vegetables and rice, smoked fish and cassava. Not much of anything, but in all the time he'd lived there, Hock decided that you didn't need any more than that.

At first glance, the Lower River seemed to have no population, because people stayed out of the sun. They crept in the shadows, in the sheltered courtyards of their huts, under the trees, in the elephant grass, on the riverbank.

After a year, Hock understood the inflections of the weather. It was not the stifling, squalid place of its reputation; it was dense and subtle. The heat enlivened him. The smells were of wood smoke and stagnation and the perfume of the water hyacinths in the river, sweetish with decay; the sun-heated dust was like talcum.

Hidden in the high grass was Malabo, inland from the river in Ndamera District, on the road to Lutwe. To the south, the tall trees in the distance were the mopane forests in Mozambique. By tradition, the people of Malabo were allowed to keep boats on the landing near Marka—one of them, a large hollowed-out log, could hold six paddlers. It was a day's paddle through the Dinde Marsh to the main channel of the Shire, and three days to the Zambezi.

Teaching at the primary school he'd helped to build at Malabo, Hock had become popular in the district, and when the local member of parliament paid a visit to Nsanje, he'd asked to meet Hock, to verify what the villagers had told him—their requests for a clinic and road mending and a new roof for the market. The MP had a second family in Zomba, so he seldom visited the district.

Hock served as a counselor, wrote letters for the villagers, sent messages, and read letters for those villagers who couldn't read, whispering the words for the sake of privacy. All the languages in the region were written phonetically, so he could convey the meaning even when he didn't have any idea of what was written on the torn-out copybook page.

In the first year, he improved the existing school building, bought sheets of corrugated pressed fiberglass for the roof, and put up a new brick latrine they called the *chimbudzi*. In his second year, he organized brickmaking and built a second block of classrooms, with a wide veranda that served as a stage where he conducted morning assembly.

The villagers had pitched in. His fellow American teacher hated the Lower River, and Malabo particularly, but got no sympathy from Hock and begged to be transferred. So Hock was alone, out of touch; he seldom left the district, and the telephone at the boma was unreliable. By the light of a Tilley lamp Hock corrected copybooks and sometimes read. He had never forgotten reading *The Death of Ivan Ilych,* especially the death scene, because of the fizzing and flickering of the lamp. Hock learned the Sena language and was one of those volunteer teachers about whom the other Americans talked with respect tinged with satire, because they never saw him, and no one wanted to go to the Lower River.

For the Sena he was the *mzungu,* then the American, and at last Snake Man. He fell in love with a Sena woman who was a student teacher in Port Herald. Her name was Gala. She had dark, slanted, almost Asiatic eyes, suggesting Zulu ancestry, a thin face, a perpetual frown that showed she was trying not to laugh, and usually a head wrap that contrasted in color with her long gown-like dress. He invited her for tea, welcomed her into his house, and urged her to sit on his bed, where he joined her. But when he embraced her, she resisted him so strenuously he knew she was not a coquette but was defending her virtue, and he was ashamed. She explained that she had been promised to a man from her village near the boma, and that if it became known that she slept with Hock, the man would reject her and not hand over the bride price of three cows her father had demanded. Her fiancé was a party official, and she suggested that he was well connected.

Still, Hock had considered wooing her, persuading her father that he was worthy, and perhaps marrying her, becoming a resident, staying in the country, raising a family, spending his life there.

The term was two years. Hock stayed almost four—later judged to be a record for any foreigner in the hot, miserable, bug-ridden, swampy Lower River, among the half-naked Sena people and their procrastinations.

The happiest years of his life.

4

THE LOWER RIVER remained in his mind in the way that the notion of home might persist in someone else's. When all hope is lost and everything is up the wall, he thought, reassuring himself, I can always go back there. As for Gala, because he'd loved her and been denied sex with her, he'd never stopped thinking about her—perhaps his desire persisted as a yearning through all those years because fulfillment had been thwarted.

What was it about having lived in Africa that made him so certain of it as a refuge? Africa cast a green glow in his memory, and its capacity for happiness occupied his mind. He had been much more than a mere visitor or resident. He had worked there, he was invested there, he felt proudly proprietary about Africa, though it was something he believed so strongly he never spoke about it. He was obscurely offended when he read of a celebrity who'd started a school in Africa, or a billionaire who'd funded a medical intervention, or an actress adopting an African child, or an actor involving himself in a pacification effort among warring tribes. That was the effect of Africa, of the people and the great spaces, and its simplicity. Maybe outsiders felt that in this green preindustrial continent it might still be possible to avoid the horrors that had come to Europe—war, machines, materialism, frozen food—to develop a happier place. He often felt that, as well as a sense of responsibility, almost the conceit of ownership. As long as Africa remained unfinished, there was hope. But the name Africa—grand and meaningless—was just his code word for the Lower River.

He was alone again after almost thirty-five years.

He'd made an early success of the business; he'd been happy as a father and husband. But the business was destroyed by imports and cheap competition, and his family had fallen apart. These weren't failures. You had to adapt and go on living. He had enough money to see himself into his old age, yet he wanted more than that: the joy he'd known as a young man in Africa. Nothing he'd gained in his life had matched the pleasure he'd known then. Even at the time he'd thought, I have everything I want.

Looking back, he saw that it had all been a digression—business, marriage, children. Now, at sixty-two, he had money, he had all the time in the world. Apart from reading—travel, some natural history, snakes—he had no recreations. His family had been fractured, the parts dispersed. No one needed him.

For years he'd thought of going away, but he never had. A vacation was a burden, idleness was a burden, and he had a store to look after. But when he found a buyer—the electronics chain, specializing in cell-phone technology, which saw potential in the location—he had no excuse for procrastinating.

Now he had a plan. He had a destination—Malabo. He even had a departure date, yet he was uneasy about leaving, uneasy just thinking about it. Something important remained to be done, but what? He could not imagine what it might be, yet it mattered—one of those anxious thoughts that troubled his mind when he woke in the old Medford High condo he'd begun to hate. Was it a debt he'd incurred, a promise he'd made, a threat against him in the dream he'd interrupted by waking from it?

He had never stopped thinking about Africa, yet he hadn't dared to let it preoccupy and possess him, because he'd felt it would remain unrealized, a torment. But the woman's snake had brought it all back, given his reverie a distinctive smell, the odor of earth and straw, the rich vegetable aroma of snake flesh, the crackly hum of old snake skin that had been shed and that lay like a white ghost-husk of the snake itself.

The experience of the snake had directed him, and without any help or consultation he had gone online, found a flight to Malawi and a good fare, found a connecting flight to Blantyre, a hotel there, conducted the whole business without speaking to a single soul. Using his computer, paying by credit card, he felt self-consciously secretive, as if he was planning something illicit, sneaking away, escaping to Africa.

Yet he'd wanted to share his excitement with at least one person. Not sharing it made him feel covert in a way that suffocated him and made him superstitious. He wished that Teya had been a listener, that she'd known him better, so he could startle her by saying out of the blue, "By the way, I'm leaving. Going to Africa."

I'm clearing out, he wanted to say, even if, as he knew, it was only for a few weeks.

He wanted someone to know he was going. Without a cell phone, he began to send Deena an email from his computer. He had rehearsed what he was going to tell her.

As he typed his message to her, tapping the keys, no more than two sentences into it, he imagined her reply. After such a long marriage he knew exactly what she would say. She wouldn't reply by email. She would find a way of calling him—he had a landline in his condo—saying, "That is so you, announcing what you're going to do—no give-and-take, just a flat pronouncement, and what I want to know—let me finish—is what—I said let me finish—what on earth has this got to do with me?"

So he did not send the message. He deleted it, then considered one to Chicky, and heard in his mind, "Great, giving yourself a vacation while Dougie and I stay home. Ever occur to you that we could use a vacation? You never took one when Ma and I went to the Cape year after year. Ever occur to you . . .?"

He did not even start a message to Chicky.

He wanted someone to be interested. More than that, he wanted someone to know where he was going—someone who'd still be here when he returned, someone to tell his stories to, someone to look at his pictures. He could not go without someone knowing. Leaving without a farewell was too depressing, too spooky, like a ghost dissolving, vanishing into the woodwork. Who?

Royal Junkins—Roy—he had known since grade school. Not an intimate friend—he had none—but a close friend, a bright boy in elementary school, a standout runner in junior high, a track star in high school. He was someone who actually owned a car, at a time when Hock's father said it was something they couldn't afford to give him. And Roy Junkins had given Hock rides whenever he'd seen him waiting for the bus. Hock's house in the Lawrence Estates was not far from Roy's on Jerome Street, but it was years before they visited each other's house. Anyone from Medford would have understood this immediately. Jerome Street was black, the Lawrence Estates white. It was not unthinkable, just awkward for a white person to stroll down Jerome, just as awkward and unlikely as a black face in the Lawrence Estates. But they were friends on the neutral ground of school, and it was Roy's car they used for the senior prom.

Roy had gone to college on a track scholarship in Rhode Island, and after that he had disappeared, reemerging in the 1970s with stories of California and foreign travel and hints of having made and lost a lot of money on drugs. In the way that Roy had turned up at school, always with a good story, he then visited Hock at the store. He too had been to Africa, he said, purely on a whim, in one of his flush years; and he was one of the few people to whom Hock had confided his happiness on the Lower River.

After years of roaming in the wider world, of travel, of marriage, of fatherhood, Roy had returned to Jerome Street, where he lived with his sister. He was a teacher, a drug counselor, an adviser in agencies that dealt with at-risk youths—Roy's description of the restless boys—and right up to the end he had stopped into the store, sometimes to buy a shirt or a sweater, but more often to while away the time, talking with Hock about high school, the countries he'd been to, whatever was on his mind. Roy could see that business was terrible, and it seemed to Hock that Roy was taking pity on him. Roy knew about failure—he could see that Hock was facing the end. But Roy had grace, and an easy, forgiving manner, and always a smile, and he'd never hid his admiration for Hock in having been a teacher in Africa, something Roy wished he'd done.

In the final weeks of the store, Roy Junkins was one of the more frequent visitors, though in that period, which was also the period of Teya and the snake, Hock never mentioned the python. The snake was his secret satisfaction. But casting his mind over people in Medford who might be interested in his going to Africa, Hock realized that Roy was perfect. Roy would listen to his plans, Roy would take an interest, Roy might even miss him a little—or, at least, Roy would welcome him back. Hock was able to picture that evening in the future, the dinner on his return from Africa, how Roy would sit and smile, hearing the stories.

Hock and Roy had no other friends in common, so each would give the other his full attention. In the chance encounters with Jerry Frezza, all Jerry wanted to talk about was Teya, speculating on her wild life: Witch Camp, the Mud Ritual, massages. Hock did not have the heart to tell Jerry that she was a rather sad, lonely person, with an angry daughter, struggling to make ends meet.

"Royal is watching the football game in the front room," said the woman who answered—his sister Mae, Hock guessed. "I'll bring him the phone."

Then Hock heard rustling and Roy's "Yuh?" and Hock greeted him. Roy said, "Hey, man, how you doing?" speaking very slowly and giving weight to each word with a breath of enthusiasm.

Hock was moved by the response. Here was a friendly voice, glad to hear his.

"I need to talk to you." As soon as he spoke, Hock regretted his urgent tone.

"Go ahead, my brother. I'm listening."

"It's better if I see you."

"That's cool," Roy said in his easygoing way, as though used to hearing desperate requests. His history of drug use, and his subsequent sobriety and study after that, had qualified him to become a drug counselor. And Hock had the feeling now that Roy, with his heightened sense, had him pegged as a person with a problem.

"Roy, I want to share some good news with you."

"Man, that is just great."

They agreed to meet the next day at the Chinese restaurant in West Medford. It had replaced the shoe repair shop that had stood on the corner since Hock and Roy had been in school. Roy remarked on this when they met, how he'd gotten his shoes resoled here.

"Suede shoes—very cool," Roy said.

"Wingtips," Hock said.

"You got it," Roy said, agreeable as ever.

"Thanks for meeting me at short notice," Hock said after they'd ordered their food—noodles for Hock, fried rice for Roy, some spring rolls to share.

"Ellis, I couldn't wait. I want to hear this good news."

Roy was smiling—the weary smile of someone who'd been through hard times, determined not to be brought low, a resolute smile that said, No matter what you say, you cannot bring me down. It was also a smile of encouragement and gratitude, and it had the effect of lighting Roy's face with something like love—friendship, anyway, which seemed purer for being more passive.

"I'm going back to Africa."

Roy turned his hand and tapped his knuckles on the table. "That's great, Ellis."

"I wanted you to know."

"I been there," Roy said. "It was fine."

"That's why I knew you'd be interested."

"I am beyond interested. I am down with it." And Roy smiled again. "Ghana. I had some contacts there. I just went on an impulse—well, you know. I told you all about it. It was the 1970s. And I just"—Roy straightened, threw his head back, exaggerating a posture of confidence—"I walked tall. I had my head up. Looked people in the eye. It was so great. I had never done that here."

"I always tell people, 'Africa was my Eden,'" Hock said. "I was really happy there—young, in a country that was just becoming independent. I ran a school. Really good students. I had a girlfriend."

Roy had begun to laugh. "Now you're talking. Those women were so fine."

The food was served and the two men continued to reminisce, Hock about Malawi, Roy about Ghana—though, as Roy said, he'd been there only three weeks. Yet those three weeks stood out in his mind as brighter and happier, more memorable and with more meaning, than years he'd spent elsewhere, years that had yielded no memories at all.

"I know what you're saying. Ellis, my man."

And Hock was relieved, because Roy's smile spared him from

going into further detail. This was the right man to share his secret with, someone who understood.

"You're lucky," Roy said, and continued to eat, but holding his head, cocking it slightly, in a manner that indicated he had something more to say. "Wish I could do it, but I've got—" He laughed, and his laugh indicated a weight of problems so enormous they could only be laughed at.

Hock said, "Someday you'll go back."

"That's right. Some fine day," Roy said assertively. "But you're the man to go now. Hey, give me your cell-phone number. We can talk."

"I don't have a cell phone anymore. I'm not taking one."

"That's cool." And perhaps suspecting there was a story behind it that Ellis was not telling, Roy praised him. "You done your work. You ran that store—for how long? Years, man. You put in the time when the rest of us was goofing off. You think I didn't notice? But I did. You deserve it, Ellis. You showed up every day, and now you don't have to show up no more. You can just—"

And Roy raised his hand and flicked it, a casual gesture that was like the wing flap of a bird in flight.

"Tell you something, though," Roy said, hitching forward in the booth. "I'm going to miss you, man."

It was exactly what Hock wanted to hear, what he'd hoped for, what he needed: someone to miss him. And when Roy said it, Hock felt liberated and ready to go.

"This is for you," Hock said, outside the restaurant. He took off his cashmere scarf and flipped it over Roy's head and tugged it. "I'm not going to need it where I'm going."

The two men embraced, Roy with gusto, Hock feeling tearful.

5

ELLIS HOCK CRAVED that simpler, older world he'd known as a young teacher, which was also a place in which hope still existed, because it was a work in progress. In the years he'd been away he'd often dreamed of going back to the Lower River district of swamp and savanna, yet without any confidence that he could achieve it. The dream was important to him, though: it had quieted him through the enormous digression of marriage and business. And he had just about abandoned any thought that he would return.

But that was before the present of his new phone, and the avenging weeks of Deena's anger, and the end of his business. Everything was changed, and the timing was perfect. The course of a life seems random, but all lives are shaken into a pattern that makes sense only in retrospect. Hock was a new man, or rather, the man he once was, on his way back to Malawi. Now the country was advertised as a place for holidays, with resort hotels at the lake, in the north, even some game parks. It seemed like many other travel destinations in the world, where many people starved and the tourists ate well and were fussed over.

Already, before his plane touched down, he knew his decision had been right. He relaxed, smiling out the window at the low treeless hills, the creases of green in the landscape that marked the foliage along rivers and creeks, the villages that were made visible by the smoke rising from cooking fires. From the air, the place looked just as he had left it almost forty years before. Where else could you go on earth and say that?

43

The immigration officer asked him his reason for being in the country.

Hock spoke the sentence he had rehearsed: "*Ndi kupita ku Nsanje.*"

The man said, "Eh! Eh! What am I hearing?" and reached across his desk to shake Hock's hand. "And myself I have never been there, father."

A domestic flight was leaving later in the day for Blantyre. Hock took it and stayed the night at the Mount Soche Hotel, marveling at the crowded dirty city. Loud music boomed from the cars of boys cruising, pulsing against the metal. It seemed to indicate a kind of thuggery. He saw men talking on cell phones and hoped that there were no cell phones on the Lower River.

Assuming he would be staying a few weeks, he visited Barclays Bank and used his credit card to make a cash withdrawal. The clerk, a young man in a shirt and tie, asked him if he was sure he meant to withdraw that much money, and when Hock said yes, he counted the notes twice and squared ten tall piles, tapping them, snapped a rubber band around each of them, then ducked into his cubicle, looking for a bag large enough to hold the money.

"Be careful, sir," the clerk said, squeezing ten fat envelopes under the heavy glass window.

"I'll be careful," Hock said. "I used to live here. I was here at independence. The Lower River."

"Oh, so long ago. But we have a branch at Nsanje. I think it was different then."

"Maybe not."

The clerk spoke again, but was barely audible behind the glass. "Did you say they're angry?"

"Hungry, sir," the clerk said, motioning his fingers to his widened mouth.

In the evening, walking down the street that was still Victoria Avenue, Hock saw an American flag hanging from a steeply angled pole, and a plaque identifying the newish building as the *United States Consulate*. He made a note of it, and on his way back to his hotel he passed a nightclub, the Starlight. He smiled at the well-dressed men gathered at the entrance, the women in bright dresses and high heels, some of the men getting out of expensive-looking private cars, one a Mercedes, another a white Land Rover. In his time, the men would have worn plimsolls, as they called them, and the women would have been barefoot. And no African would have owned a car, much less a Mercedes.

In his hotel room that night, the music from the nightclub and the city lights disturbed his sleep. He comforted himself with the thought that he was traveling to the darkness and silence of the Lower River.

"I'd like to see the consul," Hock said to the receptionist at the U.S. consulate the next morning.

"Is he expecting you?

"No," Hock said. "But I'm an American on tour here, and I think I should see him."

Hock was conscious of a roomful of people behind him, mostly men, probably applying for visas, and listening, perhaps resenting the access this *mzungu* had. He felt the pressure of their gaze against his back.

As he was speaking, a white man in shirtsleeves passed by the desk and picked up a file folder from a tray.

Hock said, "Are you the consul?"

The man squinted, annoyed, interrupted in his errand. He said, "I'm the PAO. Public affairs officer."

"Can I see you a minute?"

The man sighed in a way that was unambiguous—overdid the sigh, blinked in exasperation, and hesitated.

"Never mind," Hock said, hating the rebuff.

The man said, "I'm just going to lunch. And I'm busy this afternoon."

"Have lunch with me at my hotel," Hock said. "And by the way, I'm not looking for a visa. I just want a little information."

The man said, "Okay, I'll see you here in a little while."

"*Ndikubwera posachedwa,*" Hock said.

The man smiled, a wan smile, uncomprehending.

"'I'm coming soon,'" Hock said. "I was here in the Peace Corps."

"You people," the man said, and smiled again, this time with warmth.

The public affairs officer's name was Kent Gilroy, he had been in the country six months, and it was clear that he didn't like the place. But with two years to go, as he said, it was too demoralizing for him to admit it. He was impatient with the waiter, repeating his order, a club sandwich. Hock ordered fish and chips, and remarked on how busy the café was.

"Tourists?"

"All aid people. NGOs," Gilroy said. "A better class of tourist. They'd probably be more helpful to you than I could. I'm just finding my way."

"I'm going to the Lower River," Hock said. "Nsanje."

"No one ever goes there," Gilroy said. "It's not a population center."

"It never was."

"And the Sena people," Gilroy said, swallowing, instead of finishing his sentence.

"'Backward.'"

"Not popular."

"Off the map, the British say," Hock said. "To me, that was always its virtue. Even in my day we didn't have many visitors."

"When was your day?"

"Almost forty years ago."

Gilroy said, "God, I wasn't even born then. I'm sorry. I don't want to make you feel old."

"I don't feel old," Hock said. "As soon as I arrived the other day, I felt rejuvenated, as I had when I first came here. It's strange the power a white person feels in Africa. It should be the opposite, feeling like the odd man out. But no, a kind of strength is attributed to us."

"Because you're rich and successful and healthy," Gilroy said. "You can grant favors. They give you the illusion of power. I'm the PAO, so I just deal with the media and schools, but even so, I'm associated with the consulate, and that means visas and work permits. Everyone wants a ticket out."

"Years ago, no one wanted to leave. It was unthinkable."

"You should see the lines we have to deal with—around the block, three deep. How long are you staying in Nsanje?"

"Beyond Nsanje—a village. A week or ten days. But I want every minute to count. I'd like to buy some books and teaching materials for the school there. If I had a few boxes sent to the consulate, could you have them shipped down?"

"Like I said, no one goes there," Gilroy said. "I could put them on the night bus. Or bring them myself—maybe an excuse to visit."

"There was a guy who worked at the consulate here, way back, who made trips to my school—Malabo, near Magwero. His name was Norman Fogwill."

Gilroy, chewing, said, "English guy. Lives somewhere outside town."

"Fogwill—still around?"

"Yeah, old guy. Turns up at the consulate when there's a guest speaker or a movie. He introduced himself to me. I knew a guy just like him in my last post—Addis."

"You were in Ethiopia?"

"For a year. They needed me here to run the program," Gilroy said, his expression giving nothing away, and so what he said was all the more like satire.

"How was this guy like Fogwill?"

"One of those people that stays behind after everyone else has gone home."

"I wonder if he'd remember me?"

In the way that he did not want to leave Medford until he'd found someone to say goodbye to—Roy Junkins—someone to miss him, he realized that he'd be happier here if he met someone who'd known him, who would see him on his way to the Lower River.

"I see him playing chess at Mario's now and then," Gilroy said. "The coffee shop. Next to Kandodo Supermarket."

"On the far end of Victoria Street."

Gilroy said, "I can't get over the fact that these streets actually have names."

Hock said, "Haile Selassie Road. I saw Haile Selassie coming down that road in 1964—a tiny man in a brown uniform with lots of medals. The whole country was given a holiday. I came up on the train from Nsanje to see him. People watching him said, 'He's not an African. He looks like a colored'—mixed race."

"Ethiopians would agree. They're down on Africans," Gilroy said, and smirked. "The Lion of Judah in Blantyre. It's hard to believe that anything ever happened here."

"That's why I like it," Hock said. "I'm glad to be back."

Gilroy sized him up, eyeing him, as if assessing the remark. "Great," he said, and gave him a gold-embossed name card: *Kent Gilroy, Consulate of the United States of America.* "You can use this address." He scribbled a street and number on the back of the card. "It's a funny thing," he said, writing. "Lots of Americans who come here buy schoolbooks and paper and pens and stuff like that. You'd be amazed at how many. I send the boxes out and that's the last I hear of them."

"What are you saying—that I'm wasting my time?"

"No. You're doing a good thing. But it's a bottomless pit. Money, medicine, books, pens, even computers. Where does it all end up?"

"Come down to Malabo. I'll show you." With that he wrote the name of the village on one of his own name cards.

"Will I find it?"

"Ask at the boma. Nsanje, it's beyond Marka and Magwero. Near the river. Near the border."

"The end of the line," Gilroy said, and glanced at the card again. "Cell-phone number?"

"I don't have one," Hock said. "I don't want one. I never had one down there."

Hock walked him back to the consulate so he could sign the visitors' book, and approaching the building, Gilroy said, "See what I mean?"

The line of people, men and women, some old, some like students, nearly all Africans, a few Indians.

"They're all dying to leave." He shrugged. "Because it's a failed state. Whose fault is that?"

Afterward, Hock saw clearly what he had missed at lunch—that Gilroy, like the embassy people he'd known long ago, was downbeat about the country and didn't know it well; that he felt he'd been posted to a hopeless place and had to make the best of it; that he would be gone in a year or so and in a new country. Gilroy was fragmentary in the way of lawyers and bureaucrats, and because of that he was impossible to pin down, evasive, a man of no fixed beliefs.

Hock felt nothing but gratitude for being in Malawi, thankful that the country still existed, was still sleepy and friendly and ramshackle, that it had welcomed him. That day, walking along the street, strangers meeting his gaze smiled and said hello, and when he spoke to them in their own language they shrieked with pleasure.

The air was dense and hot, woven of many odors, and just a whiff brought it all back. He was walking down Hanover to Henderson, to the corner of Laws, to the bookshop, where he'd caught a glimpse of the sign *Office Supplies*. The countryside, so close, penetrated the town. You could not see the bush from the main street, but you could smell it: the wood smoke floated past the shops and seeped into the brick and stucco, the peculiar hum of scorched eucalyptus, the dustiness of dead leaves, the fields chopped apart by rusty mattocks to release the sharpness of bruised roots and red earth, all of it stinking with ripeness and decay; and on every sidewalk the sweetish feety smell of the people, the sourness of their rags. He closed his eyes and inhaled and smiled and thought, I could not be anywhere else but here.

In the bookshop, Blantyre Printery and Office Supplies, he found a young clerk and asked for the manager.

"I am the manager"—a young man in a blue shirt, red necktie, a pencil tucked into the thickness of his bushy hair.

"I want to buy a couple of these cartons and fill them with school materials. Books and things."

"This tub?"

It was a plastic container for storing files, with handles and a clip-on lid that would keep the dust out.

"This, yes, this tub," Hock said.

He selected readers, forty of them, and forty copybooks, some dictionaries, some picture books, an assortment of pens and colored pencils and rulers, a large-format atlas of Africa, another of the world. He chose hurriedly, pointing to shelves, thinking that anything he bought would be welcome.

"How much?" he asked when the two containers were filled.

"I will tally up the docket," the young man said, eyeing Hock sideways, and he made out the invoice. Though this was a lengthy process, involving several pads and the shuffling and interleaving of blue carbon paper, Hock sat and watched with contentment, liking the meticulous listing of each item, the digging of the ball-point into the softness of the pad in triplicate, the exercise of an old skill.

After he paid, Hock wrote an address on a piece of paper, saying, "Here is where I want you to deliver this. The U.S. consulate, Mr. Gilroy." And he scribbled a note to go with it, saying that he would be in touch on his return from Malabo.

The coffee shop that Gilroy had indicated, where Norman Fogwill might be, was closed when Hock passed by in the late afternoon. He drank a beer in the garden of the hotel, and as darkness fell he heard music from the nightclub adjacent to the hotel, its name picked out in lights, the Starlight.

Telling himself that he was merely taking a walk, he wandered over to the club and was at once greeted by taxi drivers, by touts, by shyly beckoning girls at the doorway. He went nearer to the entrance and looked inside—a crowd, a band, shadows, a few lights piercing webs of smoke—and a man in sunglasses said, "You're welcome. Don't be a stranger. Come inside, boss."

Hock eased himself past the loitering men and boys, and once inside the dimly lit club, he made his way to an empty table by the wall. Colored lights flickered on the gleaming dance floor. The music was so loud he could scarcely hear the waitress ask what he wanted. He ordered a beer. Before it was brought, a girl asked with finger gestures if she could join him. Hock patted the chair seat next to him.

She was small, with a mass of tight shiny curls, a pretty, somewhat impish face, and wore a dark jacket over a white blouse. Her knees bumped his as she sat, squirming, smiling, being a coquette. When his bottle of beer arrived, Hock signaled—gestures again, the music was deafening—for the waitress to bring her a drink.

The girl leaned closer and shouted into his ear, "What country?"

"United States."

"Big country," she said, still shouting.

"*Dzina lanu ndani?*" Hock asked.

"Merry," she said—at least that was how it sounded. Then, "You are knowing my language."

"*Kwambiri!*"

She touched his leg. She leaned again, her mouth against his ear. "You want jig-jig?"

Hock was startled. The girl saw his reaction and looked gratified, even strengthened, taking her drink from the waitress's tray and twirling her tongue on the straw. Hock took a breath and inclined his body toward hers and found himself shouting, "Not now!"

"Why not? We get taxi. My home is just near."

Hock said, "I'm worried about *kudwala.*"

"I not sick." She looked indignant, sitting back and staring at him with widened eyes.

"But maybe I'm sick," Hock said.

"Okay." That seemed to pacify her. "I give you—what? Massage, what you want." And when Hock frowned she said, "Let we go."

The music was so loud, Hock wondered whether he was hearing correctly. Was she really saying these things with such composure? At that moment, dizzy from the music and the cigarette smoke, Hock became aware of another girl pressing toward him from his other side.

The first girl, Merry, spoke harshly, and the girls quarreled for a moment, screeching at each other, until Hock, to quiet them, gestured to the waitress to serve the second one a beer.

"What country?" the new girl asked.

She was big, in a tight-fitting dress, with a fat face and spiky hair, and when she smiled, which she was doing now, she showed a gap in her front teeth that was as wide as a keyhole.

"Alessi," she said, extending her hand.

Merry leaned toward Hock and said, "Let we go. Please. I need money. I got a little kid."

"I have to make a phone call," Hock said. "Here, take this, for the beer." He gave each girl some money. "I'll be right back." They squawked as he left, and he realized that all he had given them was the Malawi equivalent of a dollar apiece.

He fled, feeling hot and desperate, hurrying to the safety of his hotel, where he locked himself in his room, sitting in the dark, breathing hard, hearing the music pulsing at the window, fearful of going out and perhaps meeting the girls.

6

H E WAS REMINDED on his third day of how time passed in Africa with no event to mark its passing—a meaningless slipping away of days. Once again, he woke in harsh early-morning light, thinking, I must leave. But he wondered at the urgency. After breakfast, he introduced himself to the clerk at the travel desk in the lobby and asked about a car and driver.

"You want to book now, Mr. Ellis?" the clerk asked.

"I want to know how much notice you need."

"We have cars. We have drivers. We are ready to serve you, sir."

"Good. I just have to run an errand first."

"I will be waiting you just here, Mr. Ellis."

Hock walked quickly down the hill toward Kandodo Supermarket, and approaching it he saw that the small coffee shop was open, a propped-up sign on the sidewalk lettered *Coffee Cakes Sweets*.

Inside, two old men faced each other across a chessboard. One was heavyset, with thick eyebrows, wide shoulders, his elbows on the table, hovering over the board, perhaps contemplating a move. The other man was thin, white-haired, with sunken cheeks, sitting sideways, his legs crossed, his hands in his lap. When the thin man smiled at the consternation of his opponent, Hock saw that he had one front tooth. This had to be Norman Fogwill. His narrow trousers emphasized his thin legs.

Hock entered the coffee shop. The man he took to be Norman Fogwill said to his chess opponent, "You got a customer, mate," and to Hock, "He's stumped. He has nowhere to go."

"I have an answer," the heavy man said, his accent like a morsel of unchewed food in his mouth. But he didn't move a chess piece. "You want coffee?"

"Take your time," Hock said.

The man roared and stood up, kicking his chair back, and stamped his feet.

"See?" Fogwill said, and laughed, showing his single tooth. He worked his tongue around the tooth, then coughed, shaking a cigarette out of a pack and lighting it.

"I used to smoke those," Hock said. "Springboks. I'm sure you don't remember me, but I was here in the sixties. Are you Norman Fogwill?"

"What's left of him," Fogwill said. "Have a seat. Make that two coffees, Mario."

The other man was now behind the counter, locking a chrome handle into the underside of an espresso machine.

"I'm Ellis Hock. I was in the Lower River."

"I know who you are," Fogwill said in an awakening tone. He looked pleased, but his tight smile only made his face more skeletal. "You had snakes. Big ones in baskets. I used to hump copybooks and biros down from the office. And ink for your Gestetner. Lord, there's a relic. A duplicator!"

"You remember?"

"How could I forget? It took me two days to get there in that motor, the Willys Jeep on that bloody awful road. Shaketty-boom, shaketty-shaketty boom." He sucked at the cigarette and made his mouth square and shushed out blue smoke. "I had to stay overnight and leave the next day. One night was enough for me! How did you stand it for two years?"

"Almost four years," Hock said.

"Good God. What was the name of that benighted village?"

"Malabo."

"Right. Smack in the bush. They had teachers and health workers in Nsanje, but no one replaced you in Malabo. That's a fact."

"Because I phased myself out. I taught them how to run the show."

"And a dog's breakfast they made of it, I reckon."

Hock said, "It was the best school in the district."

"Oh, right, sorry. A proper little Eton College you had down there," Fogwill said, still mocking and not seeming to notice Hock's indignation.

Hock said, "So what have you been doing for the past forty years?"

"This," he said, sitting upright, and he pulled a face, as though he'd just performed a successful trick. He called out to the man at the espresso machine. "Have I not, Mario?" But he become serious and said, "Remember my last duchess? That village beauty from Fort Johnson, Yao by tribe. We had three kids. She got fed up with the politics and swanned off to the UK. She's still there, in a nice council flat in Bristol. My kids are married. I'm a grandfather, can you believe it?" He looked teasingly at Hock and said, "You never came to town. We had to hump all your *katundu* to you in the bush."

Hock said, "I took the train up to see Haile Selassie. Ten hours in third class."

Fogwill said, "The train's not running anymore."

"I was happy in the Lower River."

Fogwill said, "Things are different now."

"In what way?"

"I used to leave my house unlocked back then."

"So you lock it now?"

"Not that it does a whit of good. I've been broken into so many times there's nothing left to steal."

"That's life in the big city."

"I live in the *bundu*," Fogwill said. "Unlike our friend here."

The man Mario had served the cups of coffee and was sitting, listening to Fogwill. Now Mario said, "Me, I'm no like the bush."

"It's a thirty-minute drive," Fogwill said. "It suits me. Besides, I can't afford anything else. The land belonged to my wife's brother. He died of HIV. I'm educating his youngest son." And as if seeing Hock for the first time, he smiled and said, "So, what brings you here?"

"Going to the Lower River."

"No one goes there now. I haven't been down there for yonks." He sipped his cup of coffee, holding it daintily with tremulous fingers. He said, "Not much has changed here. Except we don't have the old man anymore, and they kill albinos and make them into medicine, and they look for virgins to deflower—cures AIDS and the pox and heaven knows what, the dreaded lurgy, I fancy, though you'd be jolly lucky to find a virgin between here and Karonga."

"I'm going south," Hock said. The only way he had ever been able to deal with the teasing ironies of English people like Fogwill was to conceal himself in his stereotype and be as literal-minded as they believed Americans to be.

"Are you in possession of trade goods and shiny beads? Never mind, all they want is money. Or a mobile phone."

"No cell phone," Hock said.

"Astonishing." Fogwill finished his coffee and smacked his lips and signaled for another. "You look smart. I once had a safari suit like that. Stout shoes. Bush hat. You look the part."

"It's just a short vacation."

"I came for a short vacation forty years ago and I'm still here." He looked through the café window into the street. "Buggered if I know why."

He had the gargoyle features of a castaway, and the clothes too, his shirt faded and patched, his shoes torn and repaired with wide stitches on one toe, sutures of waxed twine in the leather, a specialty of the market cobbler.

As though to distract attention from his appearance, Fogwill began to tell a story about a recent night when he'd driven home drunk and fallen asleep in his car in the driveway of his house.

"The entire inside of the car was thick with masses of green beer bottles, curiously empty, and for my sins I had a whacking great bruise on my bonce. I woke to an impertinent whickering—my servant, cheeky bugger, wailing 'Bwana! Bwana! Time for your tea!' I was of course deliciously foxed . . ."

His houseboy, seeing him asleep in his car, pulled him out and dragged him to his bedroom, stripped off his clothes, and put him to bed.

That was the story in a sentence. But Norman told it as a lengthy, lisping farce, with digressions and humorous self-mockery. It was a good story, and in the time it took him to tell it, Mario served him his second cup of coffee and made his much-pondered chess move.

And Ellis thought: A story is a way of making life bearable. It was in general the English way, as he had experienced it among the expatriates. They would take a small disgraceful incident, remove the context, which was the great green frame of Africa, and make it a tale, choosing a few elements and adding droll phrases such as "curiously" and "for my sins" until it became a substitute for a stretch of monotony, or in Norman's case, forty years of futility, living in a hut, abandoned by his African wife and children. He wanted to prove that he was not humiliated, not ignored, not counterfeit, not embittered, just killing time in this seedy town of ambiguous smells. He was a character in his own comedy. If you didn't have a story, you hadn't lived. The raggedness didn't matter. What mattered was that Norman rescued a shred of dignity by relating the tale, depicting himself as a silly, forgivable drunk, tended to by a jungle Jeeves.

The manner of his telling it mattered too, in his plummy accent, made plummier by his living in the African bush. But Hock knew what those stories were worth. He could even translate them. "House" did not mean house; it meant a leaky hut. "Car" meant jalopy, "servant" meant skinny boy, and "tea" did not mean a meal but rather a crust of bread or a stale Kandodo cookie.

Hock was reminded why he had gone happily to the Lower River, why he had stayed there, why he was returning there now.

Fogwill said, "Know what you should do? Head up to the lake. A couple of nice hotels have opened up there—not the backpacker ones, but tourist lodges. You can swim, you can hire a fishing guide, you can just lie in a hammock all day and stay squiffy. You've got the money for it."

Hock said, "But I'm going to the Lower River."

"Then abandon all hope." Fogwill smiled again, and gestured, as if to say, "What are we going to do with this bloke!" But his one tooth and his sunken cheeks and frailty only made him seem pathetic.

"Or you could sample the delights of Blantyre."

"I did that last night. What's it called—the Starlight?"

"Also the Izo Izo in Mbayani," Mario said.

"Oh, come on, you're past it, same as me," Fogwill said, his eyes flashing in anger.

"What interested me," Hock said, because he was embarrassed by Fogwill's saying that, "what I couldn't help noticing, was that the girls were so well dressed. And they were wearing shoes."

"First time I ever went to the Flamingo—remember that bar, on the Chileka Road? I was courting my wife. Manager says, 'Can't bring her in here. No shoes.' I gave him a right bollocking, but he wouldn't budge. No one had shoes!"

"Was like that in Eritrea," Mario said. "Assolutely."

"He's another refugee, by way of Nairobi," Fogwill said.

Hock said, "What's the road like to the Lower River?"

"Tarmac as far as Chikwawa and then you're on your own. Shaketty-shaketty-boom. You should go up to the lake. Have a holiday."

"I didn't come here for a holiday," Hock said.

This sharpness seemed to awaken something in Fogwill's memory, because he smiled again and shifted in his chair and said, "Independence—it was the biggest day this country has ever seen. We had the mother and father of a party at the consul's house and all you teachers were invited. The place was packed. Huge celebration. I says to one of your blokes, 'Well, this is one way of getting you buggers out of the bush.' He says to me—I'll never forget this—'There's someone missing.'

"'Probably living it up somewhere else,' I says.

"He says—I can see his face now, ginger hair, freckles, those cretinous Bermuda shorts—'He's on the Lower River.'" Fogwill nodded and smiled and showed his tooth. "It was you."

"We had a celebration there," Hock said.

"Were you here in Batley's time? He was the rugger player. Remember Ray Castle? We called him Castle Lager, after the beer."

Mario tapped the chessboard and said, "Your move."

"What about Worley-Dodd? He had the Land Rover dealership. Married an Ismaili bint. And Bill Fiddes? Nyasaland Trading Company? 'This is my UK woolly,' he'd say in his pullover on those cold days when the *chiperoni* came down like sleet. And Major Moxon at the Gymkhana Club. Fred Horridge and his horrible restaurant. No sense of smell—bit of a handicap in a chef, what?"

"Norman," Mario said, making an impatient Italian gesture with cupped hands.

"Jumping Jimmy Jesus, he wants me to thrash him again," Fogwill said, and then to Hock, "Go to the lake. It's beautiful there, like it always was." But he'd kept his head down as he was speaking, studying the board, and did not look up, just grunted, when Hock said goodbye and left.

At first Hock was sorry he'd spent the morning with this man. It had meant that leaving today was out of the question, that he'd have to leave in the morning. But he softened. It was a good thing that Fogwill knew he was going to the Lower River—someone else to say farewell to, someone else to have him in mind, like Gilroy at the consulate.

And that night, hearing the music from the Starlight, the drumbeats thumping at the walls of his room, he thought how, long ago, he had toyed with the notion of courting Gala in Malabo, wooing her away from the man she'd been promised. She was lovely. They would have children. They would live on the Lower River and Hock would go on teaching—running the school, turning out brilliant students. But no—and he smiled at this: in the course of time, Gala would leave him, the children too, and he would be skinny, toothless, reminiscing in a coffee shop, killing time. Fogwill was the man he'd have become if he had stayed.

PART II

The *Mzungu* at Malabo

7

S UMMONED AT SIX from the parking lot to the travel desk in the lobby, the hotel driver laughed when Hock said that he wanted to be dropped at Nsanje. The driver wore a blue baseball cap and sunglasses, and the top buttons of his shirt were undone, a gold neck chain showing; his shoes were narrow and stylish, with thin soles. He was a city man, who would never have heard of Malabo village.

"*Muli bwanji, bambo?*" Hock asked. "*Dzina lanu ndani?*"

The man said in English, "My name is Chuma."

The sunglasses over his smooth jut-jawed face gave him a cricket's profile. He smiled greedily at Hock's watch. Hock knew that lingering gaze of admiration was like a request, but Chuma had a watch of his own.

"Let's leave at seven."

"Eight will be best. African time. No worry, be happy."

"Seven," Hock said without a smile, and the man turned deferential—respectful, with a slight jerkiness in his face of fear. All that happened quickly. Hock could see that the time Chuma had spent with other foreigners as a driver had made him overconfident. Something showy about his clothes, his ease, his laugh, his knowingness; but the correction had reduced him, moving him from familiarity to subservience. It happened again on the road: "This is the best way," he said leaving the city, to "Anything you say," when Hock told him he wanted to pass through Chikwawa. Chikwawa was a place he'd remembered well, and he wanted to see how it had changed.

Chuma lit a cigarette.

"Don't smoke," Hock said.

Squeezing the lighted tip with his bare fingers, Chuma took a deep resentful breath.

The road south out of Blantyre was paved, but it was so broken, the potholes so numerous, it did not seem modern at all, but rather like another old set of obstacles; and the holes, deep enough to trap a wheel, required Chuma to make detours through the grass and mud at the edge of the road.

The farther they got from town, the flimsier and more temporary the houses, from the solid terraces of shops fronting onto storm drains, to the tile-roofed bungalows, to the tin-roofed shacks, to the mud huts thatched with straw and the skeletal sticks of the frame showing through the crumbled mud plastering. And then the road grew worse, in some places just a strip of broken paving in a gully between two slopes, and on the slopes the stumps of trees that had been cut down, the forests stripped by people foraging for fuel.

Far ahead, toward the escarpment, the whitewashed houses of Chikwawa looked like sugar cubes, filling the valley in neat rows. But up close those same houses were stained shacks, made of painted wood and patched with plastic sheeting.

"Don't stop," Hock said.

Chuma said, "This must look different from before. How many years?"

"*Za kale,*" Hock said, because "long ago" in English didn't adequately describe the length of time.

None of what he saw from the car was lovely: the Africa of people, not of animals. And that was its oddity, because it looked chewed, bitten, burned, deforested, and dug up. A herd of elephants could eat an acre of trees in a day, leaving behind a mass of trampled and splintered limbs, yet that acre stayed green and grew back. But this human settlement was befouled, the greenery slashed and burned, or dragged away until only dirt and stones remained—a blight, a permanent disfigurement.

At the end of the badly paved road the car shuddered, slid on the loose rocks, and bumped in the deep ruts. At the margin, the tall thickened blades of elephant grass blocked the view. When they came to a bridge over a stream, or a roadside village, or a cluster of shops, Chuma said, "So many changes."

Hock said "Yes," because the man was young and proud. But the answer was no, and he was glad.

Out here the bush was still a semi-ruin, a landscape coarsening, losing its softness. He would have been happier to find that nothing had changed, because it was a place he had loved for its being itself, in spite of the aid workers and the charities and the missionaries. Now they were beyond Chiromo, in the southern province, nearing the Lower River. He recognized the flattened landscape at once, a kind of disorder even in the trees and the tall grass, and an odor of dust and smoke. It had been different from anything he'd known, not beautiful, too flat and featureless to photograph, but powerful, his first experience of the world, ancient in its simplicities.

"You like," the driver said, seeing that Hock had begun to smile.

It all came back to him again. As a volunteer teacher, in this district of small huts and half-naked people and unpaved roads—a world made out of mud—he had been content. The Lower River became the measure of his happiness; he was happiest most of all because he'd been cut off. No telephone, only the weekly mail delivery, and sometimes an out-of-date newspaper, already yellow from age, the news irrelevant, overtaken by newer, greater trivia. There was nothing to fear. No one had money. He'd hated to leave; he'd longed to return. And here he was, back again—amazing.

"Mwabvi Game Park," Chuma said. "You want to stop?"

Hock saw the entrance, the turnoff—just a barrier, an iron pipe resting across two steel oil drums, and a shed farther on.

"*Njobvu*," Hock said. "*Chipembere*."

"None of those, eh. But just monkeys," Chuma said.

"I said, don't stop," Hock said.

The car was slowing down and seemed to be sliding sideways on the heavy gravel at the edge of the road, Chuma yanking on the steering wheel as if trying to avoid a skid. Hock sat forward, bracing himself against the dashboard with outstretched hands, and as he did, the car came to a stop on the slant of the roadside.

"Puncture," Chuma said.

From his tilted seat, Hock said, "Fix it. You have a spare tire, right?"

Chuma did not reply. He pushed his door open in a sulky gesture and went to the back of the car to open the trunk lid. Hock watched him lifting out his big duffel bag and flipping up the carpet to get at the spare.

"*Tsoka*," Chuma said.

Hock said, "What do you mean 'bad luck'? You have a spare tire."

"*Palibe ujeni*," Chuma said.

"What *ujeni*?" The word meant whatsit.

"Jack. I am not having."

"We'll stop a car. We'll borrow one."

Chuma looked into Hock's face, seeming to defy him. He said, "Are you noticing any cars?"

They were standing in the sun, breathing hard, their heads pounded by the heat, knowing they were helpless. And the whine of the locusts made it worse, reminding them they were alone. Chuma's forehead was beaded with sweat. He took off his sunglasses. Unmasked, his face was weak and damp. He dug out his shirttail and lifted the whole front of his shirt to wipe his face. Hock walked a few steps, and when he looked back Chuma was unbolting the spare tire from the trunk. He set it against the car with care, and stared at it, and with sudden fury kicked it.

The only shade was a low thorn tree just down the road. Hock walked to it, but when he prepared to sit he saw a smooth termite mound caked against the lower trunk. He stood for a while, then wandered back to the car, where Chuma was scowling at the tire.

Hearing the roar of an engine, Hock looked up to see a new white van with a gold logo on its side speeding toward them in the center of the road, like a locomotive on a track. Hock waved his arms but to no effect—the vehicle tore past them, its tires chewing at the road dirt, throwing up stones and leaving them shrouded in dust.

Chuma said, "The Agency. They are giving to the people here," and in a mocking voice, "They are *mzungus* from your country!"

"They didn't stop!" Hock cursed and batted at the dust the vehicle had left. "So what's the plan?"

Because of Chuma's big sunglasses, all that Hock saw was the lower portion of his face, seemingly impassive.

Hock stood apart from him, watching the dust settle. An hour passed. He kept checking his watch, dreading that they would be stuck there in the night. Looking up from his watch, he saw a boy approach on an old bike. As the boy wobbled by, Chuma spoke to him sharply, not like someone in trouble, but in a domineering way, making the boy wince.

"What are you saying to him?"

"He must get some men and boys from the village. He must help us."

The boy looked stricken and confused. Hock showed him some money. He said, "*Ndikufuna thandiza.* We need help. You understand?"

"Sah," the boy said in a hoarse voice. He mounted his bike and rode away.

"He won't come back," Chuma said.

And for another hour and a half, under the tree, Hock believed Chuma was right. But the boy did come back, with four laughing men, who laughed harder when they saw the car, lopsided on the gravel at the sloping roadside. One of them was carrying a crowbar, holding it less like a tool than a weapon.

They spoke to Chuma. Hock heard the words "jack" and "*palibe*"—none—and more laughter. Without hesitating, the men walked into the bush and came out hugging big rocks, one apiece, which they piled near the flat tire. They repeated this, bringing boulders from the bush and adding them to the pile of football-sized boulders. When they had enough, they pushed some under the axle and the others against the wheels to prevent the car from rolling back.

Using the biggest boulder as a fulcrum, and the crowbar as a lever, they lifted the car, three of the men snatching at the bumper to raise it as the boy added smaller boulders under the axle. This took almost half an hour, the men resting between thrusts of the crowbar, examining the height of the flat tire. They asked for a spanner—they used that word—and loosened the nuts. At last the tire was off the ground and able to turn. They removed the nuts, and when the wheel was off, Hock could see the way the axle rested on a pile of boulders and fitted-in rocks, an ancient but indestructible arrangement, as neatly made and as symmetrical as a stone altar.

One man bounced and rolled the spare tire from the place where it had fallen after Chuma had kicked it. They fitted it, tightening the nuts. And when they were done they removed the boulders from in front of the wheels and pushed the car off its pillar of rocks, rolling it forward.

Hock gave them money, each man a thickness of kwacha notes. They touched the notes to their foreheads and laughed some more and bade Hock a safe journey.

In the car, Chuma said, "You gave them too much money."

"They saved our lives," Hock said, suddenly angry, because Chuma hadn't helped or so much as spoken to the men. Hock felt a pent-up anxiety from watching the primitive display, the laborious work of levering and carrying and piling boulders.

"They are just village farmers," Chuma said.

"They know more than you."

Chuma did not reply, but Hock could see that he had stung him.

Hock calculated that they had four hours of daylight left. Then they were passing the road junction at Bengula, and were following the course of the river, on the west bank, throwing up whitish dust and heading straight into the sun, toward the Lower River. By late afternoon they were in Nsanje.

"Keep going," Hock said.

"You said Nsanje. This is the boma."

The district commissioner's house was a ruin, Bhagat's General Store was boarded up, the railway station had been abandoned, but the greeny-black river brimmed at the embankment, and at this hour of the day the pelicans still roosted on the dock posts at the landing. Hock raised his eyes, looking for the bats, and was heartened to see the sky thick with them, fluttering and swooping from the riverside trees.

"The village I want is farther on."

"That is extra charge."

"It's twenty miles," Hock said.

"More money," Chuma said, with menace in the words.

"Stop the car," Hock said. The driver was so rattled he kept going. "Stop the car—I'll walk."

"It is far, sir," Chuma said, with that same jerkiness of fear in his face.

"It's not far. I know where we are." The driver glanced at him. Hock said, "No extra charge."

And down the road two miles, at Marka, Hock signaled for him to stop, and the driver said, "*Iwe*," in the familiar form—"You!" But it was an anxious appeal, like a cry of help. Then he saw the men sitting under the tree and said, "They are waiting for you."

"Yes," Hock said, but he knew better. Even in his time, it had been the usual place in Marka for men to sit, a log under a mango tree. The logs were never moved, the mango trees never cut down for firewood. Yet the men murmured when they saw Hock, and they shouted a greeting.

Chuma got out of the car but stayed back, smoking a cigarette, watching with fascinated distaste—these yokels at the edge of this ramshackle village, tearing the fiber from sugar cane stalks with their teeth. Chuma seemed uneasy, eager to leave.

"What time you coming back, bwana?"

The air was so still, his cigarette smoke clung to his face. He slapped the smoke but kept puffing on the cigarette.

"You can go," Hock said.

Chuma relaxed. He was released. The sun slanted into his face. The bush pressed up against the road, and some of it flopped over the tire tracks. The river was not visible, but its smell was in the air: the stagnation, the mud glow, the bittersweet decay of crushed hyacinths, and—strongly, part of the same heaviness, like hot damp fur—a human smell.

"I'm not coming back today," Hock said.

The great soft cloud of white dust raised by the departing car closed over it as it rocked in the wheel ruts of the narrow road, going much too fast, north toward the boma, the horn blaring at something unseen. Even Hock found the departure a strange breach of etiquette. The man should have lingered a little, eaten something, accepted some bananas or a cup of tea, handed out a cigarette or two.

"Welcome, father," one of the old men said, rising from the log.

This man gave his name as Maso, and introduced the man next to him as Nyachikadza. Hock said that he knew both their fathers, from long ago.

Hock greeted the men formally, holding his elbow as he shook each hand, then said to Maso, "I'm going to Malabo. I used to live there. Can you send a message? I'm looking for the headman."

"Festus Manyenga," Maso said. He called to a boy sitting against a bicycle, holding Hock's duffel bag, and told him to go to Malabo. "Tell Manyenga the American is here."

They knew of the *mzungu* at Malabo, they said. They had heard stories about him.

Hock said, "Maybe it was someone else."

"There was only one *mzungu* at Malabo!" the man Nyachi-kadza said.

And he explained: Hock was famous; he had attained the status of an almost mythical figure. He had built the school, which also served as the clinic for the monthly visits of the doctor. He had served as go-between for the White Father and the member of parliament, all those years ago. He'd presented them, at independence, with a dugout canoe, called a *bwato,* that could hold eight paddlers.

"Come," Nyachikadza said, and led them all through the low spreading trees and across the hard-packed dirt of a courtyard, which was being swept by a woman. This was Marka village, almost unchanged from what Hock had remembered, an important village for being near the edge of the landing stage into the channel of the great marsh.

They sat before a hut and drank tea, Hock in the place of honor, on a low stool, next to a woven mat. Hock asked about the harvest and the weather and the fishing. To each question he got the same reply, not words; the men made regretful noises, clicking their tongues, meaning, Not good, but they were too superstitious to form words for their bad fortune.

As they talked of other things—the rains, the height of the river, their children—Hock looked around and marveled at the compact village and the sheltering trees, the cooling shade, the way the sunlight speckled the ground, the children playing, kicking a knotted ball of rags. The men sat on simple benches, a woman refilling their cups from a fire-blackened kettle.

The comfort Hock felt was the comfort of a homecoming — a friendliness, the gratitude of the old men, and the dignity of a ritual welcome. He felt important, even powerful, because they knew who he was — all that had been apparent from the outset. Hock wished that someone he had known back in the States — Deena, or Roy — could witness him here, the tableau of his calmly sitting among the elders in the remote village on the Lower River. At first he'd wondered if he'd been too hasty in dismissing the driver. Now he knew it had been right.

He slipped to the mat and fell asleep. Hearing voices, Hock saw three men entering the clearing from the road. The sun was lower, the air cooler.

"Manyenga?"

"Not Manyenga."

The men were carrying a pole, holding it horizontally. A crocodile was slung beneath it — not a big one, hardly three feet long from snout to tail tip. The creature sagged on the binding, obviously dead, swollen from decomposition, its legs swinging limp, its jaw hanging open. It looked like a child's toy, but an old one, from an attic.

"*Nyama*," Hock said — meat. A croc's tail was eaten in the Lower River.

But the men didn't answer. Maso was giving them orders, obviously contradicting them, setting them straight, in an I-know-better voice.

"It was found dead in the marsh," Nyachikadza said. "Just here. Too near."

Now all the men became serious, eyeing the dead croc as though it was not merely an interloper but a menace that had been sneaked into the village.

"They are wanting to bury it," Maso said, laughing in mockery. And to the young men he said in Sena, "Don't bury."

"Bunning is better," Nyachikadza said in English.

"If you are burying," Maso said, "anyone at all can dig it out of the ground and cut its liver, and poison us."

"But the badness is," one of the other older men said, and finished the sentence in Sena, which Hock believed he understood: The crocodile has to be completely destroyed.

The men spoke in a sagacious-sounding way when they used English. Hock complimented them on their fluency. Maso said that the older people spoke English because they'd had American-trained teachers, but the younger ones didn't go to school.

"Paraffin," Maso said to Hock.

That made sense: douse the croc in paraffin, reduce it to ashes.

They muttered a little more while Hock listened, and as he did, he realized they were being circumspect, talking about money. They needed money to buy some paraffin at the village shop, where there was a drum of it. Still, they were murmuring, discussing the problem softly. Hock sat at the edge of this talk, listening to the repeated word, *ndalama*—money.

"How much do you need?"

Maso looked up and said promptly, "Five hundred kwacha."

"Okay," Hock said. It was about three dollars.

"Or one thousand," another man said. "Crocodile must be bunned."

Hock called for his duffel bag. He took it aside and unzipped it so that no one could see what it contained—the fat envelopes of money. He extracted two five-hundred-kwacha notes and zipped the bag shut. Maso took the money with both hands, bowing as he did so, whispering, "Mastah."

8

THE MOSQUITOES WERE humming in his dreams, torturing his head, whining in his ears, tickling his eyelids, inescapable. He woke clawing his hair and slapping at his eyes, and only then, just before dawn, in the thickened air like a suspension of ashes, breathing the mud walls of the hut, the dampness of the dusty floor, did he remember where he was. To keep the mosquitoes away he wrapped his head in the dirty sheet and lay back and laughed.

Someone had heard him wake. Someone was snapping twigs for kindling, a cooking fire began to crackle, a kettle lid was clapped down, and soon the clatter of enamel cups. A shy "*Odi?*" A small boy, moving forward on his knees, bowed his head and presented a cup of sweet milky tea. Hock gave thanks for his good luck.

At sunup he joined the men, sitting on a stool, eating a banana. The men were discussing yesterday's crocodile, the sequence of particular events—the talk of evisceration, mention of the liver, and instead of a burial a cremation, conducted by Maso—as though to reassure themselves that they were safe. They were speaking so quickly, Hock found the argument hard to follow, but listening closely he heard above the words the blatting of a motorbike, growing louder. He looked up as it roared into the clearing.

"Manyenga," one of the boys said softly.

The man parked his motorbike and approached Hock, saying, "The boy on the cycle said, 'The American is here,' and I said, 'I am knowing him. My grandfather was his friend.' Welcome, welcome. I am Festus Manyenga."

"Hello, Festus."

And there raced through Hock that feeling again, a lightness, a slackening in his flesh, of gratitude. He'd known the Manyenga family as important in Malabo. One of the older Manyengas, perhaps this one's grandfather, wore a pith helmet, and pinned to his long-sleeved shirt was a brass badge, lettered *Headman*.

Now the ritual of hospitality was extended to Festus Manyenga: tea, some dry crackers, the offer of bananas, and friendly talk: about the harvest, the condition of the road, the shortage of cooking oil, and the news that Hock had come—what they had heard about him, speaking of him as the long-ago figure of their elders' stories.

"I was a small boy when I first saw you," one of the men said. He was old, toothless, in a tattered shirt, with reddened eyes, his skin shiny and loose like a reptile's. "My father said, 'That man comes from America.'"

"We thought America was in Europe," Maso said.

"I never saw this man before. My ancestors, they were the friends," Manyenga said.

They talked in this congenial way, in English, praising Hock, and finally Manyenga got up and began to thank the men elaborately, taking their hands in his, repeating his gratitude, and Hock knew it was time to go.

"What do you have in the pipeline?" Manyenga asked.

Hock smiled at the expression. "Nothing special. Just to see Malabo."

"I can arrange, father."

His duffel bag was tied to the rear carrier of the motorbike, and he swung his leg over and sat behind Manyenga. They traveled under the shade trees the short distance to the main road and, after riding a few miles south, raising dust, turned onto the back road to Lutwe, which ran parallel to the Mozambique border. In Hock's time it had been a path; it was wider now but harder going. Manyenga settled the bike into one tire track and gunned it along the deep groove. After half an hour—twenty miles or so—Manyenga slowed the bike and plunged into the bush, not a road, hardly a track, just an opening in the high grass that led through the yellow bush to a clearing, a scattering of huts, the big upright baskets on legs that were granaries, the crisscrossed paths that marked the edge of Malabo.

Where the trees were greenest, on the banks of Nyamihutu Creek, a woman was beating a blue quilt suspended on a line. Near her a small girl was sweeping the smooth earth with a straw broom.

Though Manyenga had been shouting the whole way from Marka village, the engine of the motorbike kept him from being understood. Now that he pulled up at the hut, he said, "This is your home, father."

"I can only stay a few days," Hock said.

"You are welcome, father."

The woman and the girl fell to their knees and called out their greetings, and children and older boys from the other huts came running. The village gathered, hanging back. He saw that they were afraid of him—some of the older ones were terrified. Their anxious faces made him self-conscious. He wanted to reassure them. He would have handed out money, but he knew it would have created a mob scene.

"My other wife," Manyenga said of a scared-looking woman. "She was married to my brother."

"And who's this?" Hock asked.

The girl, too shy to speak, twisted her wraparound cloth in her fingers.

"Zizi," Manyenga said, and hearing her name, the girl covered her face. "My cousin's child. He died some two years ago. She was raised by her grandmother."

Seeing that the girl had gone shy, one of the small boys ambled near her, seeming to limp, and chattered at her. The boy had twisted fingers and sores on his legs and a battered face, flaky patches where hair was missing from his head. He could have been the victim of a fight, but Hock guessed he was epileptic, with head wounds from continually falling to the ground—and now Hock saw that he was not a boy at all, but a disfigured dwarf, boy-sized, in rags, who could have been any age.

"*Moni, moni,*" Hock said, greeting the dwarf and cajoling him, to distract him from teasing the girl. And rummaging in his duffel he found some candy that he'd bought at the hotel. "*Mankhwala,*" he said—medicine.

The dwarf laughed and ate it, drooling, licking his fingers, then walked unsteadily on stumpy feet, giggling because the others were laughing at him and calling out an English word.

"What are they saying?"

"His name, Snowdon."

Hearing his name, the dwarf said, "Fee-dee-dom!"

"What is that?"

"Freedom," Manyenga said in his own way, *friddom.*

"You speak English," Hock said to the dwarf, who made a face at him, then stuck out the quivering plug of his greenish tongue. He had the license of the fool, but the candy worked. "Medicine!" they cried. And though the girl did not look up again, Hock could see she was relieved that the dwarf was hobbling away.

"You can stay here, father," Manyenga said. "The roof is bad"—it was thatch, the bundles loose—"because we had so many challenges. But it's clean enough. Rest your body. My wife will bring water for your bath. Tonight we will have some chicken and rice. We can discuss your program."

Another of those words. "I don't have a program."

"Your agenda, father." Manyenga gestured, touching his ear. "Where is your mobile?"

"Cell phone? I don't have one."

"Not having?" Manyenga frowned, then drew his lips in a smile, as though expressing disbelief.

"Don't want one."

"Everyone wants a mobile."

"Maybe that's why I don't," Hock said, and saw that Manyenga was smiling broadly.

"Indeed, you are knowing what is best. You are a good example for partnering."

Partnering—yet another. It was Zizi who brought the water in a basin, with a small chip of soap, and after Hock had washed, he lay on the string bed and let down the mosquito net that hung like a bridal veil, and he dozed, hearing the boys' raised voices in the clearing, the sound of a ball being kicked. Where else in the world could you arrive unannounced and be welcomed on sight and given a bed? But Hock was still smiling at Manyenga's choice of words—pipeline, challenges, program, agenda.

Seeing that it was growing dark in the hut, he got up and went to the door, where it was lighter. The sky exploded over Mozambique in a fiery sunset. He searched his duffel for the bag of gifts, then walked toward the rising smoke across the clearing where Manyenga was sitting in a chair. Another chair stood empty beside him.

Hock distributed the presents he'd brought. The ballpoint pen he gave to Manyenga, a shawl he gave to the senior wife, a pocketknife to the junior wife, some books for the children. And he set down a large can of powdered coffee.

"America," the senior wife said, fingering the cloth.

Then the women served the food—slices from the goat leg that had been grilling on the fire, roasted corncobs, a bowl of *nsima* and stewed greens, plates of chicken and dried fish. Manyenga poured Hock a glass of *nipa,* and they toasted each other and drank.

The children sat a little distance away, and some other women were standing, holding babies in cloth slings.

Manyenga was talking, in English and Sena, and Hock nodding in agreement, though he slipped to the ground and rested his head against his chair.

He must have dozed, because he heard someone say, "Tired."

He found himself on all fours, and then was helped to his feet. Accompanied by someone with a lantern, walking beside him but saying nothing, he tottered to his hut and crawled under the mosquito net into his string bed, his flesh inert, like clay.

He woke before sunrise, as a cockcrow tore at the silence and the darkness. He could not remember ever having slept so soundly: no dreams, a whole night with his mouth open, drawing shallow breaths. They had given him a good meal, killed a chicken for him, brought him smoked fish. He had been almost tearful, thinking, Suppose it had all changed and modernized? He'd have been devastated. But the place was still simple and still smelled of the marsh and the river and wood smoke. He had dreamed of this for many years, awakening in Malabo, his real life, the only one that had ever mattered.

He listened to his compact shortwave radio until it was light, and then he walked the length of the village through the scrub. In the courtyard of most of the huts, crouching women fanned the glowing embers of cooking fires. Hock looked into the woven barrels of the granaries propped near the huts, and was glad to see they were full of dried corncobs. He saw the schoolhouse in the distance—he would save it for the afternoon. It was like seeing an old flame, the thirty-year-old now seventy-odd, thin, pinched, gone in the teeth, with a wan smile. He continued walking to the road, and past it, to the creek.

The water of the pool beside the stream, perhaps a hollowed-out part of the embankment that served as a landing place, was perfectly still, reflecting the far bank, the few palm trees, a scrap of cloud in the sky, and after a moment a slim girl stepping into it. She kept her *chitenje* cloth wrapped around her skinny legs, tugging it up a few inches so it wouldn't get wet.

As she stepped farther into the pool she kept raising the cloth, hitching it up against her legs. Now the hem was at her knees, now above her knees, still rising as she made her way into the deeper water.

She had a bundle on her head—laundry, he supposed. Maybe she intended to wash it at the nearby reach of the river, where there were rocks to lash it clean and the current was swifter and clearer, not the scummy green of this pool.

The solitary girl hiked her cloth up her bare thighs as she waded, the level of the water rising. Now the loose wrap was bunched in her fists, which held it at either side of her hips, the morning sun shining through her legs, flashing on the water as the cloth went higher.

The whole luminous process of the girl slowly lifting her *chitenje* wrap as she waded deeper into the still pool was one of the most teasing, heart-stirring visions he'd ever had. Yet she wasn't a tease. The cloth inched up with the rising water, and when it exposed the small honey-colored globes of her buttocks and she half turned to steady herself, the surface of the green pool brimmed against the patch of darkness at the narrowness of her body, a glint of gold, the skirt-cloth twisted just above it, Hock felt a hunger he had not known for forty years. He stared at the spangled sunlight in the gap between her legs.

He must have sighed, his desire was that strong, because the girl glanced over and bowed and clutched herself in a reflex of modesty. Then she turned away and was soon waist-deep in the pool, her cloth sodden, spread and floating around her like the blossom of a long-stemmed flower, as she waded away, seeming to float like a dark aquatic plant. It was the dead cousin's girl, Zizi.

Hock sat on a log watching fish nip at flies, disturbing the blur of scum in the stream. Then he returned to his hut. He shaved, wrote some notes in his journal. He unpacked his duffel bag, sorted his clothes, and hung up the empty duffel to keep it away from rats—he saw droppings on the floor, from rats nesting in the thatched roof.

All this, and it was not yet seven-thirty.

Announcing himself, calling out, "*Odi, odi,*" Manyenga visited after eight and invited Hock to breakfast. Now Hock saw how young he was, probably in his twenties, jaunty in a baseball cap and blue shirt.

"You were going about early," Manyenga said.

Someone had seen him. Now, an hour later, everyone knew.

"I slept so well," Hock said. "I hate to leave."

"So don't leave," Manyenga said.

They were standing before the hut, Manyenga frowning at the roof.

"But the roof must be replaced. I want to get an iron roof for you, but—eh! eh!"

Hock knew that grunting meant money.

"What about fixing the thatch? There's plenty of grass."

"The people who make the thatch are all dead. Even the women. Even myself I am not knowing. We are needing an intervention."

Hock knew he was asking for money for the roof, and what made him smile was the clumsiness of it—his first morning. Usually such a request came later. But Hock was not dismayed; he was more at ease knowing that Manyenga was unsubtle, and easier to watch. But he was surprised, too—it had all happened so fast.

He said, "We can talk about it."

"I'm going to the boma today. It is so far, but maybe they are having some iron sheets." He mumbled, seeming to search for more words. "It's a big priority."

Hock knew that Manyenga, in his mind, had already received the money, and bought the iron sheets for the roof, and kept the change, and perhaps put aside the scraps to sell or trade. It only remained for the transaction to take place, for Hock to hand over the money.

"I have provided this table for your projects." It was at the corner of the veranda; Hock hadn't noticed it. "You can take your breakfast here. I will find you later, father."

The girl Zizi brought the basin again and watched him as he washed his face and brushed his teeth. She returned with a plate of *nsima,* a puddle of oil in the center, and a bowl of vegetables in gravy and some tea. She stood in the shade. He spoke to her but she averted her eyes, perhaps ashamed from his having seen her hitching up her cloth in the stream.

As he was eating, Hock saw a creeping shadow come to rest: the little man, the bruised dwarf Snowdon, hunkered down by the veranda, rocking on his stumpy feet. Neglect and probably fits gave him the look of someone who'd been badly beaten. He was sad, his ugly face lopsided as if in pain, helplessly small, his wounds bright with infection.

Hock beckoned him over and gave him a lump of *nsima.* He crammed the whole lump into his mouth, crumbs on his fingers and cheeks, and chewed it with his mouth open.

"Snowdon," Hock said.

Hearing his name, the dwarf opened his mouth wide in satisfaction, showing Hock the half-chewed food on his greenish pitted tongue.

Hock leaned toward him and said, "Rubber buggy bumpers."

The dwarf hugged himself and gabbled and, sitting down and smiling, seemed to understand it as a phrase of welcome.

It was only nine o'clock. Hock smiled, thinking of the day that stretched ahead—the long overbright day of village somnolence, supine in its stillness, under trails of wood smoke and the confident boasting of the strutting crows and the *why-why-why* of the nagging shrikes.

9

OCK SAT OVER his notebook, smoothed it with the flat of his hand, poised his pen, tried to remember the date. What to say? Two lines, one about food, one about sleep; day and night. Superstitiously he avoided writing anything negative. He'd asked for this, and yet he pondered the clean pages of the notebook and his only thought was that he'd brought it from Medford, to record his memories. So far, there was nothing in Malabo he wanted to remember.

Around noon, he walked to the maize patch, picked up a hoe, stepped into the *dimba,* and began chopping the dry earth with it, scraping the weeds away. Two older boys saw him and laughed. He knew why: it was women's work. One of the boys held a rhino beetle on a length of thread; he had pierced the beetle with a needle. The beetle rose, trying to fly away, and fell heavily as the boy tugged it toward him.

Hoeing and hacking at a patch of dry shucks, Hock startled a snake. Deftly, he pinned its head down with the hoe blade, pressing it, then picked it up, and as he pinched it just behind its head, its long whipping tail caught his arm and wrapped it with the whole coil of its body.

"*Kalikukuti,*" he said. A twig snake, a juvenile, hardly two feet long.

The two boys stepped back, murmuring "*Njoka,*" snake. The one with the beetle let go of the insect, which dropped to the scattered trash of the corn shucks and scrabbled away, dragging its thread. Hock stepped out of the maize patch and the boys ran, stamping in the dust. Hock peered at the snake's odd horizontal pupil. He brought the snake back to his hut and put it into a basket on his veranda and covered it. Sitting near it, he felt less alone.

He slept through lunch. In the afternoon, he walked again to the stream, retracing his steps of the morning—perhaps this was the beginning of a routine? All the while he was followed by children, some of whom carried homemade toys of wire twisted into the shapes of cars and wagons.

They were small skinny children, all smiles—it seemed a village of children, like a settlement in a folktale. One said "*Mankhwala*"—medicine—and the rest chimed in. Hock knew they were asking for candy.

"Tomorrow," Hock said. He repeated it in Sena: "*Mawa.*" Seeing them laughing, he asked them if they knew English.

They shyly admitted no.

"Do you go to school?

"No school!"

He had intended to see the school that afternoon, but now the light was fading. Night came quickly: he'd see it tomorrow—something to do. As he watched the last long orangey tatters of the sunset, Manyenga called out, "Father!" for the evening meal. They ate as they had the previous night: the basin, the ceremony of being served by Zizi and the elder Mrs. Manyenga: *nsima,* stew, a portion of dried fish, a stinging swig of *nipa.*

Manyenga sat with him and in a tone meant to reassure him, said, "I have ordered the iron roof for your hut."

"How much?"

"Very cheap. I am knowing this man. I told him about you. His father remembers you too much. Maybe he was your student. He gave me a good price. He knows we are partnering."

Partnering? Hock said in Sena, "Lots of money"—*ndalama zambiri.*

"No, father. Not at all. One sheet for six thousand kwacha only." That was forty dollars.

"How many sheets do you need?"

Manyenga didn't answer. Hock knew the man was making a complex calculation, thinking of numbers and discarding them. At last he said, "Six," in the local way, *sick-ees.*

83

"Say five."

"Can manage five," Manyenga said readily.

After the meal, when Hock walked across the clearing to his hut, he saw a shadow on the veranda and turned his flashlight toward it—Zizi, her hand shielding her face, yellow palm showing. She knelt in the light, keeping her hand up, and he moved the beam away from her.

"What are you doing?"

"*Ujeni.*" She faltered in the half word, whatsit.

"Did Manyenga send you here?"

She didn't reply. Hock knew the answer. He said, "There's a snake in that basket," and hearing that, she stood and backed away. When she was gone he went inside and lay in the darkness, slightly drunk and levitated from the *nipa*.

The next day was the same: the walk, the dwarf at breakfast, the riverbank, a nap, another walk, writing notes; then dinner at Manyenga's, more talk of money, and bed. He wondered if time spent in such a random, unprofitable way could count as a routine. And he remembered his first weeks here—the full days of work, the hot nights by lantern light grading students' exercise books. He grew sad, admiring his younger, hopeful self.

"I want to see the school," he said to Manyenga on the third day, seeing him straddling his motorbike.

"It is finished, father."

"Maybe I could get it fixed up."

Manyenga considered this, chewing his lips, his face twisting in thought.

"Some boys are there."

In Hock's day, the school had been three buildings: a pair of classrooms joined by a veranda, an office block standing on its own, and a long brick privy, a *chimbudzi* that was also a wash house, boys at one end, girls at the other. These structures were roofed with a kind of plastic composite popular in the sixties. The cement floors were polished and buffed with oxblood-colored wax from a five-pound can.

Manyenga propped his motorbike on its kickstand and walked with Hock beyond the clearing, through the tall grass, to the

84

school. Head-high bushes had grown up around the buildings. The roof of the classrooms was mostly gone, only brittle pieces remaining. Weeds grew in the eaves. All the furniture had been removed. The table at his hut had been one of these. The windows were broken. The office was just a shell, though it showed signs that it had been lived in, mats and quilts twisted on the floor, scorch marks on the wall.

"Watch for snakes," Manyenga said.

Hock had supervised a renovation of the store in Medford. He knew a little about construction. He studied this ruin and tried to imagine how to put it back together. It was like the remains of an old civilization, more plausible as a ruin, more coherent, more venerable as wreckage.

A lovely tree dominated the scene of decrepitude, a tree Hock himself had planted, all those years ago, when the minister of education had visited to open the school—the minister had supervised the planting, but Hock had bought the sapling, dug the hole, and set the circle of bricks around it. The minister, fat in his suit, perspiring, had watched Hock slip the root ball into the hole and had lobbed a spadeful of earth into it as the children sang. Manyenga's grandfather had been one of those children, in the school uniform, khaki shorts and a gray shirt. The tree was now forty feet high, swelling over a pool of shade. Why hadn't they cut it down?

Beyond the tree lay the battered classrooms, the skeleton of the office, the vandalized latrine. Graffiti on the latrine walls was crude, but it was graffiti all the same, stick figures in unmistakable postures of copulation.

"How long has it been like this?"

"I am not knowing," Manyenga said, truly bewildered, which surprised Hock.

"We could fix it."

The windows gaped, the roof was gone, the doors were splintered but still attached to hinges. Hock mentally scythed the grass, roofed the school, imagined it with a coat of paint, laid out gravel pathways. And he put himself in the picture: he was standing on the veranda, as the minister had stood long ago, leading the students in the national anthem and giving them a pep talk.

"Didn't you go to school here?"

"I was schooling at Chimombo, near the boma. I completed my school certificate in Blantyre."

"You've done well. And you're still young."

"Yes, father."

Hock was thinking of the compound, the four huts, the motorbike, the two wives, the many children.

"I was a driver for the Agency some few years," Manyenga said. "They were bringing food and whatnot."

Now Hock understood Manyenga's buzzwords. "Why didn't you keep working for them?"

"They were cheeky. They were falsely accusing me. They couldn't cope up at all with our customs. Not like you, father."

Hock said, "Will you help fix the school?"

"I can send some chaps. They can help."

This wasn't the answer Hock was looking for, but he said, "Okay," and looking again at the ruin, he quoted a Sena proverb: "Slowly, slowly makes a bundle."

He was slashing at the weeds with a hacker the next day when the four boys arrived, creeping through the tall grass, parting the blades with their outstretched hands. None was older than fifteen or so. One said he'd just come from the creek, where he'd been fishing. They were like the young boys he'd known in the past, hungry, very thin, wearing rags for shirts and tattered trousers. They had been speaking in Sena.

"Speak English," Hock said.

"Ah!" And they laughed and covered their faces.

"The *mfumu* sent us."

So Manyenga was a chief?

"This was a school long ago," Hock said.

"It is nothing now," one of the boys said.

"But we can fix it. Then Malabo will have a school."

They were watching shyly, making sounds of breathing, not saying anything more, but the little breaths meant they were paying attention and seemed to understand.

"Who are your parents? Maybe I knew them."

They didn't reply. They seemed to grow shyer.

86

"No father, no mother," one said.

"They were sick," another, the tallest boy, said, drawing out the Sena word. He chopped with the flat of his hand. "They died."

"What about relatives?"

"We live down there"—and the boy squinted into the sun.

"How many altogether?"

The boy flashed ten fingers at Hock. "Small and big."

Hock was still holding the hacker, standing among the tall weeds and the overhanging bushes he had slashed. The cuttings on the ground were already withered, going pale in the strong sunshine and the heat.

"Help me," Hock said.

"We can try," the tall boy said. He took the knife from Hock. Another boy grasped the spare machete from a stump. They whacked at the weeds while Hock went through the classrooms to examine the wreckage. He heard the boys muttering and was gladdened by the sound of slashing. The blue sky showed through the smashed roof. The trusses were still sound—usable, anyway. The rooms were hot, sunlit, cluttered with dead leaves that had blown through the roof. Hock stepped carefully. He smelled snakes—it was an oiliness, a hanging odor of a decaying nest, the hot eggy stink.

He found a narrow tree limb and stripped it of its twigs and then poked with it and startled the snake he knew was there, a black-lipped mamba. He prodded it, let it whip and coil, and pressed its head with the end of the stick, quickly snatched it, keeping its frothy mouth just above his fist. Then he brought it outside to show the boys, a trophy they'd remember.

"Mamba," he said. "*Mbadza*."

But the boys were gone, and not only that, they'd taken the two knives.

"They are useless," Manyenga said later. He thought a moment. "Did you give them money?"

Hock said no.

Manyenga relaxed and smiled. "Ah," he said, as though to say, What did you expect?

They didn't discuss it further. Hock was not sure how to proceed. Perhaps it was all a mistake, perhaps this noncooperation meant it was time to go. All he had to do was ask Manyenga to take him to the boma, thirty-odd miles away, and catch the bus to Blantyre. But that would be so final, such a resignation, no hope of coming back. He'd put it off for a little while.

This thought induced him to distribute some small amounts of money to the women he encountered in his walks through the village. And one morning a few days later, he told Manyenga that it was time to leave.

With a pleading face, Manyenga said to him, "We need you, father."

Manyenga appeared disturbed by the suddenness. Hock had seemed at home, and now his abrupt announcement that he was leaving. Perhaps they feared his assertiveness. But he was affected by Manyenga's simple statement.

That same day the corrugated sheets of roofing were delivered, dumped at the roadside by an old van. Manyenga said they would put them on the house soon. "*Tsopano, tsopano,*" he insisted, slipping into Sena, then, "Now, now." When he spoke English, Hock felt the man was being untruthful.

Even without the boys' help, Hock went back to the school, and he slashed at the weeds and tried to tidy the classrooms and found the same black-lipped mamba in a corner of one of the rooms. Rather than disturb it, he swept the veranda, and Zizi helped with her straw broom. The dwarf Snowdon watched, flicking at the flies that settled on his sores.

Hock gave Zizi a handful of kwacha notes for helping him—just a dollar. He knew that Manyenga had sent her to stay by him, to sleep with him, and that all he needed to say was "Go inside," and she would have obeyed. She was thin, tall for a Sena woman, with a shaven head and skinny fingers, bony wrists, almost shapeless, small breasts, long legs, with wide feet. Those feet and the way she sometimes stood reminded him of a water bird, a heron perhaps. With a bath and stylish clothes she could have passed for the sort of model he'd seen in magazines—bald, with the starved angularity of high fashion. But she was hungry and hollow-eyed. She shadowed him, never coming too near, never quite sure what he wanted, yet eager to please him.

Snowdon just watched, and sometimes giggled, or held tight to a knife and wouldn't hand it over, jabbing at Hock, teasing him.

Hock kept working at the margins of the school, conspicuously, to attract attention or curiosity, perhaps shame the villagers into helping. No one helped, though sometimes a woman came looking for firewood, taking the splinters he chopped, or boys who scrawled with charcoal on the walls of the office, where they might have slept some nights.

It was as though he'd arrived and was living without being seen: an invisible *mzungu*.

10

THE NIGHT SKY was different from any other, a cloudless dome of bright blobs and pinpricks, and around a bald pitted moon were star clusters bright enough to read by. Every waking hour he was reminded that the world he knew was distant and inaccessible, so remote as to seem like another planet. He was immobilized in a vegetating settlement on a distant moon of that planet. In Medford, at the store, he'd often thought of the Lower River as a place he could easily travel to, if he'd only had the time. It was a matter of buying a ticket, making a few arrangements, withdrawing money from the bank, and setting off—a taxi to the airport, a blur of flights in a narrow seat, and then Malawi—Blantyre, Nsanje, Malabo. A jump across the world.

But here was a paradox: the way home from here was so hard it was nearly impossible to visualize from the depths of this place. He could imagine the narrow path out of the village, and the stony Lutwe road, but after that his imagination failed him. He had put himself into Manyenga's hands; Manyenga had guided him here. He had surrendered to the gravitational pull of the Lower River, and from here the whole world was hidden, as though he were not just on a faraway moon but trapped on its dark side, in an underworld. He'd arrived as if having squirmed through a thicket of baffles and finally the funnel that was the bad road, depositing him in a narrowness of bush and dust. He had no idea how to get out. A clear way was not apparent. No electricity meant early nights and twelve hours of equatorial darkness, no computer access, no Internet, no fax machine. He had asked to be disconnected, but that had been before he'd arrived. Now he was buried in utter silence, or else the mumble of "not possible." At first the disconnection had been an amusement. He'd even rehearsed his telling the tale to Roy or Jerry or Teya—how cut off he'd been, how remote, "another world," "lower depths." It astonished him to think that there was still a place on earth that lay outside the great transit of information or international chat. Long ago, much of Malawi had been like this—much of the world lay in darkness. Then, it had not been so remarkable to be isolated. He'd accepted it as normal.

Nowadays, such isolation was a novelty, and that was how he regarded it, as news to bring home—no phone, no mail, no juice at all. The separate villages in the Lower River were cut off from each other, the boma seemed as far away as Blantyre, and not only far but forbidden, the haunt of predators—tax collectors, party officials, thuggish boys—from whom villagers hid as from snakes. The stone under which they lay never moved.

Hock had taught English in Malabo, and though he was no reader, he'd boned up on the set books: *Great Expectations* had been one, and an African novel about independence, Wordsworth's poems, an abridged and simplified *Julius Caesar*. It now seemed extraordinary that he'd talked about them so earnestly in that ruined, roofless school. Only one other person had been able to teach them, Gala, and she'd gone off to a teachers' college in the hills outside Blantyre and earned a higher grade of teaching certificate.

Hock's own reading was, as he called it, "mind rot." He read detective stories, thrillers, "trash," he said, dismissing it all. Yet he persisted. He read science fiction and consoled himself with the thought that even though it might be regarded as trash, its redeeming feature was that it was based on a sort of speculative science. Science fiction spoke of the world of perhapses: perhaps we would find another habitable planet, perhaps we were not alone in the universe, perhaps on another orbiting rock elsewhere in darkest space lived loping plant-like creatures awaiting contact over great intergalactic distances . . .

Such reading was futile, frivolous, self-deceiving. You didn't need to devise a rocket journey to another galaxy to find alien life forms, for while the science-fiction writers were squinting into space, imagining insectile creatures and sentient sticks of matter and crystal cities and greenish almond-eyed mutants in boots—all of this fantasy—there were people in Malabo who were more remote, more cut off, less accessible than Martians or moon creatures.

Scientists had dreamed or imagined outer space into being and made a reality of space travel. But no one else on earth ever thought of the Lower River. Malabo was more distant than Mars. It was perhaps not all that remote in miles, but it was unknown, so it was at the limit of the world. Because of its isolation it was absurd, fantastic, unreal, a place of the naked and the misshapen. Alone in Malabo, Hock concluded that the villagers were unlike anyone he knew—they were different, too, from the people he'd lived among here years ago. They had changed, regressed drastically in their small subterranean hole in the world through which a river ran as dark as any in classical myth. The villagers on this riverbank did not look like other people, they did not think about the wider world, they did not talk like anyone else—and when they did speak, they didn't make sense. They didn't walk like other people, or eat or drink like anyone he'd ever known. And so from the beginning he saw that they were different, and what was more disturbing, they saw that he was different—utterly unlike themselves, a visitor from a distant place that was unknown but whispered about, impossibly far, unreachable from here, where they lay buried in their belowground river world.

At night, looking up, he was dazzled by the masses of stars and the winking planets and the streaking long-tailed comets, the big moon that at times looked as though it was made of bleached coral; and it seemed that those bright stars and that crusted moon were nearer than Medford.

Time, too, was retarded—or else crazed, circular, inverted, as it might be in deep space, one of those black holes into which the science-fiction writers tucked their voyagers. Hock could not remember when he'd arrived. He could not count the days that had passed, even the names of days had lost their significance, since they were indistinguishable. Market day was no longer observed, because there was nothing to sell. Sunday didn't exist in a place where no one went to church, and the church itself had fallen into ruins. He remembered the progression of his first day—his nap, the meal, the sound sleep. He remembered his first glimpse of Zizi, of the dwarf, of Manyenga's initial demand for money. After that it was sunrise, heat, sunset, the night sky, the stars, the suggestion that he was on another planet—that he was lost.

Some days he'd forgotten why he'd come, and Manyenga would show up for money, and only then would he think, I must get away.

Manyenga said after breakfast one day, following Hock so that no one would hear, "What are you looking at, father?"

"Nothing," Hock said, bewildered by the ambiguous question.

"In the night, father. Looking with your eyes."

How had they spotted him at midnight in the grove behind his hut, his arms crossed, his face upraised? Hock was reminded that he was happier in Malabo at night. He'd never used a flashlight, because any other light would have dimmed the stars. Standing in the darkness, he had not moved, only gaped at the sky. Yet they knew—they knew everything. Someone had seen, and here "someone" meant everyone.

"*Mphanda,*" Hock said. "I like to look at it."

Instead of placating Manyenga, the answer seemed to disturb him. Hock had given the Sena name for the Southern Cross, their word for the ridgepole of a house, which is how it looked to them. He realized, too late, that he should have said, "Not looking at anything special." But he had been specific in identifying the stars, and he knew such a reply was suspect, witch-like, as though the murmur of an element in a spell that might relate to a person's house.

"Some people think the stars can control us," Manyenga said.

"Which people?"

"Many people. Even those people at the Agency where I worked. One *mzungu* lady with much schooling, she herself said so."

"Do you think so?"

"I am a simple man," Manyenga said, and saying this, he had never sounded more complicated or crafty. "Myself I don't know these things. But you, father, you are the expert."

He said *exputt,* which could have been "expat" or "expert."

"I was just thinking how far away we are," Hock said.

Manyenga laughed, whinnying *Eh-eh-eh* in his throat, genuinely amused.

"Far away from what, father? We are here, right here in the middle of the world on our great river. We are having—what? We have food, we have water, we have *ujeni*, the river. I have my big wife and my little wife and my children." Manyenga stamped his foot in the dust and said again, "We are here!"

"At the center of the universe," Hock said.

"Yes. In the middle. We are having everything."

With a thin querying smile, Hock said, "You have everything?"

"We have much," Manyenga said, and he was returning that thin smile. "And you have much."

Hock didn't reply to this. He knew what Manyenga was saying: You belong to us.

Manyenga was hesitating. Finally he said, "You tell me you are observing the ridgepole. So what are the stars saying to you?" And he laughed. "That is what the people are asking. Not me. I know you are just taking refreshment in the cool air. But they are asking, 'What are the stars saying to the father?'"

Hock couldn't say "nothing." No one would believe him. Nothing was a concept no one understood. Every act, every word, every event had a something to it, a direct cause. The fall of a branch was motivated by someone; a dead animal was always an omen; a person's illness or bad luck was caused by someone who not only had a grudge but had the power to bring illness down upon that victim, or sour the person's luck.

Someone staring at the night sky was studying the heavens, monitoring the approach of events, conspiring with the stars to bring misfortune upon an enemy, wishing to visit destruction on someone.

"They are fearing," Manyenga said.

Hock said, "Fearing what?"

"The *mzungu*. The father."

Hock said, "Sometimes I can't sleep."

"And they are saying that, too. The *mzungu* is awake when we are sleeping. He is like the *fisi*."

Hock laughed at the word. "They think I'm a hyena?"

"The *fisi* is awake at night. They are fearing for that reason, too. A sorcerer can be any animal. And they presume you are looking for a lightning bolt in the sky."

"Why would I look for a lightning bolt?"

"Because you are a friend of the snakes, and the lightning is a snake from the sky, as the rainbow is a snake from the earth. A sorcerer can be able to join them, heaven and earth. You think we are stupid?"

It was impossible for Hock to tell whether Manyenga was teasing. Hock had heard of the rainbow as a snake, rising from the river or a pool, but the lightning as a snake from the sky? Was that something new, or a resurrected belief of a people who felt they had been bypassed? He was from another world, and knew he needed to be careful: he was ignorant here. The remote village had strict rules and fixed beliefs and many suspicions. In the forty years that had passed since he'd last been here the villagers had drifted farther off, they were more distant, the shadows deeper. Or was it all, he sometimes wondered, a shakedown?

"What was this Agency, the charity you worked for?" Hock asked.

He was merely trying to change the subject, but Manyenga was silenced by the question; he stared at Hock as if this question was somehow related to his inquiries about the stars, the suspicions that Manyenga had voiced.

"They were from Europe," Manyenga said. "And some people from America."

"The Agency was the name of their charity?"

"Why are you wanting to know?"

"I have friends who give money to these people. I can tell them their money is useful."

"The money is rubbish," Manyenga said. "They don't give it the right way. They were cheating me."

"I'm just asking what the organization was called."

"And they were false witnesses," Manyenga said.

"Did they come here to Malabo?"

"That was the badness. They promised to deliver us. But they were telling blue lies."

Manyenga had grown angry, and looked sullen as he spoke.

Hock was reminded again of how this simple conversation about the stars had veered off course.

"Never mind," Hock said, and began to walk away.

Following him, toeing the dusty path with aggrieved steps, Manyenga said, "And they were causing trouble."

"What kind of trouble?"

"And bringing deadly diseases," Manyenga said, still treading angrily. "They were false friends." He tugged the loose sleeve of the khaki shirt that Hock wore as protection from the sun and the insects. "But you yourself are not like that, father. No, indeed, you are being a true friend."

In spite of trying to keep a straight face, Hock found himself smiling, with a slight heave of laughter in his throat, because he knew what was coming next.

"And those people who were whispering when they saw you at night observing the stars of the *mphanda* in the dark sky—no!" Manyenga, overdoing it as usual when he pretended to be indignant, worked himself into a fury, popeyed, clawing the air with his fingers. "I told them, eh! He is our father and our friend. He will never make magic against you. Don't! I am telling them"—he made a chopping gesture with his big square hand as a froth of spittle flecked the corners of his mouth—"don't be fearing."

"Thanks, Festus," Hock said, but no more than that.

"Please, father. Do not thank me for saying the truth. How can I lie? It is not natural for me."

"People here used to know me," Hock said. "No one knows me now."

"I am knowing you, father." Manyenga whipped his hand, snapping his fingers for emphasis. "I am knowing you too much."

"But if the people I'd known before, long ago, were still alive, you wouldn't have to tell people about me."

"Some are alive."

"Who?"

"Elders." He named a few families, mentioned people whom Hock didn't know. He listed the men in the riverside villages of Marka and Magwero, whom Hock had met that first day—children, grandchildren of men he'd known.

"And the teacher, that old woman."

Hock shook his head and squinted for more.

"Gala Mphiri."

Hock regretted his show of surprise, the "What?" that escaped him as a grunt. But he couldn't help it—the name was an echo of the name in his mind.

Manyenga didn't smile. He held the smile back, kept it in his mouth. He knew he had made his point. And it was then that he asked for money.

11

A S A YOUNG TEACHER in Malabo, stricken with a love hunger he had never known before, he had desired Gala, had to have her or he would be ill. She was aware of his hot gaze, often turning her head to look aside and smile at him, sensing his eyes on her. It was also a measure of his happiness in Malabo that he wanted her. She was slender and strong, she was aloof, striding alone from her hut to the school—white blouse, long dark skirt, red sandals. What would I give up to have her? he sometimes thought, answering himself, Everything. He would stay there, become a Malawi citizen, live in the bush, raise children, never return home. Some people did that, Fogwill for one, which was why it had been such a shock to see toothless Fogwill in Blantyre: the man he might have been.

But Norman Fogwill had married a village girl who wanted brighter lights, and Mrs. Fogwill, a Yao villager from the lakeshore, had left the country to live in England. Gala was a different sort. Hock guessed that she would never leave, but it surprised him to know that she was still alive.

She was not more than twenty at the time of independence. She had the flattish, vaguely Asian face that some Sena people had, the high cheekbones, the slanted hooded eyes. Her shaven head revealed its sculptural symmetries, her neck was slender and fragile-seeming. She was very thin, with tight muscles in her arms and legs that gave her a loose springy walk, her small high buttocks beating against her swinging skirt or her wraparound, the red *chitenje* she sometimes wore.

Hock had hesitated, but he had been confident that he would persuade her to marry him. He hoped she would sleep with him first, but so what? He could offer her everything. It was only a matter of time. How could she refuse? He knew the power a *mzungu* had in the Lower River—something magical, almost god-like. He didn't want to think how he'd overwhelm her with his aura of being a white man in a remote place that had seen so few of them—always armed, in Land Rovers, wearing boots and shouting, sturdy, pink, and indifferent among the naked skinny Sena people. Some of them, the toughest, were Portuguese planters who had wandered over the border at Villa Nova, or crossed the river looking for animals to shoot. None had been teachers, like Hock. They had never seen anyone like him.

"We need to discuss the syllabus," he'd said.

"I am ready."

"Come to my house."

"Yes, I will pop in."

The day she dropped by his house, he sent his cook to the market. The cook was so surprised that in the midst of his sweeping he left his broom in the bucket. Hock made tea, he talked, he offered her cookies, he procrastinated, he knew night was falling but did not light his lamp. He tuned his shortwave radio and got music from Rhodesia Radio.

"Beatriss," Gala said.

The word was unpronounceable on the Lower River. The Beatles had just reached southern Africa. Hock poured the only alcohol he had, two glasses of warm vermouth from a dusty sticky bottle.

"What is this?" She sipped and made a face.

Behind her head, out the window, across the clearing, the sky was alight in the thickened flames of sunset, and a lamp was glowing on the veranda of a hut, the orange flare in a glass chimney. Night thickened around it. Hock wanted darkness, his face hidden, his jittery fingers unseen.

In the darkness of his own house, so far from home, among people he liked and trusted, he was surprised at his eagerness, even more surprised by how he seemed—single-minded, slightly breathless, all his attention fixed on Gala. She sat on the creaking rattan sofa opposite, her small rounded head framed by the window and the glow from the distant lantern, her face in shadow. He knew she was smiling by the way she asked about the vermouth, sipping it, the smile an indication of her uncertainty, the sweetish medicinal taste.

"It is wine?"

"A kind of wine."

"From Portuguese East?"

All the wine they knew there came as contraband from Mozambique, and the empty bottles were coveted as containers, used as lamps or as water bottles in canoes.

"From Italy. You like it?"

She shuddered, she laughed—a new taste in a culture where all tastes were age-old.

"It is alcoholic, like *kachasu*." It was the polite word for *nipa*.

"You drink *kachasu*?"

"Myself I never take."

She wasn't drinking, only sipping. Hock thought, If she drinks a glass or two, she might get woozy enough to listen. But the vermouth was warm, syrupy even to him. She was politely pretending not to dislike it, to accommodate him. For months she had been a friend, a fellow teacher, but this was the first time he'd been alone with her in the dark.

"If only we had ice," he said.

"Ha! Ice in Malabo, a miracle," she said. "Even the word we are not having."

"Next time, I'll get some ice from Blantyre," he said, standing up, delivering the statement like a piece of news, using it as an occasion to take three steps to the sofa, to sit next to her.

The crackling of the brittle rattan seat under him, the shiver of the frame as she moved aside, stirred him, as he draped his arm across her shoulder, stroking the white blouse.

"Put the light, please," she said.

"I like it like this."

She held herself and said, "I always imagine snakes coming in the dark."

"The snakes are afraid of me," he said.

"But not of me." And she sniffed for emphasis. She was quick like that; no one else in Malabo would have had that answer.

"I'll protect you." He hitched nearer and settled his arm on her. She shrank, even under his light touch.

In that moment he became aware that she was humming the music that was playing on the radio, the song a throbbing murmur in her throat: She loves you, yeah, yeah, yeah. She didn't know any of the verses but she had the rhythm perfectly, and now it was rising in her throat, ringing softly in her head.

He touched one of her breasts, shaping its softness through the cloth of her blouse. Breasts had no magic in Malabo—most of the women went bare-breasted. Gala didn't object. She patted his hand as though in chaste friendship.

"I like you so much," Hock said.

"Alice," she said, her version of Ellis, but nothing more. She held her face away, as if anticipating that he'd kiss her. But though her body was turned to the opposite wall, she held his thigh, seeming to steady herself. And she was canted against him, in his arms, as he stroked her breast. It fitted his hand and the underside had a softness. Her breast was as firm as fruit under her modest buttoned blouse.

He moved to touch her between her legs, but she resisted with such sudden force it was as though he'd pinched her.

When he had soothed her, she resumed crooning, a new song now, the Beatles again, he didn't know the name. As she sang in her throat and her nose, groaning, moving just perceptibly to the music, she steadied herself, slipped her hand between his legs and pressed, and he almost fainted with pleasure. He let go of her breast, put his mouth on her neck, and was glad for the darkness.

The Sena had a peculiar way of eating, not just gathering the lump of steamed dough and splashing it into the stew, as other Malawians did. Instead—perhaps to prolong the anticipation of eating, they were always so hungry, and food was so scarce—they broke off a corner of the hot dough, held it in their fingers, and kneaded it like a pellet, using the heel of the hand, smoothing it, making it into a small ball, then flattening it again, working it more with the fingers and palm, savoring it, sharpening their appetite in the delay, bringing it to perfection, breaking it down. The act, like mastication, was done without hurry, using only that one clean hand, continually pressing and squeezing, massaging the lump.

He had seen Gala eat this way. And this was what Gala was doing now, working her skinny fingers and her hard palm on him. What would have seemed gross and obvious in daylight was, in darkness, a bewitchment. He let her continue, saying nothing, then held his breath, and when the quickening pain of the release was too great, he caught her hand and held it and sighed.

She was listening, looking away, her head erect, alert. She had stopped humming, though the music still played.

"What is that?" Her fingers were inquiring on his lap.

He didn't want to say, and his deeper silence seemed to animate her. She laughed softly. She tapped and traced the way she did with her fingers on food.

"Wet," she said. "Is wet."

He clapped his knees together like a startled girl, and placing his damp hand on her much cooler one, he lifted it away.

"I want to see," she said, turning to him. She was whispering. "What is it?"

"You know."

"I have never."

In the darkness she was not the bright schoolteacher with copybooks under her arm, but an African of wondering bluntness: *What ees eet?* And *Ees wait* and *I hev nayvah.*

She searched in her carrying basket, and the next thing Hock knew she was laughing, softly waving the beam of her old chrome flashlight around the room and into his eyes and onto his pants. She let out a sound that was not a scream but much worse, a low agonic moan, as if expelling her last breath: a terror of dying where she sat.

The yellow light had fallen across the room in the crease between the wall and the floor where a puff adder lay like a strange misshapen hose, tensed and swelling, its blunt flat head lifted from the gritty floor, its eyes glinting at them.

"Don't move," Hock whispered. "Keep the flashlight on him."

The wide froth-flecked mouth of the snake was slightly parted, spittle coating its narrow lips. Its shadow gave it extra coils, so it seemed a great knotted thing fattening against the far wall.

"He can't see us behind the light."

But Gala's shoulders were narrowed in fear, and her hand shook so violently that Hock was afraid she'd drop the flashlight. The flickering beam seemed to disturb the snake. The wedge of its head lifted to sample the air with its darting tongue.

Taking the pillow from behind Gala on the sofa, Hock hitched forward, and when the rattan squeaked, the snake tensed again. Hock tossed the pillow in front of it, and the snake sprang at it, leaping full length from the last coil of its tail, and striking it, imprinting a clean parenthesis in spittle of its mouth shape on the cloth.

Gala yelped in terror as Hock snatched the flashlight from her. He kicked the lengthened snake across the room, where it gathered itself again and made for the open door, thrashing back and forth, its mouth still gaping for air.

"It's okay," Hock said. "It wasn't a big one. And not poisonous, though they bite."

"All snakes are poisonous," Gala said.

"It's a puff adder, not deadly. And it's gone."

"I should never have come to this house." Gala fretted breathlessly, reproaching herself.

Hock walked her back to her hut, which she shared with another teacher, since it was, like his, a hut provided by the school. Her home was in an adjacent village, nearer the river, where her father had a fishing canoe in a small compound on high ground in the marsh.

Too upset to speak, she turned away from him at her hut and uttered a formula of words in Sena, which could have been a curse or a prayer.

Yet it had all excited him. After that, Hock could not think of her visit, and her embrace, without thinking of the snake—the desperate bright-eyed thing coiled in the room all the while they'd spent body-to-body, her hand moving on him.

He did not mention any of it again. She was oblique with him, but still friendly, more familiar, as though strengthened by the episode. Hock guessed that she was so sure she'd made a mistake, she was confident she'd never do it again, and her resolve made her franker with him.

One day he said, "I need some help with the report cards."

"But I am busy." She laughed. She would never have said that before.

It was odd for him to think that he had no power over her, no influence at all; even odder that she giggled at him instead of offering to help. And yet—in her eyes, anyway—hadn't he saved her from being bitten by a snake?

A month or more went by before he risked inviting her again. In the meantime, he bought her some ointment at Bhagat's General Store for a wound on her leg. When she accepted the tube of medicine, he concluded that all was well. He'd asked her to his house. But when she was with her friends, or the other woman teacher, Grace, she mocked him gently or pretended not to hear him, twisted away from him in a dance step that only aroused him more.

In time, he thought, she'll give in, she'll listen. What else was there for her on the Lower River? Her father was a fisherman, her brother helped him mend his nets; only Gala had an education, because she had no practical skills that would be of use on the river.

Surprising her one day in the classroom after the students had left, he shut the door and leaned against it and said, "I want to talk to you."

She said nothing at first, keeping her gaze on the copybooks she was stacking.

"You can talk," she finally said, though she didn't look up.

"I want to see you."

"Aren't you seeing me now?"

"In my house."

"Sorry. I cannot."

"Tell me why."

Adding another copybook to the stack, she said, "I am betrothed."

"To be married?" He was stunned.

She said primly, "What else?"

"Who's the lucky man?"

"Mr. Kalonda. I think you are not knowing him. He has an official post at the boma."

"Married," he said, fixing the word on her. "How long have you known him?"

"For some two years, but he was in discussion with my father about the *lobola*."

The issue was always the dowry, the bride price, never love. Among the Sena it was the man who had to come up with money or a cow to compensate the parents for the loss of their daughter.

"Do you want to marry him?"

"A girl must marry," Gala said. She sighed and slipped the copybooks into her basket. "That way her parents can earn. If she has a man without being married, the parents will not get any money."

"Was he your fiancé when you visited me that day?"

"You tricked me," Gala said. "And your snake threatened me." Now she was her mocking self, and seemed even more confident having told him of her betrothal. But he wanted her. Her eyelashes were long and black and glossy, her skinny fingers clutched at the basket, chips of pink on her fingernails, the wound healing on her leg.

"What will I do without you?"

She saw that he was teasing—what else could he do? He was sorrowful, having heard her news. He could not show her his sorrow. Anyway, she seemed to know, but there was nothing to be done.

"You have your snakes," she said. She stood up. "Please open the door. I have to go to my home."

Hock hesitated, then opened it. But she did not leave. She walked toward him and onto the veranda, where she turned.

"I like you, Ellis," she said. "I know you like me. But nothing can happen now. I have a fiancé. If he suspects that I am not true to him, he can refuse me. My parents will get nothing. And they are needing."

She did not wait for a reply—he didn't have one, in any case. She hurried away, and he told himself that in these determined strides, and all this talk of money, she was less desirable. He knew she was unattainable, and still virginal, strong, certain, unsentimental, doing her duty as a daughter and a village girl, following protocol and marrying the civil servant. Her parents would get a cow, and some money. Her whole life lay ahead of her.

Gala's rejection of Hock made his leaving easier, and when the message came that his father was ill, he swept away without looking back. Burdened by the family business, he was sure that phase of his life was over, his four years in Africa under the starry sky. But as the years passed, he often thought of Gala on the sofa, her head at the height of the window, the daylight waning, and the fiery sunset giving way to darkness; the whispers in the dark, the radio music, her touch, unmistakable—squeezing the life out of him; and the snake, dazzled in its darkness, frantic, rising to strike.

In his life as a man it was perhaps the sharpest desire he'd ever felt. Even the memory of it years and years later was capable of arousing him. And what was it? Just a touch, no more, but unforgettable, unrepeatable, magic.

12

THE SOURCE OF Hock's contentment, years ago, had been his trust in their innocence. He had been happy when he had never suspected anyone in Malabo of having a darker motive. Grateful, he'd felt blessed. Now it was a struggle that made his head hurt. Hock was so suspicious of Manyenga and those he influenced that he was wary of announcing his intentions, or so much as speaking casually. The consequences were obvious. If you know what's in a man's mind, you have power over him.

The other side to this was their obliqueness—the villagers in Malabo never said anything that might reveal how they really felt. This trait made them seem mild, but they were deeply suspicious of him now, too, nor were they innocent. And he had come with the best intentions, had handed out money, had shown that he wanted to help. He even picked up a shovel and a slasher and cleared the schoolyard for the restoration of the Malabo school. But in their general glum strangeness they didn't trust him.

What does he want? they seemed to think. He saw the question in their guarded smiles, their sidelong looks, their narrowed eyes, the way they floated a suggestion—"We can manage better if we have a new well"—and glanced to see whether he'd bite. He could no longer be truthful; they would mistake the truth for a ruse.

He didn't want anything from them, but he knew what they wanted from him. Simple enough: an unending supply of kwacha notes. Because the money was so devalued, the denominations of bills so small, even a modest sum, fifty dollars' worth, was a whole big bag full of paper. And along with the need for money was the need for him to be a witness to their distress, or so he thought. They seemed to want to prove to him that they were worthy of this charity. Yes, it was a shakedown.

When he had nothing left, he'd go. But he resisted telling them anything of his plans, and he was sorry he'd shown so much emotion when Manyenga had told him that Gala was alive. Manyenga had uncovered one of his secrets, that he still had a feeling for the woman he'd known so long ago, a memory he had not shared with Deena in the many years of their marriage.

"You want me to take you to her?" Manyenga said a day or two later, tossing his head. "I can arrange it."

He didn't need to say Gala's name. He knew what Hock was thinking, and was exploiting it. Hock reminded himself that Manyenga had lived among the aid workers for whom he'd been a driver. He had learned to read the gestures and expressions of Europeans; he knew all about *mzungu* reactions. He knew when to be silent and when to intervene. It was his mode of survival. Europeans could be obvious when they were anxious. He had been their fixer. *Festus, see what those people want—Ask them the price—Find us a place to stay—Get us some food here—Talk to the chief—Meet us with the van—Deliver that message.*

Manyenga had been their man. The relationship had gone wrong in the end, Hock was sure of that, because in his greed and laziness Manyenga had gone too far. Believing he knew them, he became overconfident, incautious, reckless. They had misjudged him, and he hadn't known when to stop. Even in his dealings with Hock he didn't realize how obvious he was.

That was a lesson to Hock, who did not want to be obvious either, who had always hoped he'd be able to slip back into the village, hardly noticed, to pick up where he'd left off.

So to Manyenga's presumptuous question he replied, "Take me where?"

"To the woman—Gala."

"No," Hock said. "It's not important."

That baffled Manyenga. He had a habit of picking his nose when he was especially reflective. He scrunched his face, his thumb in one nostril, and his bafflement gave Hock time to think.

Hock was not alone. The skinny girl Zizi still brought him

hot water in the black kettle for tea in the morning. She carried his laundry away, the bunched pile in her thin arms. Whether she washed the clothes herself he wasn't sure, but it all came back to him folded, ironed as he instructed, with the clumsy hot-coal iron. It wasn't the crease that mattered; what was important was that they had been heated. The whole of the Lower River was buzzing with blowflies. These putzi flies laid eggs on damp clothes on the line. Ironing killed the flies' eggs and the possibility that they'd hatch from the warmth of his wearing the clothes and burrow into his skin, the maggots in his flesh that had become boils he'd suffered in his first year with unironed clothes at Malabo.

Zizi knelt and swept with the twig broom, she dusted and fussed, and she clucked when she knocked things over. But he loved to see her happy, stretching in the heat, muttering "*Pepani!*"—Sorry!—as she brushed past him. Although he did not tell her what he wanted, he trusted Zizi. Her large dark eyes and long lashes spoke of innocence, and he could see that she looked to him as a protector. When the bratty boys in the village teased her for being a virgin, she sidled nearer to Hock and the boys were silenced, abashed, because while they were suspicious of his intentions, he knew they feared him, understood that as a stranger he was strong. Zizi knew that he didn't despise her.

And Snowdon, with his scabby face and twisted fingers and clumsy feet, he too looked to Hock for protection, since dwarfs were often murdered and their bodies used to make medicine. Snowdon could see that Hock was taken by Zizi—in a way that surprised and embarrassed Hock. He guessed it one late afternoon as Hock sat on his veranda watching Zizi crouching, sweeping the dust and leaves from the courtyard, cleaning it the way Malabo women did, claiming the shady front of the house by tidying the ground. Snowdon toiled over to her on his damaged feet and pinched her shoulder.

Zizi twisted inside her *chitenje* wrap, loosening it, then stopped to adjust the cloth, drawing it closer and retying it, edging away from the dwarf.

"She is beautiful," Snowdon said in his screechy voice, glancing slyly at Hock. "She is"—and here he twisted his mouth and spoke his one English word—"fee-dee-dom."

Another one who had had a clear glimpse of what lay in Hock's heart.

Wide-eyed, her lips pressed together as though for balance, breathing anxiously through her nose, Zizi stood, presenting him with a tin bowl of chicken and rice. She was black and slender and emphatic, like an exclamation mark in flesh, upright before him, her wrap slightly slack at her small breasts, standing on large feet, bobbing slightly as a clumsy courtesy and a show of respect when she handed over the hot bowl of food.

Hock loved being barefoot on his wood plank veranda, drinking warm orange squash, sitting in his shorts, eating the tough chicken and sticky rice, peeling a juicy mango, treating himself to one of the last chocolates in his stash, while Zizi watched him from the edge of the veranda, the dwarf gnawed his fingers, and mourning doves moaned in the twisted thorn tree. He felt like an animal then, a happy animal, with food in his paw, his face smeared.

But he was alone. And on hot afternoons like this it was easy for him to believe he was the only foreigner on the Lower River, the last living *mzungu* on this hot dusty planet, with his retinue, the skinny girl, the dwarf, and his snakes. He was so content in this role as the last man, he had stopped tuning his radio and ceased to take an interest in the news. He rediscovered what he'd forgotten from before: stop listening to the news, and let two weeks go by; tune in again, and you realize you've missed nothing, and so you were cured of the delusion that you needed to stay current. The news didn't matter, because nothing was news. Nothing mattered. No one was interested in Malabo—this was why the people in the village must have suspected him of having a deeper motive for visiting. He wanted something from them—why else would he come all this way to live in a hut? Altruism was unknown. Forty years of aid and charities and NGOs had taught them that. Only self-interested outsiders trifled with Africa, so Africa punished them for it.

He was much harder to read than any of the other outsiders because he was alone—there was an implicit boldness in that. He had no context, no vehicle, no way out. He was a stranger, a solitary, and the only way to his heart was to confront him with a skinny girl, like the traveler to whom they would offer a bowl of food or a drink from a green coconut, as though to test him, to see if he was really a man, and also to disarm him, to delay him, to confine him, to obligate him.

Did Zizi know she was being used? At times he stared at her with an old hunger—he could not help himself. She set the food on the wobbly table and he reached for it and snagged her fingers and held on, tugging a little. He watched her anxious eyes widening, her pressed-together lips, her nostrils opening for air, and it sometimes seemed to him that her ears moved, twitching to hear a danger signal. She stood, her feet together and overlapping slightly, one big toe clamped on the other.

Her hands were marked with her history. Her fingers, though slender and delicate-looking, were like twigs to the touch, callused and rough at the tips from handling firewood and heated pots. The backs of her hands were scaly, slick, and with her hard palms seemed almost reptilian. She was not old—sixteen?—but she'd been working since the age of six or so, carrying wood, picking maize, thumping the corn with the heavy pestle pole. Like any old woman she could carry the hottest tin container in her bare hands. The work had hardened her hands, and though they were graceful from a distance, holding her hands in his, Hock could feel only the thickened and dead skin that made him think he was holding a claw. And he knew that her fingers were so desensitized by heavy work, she could hardly feel warmth from his. Still, he held on to her hand, and knew her life better. He wanted her to know that he cared for her.

A choking sound from the doorway made him turn. Snowdon was gagging on a clot of mucus in his damaged nose, watching them with his whole ruined face.

Zizi's wordless way of responding to the intrusion was a sudden eyebrow flash and the scratch of a quite audible sniffing.

"Send Snowdon to get some water," Hock said, because he did not want a witness to this, not even the dwarf, who was despised by the village.

Zizi was loud, heckling the dwarf with instructions and smacking the bucket for effect and chasing him down. And after the dwarf had tottered away on his almost toeless blunted feet, Zizi returned, her arms at her sides, twisting her *chitenje* wrap in her fingers.

Hock said, "Tell me, do you know a woman named Gala?"

Zizi's yes was a lifting of her eyebrows and an intake of air at her nose.

"Does she live in Malabo?"

Zizi frowned, half closed her eyes, and allowed her head to tilt once, sideways just a little, as though reacting to an odor on a rising breeze.

"You know where she lives?"

The eyebrows again, and the widening eyes that made the face lovely and innocent. All this time she had not opened her mouth.

"Nearby?" The Sena word was one of Hock's favorites, *pafoopy*.

A scarcely perceptible nod that was unmistakable, and she drew in her chin for emphasis.

"How do you know her?"

Zizi went shy and knotted her fingers. She swung around as if to see whether anyone was listening, and then in a croaky voice she said, "My *gogo*," and then, unexpectedly in English, "My granny."

After she'd gone, Hock realized that she had taken him into her confidence. She hadn't wanted anyone to hear her. Perhaps she was the one person he could trust.

The presence of this tall skinny girl relieved his days, and when he considered that she was the granddaughter of Gala, he thought, Of course. "Auntie" meant many things, but "granny" meant only one: they were directly related. He could now discern a strong resemblance between Zizi and the Gala he had known as a young woman in Malabo, when he'd been a young man—two people in their twenties in a country that had just awakened from more than half a century of colonization. It had been a drama in Blantyre, a big event that Fogwill clearly recalled, the Duke of Edinburgh present as the Union Jack had been lowered. In Malabo it had been a party, schoolchildren dancing, villagers singing, and two days of drunkenness.

"But we are the same," an old man had said to Hock then. "Maybe wuss."

"No more British," Hock said.

"In the Lower River nothing change."

The man who had said that was Gala's father, whom Hock had met at the dance performance.

"Gala's not coming?"

"We are Christians. Myself, I was baptized at Chididi Mission," the old man said, frowning at the bare-breasted girls, the sweaty stamping boys in the *likuba* dance, the spectators with fire-brightened eyes. The celebration had been a shock in the Lower River. It was not a patriotic display, with banners, parades, or the pious speeches of the large towns. It was two days of debauchery, a feast of smoked fish and rice, jerry cans of home brew—the frothy porridgey beer that women made of fermented corn—the riotous boys, the shrieking girls. Hock had been startled by the sudden eruption of hilarity, and he'd been afraid, too, because it was his first experience of Sena recklessness, a wild streak, and the binge drinking that had tipped into brawling and rape. Some boys had howled at him for being a *mzungu*.

Then it was over. No one spoke about how the independence celebration had gotten out of hand.

All that was in the distant past. He remembered the old man saying *We are the same* and *Maybe wuss*. But it didn't matter. They were themselves. In most respects the Lower River had not changed. Perhaps they had never wanted to change and, in helping him put up the schoolhouse, they were merely humoring him.

That seemed to be a feature of life in the country: to welcome strangers, let them live out their fantasy of philanthropy—a school, an orphanage, a clinic, a welfare center, a malaria eradication program, or a church; and then determine if in any of this effort and expense there was a side benefit—a kickback, a bribe, an easy job, a free vehicle. If the scheme didn't work—and few of them did work—whose fault was that? Whose idea was it in the first place?

That was probably Manyenga's complaint: not that he'd cheated the charity he'd worked for, but by their very presence they'd taken advantage of him.

He could make the same objection to Hock, who (Hock argued) had arrived and tempted them with his wealth. Manyenga wasn't at fault. Hock had asked to be fleeced by simply showing up, with his implausible story of how he'd once been happy there.

So he had to leave, there was no point in staying, but he could not leave until he had visited Gala. He needed to satisfy himself that he'd seen one person he'd known before, who would recognize him—especially Gala, someone he had loved.

13

IN THE TALL, fixed, vigilant way she stood when she was idle, Zizi reminded him of a water bird, head erect, her arms tucked like wings, one skinny leg lifted and crooked against the other, like the elder sister of those stately herons at the edge of the Dinde Marsh, the thin upright birds planted in the mud on big feet. Zizi's feet were much larger than those of other girls in the village. She was perhaps only sixteen, but for her whole life she'd gone barefoot. Her splayed feet and thin shanks made her seem even more a water bird.

She blinked the flies away and sniffed, a slender sentinel, solitary, looking unloved. When Hock appeared on the veranda in the morning, she flew across the village clearing for the kettle of hot water, the dwarf chasing her with his hopping puppy-like gait.

Just a few days had gone by since Zizi had told him who she was. In those days, though, knowing he had to see Gala, he'd decided to leave Malabo for good and put the Lower River behind him. His decision to go made him impatient with the place; he was unforgiving. It was all hotter, dustier, more ramshackle than he remembered. No one was sentimental about the old days—few people were alive to recall them, and the elders were all dead. These days, an elder was a thirty-five-year-old, like Manyenga, still a youth in Hock's opinion, though a chief. And Manyenga ruled a decaying village.

Memory mattered, and it demoralized Hock to think that there was no one alive who knew the vigorous village that Malabo had been, and if the unashamed booze-up at independence had scandalized Hock, it at least had shown the vitality of the place. Hock wanted to meet someone who remembered him. In a significant way he was (as he saw it) seeking permission to go home.

But he needed to be covert. If word got out that he was seeing Gala, the villagers would look for a reason why. They might guess correctly that he was making his farewells, and if they knew he was leaving, they'd fuss, they'd make excuses for him to stay. He knew that he was not welcome, merely tolerated, and yet the paradox was that they did not want him to leave. He was a nuisance in the village, as all guests and strangers were, because they were parasitical and had to be catered to. Meager and hostile meals usually drove them away. But Hock had money. If he left, they'd lose it. He was like a valuable animal that needed special attention, a creature prized for its plumage, resented for its upkeep, even as its gorgeous feathers were plucked out for their adornment.

He watched for a chance, and one morning, three or four days after Zizi's revelation ("My granny"), she had returned with the kettle, and he saw the dwarf in the distance, out of earshot. He said hurriedly to Zizi, "I want to see your granny."

Zizi showed no surprise; she did not react. Had she heard him?

"Can you take me to her hut?"

She faced him, flashed her eyebrows, sniffed, and continued to pour the hot water into the teapot.

"Today?"

She clicked her tongue against her teeth, a yes.

Only after she'd gone to pick up the bowl of porridge from Manyenga's fire did Hock consider that Zizi had never said no to him, never refused him anything, never asked for anything, had always submitted—silently, waiting for him at the edge of the veranda like a shadow, anticipating that he'd want tea, bringing him food, dealing with the laundry. And she seemed to imply, by the way she shadowed him, that she needed him for protection from the noisy boys in the village, those turbulent orphans; protection from the dwarf and from Manyenga, who acted like a tyrant toward all the children and the women, too.

I'll find a way of giving her money, he thought. I'll take care of her. She'll be my project. Perhaps she was justification enough for his trip back to Malabo. Finding that the place was uninhabitable for him, he'd encountered someone worthy, to whom he could be a benefactor.

Like the crooked shadow of a bat in flight, a dark thought fluttered through his mind that he could ask more from her. But reminding himself that she was barely sixteen—that his daughter was thirty-two—he only smiled, and the next time he passed the mirror in his hut, he peered into it and laughed at the pink sweaty face, the damp hair, and the bright exhausted eyes.

That day Zizi stayed close to the hut, and when the sun was high at noon and the dwarf was dozing under the maize basket of the granary, Hock said, "Let's go."

She knew immediately what he meant. Alert and attentive, she anticipated his movements, and she set off ahead of him, crossing behind the hut and through the maize patch in the somnolence of the hot noontime when nothing in Malabo stirred and the parched leaves of the mopane trees hung like rags.

The bush at the edge of the village was low and thin, offering no shade. Between the spindly shrubs and stunted trees, the narrow path was littered with corn shucks and twists of trampled fruit peels that monkeys had gnawed. Hock knew from the noon heat, the packed earth, and the withered layers of leaf trash that it was a snakey neighborhood. When Zizi hesitated, muttering "*Njoka*," he was not surprised.

He stepped around her, broke a branch from an overhanging tree, and prodded the snake, which glided away beneath the dry litter.

"Mamba," she said.

"Not a mamba." He hadn't had a good look, but he wanted to seem knowledgeable to this young girl—wanted to impress her! He laughed and said, "Wolf snake."

She put her fingers to her mouth and giggled in fear. "You go first!"

The path was distinct enough, but he could not see ahead. The bush obscured the distance in a twiggy web, and the land was so flat he had no idea where he was going. But it had always been like this—the same bush, the same snakes, the same heat, the biting tsetse flies leaving itchy sores all over his ankles. Away from the river and the marsh the soil was crumbly, dry, and stony. Dust coated the leaves, and the sun knifed through the scrubby trees. Hock stopped to get his breath, to lift his shirt against his sweaty face.

"Not far," Zizi said.

He was looking at her bare feet, her skinny legs, her flimsy *chitenje* cloth wrapped around her body. Apart from the dew on her upper lip and a kind of frost-textured sweat streaking her neck, she did not seem in the least fatigued or overheated. And there he stood in heavy shoes, khaki shorts, a drenched shirt, and his red baseball cap. They were alone, and the veiled bush made it seem that there might not be anyone for miles. And the bush itself, the solitude, roused him. Even the way Zizi stood, twisting her fingers and breathing, excited him. The heat most of all, the glare, the baking in sensuality—and the glimpse of the snake that had sped his pulse made her more watchful, keeping close to him.

His hand trembled as he touched her bare shoulder. She said nothing. He draped his arm so that his hand was slung over her breast. His dangling fingers grazed her cloth, the nipple poking beneath it. There was no softness; her shoulder was a polished knob, her small breast like a compact muscle.

With a feline expression, Zizi turned away, half smiling, half fearful, listening, her head slightly raised, as if to protect him from being seen holding her. And then, almost overcome with desire, Hock released her, and she sighed.

"How far?" he asked.

"Near. I can hear."

What she heard—what he saw, forty yards down the track at the opening of the clearing, another village—was a woman pounding maize, the slow *thud thud thud* of a heavy pestle pole clouting maize in a wooden mortar.

The working woman was not old. She was bare-breasted, shapeless in her cloth, which was flapping loosely from the effort of lifting and dropping the thick pole into the mouth of the mortar. She was facing away from them, toward a large cottage-like hut—a tin roof, a veranda, curtained windows, a number painted in white on the smooth mud wall, the pale twig framework showing through a fallen-away patch of plastered earth, like bones revealed in a starved carcass.

Before Hock could call out, Zizi cried "*Odi!*" as an announcement.

Deafened by the butting thud of her own pounding, the woman did not react, but a shadowy figure on the veranda greeted them and stood, clapping her dry hands in welcome.

The woman standing over the mortar caught the four-foot-high pestle pole in the angle of her bent arm and wiped her brow with the back of her hand. Seeing Zizi, she smiled, and Zizi in return jerked her body in a low genuflection.

"My auntie," Zizi said, and as she was saying "My granny," there was a barking sound from above, laughter like the clack of wood.

An enormous swirl of cloth rose from the veranda, a woman inside it, heaving herself from an armchair, and she swung around to face Hock. She wore a shallow green turban, and her dress fluttered over her bulky body, but even so, Hock could see her great stretched breasts flopping beneath the folds. She was dressed in the old style, the hem of her smock-like dress reaching to her ankles. Her face was puffy and dull, like scuffed shoe leather, the skin around her eyes purplish from age, her bare arms blotchy, and when she opened her mouth wide—laughing in satisfaction—Hock could see that several lower teeth and at least one upper tooth were missing.

Gala, grown old, was monumental but battered, heavy-breasted, plodding toward him on the boards of the veranda on thick fat feet, showing him her yellow palms in greeting.

She shook his hand in both of hers and kept laughing, saying, "Ellis, Ellis," the name that sounded like Alice.

"Remember me?"

"Yes, I do indeed!"

From that big, coarse, and aged body, from the cracked lips, a voice of refinement—astonishing, correct English.

"Come sit here," she said, indicating a plank bench on the veranda, and she ordered Zizi and the other woman to bring drinks. "What will you have? Water? Tea? We have orange squash as well."

"Tea," Hock said, fearing the water.

Gala dropped herself heavily into the armchair and took up a fly whisk. She batted a brush of horsehair around her head and smiled at Hock and peered with watery eyes. Her eye shape had not changed, still hooded and Asiatic, but apart from her eyes he could not find anything else of Gala in this fleshy old woman.

"Now tell me about your journey," she said, lapsing into the local approximation, *jinny*.

"You're surprised to see me?"

"To see you, yes," Gala said carefully. "But I heard you were at Malabo."

"You knew I was there?"

"You arrived on the fifteenth, not so?"

Hock had lost track of time, yet she was precise.

"I didn't know you would come here to pay a call and reacquaint yourself."

He was baffled by the sensible and fluent voice in that big battered body. *Pay a call* sounded so formal, involving doorbells and visiting cards and teacups and overstuffed chairs with doilies, and here they were on the rough plank porch of a mud hut.

Gala looked like a market mammy, someone he might find behind a table heaped with bananas and mangoes, or eggs in a basket, fanning herself with a palm leaf, feet wide apart, her cloth wrap drooping.

Yet she said, "It is rare that we get visitors here, except the tax collector, or the boys from the ruling party soliciting donations." Then she laughed, with a slight choking sound, *kek-kek-kek*. "You look fit."

"I'm okay."

"My granddaughter is looking after you."

"You know that too?"

"Her mother has passed on from the scourge of eddsi"—AIDS was a word that no one could pronounce. "The Lower River has suffered. Even Malabo has suffered."

But Hock saw a different connection—a revelation. He said, "So it's not a coincidence. They knew about you and me?"

"We are part of the local legend," Gala said, laughing again, *kek-kek*. "It was a source of pain for my late husband. I was a marked woman because of my friendship with the *mzungu*."

"And that's why they chose Zizi?"

"Some people might think so," Gala said, and screwed up one eye against the sun.

So it was a setup. He should have known. They had assessed his weakness, his sentimentality, and he reflected on how shrewd they were, how predictable he was: just minutes ago he had embraced Zizi with hot hands on the bush track.

With exaggerated dignity he said, "I might not be staying much longer in Malabo."

Gala flicked at her head with the fly whisk, then said, "So—hah!—what do you think of your village?"

"It's changed," he said.

"Maybe it hasn't changed," Gala said. "Maybe it was always like this."

"Forty years ago it seemed like home to me."

"That was a special period," she said. "Maybe you could call it an era. People were hopeful in a way they hadn't been before. After some few years the hope was gone. You had left by then, back to your people."

"I thought of the Sena as my people," Hock said. "What happened?"

"Nothing happened. That was the badness. People expected a miracle, and when the miracle didn't come they were angry. You see these young people in Malabo—all over the Lower River. They are so angry. What do you think?"

Hock, staring at her, was thinking that he was about her age, and yet, for all her fluency, she was a physical wreck, decrepit in spite of her wisdom. What he could see of her eyes was clouded, not blind but dim-sighted and milky from her hard life in this sunlight.

"Zizi isn't angry," he said.

"I raised Zizi," Gala said. "My children were not angry. I sent them away for their own good. My firstborn is in the UK, a pharmacist. Another is married, in South Africa."

"How many children do you have."

"I have borne a total of eight, but two died in infancy. One more from dysentery, another succumbed to malaria. I myself am troubled by malaria. I hope you are taking precautions."

"I take a pill every day."

"The headman, Festus Manyenga, he was with the Agency in a malaria eradication program. Also some food delivery."

Her mention of the man gave him an opportunity to ask, "What do you think of him?"

Laughing, she said, "Festus was so puffed up when he worked for the Agency. He was the driver—not a very elevated position, you might say. But he had a smart uniform. He took advantage. His vehicle was so big and expensive. He treated it as his own. He pinched from them. Have some tea."

Zizi held a tin tray, a cup trembling on it, as her aunt poured tea for Hock.

"I think we have some biscuits," Gala said. She was making queenly gestures from her armchair. At last, with a frown and a dismissing hand she indicated that Zizi and the aunt should leave. In a low serious voice she said to Hock, "I hope you are being careful in Malabo."

"Doing my best," Hock said.

"Please take care."

"You sound worried."

"I know those people." She leaned forward. "They are different from any people here that you knew before. We were quite cheerful. Independence was a joyful occasion for us. The school was new and it was something wonderful."

"When did it fall apart?"

"Some few years after you left."

"I used to think how happy I'd be living here," he said in a soft speculating voice that implied, *With you.*

"You made the right decision by going home. You have a family?"

"A wife, a child," he said. "An ex-wife. An angry child."

"Angry or not, your child is forever your child."

He could not explain why he felt differently, and that when he had left home he had said goodbye to his friend Roy and not to his ex-wife or his daughter. He said, "Are you warning me about the people in Malabo?"

"You are wiser than me," she said. "But this is my home. These people know you only by name and reputation. They know you don't fear snakes. Apart from that, you are a stranger here."

She seemed so ominous, saying it in her deep voice, he laughed to lighten the moment. But she kept her head lowered in that confiding posture.

"They will eat your money," she said. "When your money is gone, they will eat you."

He flinched at this, and was sorry he showed his surprise. It was a far cry from the homecoming he'd expected, and a shock coming from this articulate old woman, who clearly had suffered. She was ill and overweight and short of breath, and having gasped that warning, she'd exhausted herself and was panting.

"So I can't trust anyone?"

"You can trust me," she said. "You can trust Zizi."

"She's, what, sixteen?"

"More than that. Soon to be seventeen, but still a girl, still *mtsikana*." It was a village distinction, a girl who had not been initiated—a virgin.

"No *chinamwali* for her?"

"I didn't agree to the initiation. Festus was so angry!"

Hock glanced at the girl. "Pretty young."

"I was not much older when I met you. Eighteen."

"I had no idea. You were a teacher."

"Anyone could be a teacher in those days," Gala said. "But as you found out, I was promised to Mr. Kalonda. Zizi is not promised."

Hearing her name, Zizi became watchful and solemn. She knelt with her auntie at the edge of the veranda, as though awaiting instructions. Zizi seemed anxious, hopeful, her dark, white-rimmed eyes lighting her smooth face. Her shaven head gave her a distinct nobility as well as an air of ambiguity, an apparent androgyny, the slender boy-girl with breasts and big feet. Hock was glad that Gala had praised her, and even seemed to encourage him, because he had already come to depend on Zizi with mingled helplessness and desire, feeling more like a lost boy than a man, as he sometimes said, on the shady side of middle age.

"My friend," Gala said, "I am so glad to see you. But I will also be glad when I hear you are safely far away from the Lower River . . ."

She hadn't finished. She had lifted her arm to make a point—to give him another warning, perhaps. He could see it in the way she took a deep breath to sustain her through a serious utterance. She had begun to say, "Do not believe . . ."

Then the *bap-bap-bap* and the shimmy of a loose muffler of a motorbike rattled into the stillness, waking a terrified dog and throwing up gouts of white dust, Manyenga skidding to a halt in front of Gala's hut.

"I was getting worried," Manyenga said, wrestling with the handlebars and killing the engine. "But here you are, seeing your friend."

Lifting herself from her posture of warning, Gala relaxed and clapped her hands to welcome him. She spoke all the formulas of ritual greeting, the repetitions, too, in a mild submissive voice, calling him Festus, ending by offering him a cup of tea.

"I can't stay. I must help this big man," Manyenga said. Then with his teeth clamped together he hissed at Zizi in Sena. Without a word, she slipped off the veranda and turned to head down the path. She lifted her knees when she walked, seeming to march.

Manyenga climbed onto his motorbike and kicked the starting lever. His voice rose as the engine revved, but still it was inaudible. Hock had begun to follow Zizi, but Manyenga gestured for him to ride behind him.

Hock waved to Gala and was sped down the path, past the marching girl, to Malabo.

At his hut, dismounting, Hock hated that he'd been spirited away. Manyenga didn't shut off the engine. He tossed his head as a casual acknowledgment. But before he rode away he shouted at Hock.

"What did you give her? A present, eh?" In the risen dust he'd thrown up, he pushed at his nose with the back of his hand, and it seemed a hostile gesture. "What have you got for me?"

Hock fumbled in his pocket and found a broken peanut shell and gave it to him, holding it over the man's open palm.

"Eh!" he grunted when he saw it. "Groundnuts! You are so funny, father."

After he'd gone, Hock waited in the shade for Zizi to return. Idle there, he replayed the visit and remembered seeing a book on the floor beneath Gala's armchair, a book of frayed pages, fat with mildew, the cracked spine looking chewed, like a relic from another age. He wished he had looked more closely. It was probably a Bible.

When Zizi slipped from amid the tangle of bushes at the margin of the maize patch, Hock was glad. But the day had disturbed him. Now he knew the limits of his world here, how narrow they were.

14

H E DID NOT want to think that Africa was hopeless. Anyway, Africa didn't exist except as a metaphor for trouble in the minds of complacent busybodies elsewhere. Only the villages existed, and he was now convinced that there was something final about Malabo. He had believed it to be static and inert. But the village, all of it, seemed to be sinking, the thirty or so huts, the low bush and splintered stumps, the withered mopane trees and their twitching leaves, the smoke smell, the smoothed and swept portions in front of the huts, the dusty tussocks of weeds. The place was flattening, soon to be a ruin, like the failed schoolhouse, the fallen church, none of the ruins or huts, even now, higher than Hock's head. The whole of the village was like a rubble of foundations suggesting the settlement it had once been. Or maybe it wasn't final but would just go sprawling on like a termite mound, mimicking its stick-like people.

Waves of sadness weakened him as he blinked in the heat shimmer of the small dusty village that had once been his greatest hope. It was not a mistake to have come, but it was a mistake to remain. Gala was right, he had overstayed his visit—time to go. He tore a page from his journal and wrote a message to the consulate in Blantyre, saying that he was unwell and needed to talk to the consul. He found an envelope. Stepping off the veranda of his hut with the letter in his hand, he heard a whistle.

The clean white paper, so rare in Malabo, brilliant in the sunlight, had been spotted from fifty yards away.

"*Kalata,*" Manyenga said, materializing on the path, as always trying to push him back with the force of his voice. And when he put his hand out, palm up, Hock imagined that at one time a cheeky *mzungu* at the Agency had done that to him. Manyenga must have been working on his motorbike—his hands were smeared with black grease. "We will post the *kalata* for you."

"I can do it, Festus."

"The big man does not post letters. His people carry out the workload. They brush the glue on the stamps. His people post the letters. Give it, my friend!"

Too feeble to protest, Hock handed it over. Finger streaks of grease imprinted the pure white envelope, which he knew would never be sent.

Hock had abandoned any idea of improving the village. The school would remain a roofless shell, a nest of snakes, the office a hideout for the orphan boys, the clinic a ruin. The side road would grow narrower from the dense encroaching elephant grass that flopped over at its edges. The villagers would subsist, the weaker ones would die. The river was invisible, and all he had seen of it was the heaviness of the marsh and the water hyacinths that piled up in a mass of leaves and flowers that filled its channels. The nearer creek was stagnant, a constant whiff in the air of decay. The boma seemed as distant as Blantyre, an unwalkable distance.

The next day at breakfast he said, "I'm going to pick some bananas," using that as an excuse to take a stroll, to feel less trapped.

Though he had not spoken to anyone in particular, his words reached Manyenga, who confronted him, speaking as though to a child.

"The big man cannot pick bananas!" Manyenga said. "You must not do, father. The kids will fetch them." And he called to a small boy, saying, "*Ntochi!*" He never spoke to the dwarf Snowdon.

Hock's running an errand or going for a walk were indignities, not befitting a chief. So they waited on him, the whole village enlisted as his helpers, and they kept him captive. They were no longer afraid of him. He would rise from his chair on the veranda and as soon as he stepped into the clearing he'd hear a sharp whistle that signaled, He's moving.

The earth, his life, his brain, had slowed in the humid heat of the Lower River. Half cooked, drowsing during the day, he was more wakeful at night. He came to understand the sharp squawks and chirps, the warbling and whickering of some birds and the bub-bubbling of the mourning doves at sundown. These noises gave way to the raw coughing of dogs, or the untuned string of a locust at dusk, until in the pitch black of his hut at midnight when he was wakeful all sounds ceased except the most disturbing one, the gabble of a human voice, five or six muttered words, the more alarming for being flat and unintelligible, always like a command. He found no reassurance in the voices of Malabo, only warning, as though they were always speaking about him.

He became accustomed to Zizi bringing him news, or sometimes warnings. Boys in ragged shirts would wander past his hut, going slowly, tilting their heads, giving him sidelong glances. Before he asked who they were, Zizi would hiss through her teeth, "Bad boys. They are wanting." One day, hearing a commotion, Zizi squinted into the emptiness of the village, as though conjuring a vision. "They are killing a goat, but he is not dying." She might mention that someone was brewing beer, or that visitors had come to Manyenga's compound—the delivery of medicine, the arrival of a relative. Another day, she reported a death, but it was not the death of the man that she described; rather, she told how Manyenga's family had gone to the dead man's hut, at the far side of the village, and they had stripped it of all the pots and knives, taken his hoe and his ax, his mirror, his mats and baskets, then set the house on fire, something that Hock had once witnessed, the ritual raid the Sena called "erasing the death."

"What will Festus do with the hoe and the ax?" Hock asked, to see what Zizi would say.

"They will sell them, because they are lazy."

No government officials ever visited the village, no missionaries, no aid people, no foreigners, no health workers. Hock inquired. Zizi shook her head.

"But the Agency," she said, "they have food for Festus."

"What's the Agency?" It was a recurring name. Gala had also mentioned it.

She couldn't say; it seemed she didn't know. She shrugged and pointed to the sky.

Sorting papers early one morning, still in his hut, disconsolate that he had stopped his diary, because every day's entry was the same two lines, he heard Zizi calling to him, clucking through the window.

"A doctor has come."

It seemed a blessing, it gave him hope. "Where is he?"

"At the clinic."

Like the school, the two-room clinic was a ruin—no roof, the doors and window frames torn out and used for firewood. What remained was a set of brick walls that dated from Hock's time as a teacher in Malabo, one of the buildings put up at independence. Every month, a doctor or a medical missionary would arrive in a Land Rover from the boma, or Chikwawa, or farther afield; word spread and within the hour a line of people formed to be treated or to ask for medicine. Hock always went to the clinic to hand over letters to be posted, or to obtain chloroquine for students who were down with malaria. He'd been treated, too, for tonsillitis, for an infected knee, and once he'd had a chigger dug from beneath the nail of his big toe, a fat leggy flea that had writhed and kicked on the blade of the doctor's lancet. "Cheeky bugger," the doctor had said, smiling at the flea, wiping it away.

That a doctor had come to the ruins of the clinic today seemed an unexpected miracle, but for Hock—usually to his sorrow—Malabo was a place where the unexpected often occurred. Yet this was news. No matter who it was, a doctor would have come from afar, and would have a vehicle. There was no other way for such a person to reach the village.

So Hock flung his papers aside and left his hut, walking quickly, overeager, finding himself gasping in the heat—he was not used to hurrying, and the sunlight slashed at him. Zizi stepped ahead of him, taking long strides, seeming to dance. She wore her purple wrap, and the turban wound round her head against the sun gave her stature, made her seem exotic and stylish, as Hock followed.

The sight at the clinic was old and familiar, even uplifting: hopeful villagers waiting at the open doorway, a long line of them, forty or more, women carrying infants in cloth slings, men squatting, some boys, their hands on their brows to shield their faces from the sunlight—all gathered here to see the doctor, as in years past.

"Where's his vehicle?"

"He has no vehicle," Zizi said.

When the people in line saw Hock, they seemed to recoil, looking away, as though self-conscious or fearful. He was cautioned by their apparent fear, so he kept apart from them and walked slowly to the gaping window—no glass, no frame—at the back of the derelict building.

Stretched out, in the surrendering posture of a patient, a man in shirtsleeves and brown trousers lay on a straw mat, half in shadow, half in bright sunlight, in the roofless room. With his hands clutching his face, he looked as if he was grieving.

Kneeling beside him, a smaller man attended to him, working closely on his ankle. He was no doctor. On his head was a grubby fur hat, over his shoulders a stiff cloak of animal skin that might have been a leopard; he wore old black track-suit trousers as well, and what looked like a woman's satin slippers. He held a knife at the patient's leg, and Hock saw that he was making a continuous cut in the man's ankle, jabbing from time to time to go deeper, until he sighed and rocked back on his heels, revealing the wound he had made, an open anklet of bright blood.

He set his knife down and adjusted his hat with wet fingers, leaving a gluey bloodstain on the fur. He reached into a bucket by his side and pinched out some dark ashes—the dust of powdered charcoal—and after wiping the ankle he rubbed the ashes into the groove of the wound. Almost without pausing, he took up his knife and cut the man's other ankle, encircling it, pushing the blood flow aside with his thumb, finally plunging his hand in the bucket and, his sticky fingers blackened, pressing the ashes into the wound. He shuffled forward on his knees and began again: tugged at the man's right arm, flourished his bloody knife, cut into the wrist.

"Doctor," Zizi said, giving the word three syllables.

Hock leaned toward her and whispered, "Ask someone what he is doing."

She slipped away, and before the man had finished the wrist, Zizi was beside him, her head lowered.

"Snake doctor," she said in her language.

Without thinking, Hock groaned—too loud—and the little man in the fur hat drew back, his face upturned, scowling at the window. Startled by the sight of the *mzungu* and the turbaned girl, he made a scouring sound in his toothless open mouth, a harsh cat-like hiss.

At dusk the next day, framed by a volcanic sunset, Manyenga visited Hock at his hut to announce that he had been seen with Zizi at the clinic. And why?

Hock said, "I thought he was a doctor. I needed some aspirin."

"I enjoy your sense of humor, father! Sure, he is a doctor. Better than a European doctor. After he does his work, a person is protected for life."

"Protected from what?"

"From the bite of a snake," Manyenga said, and he raised his fists to his face so that Hock could see the old raised scars that circled his wrists. "You see, we are not fearing you!"

A thud like that of a woman bopping her pestle into a mortar woke him in the darkness one night some days later, pulsing under his hut, the very soil jarred by its steady beat. He felt the thud in his body, prodding him, and was then wide awake. He walked to the window and the thudding entered his feet. Seeing nothing, he went to the door and as always was amazed by the crystalline brightness of the stars, some blobby, some pinpricks, their milky light shimmering on the leaves of the trees, the starry glow on the bare ground coating it with fluorescence.

Still the thudding, a sickening repetition, pushing at him. And then he saw the fire jumping at the edge of the village, in the football field where the orphan boys sometimes kicked a ball between two overturned buckets that represented a goal mouth.

As soon as he stepped away from his hut, Hock became self-conscious in the bluish light of the stars. He looked for Zizi. But she seldom slept near his hut. She seemed to drift off after he'd gone to bed, showing up in the early morning, probably at a signal from Snowdon, who crept to the veranda before dawn.

Yet Hock was not alone. The football field glowed yellow in the firelight. The *ta-dum ta-dum* of the drum being slapped, the *plink-plink* of the plucked finger harp like the shrill notes of a xylophone made of glass, and the far-off yodeling of women mingled with the growls of men. It seemed the whole village was awake.

Had he been a first-timer on a bush walk, down here to look at hippos in the river or to go bird watching in the marsh, he might have seen this as a colorful nighttime get-together. He smiled briefly, the naïve thought of a party crossing his mind, and then he went grim again, picking his way to the fat baobab stump forty yards from his hut. He crouched at the stump. He knew what he was watching, and it was not a party.

In his day, this ceremony had been performed outside the village as an expression of the secret society of men, directed by the chief. It was so hidden that he'd only heard the drumming those nights and seen the exhausted faces the following morning. He'd inquired and been told it was "the Big Dance," the Nyau or image dance—maybe a wedding, or a funeral, or an *ujeni* ("whatsit"), they said, meaning something forbidden or not to be spoken about to a *mzungu*, or an outsider, or an uninitiated girl.

He knew what he was hearing, and he could see the dancers gathering and stamping their feet in time to the drums and the tinkling finger harp, now tripping faster, *plinka-plinka-plinka*. He knelt and held on to the stump for balance and to ease the weight on his knees. He'd sometimes see a snake here at the stump, a puff adder that swelled to the thickness of his wrist, but snakes didn't stir at night.

He was more concerned by the crowd gathering around the leaping fire, the sharp gunshot crack of the burning branches, the sparks flying up in clusters—some carried into the sky, borne by the uprush of heat and flames. He had never overcome his fear of an African crowd, how it might grow from a handful of people to a restless sweaty mob. He'd seen such mobs at political rallies in his first years, the crazy mass of yelling men and yodeling women. Once, on the bus to Chikwawa, he'd witnessed a group of men at a roadblock. Laughing with a superior-sounding anger, they boarded the bus and used thick clubs to beat the Sena men who were not wearing the party badge that showed the president's face. He'd seen one man, begging for his life, kicked and trampled into silence.

The Big Dance, for all its apparent order, was no less menacingly mob-like. It seemed that every man and boy in Malabo was on the field. The women were audible in their ululation, but they were distant, unseen, nearer the huts. Even the orphan boys, in their rags and shaggy hair and torn T-shirts, were stamping to the drumbeat.

Yet just as all those men, sweaty in the firelight, seemed on the verge of rushing apart in a frenzy of aimless rage, a figure appeared before them—Manyenga, like a hectoring choirmaster. He was chanting a word, unintelligible to Hock, and the rest of the crowd took it up as a cry. As they repeated it, they seemed more unified and solemn.

Manyenga took his place on a chair at the edge of the stamping, chanting men, and a masked figure danced before them. The mask was not made of carved wood—the Sena seldom carved; they made wide dugout canoes and shovel-like paddles and sometimes house idols of wood, but not masks. For ceremonies they wove bamboo strips into a frame and covered it with bark and leaves, and that was their conception of a mask, a fluttering headdress of dead leaves.

This was just such a mask—twisted together and ragged, not a face but a deliberate fixture. Knotted to it were scraps of pale cloth and plastic, the flimsy rippings of a white garbage bag, a large swollen beast's head with a gaping mouth. Hock could see the face of the dancer staring wildly out of the mask's mouth.

Another dancer met this masked figure in the center of the dance area, brightly lit by the bonfire. This second, opposing figure was cloaked in a dark cape, and instead of a mask its head had been entirely wrapped in a ragged cloth, like a monster with a filthy bandage around its head.

The masks were the more hideous for being so crude. The wooden or dead-leaf masks Hock had been shown by Sena elders in the past had an aesthetic appeal, were well made and symmetrical. But these masks, one of shredded plastic, the other of rags, frightened him with their coarse construction, as though they'd been twisted together by angry men in a hurry, using the castoff scraps from a trash heap. They were clumsy, insulting, grotesque, and terrifying for being so badly made.

Snowdon grinned in the light of the fire, delighting in the noise and flames, as the two figures sparred in a mock struggle, the tall man in the ragged mask of white plastic, and the squirming figure in the cloak and faceless wrapped head. They were also dancing, obeying the rhythm thumped out on the drums.

After less than a minute of this, Snowdon waved a red object at the dancers, and seeing it they faltered, hesitated, disengaged. The dwarf was too small to do much more than gesture with the red object. At the urging of Manyenga, still in his armchair, a bystander took the thing from Snowdon and placed it on the head of the white-masked figure.

Hock recognized it as his own, the red baseball cap he sometimes wore. But if that was meant to be him, the white-masked *mzungu* figure in the baseball cap, who was that other cloaked, contending figure with its head wrapped in rags? When the dancers resumed, stamping in a circle, it occurred to him that the second figure had no arms and merely swayed, and he took it to represent a snake.

The snake seemed to be getting the better of the Hock figure, backing him up, making him dance in retreat, shuffling and leaning forward like a mamba intending to strike.

He was sure of this when he heard the word *njoka*—snake! —shrieked by some of the boys, and the drawn-out 'zoongoo mooed by the men. The snake advanced to the plinking of the finger harp. The white-masked figure retreated to the sound of drumbeats and then skipped past the snake, confronting it. The movement was too crude to be balletic, yet there were elements of subtler dance steps, as though with some refinements this could be staged as a drama—the struggle of two masked figures in the firelight, to the counterpoint of drum thumps and finger pluckings.

He was fascinated and appalled to see this battling creature with the horrible face in the ridiculous headdress fending off the snake. The snake Hock took to be sexual, though he knew he was noted for his fearlessness as a snake handler. The bystanders cheered the thrusting body of the snake, the evasions of the masked man.

Is that how I seem to them? Hock wondered—a cringing figure

with a beaky nose and peeling skin, dancing away from the confrontation? Each time the snake pretended to strike, driving the *mzungu* figure backward, a cheer went up, the drums grew more insistent, and the *mzungu* spun around. But the snake had the advantage, moving smoothly, its whole head a ragged bandage; the *mzungu* stumbled on two uncoordinated feet.

And what did it mean when the snake twisted aside and a boy dressed as a girl—a rouged face and smeared lips, a tattered yellow dress—approached and these two caricatures began to dance as a pair, as the *mzungu* figure twitched behind them? Had they been clowning, Hock might have been reassured. But it was late, the fire was hot, the drums were loud, the plinking of the finger harp pierced his heart. This was not clowning.

All this talent, all this energy at night, from those who were so sleepy in the daytime. The spectators, men and boys, were emboldened by the music, perhaps, excited by the towering fire. Faces gleaming with sweat, golden-skinned in the light of the flames, they reached toward the dancing figures, shuffled forward, crowding them.

The boy in the yellow dress taunted both the masked figures. He was not masked, though he was luridly painted, his features exaggerated with the greasy makeup.

The sight triggered a memory. In his first year in the Lower River, just after the school at Malabo had been finished, Hock had gone back to school late after lunch. He'd been disturbed by a letter from home, a clingy letter that had made him furious. As he'd approached the classroom, he heard an unfamiliar voice, and laughter. He paused before entering, sidling up to the door, and saw one of the boys pacing at his desk and muttering in an imitation of him. A cruelly accurate imitation, approximating his stammering um-um-um in an explanation, his nodding head, his way of pacing, turned-in toes, knees lifted. And he'd been abashed. So as not to embarrass himself further, he made an announcing noise, waited for the scuffling to diminish, and entered the classroom to see that some students were solemn, some tittering. When he tried to resume the lesson, he found he did not have the heart to continue. Instead, he assigned them an essay topic and gave them the hour to complete it. Afterward he fled to his house and the letter from his father.

That was how he felt now, at the sight of a man in a mask that was meant to represent his face, a snake that he took to be an adversary, and a boy in a ragged dress, which baffled him.

Never mind what it meant to them. It horrified him in a way that was more alarming for being meaningless. His face reflected in a mirror had always disturbed him. As the subject of a Nyau dance he believed he was being ridiculed, and he remembered Gala's warning. As for the boy he'd found mimicking him in the classroom, he'd never trusted him after that.

The drumming became a thunderous pounding of hand slaps. He backed away from the baobab stump, into the shadows, and withdrew to his hut.

15

HARDLY SEVEN, AND the morning sun slanting through the twiggy trees had filled the clearing at Malabo with stifling humidity, like an invisible smothering presence that bulked against his face, leaving his neck clammy and his body weak. The earth itself was baked dry and crisscrossed with paths pounded smooth by bare feet. The foliage of the mopane trees faded to yellow, the thorn acacias coated with dust.

Squinting into the distance, because a dog had begun an irritable bark, Hock saw a shimmering spectral blob in the heat, coming closer, resolving itself into two figures, large and small, Manyenga and a skinny burdened girl hurrying behind him.

"Morning, chief," Hock said.

"But, eh, you are being a big man as well, father," Manyenga said.

And he smiled seeing Hock sitting as usual at his table on the narrow veranda, Zizi squatting on her heels near him, the dwarf crouching a little distance away by a low bush, gnawing his fingers.

The way Manyenga stared put Hock on his guard. The anxiety, the calculation, something approaching fear, that he'd noticed in the young man on his arrival was gone. Now Manyenga gazed directly at him, looked him up and down, narrowing his eyes, without any hesitation. He was at ease, friendlier, more familiar, and less reliable.

Hock saw himself with Manyenga's eyes, an old *mzungu*, attended by a skinny girl and a dwarf, a portrait of inaction, like a ruined chief on a rickety throne. He'd stopped shaving, his clothes were stained. The tableau somehow illustrated his life at Malabo—not at all what he had imagined, but tolerable because nothing was expected of him beyond greeting the villagers, and not complaining, and giving them money now and then. There was no point. He had to leave, to get away, if only to Blantyre, to collect his thoughts and decide his next move.

"You were seeing us at the dance," Manyenga said, gesturing to the girl to set down the plate of porridge and the mug of milky tea.

"How do you know?"

It was a breach of etiquette for an outsider to observe the Nyau dance. In spite of himself, Hock could not be indignant at being questioned. He was abashed, as though he'd seen someone naked in the village; he'd had no right.

But Manyenga was nodding with a slyly satisfied face—a smile that was not a smile. "We were celebrating you," he said. "We were thanking you, father. And you were there."

Hock said in Sena, "A ghost doesn't miss a funeral"—a proverb he'd learned long ago, one he'd often quoted in Medford.

"You are knowing so much, father."

"But I have to leave today," Hock said, and took another breath, because his chest was tight—the heat, the scrutiny of the strong younger man. "To go to Blantyre."

All night he had been pondering this possibility, even practicing the form of words. Nothing had gone right. He knew he had been cheated out of the money for the roofing, he was being overcharged for room and board, the school would stay a ruin. The boys had abandoned him—but they were orphans, there was little hope for them. No, perhaps they were counting on him, but if so, it was all hopeless. His waiting to be fed, breathless in the morning heat, drawing shallow breaths, his face glowing with sweat so early in the morning, had shown him the futility of it all.

"I'll need a lift to the boma." His idea was to find the departure times of the buses to Blantyre, perhaps catch one that day, just to be away.

"As you are wishing, father," Manyenga said, with another nod and that ambiguous half-smile. "But you were watching our dance without permission. That is a trespassing. According to custom you must pay a fine."

"I understand."

"A heavy fine. Sorry, father."

"In that case, I need to get some money from the bank. I'm almost out of cash."

Instead of looking greedy and grateful, Manyenga frowned, seeming bewildered, but he lifted his hands in an accommodating gesture, as if to say, Anything for you. Then he clicked his tongue at the serving girl.

"Bon appétit," he said.

And again Hock remembered that the man had been a driver for a foreign agency.

"The boma is far. We must leave soon," Manyenga said.

Hock was encouraged when the man kept his word. They left on the motorbike later in the morning, Manyenga driving. Hock, sitting behind him, had his passport and all his important papers. Revving the engine with twists of his hand, Manyenga told him to hold on, and he skidded away. But not fifty yards into the journey, even before they reached the road, Manyenga swerved and screamed, "*Njoka!*"

Hock twisted around, looking for the snake, and lost his balance and fell, bruising his side. Winded, he lay in the dust, wondering if he had broken any ribs.

"We cannot go," Manyenga said, righting the motorbike, helping Hock up from the ground.

Manyenga's brow was heavy, his face dark with fear. Hock knew of the prohibition against traveling onward after a snake has crossed your path. Manyenga's mood had changed from agreeable to anxious. He seemed tense, nearly angry.

"I didn't see a snake," Hock said.

"It was so big! A green mamba—they match the leaves," Manyenga said. "We must obey."

Hock was too bruised to argue, yet annoyed that the man was describing a snake to him that he had not seen. He limped back in the sun to his hut, and there he sat, wondering how to overcome this man. He suspected it was a ruse. Yet he was hurt. And realizing that he'd been forced to lie to Manyenga to get to the boma made him uneasy. The lie indicated that he was afraid to tell the truth—that he simply wanted to go to Blantyre and plot his next move, to go home.

He went to his duffel bag and felt for his pouch of money. He found the fat envelopes and saw that some money was missing, and he laughed, mocking his own stupidity. That was why Manyenga had reacted that way. He knew that Hock was not going to the bank for money. Manyenga knew he had money, that he was lying.

Hock looked up and saw the dwarf staring at him with red-rimmed eyes, a wet finger in his mouth.

Aching after the fall from the bike, he rested. The following night the Nyau was danced again. Hock's head throbbed. The very sound of the drums echoed in his skull, pained him physically, pounded inside him. He had a fever—he knew malaria, the flu-like symptoms, the headache. He found his bottle of chloroquine and, unable to locate his water jug, chewed three tablets and lay in his string bed, the drums beating against his eyes and ears, his sore body, his sore head. The mosquito net killed any movement of air and trapped the heat.

Then days and nights were one. He did not know how long he lay shivering with chills, gasping in the heat, his heart flutter-ing, his head like an echo chamber. He heard a wild commotion, screeching, insistent drumming, the ululating of frenzied women. His eyes seemed scorched, and his skin felt raw against the sheets. The slightest brush of the mosquito net caused him discomfort. It was not like skin at all, but like tissue that was easily torn.

He suffered most when sunlight shot through the windows of the hut and caught him on the face. In the night his teeth chat-tered. Though he was wrapped in a thickness of sheets—there were no blankets—he could not get warm. He continued dosing himself with chloroquine.

"Quilt," he said to Manyenga when one day the man's face ap-peared in the wrinkles of the net, but the word meant nothing to him.

He felt sorry for himself, became tearful. No one cared, but he was comforted by the sight of Zizi and the dwarf on his veranda, standing vigil, it seemed. He heard Manyenga's voice, an assured murmur, and he envied the man his strength. But it was only a voice—he did not see him.

When, before dawn one day, the fever eased, he could think more clearly, though he was still lightheaded and weak. The sickness made his situation plain, stripped it of sentiment. He saw the foolishness of his decision. He had come expecting to be welcomed; he'd wanted to contribute something to the village or the district. But no one was interested. Why should they care? They had managed very well without any amenities. They were much worse off than he'd seen them long ago, more cynical and somehow shrewder as a result. Cynicism had strengthened them.

As a young man, he'd compared malaria to the flu, and in four or five days he'd ridded himself of it. Older, he found the ailment to be like a fatal disease. He lay in bed, too weak to stand, straining even to roll over, and his lack of appetite weakened him more. He understood how frail he was, and the danger of being sick in this remote village. His dreams were fractured and irrational, ugly beaked birds figured in them, crowds of noisy people, great heat. In one dream he imagined that he was visited. He heard inquiring voices, American ones; he heard a car, the thumping of a large vehicle in the compound, the straining of gears as it drove away. The nightmarish part of the whole episode was that he had been ignored.

In his sickbed, he felt a clarity of mind and a sense of resolve. He'd made a mistake. As soon as he was feeling better he'd find a way of escaping from Malabo.

Zizi brought him the tea and bananas he asked for, but it was an effort for him to eat. He kept on with his medicine. It consoled him to see her and the dwarf right outside, their heads silhouetted at the window.

At last he was able to stand, to eat a little porridge.

"I'm going," he said, and was not sure whether he was speaking in Sena or English. He called to Zizi: "Get the chief."

Manyenga was soon striding across the brightness of the clearing, mopping his head, seeming relieved that Hock had recovered. Hock was standing in the shade of the veranda, swaying slightly, still unsteady on his feet. Behind Manyenga, her short legs working fast, a girl carried a pail of small greenish oranges and some dried fish wrapped in the torn pages of a South African illustrated magazine.

"Eat, father," Manyenga said.

"I need to drink more. Bring me a kettle of hot water for tea."

Manyenga, suddenly fierce-faced, ordered the small girl to fetch the kettle. And then he relaxed and stood closer and inclined his head toward Zizi and said, "She likes you, father."

"Really?"

"Too much."

"Zizi should be in school."

"But the school fees," Manyenga said. "That is the badness."

Hock was too faint to reply and had to sit on the straight-backed chair on the veranda, where he slumped, breathing hard.

"You must rest, father."

Then Hock remembered. In a croaky voice, he said, "I heard noise when I was sick. What was the noise?"

"*Kufafaniza imfa.* A man died. His goods were taken. His house destroyed."

"You erased his death."

"You are so clever, father. You are knowing so much about our customs, eh-eh."

Hock said, "I have to leave. I'm going home."

"This is your home, father," Manyenga said.

Hock shivered as he had in the worst of his fever. He hugged his body, to warm himself, and moved to get his blood up, and that was when he saw the plastic crates. He recognized them as the containers of school supplies he'd asked the American consulate to send.

"When did that come?"

"The Americans fetched it here in their vehicle."

"Did you tell them I was here?"

"You were so sick. We did not want to trouble you."

"What did you tell them?"

"*Ujeni,*" Manyenga said—whatsit. "This and that."

Hock guessed that he had said nothing of his presence, nothing of Hock's lying in the hut with a high fever.

He went cold again, and he could not tell whether it was the recurrence of his fever or the faint brush of terror at feeling abandoned. Nothing that Manyenga had said was menacing, yet Hock was so weak, so feeble in response, he felt he was no match for Manyenga.

"I have a very big question to ask you."

"Go ahead," Hock said, "ask me."

"Not now. At the proper time. We will have a ten-drum *ngoma* tomorrow. Then — " He smiled and gestured with his hands, spreading his arms, meaning, it seemed, that all would become clear.

After he had gone, Zizi peeled some of the oranges and put them in a tin bowl and served him. He gave some to the dwarf, who ate messily, chewing as he always did with his mouth open and grunting, his face and fingers smeared with the juice.

Zizi ate with dainty grace, separating the orange segments, chewing, her eyes cast down.

Refreshed by the fruit, having eased his stomach pain, Hock was suffused with a feeling of well-being, sitting in the shade, the sun whitening the earth, heating the motionless dusty leaves of the bushes next to the hut, curling the dead leaves on the ground. A strange conceit occurred to Hock as he straightened himself on his chair — that he was a chief, as they said, with his retainers, the serving girl and his fool, at his feet.

"It's time for me to go," he said in English. "I have no business here."

The dwarf grunted. Perhaps he was muttering "Fee-dee-dom." Pincering with the broken nails of two skinny fingers, Zizi covertly picked her nose, and Hock sat, finding a scrap of contentment in the absurdity.

Remembering that his stash of money had been raided, he went back to the school the next day — the hot interior, the heaps of dead leaves — and poked around for another snake. He had let the twig snake go. He found a small puff adder and brought it back to his hut. He eased it into a basket and put his envelopes of money inside with it, saying "*Mphiri,*" making sure that Zizi and the dwarf saw what he was doing.

Sleep and more fruit, and some bread with the dried fish, restored him. It only remained for him to get his strength back. Living there was a daily intimation of death, and these days he felt like a corpse. The fever had subsided, leaving him gaunt. I might have died, he thought, and reflected on Malabo as a terrible place to die—alone, in this heat, among strangers.

In that mood of abandonment, the aftermath of his fever, he wondered where he had gone wrong, to find himself trapped, at the end of a narrow road of deep sand, in a small hut, in this obscure village. He lay, looking for a clue, because he now felt he could not go any farther, nor was he confident of being able to escape. The fever had not killed him, yet it seemed an intimation that he was destined to die here.

He reviewed his moves, working backward, and saw that it was not the obvious wrong turn, the error of having come here suddenly with money, naively thinking he could help to improve the lives of these people. Not the warm fantasizing emails, not the ending of his marriage, not his solitary life—most people were solitary. Not the obligation imposed by the death of his father, not the burden of business or its failure—everyone worked at a job unwillingly, and there was always a little sweetness to be had in any life of monotony.

It was an old turning, perhaps the oldest, one he'd first regarded as a victory, the happy decision to become a teacher in Africa, long ago when he'd seen the undisturbed bush at is most beautiful. He knew now where he had gone wrong. It was at the very beginning of his life as a man. He should never have come to Africa in the first place, never trifled with these people, never involved himself in their lives, mistaking their hopes for his own. Yet he had, and it had destroyed him.

PART III

Downriver

16

THE TEN-DRUM *ngoma* that Manyenga promised was announced by boys wagging torches of oil-soaked rags flaming on poles, and the boys, Hock saw, were two of the orphans who'd abandoned the work at the school. They'd scuttled away then; they were marching in a stately procession now. They beckoned, then turned to lead him, and with the torches held high, preceded him across the field to Manyenga's, Zizi and the dwarf following.

"Welcome, father," Manyenga said, showing him to a chair and offering him a glass of *nipa*. The rest, all men and boys, were seated on the ground, a few cross-legged on woven mats. A piece of meat, an angular blackened leg, was dripping on a spit, and Manyenga's elder wife was stirring a sludge of sodden, dark green leaves in a large tin pot. Several of the men were very old, staring into the fire, their eyes wild with the glow of the cooking fire, sputtering under the meat.

"Goat," Hock said. "Mutton."

"It is an impala for you," Manyenga said.

"You poached it."

"God provided this bush meat to us because we are hungry."

Manyenga introduced the men as chiefs from nearby villages, and Hock recognized them as some of the men he had met on his first day at Nyachikadza's hut, when they had decided to cremate the small dead crocodile with the poisonous liver. He remembered his excitement at arriving at the Lower River; he was ashamed at the memory of his innocence.

"And those boys," Manyenga said.

As he was waited on by women and small boys, the conceit he'd had the previous day of being like a chief returned to him. He sat contented, picking at the shreds of meat on his plate, hearing Manyenga praise him.

"Now, father"—and Manyenga called one of the boys over. "This young chap is needing something to go to South Africa for work."

"*Salani bwino,*" Hock said, as a formal farewell.

"But he is needing *ndalama,*" Manyenga said. He used a Sena word as a euphemism, because "money" was too blunt.

The boy stood straight, bug-eyed with fear in the firelight, a scarecrow in his too big shirt and torn trousers, his bony wrists pressed against his sides. A yellow pencil stub stuck into his dense hair, the pink eraser protruding, was like a badge of scholarly seriousness.

"What's his name?"

"Name of Simon."

"How will he go? Bus from Blantyre?"

Manyenga rocked a little on his heels and grunted at the idea of such a straightforward way of traveling. The others shook their heads and clucked.

"Down the river, father. From Magwero. Through the Dinde Marsh to Morrumbala. To Mozambique. Zambezi River. Then Beira side, if he is finding a lorry. Then catching a bus—and what, and what—to Maputo. Then—" Manyenga shrugged, hinting at much more. "A jinny, father. A challenge."

"How will he get to Magwero?"

"Marsden will lift him on my motorbike tomorrow."

The very thought of such a trip, trespassing over borders, saddened Hock, as the thought of humble, perhaps hopeless struggle always did. He'd expected such struggle, but he hadn't imagined so much would be expended in the effort of leaving Malabo and the Lower River. It made Malabo so remote. He was part of that remoteness.

"How much?"

"What you are willing, father."

Hock nodded, hoping to appear noncommittal, but he knew that they had read his mind. They were masterly at discerning the nuances of gesture, a mere eye blink or a way of breathing revealed a state of mind. It was not sorcery; they were illiterate, and so they could read perfectly with every other sense. Hock thought that anyone who said literacy made a person brighter was wrong. Being illiterate, not speaking a language well, out of your element and perhaps feeling insecure, unnerved, and suspicious—all these made a person much more observant.

Because they saw that he had been moved by the boy standing there, and knew what he would do, they filled his glass again with *kachasu* and toasted him. They sent the unmarried girls, among them Zizi, to serve him more food, a cut of the impala meat, platters of grilled fish, and roasted slices of cassava.

The older girls, including Zizi, were bare-breasted tonight. Hock felt that they somehow knew this nakedness meant more to a *mzungu,* that they were appealing to his foreigner's weakness, teasing him and looking for a reaction.

After the girls served him, the women sang, clapping their hands, and the girls sang with them, and danced before him, standing in a line. He knew some of the words: "Our father, our chief, our *mzungu* in Malabo." Their skin shone with perspiration, and dust clung to it, creating a weird plastery cosmetic. Their growly harmonizing resonated in the pit of his stomach. He could separate Zizi's voice from the others; it stirred something in him—a purring within him that answered her.

On any other night he would have excused himself and crept across the clearing to his hut, flashing his torch. But he was the guest of honor—Manyenga kept calling him *nduna,* minister— and could not leave, could not rise from his chair, was not allowed to choose his own food. They insisted upon waiting on him, the eager men, the solemn girls, the skinny boys, the cackling women, filling his plate, topping up his glass.

At last he called to the boy Simon, motioning him to his side. He gave the boy some money, folded under his fingers.

Everyone saw. Manyenga said, "You are our *nduna,* dear father."

During the night, under the folds of his mosquito net, he conceived his plan. Then he dozed, and when he woke he thought it through again. It was so simple and spontaneous and seemingly foolproof he could not add to it or find a flaw. All he needed was an accomplice, and he knew he had one. After that, in his excitement, he could not sleep.

Or perhaps he *had* fallen asleep. The bump and scrape of bare feet on the veranda planks startled him, made him remember his plan. He got up quickly, pushed the curtains of the netting aside, and whispered to the figure at the window.

"Sister, come here. Inside."

But Zizi froze at the words, which she'd never before heard from him. He cracked the door open, reached for her wrist, and she allowed herself to be drawn into the room. Her hard fingers tightened in his as he tugged further.

"Quick, get into the bed."

Her face swelled with thought and became expressionless. She drew in her lips and pressed down, and she wrapped herself in her skinny arms, confused but stubborn.

Hock took her by her shoulders. Her skin was cool; she must have been crouching by the door awhile in the darkness. She dug her big toe against the floor. She was not resisting, she was bewildered. *Quick, get into the bed!*

She allowed herself to be helped beneath the mosquito net, and she sat and drew her long legs under the damp sheet that served as a coverlet. It all happened so fast that in spite of himself Hock was aroused—there she lay, the skinny shaven-headed girl in his bed, her fists jammed under her chin, her eyes wide open, looking anxious but not fearful. But Hock felt less like a lover than a father, tucking his daughter into bed. She seemed fragile on her back, her head on the crushed pillow, so dark against the sheets.

"Don't be afraid," Hock said. "Just stay here. If anyone knocks on the door, don't say anything. Turn over, don't let them see your face. Keep the net closed."

She raised her head a little. "You are coming back?"

"Yes. I'm coming back to get you."

He kissed her lightly, and tasting the warmth on her lips, kissed her again, bumping her teeth in his eagerness. And for the first time in the course of making his plan he hesitated, considered abandoning it, to stay beside this pretty girl. She would have allowed him.

"Don't move," he said.

Zizi began to sing in her throat, a frantic murmuring, as she did when she was anxious.

"I'll be back," he said.

He hated his lie, but it was the only way to get her to stay in the bed, under the mosquito net. And he hated his lie, too, because he was tempted to change his plan. In a crowded vision, standing in the hut, he was confronted by images of his life with her, the flight to Boston, his proud explanations to his friends: *I'm her guardian. She deserves a better life. I knew her family.* The clothes he'd buy—he saw her wearing them. He saw her sitting at his kitchen table drinking a glass of milk, saw her with an armful of books on the steps of a college. A good daughter. Smiling, because she seldom smiled here.

Those thoughts made him grim as he picked up his bag and slipped into the darkness, locking the door behind him, passing behind the house, cutting through the maize patch, a roundabout way to the road. And then he walked fast, trying to make time before the sun rose.

He reached the six-hut settlement of Lutwe as the sun, just bulging at the horizon, rinsed the darkness from the sky, and the day grew light, a pinky glow behind the trees, the sky going bluer. And before the sun blazed at the level of the low bushes Hock was at the crossroads. There he waited until he heard the rapping of the motorbike, and the warble of its rise and fall on the uneven road.

Seeing him, the driver of the motorbike slowed and came clumsily to a skidding stop. The boy Simon was seated on the back.

"Father," said the driver—Marsden, Manyenga's nephew, who'd been at the ceremony—and then he corrected himself, "*Nduna,*" and, correcting further, attempted "Meeneestah."

"I'll take this boy to Magwero," Hock said.

Marsden said nothing but was clearly baffled. The engine was idling. He brushed at the flies settling on his face.

"It's all right," Hock said. "You can walk to Magwero. Or you can wait here and I'll pick you up on the way back."

"Chief Manyenga said to me—"

"This is the revised plan," Hock said. "The new plan." His words made the boy blink, and he was still batting the flies.

"The chief said—"

"I'm the chief."

Marsden cut the engine, and both boys got off the bike, Marsden propping it on its kickstand as he swung his leg over. When Hock mounted it and stamped on the lever to start the engine again, the boys seemed bewildered. They backed away as though in fear from a thief, their thin bodies tensed in their loose clothes, on the point of fleeing.

Hock said, "Get on, Simon, you have to catch your boat."

The boy got onto the back seat and steadied himself by holding Hock's hips.

"Luggages," Marsden said, handing Hock his bag.

"Thanks—almost forgot," Hock said, and smiled. He'd begun to believe the lie he'd told them about coming back.

"Maybe they'll miss you at Malabo," Marsden said. He knew it was forbidden for Hock to leave the village without supervision. Hock was theirs. The whole village knew that.

"It's all right," Hock said. "They won't miss me."

They'll go to my house—and with this thought he saw them at the door, gingerly knocking—then see the lumped-up body under the mosquito net. They would whisper, "Sleeping," and would go away. And not until midmorning, when Zizi got tired of lying with the sheet over her head and might be looking for Hock, would they realize that Hock had gone. By then he would be in the dugout, and the motorbike would be parked at Magwero, and the boy Marsden would be waiting under this tree at Lutwe, and in all this confusion Hock would be well into the marsh, headed downriver, passing Morrumbala into Mozambique. That was the plan.

He forgave himself for not having tried to escape before this when he saw (struggling with the bike, pulling it again and again into the deep dust of the wheel ruts) the distance to the main road and the—what?—twenty miles to Magwero, twenty sweltering miles even at seven in the morning, for as soon as the sun was up, the heat gagged him and his face was pelted by insects.

Still, the road was free of traffic, and the only people he saw were women walking to market with big cloth bundles on their heads, and men with sacks of flour or rice flopped over the crossbar of their bikes, not riding the bikes but pushing them.

He had not forgotten the mango tree and the plump smooth log under it at Magwero, and when he saw it ahead he was excited. Some men were sitting under the tree, two of whom he recognized from his first day. He called out to them as he rode past, steering the bike to the village, and beyond it to the landing.

In the morning sun, the gnat-flecked rays diffused by the tall marsh grass, eight-man canoes—wide hollow logs—were drawn up on the embankment, and the smaller dugouts and fishing canoes bobbed in the scummy water on mooring lines. At one large canoe that lay partly in the water, men were arranging sacks of meal and crates of mangoes.

Hock greeted the men and said, "This is the boy who is going downriver."

The men loading the canoe did not react. They were already perspiring from their work, their sweat-darkened shirts clinging to their bodies. One of them glanced at Simon, but without interest.

"What time are you leaving?"

"Later."

Hock said, "We have to go now."

It was a meaningless sentence, because "now" never meant now. It meant soon, it meant sometime, it meant whenever. It wasn't an urgent word; it also meant never.

Hearing it, one of the men bent over and, sweaty-faced under a dusty sack, spat onto the slimy mud of the embankment.

Hock said sharply, "Who's the owner of this *bwato*?"

A man in a crushed straw hat, wearing thick-lensed glasses, peered at Hock and said in English, "It is my."

"You know me?" Hock asked.

The old man shook his head. "But my father, he was knowing."

Hock drew the man aside. He said, "The boy has to go right

now," and tapped his watch. "And I'm going with him. How much do you want?"

"But the cargo," the old man said. He scratched at his knuckles, loosening skin.

"How much?" Hock could see through the trees to the nearby village, where women were ghostly in the smoke of cooking fires. Men and small children had gathered on the embankment to watch. They must have followed the motorbike, which leaned on its kickstand near the canoes.

"We were expecting the boy, but not you, father." The old man was peeling dead skin from his knuckles.

"Five hundred," Hock said.

The old man had two yellow upper teeth. As he worked his jaw his tongue floated around them, seeming to tickle them. His thought process was visible in his chewing. He said, "Seven hundred."

"Tell the men to cast off," Hock said. He handed the old man the fat sandwich of folded-over money, all small bills. And he called to Simon to get into the big canoe.

It worried Hock that too much time had passed in the palaver, but once he and the boy were on board, and the two paddlers were beating it backward from the bank into the bobbing density of water hyacinths—the boy, feet apart, poling—he saw that he'd gotten away quickly. The village watched them go, the ghostly women at the smoky edge of the trees, the men standing near the unloaded piles of grain sacks and the crates of fruit. And there was the parked motorbike, the guarantee that no one from Malabo would arrive here anytime soon; it was the only vehicle in Malabo. And so he'd stranded Zizi in his bed, Manyenga in the village, Marsden at the Lutwe crossroads—and he was away, cheered by the men digging their paddles into the water, pushing the canoe through the narrow channel between the glistening water hyacinths, a profusion of stems and leaves and blossoms so tangled it seemed you could step out of the canoe and walk across this floating platform of green marsh weeds.

Confident that he was safe, Hock leaned against the blunt bow of the canoe, resting on a sack of flour, and fell asleep, lulled by the rocking of the boat, the regular splash of the paddles. It was as though he had at last freed himself from the pull of gravity, not just escaped from Malabo but twisted away from the clinging people, the reaching hands, everything represented by the muddy embankment, which seemed like the edge of an alien planet, and was now bobbing through the sickly light in the soup of its atmosphere.

Exhausted by the early start and the effort in all his harangues—Zizi, the motorcyclist Marsden, the boy Simon, the elderly canoe owner—he lay in the boat asleep for over an hour. He woke with the sun full on his face, and gazing up he saw the long spikes of marsh reeds overhanging the bow as the big dugout glided past.

The two paddlers were angled against the gunwales of the boat, one on either side, the boy Simon thrusting with his pole. Hock peeled an orange and, throwing the scraps of skin into the channel, saw they were being sucked toward the stern.

"We're going upstream," he called out. "No—that way!"

The men kept their rhythm of paddling, chopping the water, their cheeks streaming with sweat.

"This is the channel," one of them said in Sena. "We have to pass through the marsh to get to the river."

In his second year in Malabo, he'd been taken fishing for tilapia in the river. They'd crossed the Dinde Marsh and entered the fast-flowing stream of the Shire River in less than thirty minutes. He explained this in a halting way to the paddlers, who listened while shoveling water with their paddle blades. Speaking about the past here was like speaking about a foreign land—happier, simpler, much bigger and highly colored, seemingly aboveground.

The man who had spoken before said, "That was years and years," and he gestured to mean the years were gone.

"So the river changed?"

The man who had been silent said, "The river is a snake."

The great marsh and its wall of reeds was an obstacle, or rather, a set of obstacles, the channel zigzagging through it without any logic or pattern, a maze in which they were pushing themselves, always upstream, slipping through narrow openings and up the widening channel, against the current. The grunts of the men and the smack of the paddles kept him awake as he peered ahead for the opening of the marsh into the river. Here and there, men in small canoes were surprised, as they fished, to see the big canoe and the red-faced man in it. And as they bobbed in its wake, staring at the *mzungu,* he noted the few possessions they had on board: the water bottle, the torn net, the dish of bait, the pathetic catch—a basket of small shiny fish.

He was fleeing, he knew. He could have ridden the motorbike to the boma, but he would have been seen and probably detained. The river was better—he could lose himself in the bush. He wanted to get away, to vanish across the Mozambique border. The thought of distancing himself from Malabo excited him; the idea that he was breaking free of Malawi made him joyous. He had a change of clothes, his little radio, his passport, his money: everything he needed.

In the stern the boy Simon was asking a question. Hock didn't hear the question, but he heard the answer.

"It is there."

The boy said in English to Hock, "Reevah."

Sunlight spanked the water ahead with such brilliance the current showed as muscles beneath bright scales on the turbulent surface. The boat nosed through the last thinning wall of reeds and shot out of the mouth of the channel, where it was caught and tipped by the wide flow of the river. The bow was yanked into the current and then the whole dugout was carried sideways along the stream. One of the paddlers wiped his face on his shirt as the other used his paddle blade as a rudder, steering the boat away from the tall bank of reeds. And just then, in a scoop in the reeds, a little bay, a hippo raised its blotchy head and was so startled by the boat he opened his jaws wide. Hock could see the reddish flesh of the mouth and the blunt pegs of its thick round teeth and the raw mottled skin of its fat body. He yelped—his first cry of joy in many weeks—and he pointed.

"You!"

Paddling more easily now, the men kept the boat in the current, sliding its beam crossways in the stream from reach to reach.

"We eat them," the first paddler said in Sena.

"People here never ate them before," Hock said, and again in speaking of the past he seemed to be referring not to another time but to a distant country. "What is your name?"

"Lovemore."

"Why do you eat hippos, Lovemore?"

"Because we are hungry."

The other paddler gave his name as Dalitso—blessings—and it was he, not Lovemore, who spoke a little English. Hock offered some of his oranges and tangerines to them, but they refused all food. Simon ate an orange, removing the peel in fastidious pinchings, such delicacy in a dugout on a river flowing through the bush.

The paddlers drank water from their plastic jug, and they rolled cigarettes and smoked. Hock knew from their glassy eyes and their concentration that they were smoking weed.

"*Chamba*," he said.

"*Mbanje!*" one said, using the slang word.

Even in the hottest hours of the day, as Hock dozed under the shirt he spread across the gunwales for shade, the paddlers kept on, fueled by the weed smoke. The banks of the river were more clearly defined now, steep and sculpted flat, like the walls of a ditch. They could not see beyond them—no trees were visible, no high ground, only now and then a break in the bank where a green stream leaked out, or a sandbar at the edge where a small bumpy green croc was sleeping.

"Where is Mozambique?" Hock asked.

No one spoke, though one man jabbed his paddle at the opposite bank.

Toward midafternoon Hock saw an island of low huts, thatched with black decaying bundles of straw. Wondering whether it was a Sena settlement, he asked idly, "Who lives there?"

"Dead people," one of the paddlers whispered.

Hock blinked and an ache of fear tugged at his throat.

A mile or so below that island—of graves, of ghosts?—they came to a wide muddy embankment where the broken hull, bare ribs, and rusty ironwork of a large wooden boat had been pushed onto the foreshore to rot. It was the only sign of habitation he'd seen since leaving Magwero. As they drew closer, he could see a shed, a sloping landing, and a man at a table under a mango tree. The man wore the khaki shirt of officialdom, including a brass badge on his pocket.

"Mozambique," the paddler Dalitso said, easing the dugout against the landing.

Hock climbed out, glad for the chance to walk, relieved that the day had gotten him this far from Malabo. He helped them haul the boat onto the landing, then climbed the embankment and walked toward the man at the table.

"Passport," the man said.

Hock took it from his pocket, smiling at the frontier—the man in his clean shirt, the table, the stamp and ink pad.

"You speak English?"

"No any Englis." He examined the passport, moving the pages with his thumb. "Visa—forty dollar."

"So you do speak English."

"Visa," the man said. He held up four fingers. "Forty dollar."

Why am I happy? Hock asked himself. I am happy because no one knows me here.

At the small shed beyond the frontier post, Hock bought a box of salted crackers, a can of beans, some bottles of beer. He saw that the paddlers were building a fire, preparing a meal of *nsima* and stew, fussing with tin pots, scraping at the thick water-and-flour mixture.

He offered Simon a bottle of beer and sat with him on the embankment, on plastic beer crates, facing the river and the reddening sun. Already the day was cooler, and the slanting sunlight gilded the swarms of insects that streamed over the river like flakes of gold.

"Thank you," the boy said, swigging beer.

"Tomorrow where do we go?"

"To Caya, on the Zambezi."

"And then?"

"Find a lorry to Beira. Or maybe a bus."

"How far to Beira?"

"One overnight. Then a bus to Maputo. Maputo, it is the capital city. Then Jo'burg."

"I want to go."

"It is your decision, father."

"I helped you with money."

"Yes, father." Simon drank his beer slowly, a small mouthful at a time, as though rationing himself. He said, "I want a bright future for myself. I want to help my family with money. They are suffering too much. Maybe I can help my country, too. I can work, sure. I am willing and able, that is the goodness."

"Did you learn English at the school in Malabo?"

"No, in Chikwawa. We have no school in Malabo. We have nothing in Malabo."

Hock was about to lecture him, to tell him that once, many years ago, there was a school in Malabo, which had a library and teachers. There was a clinic, a monthly visit from a missionary, a plan for digging a well, and another plan for electricity. There was a church that was sometimes used as a village hall. But he said nothing, only smiled, and when he finished his bottle of beer he said, "Ask these people if they have a bed for me."

"I will ask."

Hock tuned his little radio, found some faint music, and listened, growing sad. The sound of the radio made him feel more remote, as though he was listening to the earth from distant space.

"They have a bed for you, father." He led Hock to one of the nearby sheds. Seeing Hock with the radio to his ear he asked, "How many kwacha does that wireless cost for buying?"

"I don't know," Hock said. "Here, you can listen. You might learn something. You sound like a self-improver. Give it back to me tomorrow."

A woman opening the door of the shed said, "*Ndalama.*"

Hock gave her five dollars. She tucked it into the fastening across her breasts and handed him a small towel. This he spread across the hard pillow on the shelf that served as a bunk, two planks that had been fixed from one wall to the other.

He lay in the hot stifling darkness. The small room stank of kerosene and dirt, and it was airless, the door closed, the bolt shot. It had no windows. It was obviously for storage, not a bedroom. Yet he was tired, and he slept, and when he woke and walked into the freshness of the morning, the river sparkling, he was happy again.

But the dugout was gone, the boy was gone, the man in the

khaki shirt at the small table under the tree, gone. It was just another riverbank. Hock hurried to the landing and saw at the foot of it a woman washing clothes, slapping them, twisting the muddy water from them.

"Where are they?"

Even without English, the woman, seeing his confusion, knew what he was saying.

She pointed downriver and laughed and went on slapping the clothes against a large stone.

17

THE MUD AT the embankment was thick and dark, a slippery mass of insubstantial fudge, crawling with beetles and littered with chewed fish bones and fruit peels. For most of the morning Hock squatted there, slapping at the tsetse flies biting his ankles and watching for a boat, any boat, to take him away from the landing. The sky was cloudless, and empty except for the black profile of a gliding fish eagle, and nearer, the lovely trilling of a swamp warbler swaying on a reed. Yellow butterflies fluttered to the garbage heaps on the mud bank, settled on the rusted cans and the foul mass of plastic and sodden paper and broken bottles. He was not dismayed, but he felt the fatigue of being dirty and yearned to wash his face.

Though just yesterday Zizi had willingly crept into his bed, he was saddened by the thought of her, yet relieved to be here and not there. He'd crossed a border. This looked like a dump, and the settlement was just a camp, a portrait of abandonment in the bush, but it was a frontier, and he was on the right side of it, on his way home. With this thought at the front of his mind, he looked around at the placid river, the garbage, the wooden windowless shed where he'd slept, the hulk of the large wrecked boat with its still intact wheelhouse—the stink and decrepitude of it all—and he laughed. He was in the middle of nowhere, but he was free.

Just then he saw a dugout bobbing in the stream at the far bank. He stood up and whistled, with his fingers in his mouth. For a moment he thought the paddlers on board hadn't heard, or that they were afraid. But like a compass needle swiveling in liquid, the narrow canoe turned to point at him, and it slid toward where he stood on the bank.

The paddlers were children, hardly more than ten or eleven.

He greeted them, and when they remained stony-faced, either afraid or unfriendly, he asked whether they could speak Sena.

They nodded yes, they could speak the language.

Hock said in Sena that he wanted to go to the far bank, and the boys' reaction was expressionless again, implacable, and so he explained, "To your village."

They seemed to understand the word for village, but did not reply to it, or say that he would be either welcome or unwelcome there. Still, they floated nearer, and that encouraged Hock to step to the river's edge.

He threw his bag into the dugout and, up to his ankles in mud, he stepped in and held on. The boat rode lower in the water with him in it, was more stable with his weight holding it deeper.

The skinny boys thrashed with their paddles, one of the paddles merely the splintered portion of a short water-blackened board. Hock asked them their names, and they grunted some words he did not understand. But random incoherence seemed to be the theme of his escape. No record had been made of his passport details by the man in khaki. The washerwoman had laughed as she told him that his friends had left without him. The boy Simon and the other canoe were gone. He was in a small dugout in the middle of the river, still the Lower River, miles above the Zambezi, into which it flowed, the two small boys steering and slapping with their clumsy paddles on this hot morning.

I don't exist, Hock thought. No one knows I'm here, no one knows me, no one cares, and were this flimsy canoe to turn over, or be flipped by a hippo, no one would ever find me; no one would know I died. The world would continue to turn without me, my death would be unnoticed, would make no difference, because I am no one, no more than meat.

He saw himself with the eyes of a hawk that was passing high above, soaring without moving its wings, looking imperturbable, graceful in its effortless gliding. I am a speck, no more than that,

Hock thought. I am a bug on a twig floating down a dark river. Less than a bug.

A basket at his feet held three tiny fish: not bait, though they were small enough for that. It was perhaps the day's catch, a peeled stick inserted through their gills, holding them together like a kebab. The boys would have started fishing before dawn. This was all they had to show for those five hours or so.

The river narrowed. It had been fifty yards wide at the border post; now it was less than forty, and swifter because of that, rushing past sandbanks on which Hock saw the unmistakable signs of large crocodiles, the parallel paw prints and claw marks, the groove of the dragging tail between them.

Hock pointed to an overhanging mud cliff that had been hollowed out beneath by the rushing river, using it as a landmark. He said, "Malawi?"

"Nuh," the boy said, jerking his head, but still stroking with his paddle.

"Mozambique?"

The boy clicked his teeth, but that didn't mean yes; it meant the question was annoying and perhaps meaningless.

The reeds, the marsh grass, the greasy weeds, the sandbanks, the blackish water—none of it was different from what he'd seen upstream. No high ground was visible beyond the steep riverbanks. But he was moving, and no one knew him. He had escaped Malabo, and he was watchful for whatever might come next.

The pull of the current consoled him with the notion that he was being drawn to safety. All he had to do was surrender to the flow of the river, the Lower River, bearing him southward through the bush.

After about an hour he saw in the distance downriver a single straight-sided humped-up mountain, solitary, like a granite monument, headless shoulders risen in the marshy plain. As they drew closer in the canoe it seemed like a citadel of tree-clad stone, its steep sides and cliffs formed in the shape of fortifications. It was such an oddity—its great size, its unusual shape—he asked its name.

"Morrumbala," the boy in the stern said.

Hock knew the name but had never seen it. The war against the Portuguese had prevented him from traveling this far into Mozambique, so it was all new to him, a strangely hopeful sign. It lay in the distance, beyond the far bank.

As Hock stared at it, the sun striking the trees on its sheer sides, the sunlit green as luminous as fresh lettuce, pulpous and pale yellow in patches, he did not notice the canoe drawing away from Morrumbala, closer to the near riverbank. Only when the canoe bumped did he look up and see that they'd been pushed by the current against a pair of poles sticking out of the mud. Lashed to the poles was a water-soaked board that served as a crude pier, and another board, a walkway to the high grass at the bank.

A boy of four or five, wearing just a shirt—his bottom bare—saw Hock and began screaming in fear. He ran from Hock as from a demon, as the paddlers laughed—their first full-throated cry—and the small boy screamed out, "*Mzungu!*"

His fright seemed to relax them, and they were still laughing as they tied the dugout to the poles and led Hock onto the bank and up a path to a clearing.

He had seen many villages like this, the squat square huts arranged around the perimeter of an open space of smooth packed-down earth. From the condition of the fraying thatch on the hut roofs, and the exposed framework on the mud walls, and the rags hanging on clotheslines—from the sharp stink of smoke and dirt—he knew it was a poor village. Yet it was orderly, and there was something else—unusual, even remarkable—for though it was full of people, they were all very small, all of them, he saw, children in tattered clothes, the sort of T-shirts and shorts and trousers that were sold cheaply at the used-clothing markets, the shirts with American names on them, schools, the logos of well-known companies, names of cities, too, and famous universities.

The small boy who had been screaming was scooped up by a girl of ten or so—she could barely lift him. He buried his face in her shoulder.

"Where's your father, your mother?" Hock asked the paddlers.

One boy turned away in alarm, his rags making his fear pathetic. The other boy faced Hock and scowled, saying nothing, either insulted or afraid.

"The chief," Hock said. "*Mfumu.* Where is your bwana?"

The boy made an even sourer face, thrusting out his lower lip, showing a kind of threat with its inner pinkness, and began to speak fast, turning his back to Hock as he talked. Finally he walked away on his toes, in disdain, holding upright like a symbol of prestige the stick with the three small stiff fish that he'd taken from the canoe.

Hock sat on a discarded plank in the shade of a tree and watched a small girl poking a fire under a blackened pot, perhaps cooking, perhaps playing; another small girl holding a baby at her hip; infants crawling in the dust, picking at dry tufts of grass. More children were occupied stacking firewood, most of them boys, but the pile they made was so random—no more than a scattered heap—that looked like play, too, a game of tossed and broken branches. Some other, bigger boys sat under a tree on the far side of the clearing. Children and more children. They all wore faded T-shirts of various colors, much too big for them, some serving the smaller girls as dresses—T-shirts as shapeless frocks, one saying *Niagara Falls,* another *Yale.* They were dusty-faced and their hair was clotted with white bits of lint, and many of the children were unnaturally skinny, the infants potbellied with spindly arms and legs.

They seemed indifferent to Hock, and they were silent, going about their chores or absorbed in repetitive play. When Hock got up from his plank and walked through the village, they took no notice of him.

The border post on the river now seemed to him something defined and certain: the table, the sullen official with the stamp and ink pad, the battered sheds, the broken boat, the muddy embankment, the rapacious shopkeeper. It was on the map, or at least seemed so, an entry point. It was a ruin but it was not a horror, only futile-looking, decaying with the accumulation of garbage, and the rise and fall of the river, not maintained, conventionally ugly, as most of the depots on the Lower River looked, including the boma at Nsanje and the landings at Magwero and Marka. People congregated at the landings, but few people lived at them.

Compared to the border post, even to Magwero, this village of children was whole, coherent, and some of it was swept clean—Hock could see small girls with twig brooms pushing the litter of leaves and peels to the side of the courtyard in front of the huts. None of the huts was in good shape—the usual bruised walls, the skeletal frame of branches showing through—and yet the village was inhabited, strangely so. Everyone he'd seen so far was young, some very young, mostly small children, the little girls holding infants, small boys playing together, the older boys watchful. And because most were so young there was a buzz of vitality in the village, a hurrying; running boys, skipping girls. Some played with crudely made toys, formed of twisted wire, or hanks of knotted rags that served as balls to kick, and some limbless dolls, plastic torsos with cracked heads—white dolls.

This village made sense because it was full of lives being lived outdoors; it was visible and vital. Pots simmered over fires, and oddly, some small girls were taking turns with oversized mortars and pestles—the pestles much taller than they were and so heavy that some of them had to be hoisted and dropped by pairs of girls.

It could have been a summer camp or a school; it had that look of monotony and order, all the children occupied. But most were working, even those he had taken to be playing. The girls wore large T-shirts to their knees, some were cinched with rope at the waist to make a dress, others draped over them like nightshirts, or like smocks. Many of the small children wore a T-shirt and nothing else, and though the boys' T-shirts fitted them better, all were faded and worn—*Westfield High School* and *UConn* and *Bob's Bluegrass Bar* and *UCLA* and more. Once-white ones were gray with dirt, many had chewed collars and slashes, and some were shredded to rags.

Taller, much bigger than any of these skinny kids, Hock felt a sense of safety, the instinctive confidence of the tall man, a giant among dwarfs, reassured by his size and the fact that he'd escaped from Malabo, and gotten away from the border post, and was now six or seven miles downstream, probably in Mozambique but on the west bank of the Lower River. There had to be a path that would lead to a wider road and a truck route and a town.

It was just after four. He'd eaten the last of his crackers and beans in the morning, waiting on the riverbank, and nothing since. His hunger sharpened with the odor of cassava roasting on a grill over a fire, tended by a small girl on her knees. She turned the dark, roughly carved root slices with a forked stick. After watching her for a while, Hock got up and walked over to the fire. The girl shrank from him, though stayed kneeling, fanning smoke from her eyes, rearranging the slices, moving them to the side of the grill farthest from Hock.

Instinctively, as he reached, Hock looked for an adult, anyone his size, who might object, and seeing only children, he picked up one of the pieces of cooked cassava. It was hot, he bobbled it in his palm, then blew on it and took a bite. He had not realized how hungry he was until he ate the thing, stringy, dense, tasting of wood smoke. He wolfed it down and wanted another.

The girl tending the fire (her T-shirt was lettered *Colby Chess Club*) had turned toward him but with averted eyes, gazing past him. Hock looked around and saw, on a log in front of a hut, three big boys staring at him. He was surprised and disconcerted to see that they were wearing sunglasses, three bug-eyed boys in T-shirts and trousers. Something in their posture gave them an air of authority, even hauteur, and the sunglasses seemed, if not menacing, then unfriendly, intentionally ambiguous. Their clothes were clean, and that unusual fact made them seem stronger and put Hock on his guard. One of them wore a black baseball cap with the words *Dynamo Dresden* stitched in yellow on the front.

He'd been dazed and dulled by the effort of getting away from Malabo, and the canoe trip to the frontier had tired him. He hadn't expected to be abandoned by Simon — after giving him money and sermonizing about his future, the ungrateful rat — hadn't expected this, a village of children.

Hock was still hungry but, sensing disapproval from the watching boys, instead of taking any more food from the fire, he walked up the slight incline of sloping earth and dead grass to where the boys sat in the afternoon sun.

"Hello, how are you?" he asked in Sena, certain they would understand; the language was spoken all over the Lower River.

They simply stared, or seemed to, in the stylish unrevealing goggles, as though they hadn't heard or didn't know the words.

"Where is your chief?" Hock used all the words for "big man" he knew, not only *mfumu* and *nduna,* but also *nkhoswe,* the elder who traditionally looked after all the smaller siblings—nephews and dependents.

"No chief," the boy in the middle said in English. He was a skinny sharp-faced boy with wet insolent lips and he sounded triumphant. "No *nkhoswe*."

"No bwana?"

"You are the only bwana."

Hock felt a thrill at the idea of a village in the bush with no one in charge.

"What is the name of this village?" he asked.

The boy wearing the black cap lettered *Dynamo Dresden* said, "It is Mtayira."

"I don't know that word."

"It is The Place of the Thrown-Aways."

So precise, the sad name.

"Where is the road?" Hock asked. He spoke in Sena, to be sure, for the word *njira* meant any road, big or small, even a footpath.

"No road," the sharp-faced boy said, crowing in English.

"You speak English. Did you learn it at school?"

"Not at school, never."

The truculent and unwilling tone and the sulky *nayvah* in the boy's response annoyed Hock, who said, "I haven't eaten anything all day. I need some food."

"We have no food for you."

The three pairs of sunglasses were pitiless. And none of the boys had risen, in itself an act of defiance, for on the Lower River, even in the disgrace that was Malabo, the children stood up in the presence of adults. Hock turned toward the cooking fire and saw that the girl had gathered all the cassava and was carrying it away in a tin bowl, moving quickly on short legs across the clearing with the head-bobbing walk of a child.

"I'm hungry," Hock said in a mildly protesting way.

"We are more hungry," the same boy said.

"If you help me, I'll give you money," Hock said, and was at once uncomfortably aware of the pleading note in his voice.

"We want dollars," one of the other boys said, a new voice that was a growl.

Hock laughed at the idea that he was negotiating with a boy in a baseball cap who was no more than fourteen or fifteen years old, in a bush village on the river, a sullen boy in sunglasses.

"Twenty dollars," the boy said.

Hock felt pressure on his legs, a rubbing and pushing, and saw that a crowd of children had gathered around him. Instead of standing at a distance, as children always did by tradition, out of respect, these children stood close to him, chafing him, hemming him in, preventing him from moving. It was as though he was standing in thick bush grass up to his waist. He could sway, but he could not lift his legs. He'd put his bag between his feet and could feel it against his calves but was unable to reach it.

"What do I get for twenty dollars?"

"Some food to eat."

"Is that all?"

"Some tea to drink."

"I need a place to sleep," Hock said.

The children jostling at his legs made him totter and almost lose his balance. He lifted his arms and waved them to steady himself, feeling foolish.

"Maybe we have a space."

"I want to be your friend," Hock said.

"We do not know you at all." It was the growly voiced boy.

"Please tell these children to move away."

The boy spoke to them sharply, but they responded by chattering, laughing, gesturing.

"They say that you must go, not them," the boy said, and the children laughed again, as if guessing what was being said. And when they laughed, jeering, careless, Hock became worried.

He reached through the tangle of small bodies and found the strap of his bag and lifted it, hugging it, protecting it with his arm. Everything he owned was in it—not much now, he'd left most of his clothes in Malabo, and Simon had stolen his radio. But he had the essentials—medicine and money and a change of clothes.

The worst thing you could do in these circumstances, he knew, was to pull out an envelope and show money to such a crowd of rude catcalling children. He said only, "See? I have it."

The middle boy gestured, and the boys on either side of him snarled what sounded like an order, or abuse. But the crowd of children did not disperse at once. They chattered some more, they made insolent noises, they poked and pinched at Hock's legs and tugged at his bag to taunt him. And only then did they move away, at first slowly, then running, chasing each other, leaving Hock short of breath, his heart beating fast.

Hock knew from his Medford store that there is a way a person handles money that shows familiarity, not just the deftness of a clerk at the cash drawer, but also in a bush village like this, in the practiced movements of someone's fingers—a response of hands more than eyes. The boy had taken the twenty-dollar bill, had smoothed it and folded it in half, hardly looking at it, and Hock knew that the boy had experienced American money, handled it easily, his pinching fingers testing the paper, making it speak.

In return for the money, Hock was given a mat in a dirty hut at the edge of the village. He sat before it in shadows, eating a plate of roasted cassava, some bananas, and peanuts boiled in their shells, glad for the cup of boiled water into which he had swirled some tea leaves. He ate slowly, to prolong the pleasure.

The sunset was a syrup of golden red dissolving the clouds in the pools of its light, lovely over his squalid hut, lending the mud walls a pinkish glow.

18

SITTING CROSS-LEGGED IN the broken wattle-and-daub hut that had no door, Hock remembered an incident from his second year in Malabo. One of his students, a girl sleeping in a doorless hut like this, was attacked by a hyena that had padded in and begun to eat her face. Her struggling did not deter the creature, though an ember from the dying fire, thrown by the girl's mother at the hyena, the sparks setting its fur alight, repelled him. Two days later, at the filthy clinic where her severe wounds had gone septic, her head yellow and swollen tight with infection, the girl died.

From that day, Hock could not sleep in Malabo without barricading his door. For decades in Medford he'd hardly thought of that event, but this night in the village of children he sat in the doorway of the hut, heavy with fatigue and a sense of grievance, feeling wronged, not by the imposters in Malabo but by his divorce, thinking angrily of Deena's demanding the house, his daughter's abusing him and then wanting her cut of her inheritance in advance, believing that he would marry again and have more children—and here he was, indignant, sitting on the dirt floor of a filthy hut alone in this underworld, on an obscure reach of the Lower River.

Only as dawn was breaking, brightening the wide blades of elephant grass and the delicate tassels on the banks of reeds in the marsh at the edge of the river, and with the night animals dispersed—the feathered girlish shrieks of the birds seeming to drive them off—did he slump to the ragged mat at the back of the hut and sleep until the midmorning sun scorched his face.

The thought of the tangle of children and the insolence of the cruel sharp-faced boy roused him. His bag served as his pillow. The sight of the leather and canvas bag, his companion since leaving Medford, moved him—it was bruised and worn, faded from Malabo, stained from the puddle of bilge and fish guts in the big dugout, wet from yesterday's canoe, crusted with mud. It had the humble and mute look of loyalty; just a bag but also a talisman. It reflected the beating that he had taken. He snatched it up and felt stronger as he walked away from the hut, heading across the clearing and down the sloping path to the tall reeds. He knew the landing was there, and the Lower River that flowed south into the Zambezi. He'd find a boat, and a way out.

The children had awakened, the fires were smoking and sending up smuts, and a blue haze of wood smoke curled in the windless air of the village. What had seemed at first to him an almost charming place of industrious and innocent children now was a vision of pure menace—stupid unreasonable children, and too many of them, hungry, irrational, impulsive, and somehow resentful, seeing him as an enemy. And the smoke stinging his eyes in the unbreathable air made it all worse.

He expected one or two of them to interfere with him on his way to the riverbank. But as on the day before, they turned their backs on him. Why did it seem a greater hostility that they ignored him rather than faced him with insults? He was shamed by his memory of bantering with them like the silliest safari tourist, believing he could deal with children. His years of teaching had shown him that, misleadingly so. No, he was the father of an ungrateful and spoiled child—that's who he was, and here were more of them.

Yet in another sense these children were like a separate species altogether, feral and damned. A village of adults might have listened, might have been persuadable, might have understood his predicament, his need to get down the river and go home. But these children had an infantile indifference and probably no thought of him except when he was close by. They had no notion of his plight, perhaps no idea of what home or attachment meant; they were too small, too abused, too rat-like and lost. They had no sympathy, either, and if they seemed to him like an alien species—cold, weird, cruel, hungry, blighted, dim, with dirty feet—then he must have seemed to them like a hairy giant, big and pale, in a sweat-stained shirt, clutching a bag, who'd come ashore to pester them.

A fat stick of wood landed near him, hard, clacking on the stones—someone had thrown it. He whirled around and saw a small boy laughing, and just in time to bat another stick away. What to do? It was foolish to lob a stick at one of these tormenting children, and when he reprimanded the laughing boy, saying, "Stop that!" the other children hooted at him. They were small and unafraid and looked compact and indestructible.

So he walked on, and glancing back he saw a boy behind him, mimicking the way he walked, feet apart, arms swinging—and there was more laughter.

The children were fearless. He walked faster, trying to be obvious in ignoring them, but when he got to the riverbank he saw that the canoe was gone. The river was dark green and depthless in the morning light. The buoyant clumps of ragged hyacinth—flowers and roots—in the wrinkles of current scarfing through the reeds showed the speed of the river's flow. Swimming was out of the question. There were hippos, crocs, snakes, and just as dangerous, the burrowing bilharzia snails. The Lower River was as the people on its banks said—a snake, a poisonous one.

A kingfisher came to rest on a reed, and there it swayed. When it flew off, Hock felt a pang at the ease of its departure. He hoped to see a passing dugout, the sort of boat that had brought him here. But he knew that because the border between Malawi and Mozambique was so close, this was essentially a no man's land, avoided by most travelers and many fishermen.

Unshaven and dirty, his shirt wet against his body, his trousers heavy with dampness, the cuffs muddy, he sat on his bag and batted at the mosquitoes around his head. Hunger, and the lumps of undercooked food he'd eaten the night before, made his mouth foul, his teeth slimy, and the morning sun slanting in his eyes made his head ache.

The river surged past him, gulping and chuckling in the muddy hollows where it undercut the bank, and he was teased by its speed, seeing the torn vines spinning downstream. Meditating this way, he began to find his old composure, the strength he often felt in solitude. Yet he had to fight the other thoughts—that he'd been a fool to return to Malabo, that he should have raised an alarm there, that he'd abandoned Zizi with the lie "I'm coming back," that it had been a mistake to attempt an escape downriver instead of to the boma at Nsanje.

Breathing deeply, making his intake of breath a hopeful prayer, he calmed himself, vowing, I will find a way out and never come back. But at some point in this meditation he must have let out a sigh or a sob, a sound revealing of weakness, because no sooner had he released it than another sound rose as a mocking echo, and another, and a flutter of low laughter and tongue clicks and whispers.

He turned and saw twenty gleaming faces, boys in front, girls behind them, some holding infants, all of them blocking the path. They laughed again, and now his heart beat faster, making him hotter.

He stood, tottering, and began to move—he was at the edge of the bank—and they stood too, advancing on him, crowding him so that he had to step back. And when he slipped on the mud and struggled to maintain his balance, they advanced again, a low wall of chattering children in dirty shirts, pressing him back to the muddy lip of the embankment.

The river flowed just below him, swirling against the two poles that served as a mooring, curls of green current encircling the uprights. While he watched, a large wide-winged dragonfly shot back and forth between the children and him, finally coming to rest at the top of one of the poles, where it became still and insubstantial. Then it flew off, and the sight of this insect floating freely through air, landing, then flitting away, gave Hock another pang and filled him with despair.

Seeing that he had edged back, the children pushed forward as in a game, and now, standing at the bank, Hock's heels were just above the water.

He recognized some of the children—the girls he'd seen the day before tending the cooking fires; the small skeletal boy who'd mimicked his walk; the several girls carrying infants, drooling dirty-faced infants covered in brown flies; the small boys who'd been kicking the rag ball; the girl whom he encountered grilling the slices of cassava. He had spoken to some of them. None had been friendly, but neither had they been openly hostile. Where he was concerned, they had, it seemed, engaged in careless play. But now in a mass they were implacable, blocking the path, forcing him to inch backward, blank-faced in his helpless indecision. He hated them all, even the infants.

He wished for a snake, any snake, big or small. Twig snakes and adders sometimes lurked at riverbanks, to pounce on mice or frogs. He would snatch up the snake and brandish it as a weapon. The children, who were not afraid of him, were terrified of snakes, and they'd run.

They saw him searching the tufts at the embankment edge, and what he saw disgusted him: twists of their excrement and the crudded leaves, for this was also their latrine; they squatted here, too lazy to dig a pit near the village. And they were so small their bare bottoms did not extend far enough over the edge of the bank, so they fouled the edge where he was standing.

"Enough," he said, his voice an involuntary shriek, and raised his hand. "Go back."

He looked for pity in their hesitation, but soon they were laughing, and repeating, "Enough! Go back!"—*Nuff! Go beck!*—and thrusting their dirty hands at him, moving toward him, so near that he clung to the mooring posts while holding on to his bag.

More children had gathered behind the ones in front, the first to arrive, and now there were thirty or forty in torn and dirty T-shirts—*Las Vegas, Red Raiders, Willow Bend Fun Run, Rockland Lobster Festival*. They were enjoying his fear, the sight of him growing frantic. They knew the river was deadly, filled with crocs and snakes and hippos, and if he fell, the steep side of the river would trap him.

"Please," he said in their language.

Seeing his helplessness, his humiliation, they laughed, they screeched, they repeated the word, mimicking his nasal voice.

He thought of lashing out, perhaps hurting one or two of them with a slap or a punch, but there were far too many of them, and if he injured anyone, he'd be in worse trouble. So far, all he had done

175

was show up and be meek, but that had turned him into their victim.

"I came to help you," he said. "I want to give you something—anything. What do you want? I'm from America. I can get food, I can find money for you. A boat—I can get you a big boat. Or a well for water. I can bring a machine and drill a well for you. Lights, books, medicine, what do you want?"

He had spoken slowly, ungrammatically, searching for the right words in their language. They recognized "food," and "money," and "boat," and "medicine," as he appealed to them in his begging voice. And for some seconds he believed he had them.

The small boy who had mimicked him stood up and shrieked, "We want you to die!"

"Yes, yes!" the chant went up. "*Eenday! Eenday!*"

A clod of mud flew past him, and another hit his shoulder. He hoped it was only mud, though it stank like a turd and could easily have been one.

They were all calling out now—"Die!" and "Yes!"—and delighting in the sight of the big unsteady *mzungu*, red-faced in dirty clothes, holding the tall mooring posts, gripping his bag, desperate before them. How many *mzungus* had they seen? Not many, perhaps none. And now, in a jeering crowd, they had no more fear than a dog pack and were prepared to push him over the edge and into the river.

I'll jump, Hock thought, not in those words but seeing the act, his frantic leap; I'll take my chances in the river.

He turned his back to position his feet, so he could brace and launch himself into the water. The current would take him quickly, and if he was lucky, he could climb the embankment farther downstream and hide from the children.

Still he heard the shrieks and catcalls behind him, but there was another sort of shouting too, and when he glanced back he saw that the crowd of children was thinning out, and in the middle, on the path, the boys in sunglasses were kicking at them, scattering them, making room for Hock to move to a safer part of the embankment, away from the crumbling edge.

For a panicky moment he feared they'd rush him, topple him into the river. It would have been so easy, but the tallest of the three, the sharp-faced boy in the *Dynamo Dresden* baseball cap, who had sold him his dinner the night before, stuck his hand out—in an unfriendly way, a perfunctory grip—yanking him forward onto the path.

"Thank you," Hock said with a sob, half grateful, half resentful that he was thanking them. In his heart he hated them, but he was so afraid his hatred would show, he approached them with exaggerated mildness.

The boy had started down the path, Hock following.

"Why did they want to hurt me?"

"They are children. They don't care about you."

"But I can help them."

"How can you help them?"

"Food," Hock said. "Money."

"They are having food. And there is nothing to buy."

"Water," Hock said. "A well."

"We have the river."

"What does the government give you?"

"There is no government here," the boy said, and there was a malicious smile in his voice when he added, "We are the government."

Now they were back at the clearing, and the children were watching Hock walking just behind the big boy, the two other boys walking casually to the side. Hock was looking for protection, hoping that the children would keep away. He was terrified of them, for their utter recklessness, and he rationalized his fear as no different from a fear of insects or vermin or the fatal bite of the smallest viper, a night adder.

"I could arrange for a school here."

"They hate school."

"They could learn English, like you."

The boy turned his sharp-featured face on Hock and made a cruel mouth. "I don't want them to learn English like me. I don't want them to learn anything."

The two other boys sniggered, hearing this.

"Where are their parents? Where are their elders?"

"Dead. All dead."

There were orphans' huts in Malabo. And Hock had heard of

children's villages, the result of the spread of AIDS in the country. He had imagined them structured and supported by the government, not wild and improvisational like this, reverted to semi-savagery, living hand to mouth, foraging, and yet defiant as some animal packs were defiant, and self-sufficient like those same packs.

"Some of these children are having the eddsi disease as well. If they bite you, you will die."

This the boy said slowly, becoming amused, laughing as he finished the sentence, though Hock thought only of the fatal bite of the night adder.

They left him alone the rest of the day, and the whole of the following day. He heard the children laughing—screeching. He sat in the space they had given him, hoping that they were ignoring him and not plotting against him. He had no way of telling. At intervals the children crept near to watch him. Hock took some consolation at the sight of fire finches in the branches near his hut and the metallic call of the tinkerbird, which he heard but could not see. As for the children, they were the youngest, the dirtiest, and they simply stared at him with hungry faces.

In retrospect, he was afraid of the children, and when he saw two of the big boys approach him in the dusk he felt a fluttering of fright in his heart like a trapped bird.

"Your friends are coming, this boy says."

"What do you mean?" He backed away. He didn't want the boy near him.

"This boy"—a lean, exhausted-looking boy in ragged shorts lurked behind him—"he says they are coming."

"I don't know what you mean. Who is coming?"

"Your people."

The boy seemed at once milder, kinder, much less of a threat. He was holding bananas, a cluster of four. These he gave to Hock.

"My people?" Hock took a breath but could not calm himself. "When?"

"Just wait," the boy said, and pointed casually at the last of the sunset—shreds of purple, layers of darkening velvet lit by glints of gold, sinking under the darkness, making Hock sadder. "We will see them."

On the third day, the boy wearing the *Dynamo Dresden* cap and sunglasses kicked through the small gathering of watching children and said, "You, *mzungu*."

"Don't call me *mzungu*."

"I will call you Old Man."

Hock glared at him, then gestured to the children. "What do they want?"

"They want you to go."

Hock took a stride to come abreast of him and said in a heated whisper, "I want to go. Let me go. You said you don't want me here."

But the boy wouldn't look at him, or if he was looking at him Hock couldn't tell, because the sunglasses did not reveal his eyes. All he saw was the sour disapproving mouth.

"That was the other day. That was previously." He spoke the syllables separately like a whole sentence.

"I'd like to know where you learned English," Hock asked again.

"From your people."

"I don't have any people."

"Yes, yourself you are having. They are coming. That is why we want you to stay."

"They're coming here?"

"We will see."

"When are they coming?"

"We will see."

Hock had often been frustrated by Sena-speaking people, with all their euphemisms and evasions, but much worse was his trying to make sense of conversing with someone like this Sena boy, for the fact that the boy spoke English reasonably well was a barrier to any understanding and only maddened him more. There was a point where a reasonable command of English made someone like this punk in sunglasses incomprehensible.

"I'm hungry," Hock said. "I'll need food."

The boy said nothing, only raised his face to the sky, seeming to listen, and in this posture, looking up, distracted, appeared disapproving of Hock, as though he were an annoyance, an inconvenient straggler, an adult alien in a village of children, on the Lower

River, in the marshes that were neither Malawi nor Mozambique, without a road or a well or, as far as Hock could tell, any garden.

Keeping his hand on the flap of his bag, Hock said, "But I can't give you any more money."

"I don't want your money."

"I must have some food," Hock said.

What was missing in this boy was any sympathy, none in his two companions, none in the children, in the entire village. Simple pity was something he had taken for granted in Malabo: the recognition that he was alone, stranded, far from home, in need of help. These children were feral and had no use for him, and that was worse than being exploited in Malabo. They were mind-blind and reckless.

In a low pitiless voice, without turning, the boy said to him, "Give your knife."

"I don't have a knife."

"The knife from last night."

Before his meal, in a feeble attempt to tidy himself, he'd sat cross-legged and clipped his fingernails, then carved the dirt from beneath what remained. He had no idea that anyone had seen him engaged in this sad little ritual of grooming with a chrome fingernail clipper.

Careful to remove it from his bag without showing any of the contents, he slid out the clipper and handed it over.

"The food," Hock said.

"They will bring."

Later, at the hut he had been assigned, the girl who brought him the tin plate of roasted cassava and the few bananas was one he recognized as being part of the jeering mob at the riverbank. That she was subdued, almost deferential, kneeling as she served the dish, made her seem more defiant and untrustworthy.

"Chai," Hock said.

She sniffed to show she understood, rocked to her feet, and was away for a few minutes, returning with an enamel mug of hot water into which some tea leaves had been scattered. That it was hot satisfied Hock, who feared the foul water of the Lower River.

After he finished his meal he sat in the open doorway of the hut, and when darkness fell he listened to the sounds of the children playing discontentedly, or mildly quarreling, screeching now and then, the shouts of boys, the protests of girls. And later, in the silence of the night, afraid to sleep in the doorless hut, he sat, grieving for himself. He remembered slights that had been inflicted on him—not here or in Malabo, but in his marriage, in Medford, in his business, as he had the previous night.

Instead of brooding about Malabo, his sudden escape, the theft of his radio by Simon, or about the treachery of the boy paddlers who had delivered him here to the village of teasing children and hostile bug-eyed boys, and the heat, the dirt, his hunger and thirst—instead of this, he thought only of the injustices he had suffered in his life.

The trickery of his wife, who had foisted that expensive phone on him and used it to pry into his privacies. And then, after more than thirty years, she had demanded the family house, his father's house in the Lawrence Estates, forcing him into a condo in the old high school. And her repeated messages on his answering machine: "You shit." Chicky demanding that he hand over her inheritance: "I want my cut now." When he gave her the check he said, "I doubt that I'll be seeing much of you from now on."

As those bad memories coursed through his mind, keeping him awake, grinding his teeth, slighter ones intruded—hurts, insults, snubs. "Four eyes," "Fairy," "You suck," at school. The guidance counselor saying, "Maybe your father will give you a job, because if not, you're not going anywhere." A woman in college English tittering because he'd mispronounced the word "posthumous." One of his customers saying, "You're rounder now," meaning that he'd put on weight—and the man who said it was fat. The new salesman who'd gotten a salary advance ("My rent's due") saying, "You can take it out of my first paycheck," but he never showed up to work again. Not villains, but deadbeats, mockers, smirkers. "You're still working for a living?" Teachers in grade school who'd singled him out—"See me after school"—and all the women who'd rejected him, batting his hands away. The lies he'd been told now came back to him, little twisted evasions that remained unresolved and niggling at him. Like his father, he'd been a trusting soul. He believed "I'll definitely come tomorrow" and "I'll fix it" and "That's the best price I can offer you." The pretty clerk who blocked the employee toilet with her sanitary pad, then denied it. The shoddy batch of socks from China, the repeated telephone message on the answering machine of the men who owed him money, or a delivery, until he called and got "This number has been disconnected and is no longer in use."

And there was his incriminating phone, the one he'd thrown into the Mystic River because it was full of compromising emails. The thought of those emails shamed him, those whispers, those confidences, flirting and foolish. He had betrayed himself with people he'd trusted with his inner thoughts, people to whom he had confided his love of Africa. "The best years of my life," he'd said, and they'd responded, "Cannibals and communists" or "Human life means nothing there," in an echo of doom-doom-doom, and he'd lectured them on their peculiar folkways and pieties. "I was in Malabo, on the Lower River . . ."

All of this, and more, all night.

19

HE WAS CLINGING to a steep black mountainside that resembled Morrumbala. Gripping the seams of crumbling rock with his fingertips, his arms extended in an attitude of crucifixion, he had hoisted himself up the cliff face to a narrow ledge, no more than a toehold, hugging a plastic bag that bulged with a yellowish drinkable liquid, and the fat-bellied bag swelled so tight it might burst at any second. He wore boots and a harness. He pushed open a steel door in the granite wall but saw that the space was not wide enough for him and the bag to fit through. Someone was with him, a hovering figure who looked like Roy Junkins, but he was dressed in a three-piece suit and seemed doubtful, canted sideways in an ironic posture on the ledge.

"Won't work," Hock said to the skeptical man standing beside him.

"The bud." That word woke him. The sun burned against his aching eyes, the light that had colored his desperate dream.

"The bud."

No sooner had he heard the word than he saw on the hot branch behind the boy's big shadowy head the budded protrusions, some like dark spear points and some plump swollen ones, seeming on the verge of bursting.

"What are you saying?"

"*Ndege.*"

"Bird," Hock said.

"Bard," the boy said.

"What about it?"

"Is coming."

In Hock's sleepy blur of confusion the words made no sense to him. He rolled over and the mat crunched with a chewing sound. He had been more content in his dark mountainside dream than here in the corrosive sunlight and damp earth of this hut in the village of children. He yearned to sleep again, to return to his dream.

"*Mzungu,*" the boy said.

"Don't call me *mzungu!*" His own shriek startled him and made him angrier. In his rage he was also objecting to the hut, which stank of mice and sour fermented straw and spilled beer suds.

The boy stepped back, shocked by Hock's loud shout of protest. He was not the biggest boy, but one of the three leaders, who usually sulked behind his sunglasses.

"*Ndiri ndi njala!*" Hock shouted, louder than the first time, encouraged by the boy's apparent fear. Hock pounded his stomach and made an animal noise of complaint.

"And me myself I am hungry," the boy said in a low voice.

"Bring me food," Hock said.

"The *ndege* will bring food."

Hock smiled at the word. He said, "*Mbalame,*" because that was the proper Sena word for bird, and *ndege* was—what?—Swahili?

"Tea—hot water," Hock said, still angry at having been woken from his dream. Dreams were a refuge, and though you might be afraid, you never died or felt pain. But this village was a problem, with no path and no way out. "Don't tell me you have no water," Hock said to the hesitating boy. "You drink the river!"

Without saying more, the boy walked away, and after ten minutes or so a small girl brought a tin cup of hot water with a residue of broken tea leaves at the bottom.

As Hock drank he could see at the center of the clearing the biggest boy hectoring a group of children, more children than Hock had seen before, gathered together—more than had hounded him at the riverbank. And some stragglers were still joining this group that sprawled like a church congregation. It seemed a suggestion of order in a place that Hock associated with disorder and incompleteness: idle vindictive children living like bush mutts in the ruins of an adult village, where none of the basket granaries contained maize cobs and the gardens were merely wild untended clumps of cassava. The children stood in their dirty T-shirts and ragged shorts, some of them older girls wearing *chitenje* wraps, all of them listening impassively to the vehement speech.

In his earlier years on the Lower River, such a large gathering of children would have filled him with hope—for their attentiveness, their solemnity, and what he knew to be their strength; even hungry and tired, they worked and could be joyous. Now he saw the children as dangerous, defiant, without sympathy or sentiment or any memory. The previous day they had been on the point of pushing him into the river with the force of their small skinny bodies, laughing at his plight. They would have screamed in delight to see him thrashing in the green water.

He was still bitter but would not allow himself to hate them anymore, and only thought, Let them squirm, and wished to be away, anywhere but here.

The tall sharp-faced boy went on speaking to them in a fierce formal manner, gesturing with his fist. Hock wondered whether he was the subject of the speech—he listened for the word *mzungu* but did not hear it. The word *ndege* was repeated: bird, but what bird? He could only think that it was something to eat.

A girl in a torn T-shirt walked past Hock's hut carrying a basket of bananas. Hock snapped his fingers and, surprised, the girl stopped and knelt in an obedient genuflection and handed him two bananas. Alone, she seemed frightened, though he recognized her—her T-shirt, rather, *Minnesota Vikings*—from the previous day, when she had been one of the jeering pack of children at the riverbank.

To make the moment last, Hock peeled one banana slowly with his fingertips and nibbled it, eyeing the distant crowd of children from the shade of his hut. He was impressed by the silence and concentration of the children, and fearful, too, that such a large number could be controlled by the single older boy.

And in the running commentary in his head, his narrative of the misery he'd put himself into, he thought how the worst of it was not the dirt or the heat or the thirst—though they wore him down; and not the insects or the bad-tempered children; but the uncertainty, not knowing at the beginning of each day how that day would end.

This thought was cut off by movement at the periphery of his vision, a sliding line at ground level that bunched and swelled and grew longer, through the crackling dead leaves, a bluey-green snake, a spotted bush snake from the look of it.

In the snake he saw a friend, a savior, a weapon, a creature that had come to protect him; something he could keep, something he could eat. And he smiled at the snake. He was not alone anymore.

Yanking its tail, he shook it, snapped it hard enough to slacken its coil—though he could have whipped its head off with a violent jerk. And, allowing it to strike, he caught it behind its head as it leaped full length. Holding his arm up, he let the snake coil its body around his forearm. It was a juvenile bush snake, a meter long at most, the nub of its hard tail tickling his biceps.

Finished with his harangue, the boy—still wearing his black *Dynamo* baseball cap and sunglasses—started toward Hock's hut. Some children followed close behind him, walking with unusual solemnity. Seeing them approach, Hock held his snake-enclosed arm behind his back.

"We are going," the boy said.

"Where?"

"Never mind," the boy said, and as he spoke, the children, sensing a confrontation, looked eagerly for Hock's reaction.

Hock said, "Because my friend wants to know," and he repeated it in a nastier tone in Sena, so that the children could hear.

Even in his sunglasses the boy showed that he was baffled, chewing his lips, flexing his fingers.

"What friend are you talking?"

When Hock swung his arm into view from behind his back, and lifted it, thickened with the snake, holding the snake's head with his fingers so its pinkish-green tongue darted from between its fangs, the boy drew back and some of the children screamed—screams that silenced the rest of them. And then the snake's pale throat swelled, because it was alarmed.

Hock held the snake like a ferocious glove, a gauntlet, that was both armor and a weapon. Though the children were terrified into silence, their cries had attracted the attention of the others who had gathered to hear the speech. Soon Hock faced forty or more children, and the bigger boys. But all of them kept their distance.

"Now we go," the bigger boy said, controlling himself, backing up slightly.

"Tell me where," Hock said, and held out the snake's head. "Tell him. Tell my friend. Tell the *njoka.*"

"The football pitch."

"Call me *bambo.*"

"Father," the boy said, faltering with his tongue that was thickened from fear. He stepped aside, making room for Hock.

None of them—neither the children nor the three leaders— came near him then. And he, the helpless victim, despising himself for being dirty, having put himself in this position, in an underworld of cruelty, was strengthened by clutching the snake's head, loving its frothy jaws and its curved fangs and its flicking tongue. When he swung it around and reached with his free hand to pick up his bag, the children screamed again and fell against each other.

They skipped past him, the jostling mob of them, and filtered through the thin bush of dusty yellowing acacia trees, the claws of their overhanging sticks and stems, all of the children barefoot. Ahead, the three leaders called out, "*Msanga!*"—Hurry!—so odd a command here in the stifling bush, under a hot sun. There was no clear path, but the thorn bushes and stunted mopane trees were sparse enough to allow them to pass through, creating a network of separate paths. And where the bush was dense the crowd of children narrowed into a single file, moving under the shallow canopy of brittle leaves, beating down a path in the whitened dust.

The snake contracted in coils around Hock's arm, keeping its throat inflated, because of the confusion. Hock kept to the rear, where some children muttered anxiously, frightened by the sight of Hock holding the snake.

The land was so flat and obscured by the low bush it was impossible for Hock to see ahead. Because he was so much bigger than these children, who slipped under the stinging barbs on the skinny branches, he was forced to duck and sway and sidle along.

His size, he now saw—his being an adult—was no help but only a great handicap among the children, who were numerous and ruthless, indifferent to his misery, and quick to take advantage of him.

His only asset was the snake, though his arm was heavy and hot with its weight, and slimy from its closely clinging body. His bag, swinging in his free hand, bumped against his leg. Yet he had no choice but to follow, and he suspected that they were nearing their goal, because he heard more shouts from up ahead.

Some children near him sang softly as they padded forward, and he thought of Zizi, how she sang in her throat when she was anxious. He grew sad and sentimental, hearing the humming, seeing the children's dusty legs and torn shorts, and he reminded himself that these same children had wanted him drowned and dead.

Just before noon, after almost two hours of walking, they came to a grove of trees that tickled and scratched his head, and he stepped past them into the margin of an open field, where the children had begun to gather.

He saw that another group of children—from where?—had ranged themselves along the far side, in the ribbon of shade cast by protruding branches. These children crouched, they sat, they knelt; none was standing. The whole straight side of this extraordinary empty rectangle of parched grass in the bush, about the size of a football field, was dark with other waiting children.

Approaching the boy in the black baseball cap, Hock was surprised when the boy touched his sunglasses nervously and stepped away. Hock smiled, holding the snake's head, and lifted his arm with the coils that had tightened into bulgy armlets.

"Where are we?"

The boy crept backward as he spoke. "We are being in the bush." It seemed in his fear that the boy's assured command of English was diminished, as he spoke haltingly, with a stronger accent. "At the football pitch."

"What do you do here?"

"Sometimes we are challenging them." He nodded at the children seated and kneeling at the far side of the field. "We play football. We dance. We fight."

"Whose field is this?"

The boy hesitated until Hock raised the snake at him, and then the boy shrugged and said, "It depends."

"On what?"

"On who wins."

"So it's a battlefield," Hock said. "And you fight with fists?"

"With hands. With sticks of wood. With weapons." He said *steeks,* he said *wee-pons.*

Hock said, "I really want to know where you learned English." The boy was still stepping back, seemingly reluctant to answer. Hock said, "I used to teach English."

"It is not hard to know English," the boy said, almost with contempt.

"What's hard, then?"

"To have food is hard. To have medicine. To have a mobile phone. To have good weapons."

Saying this, he stared at the snake that Hock held before him, leveled at the boy's face: the snake's lipless mouth and dead unblinking eyes and flicking tongue.

"You will die if he bites you," the boy said.

"Or you," Hock said. He saw more children entering the field from one of the shorter sides. "Who are they?"

"From the big marsh," the boy said.

And they too hugged the shade at the edge, for the sun was directly overhead and the flat dusty field of dry grass was so hot that the watery illusion of shimmering heat rose from the brownish bare patches at its center.

"What do we do now?"

"Just wait," the boy said, almost meekly, backing up, and then he turned and walked quickly away.

Hock felt he had lost all contact with his other life, or any other place, and he was reminded of his feeling that he now existed in another age, on another planet, as a despised fugitive, and not on the surface of that planet but on a river in an eerily lit underworld.

And wait for what? Some sort of spectacle? A game, maybe, an event, because all the children had arrayed themselves like spectators—solemn, expectant, facing the open field. The field had no road leading into it, but merely lay, a great trampled expanse of sun-heated dust and tussocks of grass, a deliberately cleared acre that, in its symmetry and blight, was the work of human hands. He hoped they hadn't come for a battle, yet their look of weariness and hunger made them seem desperate and unpredictable.

Dizzy with hunger himself, Hock sat, easing his grip on the snake. Holding it gave him confidence; he could face the children without flinching; he could ask questions. Yet he feared the recklessness of children, and he knew in spite of the snake that he would be overwhelmed by their numbers.

The boy he had spoken to was now standing in front of the seated children from the village, his back to the field. He seemed to be leading the children in prayer, or at least eliciting responses, the big boy reciting a line, the children repeating it. A prayer, a promise, a war chant, a threat, a lament—it could have been anything.

The children at the far side of the field simply watched, and the ones who had just arrived were settling into postures of waiting. Dressed the same, in old American T-shirts and ragged shorts and trousers—facing the empty field—all the children looked like members of a cargo cult.

Their patience was like indifference, like a form of despair, not anticipation of an event but hopelessness. When the children on Hock's side of the field were finished chanting they lapsed into silence, blinking at the flies that were settling around their eyes. None of them sat near Hock. Because of the snake, they kept away from him.

Then the snake's body contracted on his arm, its throat swelling again, and this made Hock more watchful, as though by its flicking tongue it had smelled a rising emotion in the children. Certainly the children were more tense, seeming to contract themselves, resolving themselves into more compact postures of listening. The snake too seemed hyperalert, its muscles pulsing and pinching against Hock's hot arm.

Nothing was in the sky, and yet a far-off sound, a *yak-yak-yak*, became audible and grew louder, until, like a giant insect, a helicopter burst from the dusty haze and hovered over the field, high up.

So this was the bird. The helicopter was blue and white, with a logo, a shield in gold on its side, and under it the words *L'Agence Anonyme*. And it was growing larger. What had seemed a small bulbous chopper, flying in and circling, grew as it descended, became elongated, and the updraft of its whirling rotor blades sucked a dense column of dust from the ground that became a wide brown cloud.

Even before it landed, while it was settling lower, the double doors on its side slid open, revealing its interior. Then two things happened, surprising things. First, music began to play—rock music, very loud, a pounding rhythm, *yada-boom, yada-boom, yada-boom*. And then, while it played, growing even louder, a group of people appeared at the opening. The two in front, flanked by Africans, were a white man in a cowboy hat and a woman in high boots—a blonde, chalky-faced, in a black skintight suit. Both of them were gesturing to the children, looking jubilant.

Yada-boom, yada-boom—where were the loudspeakers?

The children, most of them, kept their places at the edge of the field, though a handful of excited, much younger ones ran into the thickening dust cloud, staggering, seeming to choke, many of them retreating as the helicopter came to rest, its long skids sinking into the rough grass and loose dirt of the field. The two white people standing in the cabin hatchway waved, still jubilant. Just behind them was an imposing-looking African man in a spotless safari suit, taller than the white man and woman; from his assertive gestures he seemed to be issuing orders.

Before the children sitting and kneeling at the margin of the field stood up, preparing to run to the helicopter, the boy in the black *Dynamo* cap appeared next to Hock and said, "Tell the Agency to help us." He held his body away, his arms behind his back, his head to the side, as though he expected the snake to uncoil itself and strike him.

Hock said, "Help me get near—keep the children away," and he snatched up his bag and headed toward the helicopter, which had become a blur in the rising dust cloud.

Hock saw his chance to save himself, to get close enough to appeal for help. He was sure he was visible from the helicopter—how hard was it to pick out a tall white man in a bush shirt and tattered trousers, a bag in one hand, a fat snake wrapped around his right arm, which he held forward like a weapon?

The boy in the baseball cap pushed ahead of him, elbowing his way through the mass of children. Now that the rotor blades had stopped and the engine was silenced, only the music played—thumping joyous music—and the children who had been hanging back rushed toward the chopper, into the risen dust, making more dust, crowding Hock and nearly knocking him down.

"Over here!" he called to the man and woman in the open doorway. How clean they looked, how outlandish in their dress, the man in the cowboy hat and boots, the blond woman in her skintight suit. "Help me!"

They began tossing boxes and bags to the children who were nearest to them. At first they handed them over, but within seconds the children were fighting over them, and the man in the cowboy hat became frantic, flinging the bags, kicking the boxes out of the helicopter door, as though to distract the frenzied children.

The children, maddened by the sight of the bags, tore at each other.

"Please—help me," Hock cried out, waving his bag. He relaxed his other arm, and the children near him, reaching for the bags, jostled his arm, bumping the snake. Feeling its coils loosen—the snake was blinded by the dust—Hock let go of its head and allowed it to drop into the dust. The snake's whipping back and forth on the ground panicked a small knot of children, who kicked at it and stamped on it, crushing its head.

Even pushing as hard as he could, Hock made little progress against the small bodies so tightly packed ahead of him. Some children nearer the helicopter had begun to climb aboard, bracing themselves on the skids and clinging to the struts, attempting to crawl through the legs of the man and woman at the door.

Hock was shouting but could not hear his voice over the loud *yada-boom, yada-boom.* Tripped by the small battering bodies, he fell to his knees among the struggling children with dust on their sweat-smeared faces. Now kneeling, he was the height of a child himself.

He could see the man and woman clearly: the man's expensive sunglasses and clean cowboy hat, the woman's red lips, gleaming makeup, and unusually white teeth. Another man stood beside them with a video camera, shooting them, shooting out the door.

Now the man in the cowboy hat was kicking at the children, fending them off with bags of food, and the woman was trying to keep her balance. She was open-mouthed, perhaps shrieking in fear, but all Hock could hear was the *yada-boom*. She looked clownish, costumed, like the man, dressed as though for a party or a concert, in great contrast to the mass of small children in dirty T-shirts, clawing at one another.

All this time the music played, energetic pumping rhythms that drowned out the children's shouts and the woman's shriek and the voices of the men at the helicopter door who seemed to be yelling at each other. No voices were audible, but the open mouths and wild eyes made it a scene of pure panic in the growing dust cloud.

Still trying to make himself heard, Hock got to his feet and fought on, stepping over the children, pushing others aside. His effort had the absurd indignity of a dream, all irrational and unreal, and what made it more dream-like was his slowness, his pathetic helplessness, and that he was ignored, humiliated, unable to call attention to himself.

The man in the cowboy hat met Hock's eyes and lifted his sunglasses to verify with his own surprised gaze the sight of this frantic white man. He seemed to lean over, as though what he was seeing was not quite believable. He said something to the man behind him. But he had a pale debauched face, and there was no sympathy in the set of his jaw, and when he let his sunglasses slip down over his eyes and turned to throw more bags from the helicopter, at the same time kicking out at the climbing children, Hock flung himself forward.

"Help!" Hock screamed. He felt the strain in his throat without hearing the word, because now the music was overwhelmed by the roar of the engine, the chatter of the rotor blades as they began to turn. Turning faster, they stirred more dust, and the dust engulfed the children and the field while Hock hugged his bag to his chest. Two children dropped from the skids where they had been hanging. *Yak-yak-yak-yak-yak*, the helicopter rose into the sun, which cast an eerie glow through the dust; it was like a beetle swallowed by a storm cloud.

The rotor's yakking diminished, the music grew softer, and the yelps of the children grew louder as they fought over the bags and boxes strewn on the ground. Seeing that they were occupied in this free-for-all, Hock turned to go, intending to run away from the choking dust, to the margin of the field, to take his chances in the bush.

But just as he turned, he saw, emerging from the trees, fifteen or twenty motorcycles rushing toward the center of the field like a pack of one-eyed animals. Side by side, the motorcycles converged as they came closer, heading into the mass of children.

Half an hour before, Hock had been sitting cross-legged in the shade of the tall grass and shrubs at the edge of the field, the snake coiled on his arm, feeling powerful. Then the confusion—the helicopter, the loud music, the strangers at the door, the dumped boxes and bags of food, the crazed children, his own desperation. The swelling uprush of dust had slowed him, and the eruption of children quarreling over the bags and boxes, tearing them to pieces, had shocked him. The helicopter taking off had made more dust, but no sooner had its noisy rotors disappeared than the blatting of the motorcycles began.

He was in danger of being trapped by the motorcycles. Some of them were knocking children down as the riders snatched at the bags, stacking them on their handlebars, shoving the children out of the way, chasing children who were tottering with bags in their arms. He dodged a skidding bike and headed toward the emptier part of the field, and on the way managed to pick up a bag, a bulging cloth sack of what he imagined to be rice or flour or millet.

He could not run. After sprinting a few steps, he stopped, gasped for breath, then walked, his face grimy from the sweat-smeared dirt, still breathing hard in the dust cloud that hung over the field.

He half turned to see how far he had come when the boys, flailing their arms, rushed at him, shouting. Resisting, Hock felt old and feeble, unable to repel them, and afraid of the very sight of them, their angry faces, their bared teeth. One of the reaching boys grabbed at Hock's sack of flour, another boy clung to his arm—the arm where the snake had been coiled.

"Wait—wait," Hock said, trying to calm them, because he knew he lacked the strength to fight them off. "What do you want?"

They were two of the bigger boys from the village of children, the boys who had led him here, knowing in advance that a helicopter was going to arrive, carrying—who? celebrities? politicians?—to distribute food. One of them was the boy who had woken him that morning with the words "The bud."

"Wait—you not go."

"Let go of my arm," Hock said, hating the boy's dirty hand on him, his bony grip. "Take the bag of food—you can have it."

"We want you," the bigger boy said.

In spite of the long trek here, and the struggle in the field, and the confused chase, these boys were still wearing sunglasses, and one of them the black baseball hat he'd had on in the village.

"I have to go home now," Hock said, and absurdly, with a screeching insistence and pompous formality, "Don't you understand? I have appointments! I have issues to settle."

"There is no need," the boy said, holding on.

Now the other boy was clutching Hock's shirt, his fingers hooked in the strap of Hock's duffel bag. Although neither boy was as tall or as heavy as Hock, they hung on, dragging him back. The dust, dense and flecked with dirty sunlight, and the loud complaints and whines of the squabbling children in the middle of the field, made it all worse: the children's protests, the braying of the motorcycles. Hock was weakened, unnerved by the shrieking, the heat, and now unable to speak, grit in his mouth, gagging on the dirty air.

Hock was pushed hard as the boy next to him was thumped aside, and in the same moment a motorcycle roared. The other boy let go of his arm and stumbled away.

"Get on, father," the rider called out impatiently, then louder, "Get on!"

Hock swung his leg over and took hold of the man, who sped into the crowd. It was a full minute before he saw it was Manyenga, who seemed to laugh, but no, just teeth and lips set in an expression of fury, screaming for the children to back off.

20

THE MOTORCYCLE PASSED through the low wall of yellowing shrubs and parched trees on a path that was a groove hardly wider than its fat tires, but wide enough. There were no roads here, as the exultant boy had said in the children's village, yet the stony crusted floor of this sun-heated bush was crisscrossed with tire tracks. And Hock was cooler on the speeding bike, the breeze in his face. He held on as Manyenga's elbows slapped at the slender tree limbs and grubby leaves. He was grateful to be delivered from the chaos on the field and glad that he was with someone he knew, feeling like an impulsive runaway who'd been rescued from his foolishness by the intervention of an adult: saved. But as he sat on the motorcycle, which was rocking like a hobbyhorse on the straighter stretches and skidding on the sandy turns, this feeling of deliverance ebbed, and as his strength returned he was filled with apprehension: caught again.

His relief at being rescued turned to misery as he acknowledged that he had not been saved but snared, and by the very man he'd tried to escape from. Still, he hung on, and the awfulness of his situation did not hit him fully until they were well away from the children, who now seemed to him so skinny as to be half alive, desperate, improvisational, and reckless, living by their wits.

Manyenga meanwhile appeared to realize that he had traveled a safe enough distance and was not being followed. He slowed down, and seeing a baobab tree ahead, he stopped the bike under it and both men dismounted. Manyenga's sweat of exertion hit him: he stank like a wet dog.

The bark of the baobab was torn, the white flesh of the wood exposed and splintered.

"Elephants like to eat this tree for its juicy wood. It has water!" Manyenga said, and he laughed. "They can destroy it!"

"There are elephants here?"

"Why not? This is bush, indeed!" Manyenga was friendly, oblique, teasing. Then he said, "What are you doing, playing with those silly children, isn't it?"

"They gave me food," Hock said.

"What food? They have nothing to eat, only what the *ndege* from the Agency brings them."

"And you steal it from them."

"We are hungry too."

"They have cassava and bananas."

"Rubbish food, famine food. Where are their chickens? They have no gardens. Are they making relish or stew? Not at all!"

"I was here only a few days," Hock said, not knowing where this conversation was leading. He didn't want to admit that he'd been trapped by the children.

Manyenga said, "You prefer to live there with those children, isn't it?"

"I was just passing through."

"I must inform you that one German *mzungu* on the river was captured by them and after some few weeks in captivity they sold him for money. They absconded with his money and food. I know these children. They make trouble on the river. That is why . . ."

Instead of saying more he sighed—whinnied—shook a cigarette from a pack, and lit it. He pursed his lips and directed a plume of smoke into the air. He looked around and laughed, as though at the strangeness of his being there, under the tree with Hock. He had Hock's full attention now.

"That is why, my friend, the paddle boys and Simon left you at Megaza frontier station. They knew that if you were with them, the bad children would try to overturn their canoe and catch you."

"How do you know that?"

"The paddlers dropped Simon at Caya on the Zambezi. They came back yesterday. And I was told."

"So you went looking for me."

"Not at all! I was with my friends, following the *ndege*. When it flies, we chase it—for goods! But God sent me to you. I knew you must be with the children, or maybe dead."

"You know everything," Hock said, testing him.

Manyenga squirted smoke through the gaps in his teeth, hissing, and said, "You should thank me, father."

"Thank you," Hock said.

"Because I saved your life, isn't it?"

Hock wondered if this was so, and suspected it might be, but he wanted to deny the gloating Manyenga the satisfaction of it. He said, "They were afraid of me."

Manyenga laughed, wagging his tongue, and then, his laughter faltering and growing harsh, he began to cough and, coughing, fighting for breath, stamped on the ground, raising dust.

In a choked voice he said, "They are afraid of nothing, my friend," and to emphasize this he flicked his hand sharply, whipping his fingers together, making them snap. "That *mzungu* they sold, that German, was tough. But where is he now? Those children are devils. Maybe they took your things, too."

Hock said nothing. Manyenga was studying him, the cigarette in his mouth giving him a look of insolence.

"What things?" Hock said at last.

"Maybe money."

"Let's go," Hock said. "Where's the road?"

Whenever he saw that he could contradict Hock, Manyenga put on a smug expression and became theatrical, hamming the moment, pausing before he delivered his putdown. Hock was not annoyed; it gave him hope when he saw that Manyenga was predictable.

"This is the country of no roads. No vehicles. Nothing. Only" —he indicated the wheel tracks, flourishing his cigarette—"paths for footing only. Or for motorbikes."

"How far is the village—Malabo?"

"Too far." Manyenga tossed the cigarette butt away. He mounted the bike and leaned and kicked the start lever. The engine gagged, gargled in complaint, then began rapping.

"Where are we going?"

Manyenga said, "You will see," and when Hock hesitated, Manyenga's face lost all its teasing mirth and became a mask sweating with impatience. "Do you want me to leave you here?"

Hock allowed himself to be scolded. He sulked as he got on the bike, moving slowly out of pride, like a child who'd been reprimanded. He thought: That's how it is—I've been reduced to that, or less than a child, because even the children in the village were stronger than me. And now Manyenga had taken charge of him and was telling him what to do. He had no choice but to obey. He was lost here, disoriented by the river trip and the spell in the village and the hike to the open field. The appearance of the helicopter had been like a hideous dream of mockery. And now the motorcycle ride and the hostile *You will see.*

He did not know whether this trackless bush was in Malawi or Mozambique, only that if he were abandoned by Manyenga, he'd never find his way out or he'd be caught by the children again. And reflecting on Manyenga's sudden showing up in the field, he had to admit he was glad. The children had frightened him for being hungry and ruthless and fickle and unreasonable—for being children. They resented Hock, but Manyenga needed him, and that need could work to Hock's advantage. The children lived sparely, like animals, and they were especially dangerous because they had nothing to lose.

Hunched over the front of the motorbike like a workman digging a street, the bike itself resembling a jackhammer in the pounding of its front fork, and jumping in the ruts, Manyenga sped through the bush, Hock clinging to his doggy shirt. They came to a dry streambed, a bouldery trench lined with sand and stones, just a rough sluice that showed the disfigurement of rushing water and exposed rocks.

Hock got off and helped guide the bike over the big rocks.

"Is this Malawi or Mozambique?" Hock asked.

"It is having shrines there—sacred groves—and fugitives, and fruit trees. There used to be a mission on the Matundu Hills side, but they ran away. Maybe you can say it is Zambesia. But this is no country at all."

"No man's land."

"No man's land! Ah-hah!" Manyenga roared. "No man's land!"

Hock remembered that he'd always seemed like a witty genius

to his students in Malabo when they heard him utter a cliché for the first time.

After the streambed they entered higher ground, where the mopane trees were fuller of leaves—greener and taller, and their shade gave the impression of coolness. Sausage trees, too, stood with their bulbous fruit suspended. The birds were bigger and more numerous here, keeping to the upper branches of the trees. Hock knew the starling from its purple feathers, and the gray lourie from its cry: *go-away, go-away.* In one thicket of yellow-striped bamboo he saw the hanging nests of weaver birds. The leaf mulch crackled under the wheels of the bike; the earth was denser and kept moist by the shade. No dust cloud followed them now, only the blue fumes of the engine.

A small impala bounded away from them, and soon after, at the base of a tamarind tree, a troop of baboons backed away and fled on all fours like dogs, faces forward, using their knuckles for propulsion. Some of his anxiety left him, and Hock was reassured by this more orderly and fertile green Africa of shadows and animals.

Deeper in the bush a dampness softened the air, the whiff of stagnation that was a suggestion of life. A dark green moss like a scouring pad coated some of the big boulders in the shade, and in places boulders blocked the path. They pushed the bike awhile, Manyenga panting, and Hock wondered if this higher ground was part of the Matundu Hills that Manyenga had mentioned.

"So what—?" Hock began.

"The answer is no," Manyenga said. He laughed, his usual cackle. "What's the question?"

Who taught him that rude reply? What bullying foreigner said that to him, to sour him and show him how to be mean?

In this higher ground of ridges and sheltering trees, with a film of dampness clinging to the dark overhangs of the empty creekbed, Hock felt he was in another country—at least nowhere near the Lower River; far from Malabo, another zone altogether. He could breathe the air without snorting a hum of dust in his nostrils, and none of the trees looked as if they'd been interfered with—no paths either, not even the tracks of motorcycles. It was odd to see a sunny slope of sand without footprints on it, though in one corner he caught a glimpse of a fat furtive monitor lizard. The land was too stony and steep for a garden, too far from the river or any well to support a village. The heat and mud and scrubby bush and accessible water of the Lower River made it habitable, but these slopes of thick trees and toppled rocks and shade kept people away.

Gaining the top of a ridge, Hock felt the breeze on his sweaty face, as though he'd stuck his head above a fence into a wind. He looked across at what must have been the Matundu Hills, a silhouette of rounded peaks in blue haze. Below was a circular valley, a green bowl of foliage. Behind him, Manyenga was pushing the motorcycle slowly, bumping over tree roots and the protruding knuckles at the base of thick-stemmed bushes.

"Do you see it?" Manyenga asked.

"The valley?"

"The compound."

"What compound?

All that Hock saw were the smooth sides of the valley and a profusion of bushy treetops, and the word that came to him, because he was so unused to seeing such a lush unspoiled valley, was "uneaten." He could not see any road in or out, no gardens, no cultivation, nothing dead or burned, only the great bowl of green trees.

"There," Manyenga said, "that side."

A glint of silver metal, a glimpse of geometry, a fence; and then he saw it, an enclosure, perfectly square, though some of it was hidden, two of its corners. At this distance it looked like a cage in the form of a playpen, a high fence with some buildings inside it, painted green, blending with the green of the valley, easily mistaken for a symmetrical hillock. But they were houses, and studying them he saw the people, more easily visible than the houses because the people were white.

"*Mzungu,*" Hock said.

"*Azungu,*" Manyenga gasped, correcting him with the plural. He had lit a cigarette and coughed, and panted from having pushed the motorbike up the slope.

"What are they doing there?"

He sucked in smoke and coughed again and bared his teeth for air. He said, "You can ask them, father."

No road led to the fenced enclosure; the path they used was probably a game trail. Apart from this sturdy camp, no sign of any other human structure was visible—odd in a place that was so fertile-looking, but perhaps not so odd considering how far this valley was from the river and how hard this rocky soil would have been to break with a plow.

"There, that side," Manyenga said, dropping his voice while pushing the bike, guiding it along the narrow track that was damp enough to keep the prints of animals that had used it: the monkey feet—narrow, with long toes—here and there the hooves of dik-diks, an oblong that might have been a hare's paw, and clusters of dark grape-sized scat.

Hock had seen Manyenga only as bossy or smilingly manipulative, the brute or the calculator, not as he was now, cautious, stealthy, shy, almost intimidated as he approached the looming chain-link fence that surrounded the three flat-roofed buildings—prefab bungalows, painted green. A garden of purpley-pink bougainvillea near one bungalow was contained in a circle of whitewashed rocks, giving a suburban touch to this forest compound. Beyond the buildings was an open area marked with a large white-painted X on the bare ground, obviously a helipad.

"The helicopter must have come from here."

"Of course," Manyenga said. "What do you think?"

"You've been here before?"

"I tell you, my friend, I am knowing these people. And they are knowing Festus."

He was peering through the last of the bush cover, where it had been cleared for the high fence. He was peering through the fence too, which seemed absurdly strong, overbuilt, the sort of fence you'd see at a national frontier, Hock thought, something to keep undesirables out, a steel barrier topped with coils of razor wire.

"They are stupid," Manyenga said, still studying the fence. "Look at this."

"What is it, anyway?"

"They are calling it the depot."

"Where's the chopper?"

"Maybe making another food drop in the bush somewhere, isn't it? Because they are having a visit from the big people."

"That man and woman on the chopper?"

"Famous, I tell you! Big people. Pop stars! You are knowing them."

"I don't know them," Hock said, thinking of the man in the cowboy hat, the blond woman in the catsuit. "My daughter might know them."

"You can ask her. She will be so happy. Eh! Eh! 'You have seen the big people in Malawi!'"

As though talking to himself, rehearsing the improbable notion, Hock said, "When I go home, maybe I'll call my daughter. I'll tell her where I was. I'll tell her what I saw."

"Famous pop stars in the bush!"

But Hock was looking at the compound. It was like a fortress, a prison, or perhaps, given its remoteness in this empty valley, a space station—all the steel and the compact buildings, a detached and singular platform in this hidden place. On top of the buildings solar panels were propped at an angle, black squares on gleaming brackets, with a white satellite dish and a tall radio antenna. What held Hock's attention and consoled him was the neatness of the place, the idea that such order was possible. His eye had become accustomed to dirty huts and windows, the filthy underworld of the Lower River. This sight of a cared-for place was bittersweet; it lifted his spirits and saddened him, too—the clean symmetry was an aspect of his own world that he had forgotten. Encountering this compound unexpectedly gave him hope.

Hock clapped his hands to announce himself, and called out, "Odi! Odi!"

Only then was he aware of the sound of an engine that had just started up, which he took to be a generator. The rattle was disturbing, a reminder of the harshness of that other world and its motors.

He saw an African man in a clean uniform—green, like army fatigues or hospital scrubs, with a green baseball cap. The man, his back to the fence, was polishing a fat stainless-steel tank, a water tank most likely, about the size of a basement boiler and as tall as the man who was wiping it, with a cloth dampened with water from a plastic bottle. He then coated the tank with a whitish fluid, which quickly dried in the heat to a dusty film.

"You talk to him," Hock said, unable to get the man's attention.

"No. It is for you. Get some supplies. We are needing."

"Why me?"

"Because it is your duty," Manyenga said, and bared his teeth again, breathing hard.

"What are you talking about? It's not my duty!"

Even as he spoke, he saw the absurdity of his arguing in this remote valley of the Matundu Hills, beside the chain-link fence and the big half-polished tank—no apparent door, only a seamless enclosure. Hock was screaming at Manyenga; Manyenga was screaming back at him.

"I don't have a duty!" Hock shouted. "Do I, Festus?"

"You lied to me! You tricked Zizi into the hut! You stole my motorbike! You ran off down the river with those boys. You betrayed me when I trusted you."

"You didn't trust me!"

"I made you my chief minister. I respected you too much, but you did not respect me, not at all, isn't it?"

"I came in good faith," Hock said, almost weeping at the memory of his arrival in Malabo. "I came to help."

"You are talking bloody rubbish," Manyenga said, wrinkling his nose in disgust. "I saved you from these boys who capture Europeans and sell them."

Their shouting was loud enough for the man in uniform to hear over the rat-tatting of the generator. He turned from his polishing and, startled by the sight of the two quarreling strangers outside the fence, dropped his cloth and the bottle of polish and hurried across the compound to the largest of the green bungalows, losing one of his rubber flip-flops as he ran.

"You scared him away," Hock said.

But when, hearing no reply, he glanced around, Manyenga was nowhere to be seen. Hock hooked his fingers on the fence and hung there, his head down, jarred by the chattering of the generator. The whole self-contained compound, with its lawn sprinklers and its bougainvillea and its gravel paths, so hopeful a little while ago, filled him with despair, because here he was, contemplating it from behind a ten-foot fence.

The African in the green uniform reappeared at the far side of the compound, near a building, talking to a man in sunglasses. The man in sunglasses was white, the first *mzungu* Hock had seen in more than six weeks — since Norman Fogwill in Blantyre. This man wore a green baseball cap and a Hawaiian shirt and khaki shorts and sandals, like someone on his way to the beach. Seeing the man, Hock became hopeful again, as when he'd first seen the compound. He felt like an earthling on a planet in deep space who'd just had a glimpse of another earthling — a brother, he thought, and he was almost overcome by a hatred for Manyenga. Seeing another white man inspired and allowed this feeling. He was stronger, not alone anymore, and, being stronger, he was able to admit this feeling of indignation.

He waved to the man in the flower-patterned shirt, who was still talking to the African at his side — laboriously, perhaps because of the loud generator. Hock tried to call out, and his voice caught and failed him — he was too full of emotion, near tears in spite of himself. He snagged his fingers in his mouth and whistled sharply.

The white man stared and then walked toward him, taking his time, kicking the gravel. Hock could see from the casual way he walked that he would be unhelpful. His cap visor was pulled low; his sunglasses were too dark for Hock to see his eyes. The double-A stitched on his cap Hock took to indicate the agency, L'Agence Anonyme.

Before Hock could speak, the man said, "What are you doing here?"

"I need help — please," Hock said, clinging to the fence.

"How did you get here?" The man stepped back as though from a bad smell.

"With another guy, on a motorcycle."

"I don't see anyone," the man said. "And there's no road." The man was stern, and his sternness emphasized his accent, which Hock could not place.

"We pushed the bike through the bush — does it matter? Listen, I need you to send a message for me to the consulate in Blantyre.

It's very urgent. I haven't had a decent meal in a week. I've been sleeping in the bush. I'm thirsty—I need water. I need a lift out of here. All I'm asking . . ."

The man set his face and his beaky cap at him and said, "You know this is a protected area?"

"Please help me."

"You need permission to come here."

"I'll get it. I have friends in Malawi."

"This isn't Malawi."

"Or Mozambique. Whatever."

"It's not Mozambique."

"What the hell is it then?" Hock said in a shriek, his voice breaking.

"It's the charity zone, between both countries, and it's policed. So take my advice and go away."

"Can't I just stay with you tonight?"

"We are not running a hotel."

"I need a drink of water."

"This is one of our busiest days," the man said, sighing in exasperation. Hock hated the man's shirt, hated the flowers, hated its cleanness, the neat creases on the sleeves. "We've got VIPs in the field—I mean, serious people. Heavy security. And you expect me to drop everything because you show up at the fence? Do yourself a favor. Go away. That's a polite warning."

"What's the name of this outfit?"

"That's confidential. We're contractors."

"I know. The agency—Agence Anonyme," Hock said. "Okay, I'll go. But just send an email for me. Please."

"Who says we have the capability?"

"You've got a satellite dish."

"It's not operational."

"Look, I'm an American, like you."

"I'm not an American"—and saying so, accenting the word "American," Hock knew the man was telling the truth.

"Where are you from?"

"Who wants to know? Who are you with?"

"I'm alone."

"What agency?"

"No agency," Hock said. "I'm a retired businessman. I came to Malawi over a month ago. Almost two months—I lost track of time. My clothes were stolen. My radio was stolen. I used to teach school here . . ."

As he spoke, Hock could see the man backing away, and finally he turned and walked along the gravel path, snapping his fingers at the African in the uniform, beckoning him.

For a moment Hock believed that the man was summoning the African to help him. But instead of approaching him, the African returned to the stainless-steel water tank next to the fence and resumed his work, using a rag to wipe off the dried polish and to buff it, shining it, so that a whole oval patch, head high, gleamed like a mirror.

Watching him work, Hock saw his own face reflected in the metal of the shiny tank, distorted because of the curving cylinder but clear enough for him to be appalled, terrified, and now he knew what the man had seen. He had not looked at his face for a week, since leaving his hut in Malabo, where he had a small mirror on the wall.

His first thought was, I am a monkey. His hair was wild, clawed to one side but stiff with caked dust and dried sweat. The grit in his eyebrows thickened them, made them seem hairier, and the bristles in his week-old beard were darkened with dirt and streaked with muddy sweat, still damp. His eyes were puffy, bloodshot, and miserable—the sad and scary eyes of a madman. Yet when he opened his mouth in horror, he saw that his teeth were white, and this whiteness made his face more monkey-like. The filthy face pushed against the fence, the dirty hands, the torn clothes, must have seemed so desperate to the agency man. The sight of himself devastated Hock. He had never imagined that he could have been so reduced, so degraded. He had become almost monstrous in his days as a fugitive on the river—or was it in Malabo he'd begun to degenerate? If so, it was no wonder they'd taken advantage of him. He looked as though he'd lost all self-respect. Judging from this wild face in the gleaming side of the tank, which the curve of the stainless steel distorted even more, he was an unwashed fugitive, the strangest sort of white man in the African bush—a dirty one, helpless and stinking and probably insane.

Yet he still had his good wristwatch, his small duffel bag, his medicine, his passport, his money, a change of clothes. The bag was filthy, too, but it was valuable, and he saw it as a friend.

"*Bambo*—father," Hock called to the African in the uniform, raising his voice so he could be heard above the generator.

The man winced, pretended not to hear, and went on polishing the tank. Hock, unable to bear seeing his dirty face, had moved away from the tank.

"Water," Hock said. Getting no response he said, "*Madzi,*" and repeated it.

He thought he saw the African's lips form the word *pepani*— sorry—but he could not be sure. The man glanced back at the bungalow, and while buffing the tank he stooped and picked up the plastic bottle he had used to dampen the washcloth. He wiped the mouth of the bottle on his shirt and then stuck its short neck through the chain-link fence.

Hock crouched and drank, but clumsily: the water slopped at his mouth and ran down his chin. He was aware that, with the bottle tilted this way, and in his submissive posture, he was like a baby, or a zoo animal being fed through a fence. He had never felt so helpless, but he was grateful to the African, and when he finished, gagging from the greedy mouthful, he thanked the man.

Without acknowledging Hock, obviously afraid that the white man might have seen him from the bungalow, he put the water bottle aside and set to work again. He had polished enough of the tank now so that Hock could see his upper body—horrible, wild man, desperate man, crazy man. Nothing this dirty man said could possibly be true.

Back on the field, among the scavenging children, facing the helicopter, he had felt he was at a low point. In the days at the village of children, cowering in the abandoned hut, sleepless, watching for hyenas, he'd felt he was at his wits' end. And on the riverbank at the frontier, looking for a passing canoe to take him downriver, he'd felt abandoned. At Malabo, too, on the night of his decision to leave, he'd felt full of despair.

But none of these episodes could compare with the way he felt now, crouching on the wrong side of this perimeter fence, filthier than he'd ever been in his life, saying thank you to the African in the uniform for a gulp of the cloudy wash water.

"It tasted like champagne," people said at moments like this. But no, this mouthful of warm water tasted foul, and the sour aftertaste of failure lingered in Hock's throat and nauseated him.

He knew then that he had come to the end of something. He was defeated. He could not imagine anything worse than the degradation he felt on this sunny late afternoon in no man's land, his reflection in the shiny tank staring back at him.

Two white men walked quickly toward him on the gravel path. The slow walk of the man earlier had signaled unhelpfulness; this brisk stride indicated pure hostility.

"You're still here?" the first one said—the man from before, in the Hawaiian shirt.

The other one wore a bush shirt, bush shorts, and heavy boots, and seemed military and almost familiar. Both men were so clean, so intimidating, their cleanliness like strength.

"I know you," he said.

Hock said, "Please help me. Send a message."

"You're the guy from the field, from this morning, when we were making the drop." He turned to the other man, saying, "He was with those kids from the villages. He was trying to score a bag for himself. It was chaos, all his fault. We had to scrub it. That's why I came back early. He put us off schedule." He snapped at Hock, "How'd you get here?"

"He wouldn't tell me who he was with," the other man said.

"I am warning you," the man in khaki said. "Get out of here the way you came in. If we see you again, we'll shoot."

The African, listening, looked fearful, and when the man in khaki gestured, he went back to polishing the water tank, his eyes widened in terror.

That fear penetrated Hock. He picked up his bag, and for the sake of his dignity he said, "You're going to hear about this from the authorities. You'll be sorry. I'm going to report you when I get back."

"Mister, the way you look, you're not going to make it back."

Hock straightened and slung the strap of his bag over his shoulder. He stepped into the bush—he was still less than six feet from the fence, staring at the men. It occurred to him from the way they watched him that these men were unfamiliar with the bush, perhaps afraid, that they traveled in and out in the helicopter and had no sense of the path. Hock looked around, wishing for a snake—a fat one, a viper—that he could seize and shake at them like a thunderbolt.

"I'll make it," Hock said.

But when he turned, and ducked into the bush, and saw nothing but the narrow track with the faint impression of the motorcycle's tire marks, he felt tired; and dispirited, away from the men, he sat down on a boulder. Almost immediately he was stung by ants. He slapped at his legs, he rubbed his arms. He walked farther, crossing to the far side of the steep bowl-like valley, wondering which direction to take. Looking around, he saw movement, a human figure. Leaning forward to see better, he heard mocking laughter. He knew who it was.

PART IV

Snakes and Ladders

21

T HEIR OWN LONG late-afternoon shadows floated on the path in front of them, leggy torsos in the red dust. They tramped this lengthening darkness to the whine of cicadas, and before they reached the lip of the valley the sun had dropped beneath the level of the trees, and flights of mouse-faced bats filled the air, darting like swallows. While it was light enough to gather firewood, Manyenga parked the motorbike under a tree and they went in search of dry sticks. They piled the wood but waited until dark before they lit it, because the fire was to keep animals away, hyenas or baboons or biting lizards, and to repel ants and flying insects.

"Where's the food bag?" Hock asked, because he knew Manyenga had snatched one at the field.

"It is for my family," Manyenga said. He had found three green coconuts in his foraging. By the light of the fire he hacked off the tops, sawing at the sinews with his pocketknife, and they took turns drinking the coconut water and eating the gelatinous flesh. Until this moment they had only muttered. "Wood" and "matches" and "You take."

But as Hock lay near the fire on a pile of dead crackly leaves he had scraped together, his animal feeling rose up in him. He remembered the way he had looked in the shiny tank. He was not saddened by the memory of the filthy face and matted hair and stubble on his cheeks. If anything, he was encouraged now. The image of that dirty, defiant monkey face strengthened him as he lay, his head propped up by one hand so he could feel the heat of the fire.

"I hate them," he said, suddenly aloud.

"And myself, I hate them, too much," Manyenga said.

"Festus," Hock said, smiling, almost with affection.

He slept with the dust of the forest in his nostrils, hearing the chirp and snapping of nighttime insects and the odd bird squawk. Once he thought he heard the *whoo* of a giant eagle owl, or the crack of a branch, undramatic, no louder than a matchstick snapped in half.

At first light, in a racket of insects and birdcalls, with the heat beginning to rise, Manyenga rolled over and grunted. His face was a dark medallion in the sharpness of the sun. They set off through the bush, taking a new direction—north, Hock could tell; the sun was on their right. Manyenga knew the way, and after about an hour they began to see signs of disorder, the first village, hardly a village, one of those static settlements of the bush, a few huts, a wide-eyed boy, a woman fanning a fire with a pot lid, a yapping dog. And they kept going, on a proper footpath now, with the dampness of the river seeping into it, and the elephant grass too high for them to see over it.

Then a road. It had once been a road; it was lumpy with tussocks of rough grass. Vehicles had passed here long ago; the parallel tire tracks, mostly overgrown, were still visible. Manyenga settled the motorbike into one of the ruts but traveled slowly. Hock hung on, and the morning passed, the motorbike rocking him.

At noon a familiar odor of risen dust and stagnant water and wood smoke, and a familiar glare, the heavy light pressing on his eyes, combined with heat. All that and the toasted smell of burned grass, the sight of solitary trees, most of them dead, stripped of their smaller limbs for firewood, some of them no more than crooked posts. Malabo was not far: they were approaching the back road from the south, a new direction for Hock.

When they arrived at the village, Manyenga rode in a wide circle, as though performing a victory lap to show that he'd brought Hock back. Some small boys yelled, some women yodeled. And then he rode straight to Hock's hut.

"She will bring you tea."

A small slight figure was seated, in a posture of resignation or fatigue, at the edge of the veranda. It was Zizi, her head on her knees. Hearing the motorbike, she looked up, and when she saw who it was she burst into tears.

She gazed at Hock with a mixture of fear and ecstasy. Her tormented face, sick with grief, was thinner. She looked haggard, her cheeks already wet with tears, and yet she was smiling. But it was also a smile of agony, as though she didn't quite believe what she was seeing, Hock getting off the bike, slapping the dust from his bag, considering Manyenga and deciding not to thank him. Zizi put her fingers into her mouth, perhaps to stifle her sobs.

"Falling tears! That is a good sign," Manyenga cried out.

"What are you saying?" Hock asked.

"That it will rain," Manyenga said, then, "She was missing you," and he laughed at the absurdity of it. He kicked the bike into gear and gunned it across the clearing to his compound.

Zizi dropped to her knees and held Hock's legs, pressing her head against his trousers and weeping. The whir of emotion in her body penetrated his as she clung to him.

She exhausted herself with tears, then used her wraparound cloth to wipe her face, lifting it, revealing her legs as sticks. When Hock sat in the shade of the veranda in his old chair and watched her stumble away, to bring him tea and something to eat, her big feet and stiff skinny legs giving her an odd clockwork gait, he thought with wonderment how Zizi had looked, so relieved at his return, perhaps having believed that he had gone for good, or been killed.

The thought in his mind, not words but a breaking wave of warmth, was the rapture of being missed, having made someone happy with his presence. No one had ever missed him before, no one in his life. He had mentioned to Roy Junkins that he could write him in care of the U.S. consulate in Blantyre. But nothing had come. The man was silent, no letters—and a letter, delivered by the consulate, might have helped save him from Malabo. Nothing from the consulate, nothing from Fogwill. Yet Zizi was glad to see him, more than glad. For the first time, someone was grateful for his very presence.

She was smiling when she came back to the veranda with the tea and a basket holding a hunk of buttered bread, a hard-boiled egg, and a steamed sweet potato. He ate slowly while she sat at his feet, hugging his knees, not smiling anymore but looking contented.

"Jinny," she said, with effort, her tongue against her teeth.

Hock shook his head, squinting at the word.

"*Ulendo.*"

"Yes, journey," he said. "Big journey."

A reddened welt on her bare arm caught his eye. He touched his own arm on the same place to draw her attention to it.

"*Chironda,*" she said, meaning bruise, and explaining it, she made a whipping gesture.

"Who did that?"

"The big man."

"Manyenga?"

She blinked and sniffed, to acknowledge it.

"They wanted to know where you were. They said I must tell them."

"What did you tell them?"

Zizi shook her head and smiled softly and averted her eyes. When she stepped off the veranda into the dusk, Hock knew there was something she didn't want to say. She was silent for a while, and Hock finished the bread and the egg and drank another cup of tea. He had thought he would be hungrier, but he was tired and dirty and wanted only to crawl beneath his mosquito net and sleep for two days.

Zizi was digging her toe shyly into the dust. He knew she wanted to say something more. He smiled to encourage her. He said, "Speak."

"I told them," she said in a hoarse voice, "that I also wanted to know where you were."

He had begun to think of himself, in his flight down the river and through the bush, as a desperate, slowly shredding escapee, coming apart as he fled, growing insubstantial, fraying into a ghost. And even after Manyenga had snared him and carried him through the scrubby trees of no man's land, he'd felt diminished, a stick figure, a wraith—a mere symbol of a *mzungu*, not a man with a name but a fugitive flickering past, someone whose only importance was that he might have money.

They thought of him that way. He thought of himself that way.

And he was resigned to being hunted down. So he had gotten on Manyenga's bike and hung on, and let himself be carried through the bush to the L'Agence Anonyme compound and finally back to Malabo.

And there, seeing how Zizi had missed him, he became whole again. He slept, and when he woke up he believed in himself anew. He'd failed in his second attempt to escape, in this exhausting experience of snakes and ladders. But the cruel game was not over, and he'd recaptured his sense of life, as though Zizi's sorrow at his disappearance had proven to him that he was real, that he mattered, that it was not so bad slipping down the snake to Malabo as long as one person was loyal to him. Someday, he vowed, he would reward her.

He heard her singing. He had heard it before, her habit of singing when she was afraid, when she was anxious, but now he saw that she was singing softly in contentment, releasing her emotion in a muffled melody.

And when the dwarf Snowdon saw him, he chattered and smiled, drooling, pointing at Hock and at last bowing to him on his bandy legs, touching Hock's feet as Zizi had done, but the dwarf performed it with respect so exaggerated it seemed a form of clowning.

"Fee-dee-dom," the dwarf said.

Manyenga had not seen that—a good thing—but he saw how Zizi and the dwarf attended to him.

He said, "They treat you like a big man."

"Aren't I a big man?"

"At the Agency compound they sent you away with nothing."

"What did you want?"

"Food and medicine. And what, and what. They are supposed to help us, but they cheat us. They give food to those devil children, and themselves, those *azungu*, they live like chiefs. Send them away!"

"Why don't you send me away?"

Manyenga was stung. He'd come to Hock's hut to offer a few mild insults and to remind Hock of the ineffectual power of someone looked after by a skinny girl and a dwarf—what sort of chief could this be?

"Not at all," Manyenga said. "I have come for *kusonka*."

It was one of those euphemistic words that meant to start a fire, but also to hand over a sum of money.

Hock said, "You've already got a fire."

"Give money," Manyenga said, licking his lips—*geev mahnie*. The crude demand made all of Manyenga's replies like the grunts of a brute.

"Who am I?"

"Chiff."

"What do you say to the chief?"

"Puddon?"

Hock repeated his question.

"Pliss."

"I'll give it to you later, when you have food for me."

Neither Zizi nor the dwarf understood, yet they looked on with admiration, smirking at Manyenga, believing that Hock had defied the big man.

He knew he had failed, had allowed himself to be abandoned, and captured, and threatened, and rejected, and seized again—snakes and ladders. He had been starved and out of desperation had drunk swamp water. In the shiny tank at the Agency compound his face, burned by the sun, looked scorched, and he was unshaven and dirty. He had sorrowed at that face of desperation.

The one constant in his life as a shop owner in Medford had been his appearance. He was aware all those years, standing in his clothing store, that he had to dress well, dress better than anyone who entered, because he was advertising his own goods—the blazer, or the tweed vest he wore when in shirtsleeves, the cravat with the blue shirt, the dark dress suit with chalk stripes. He dressed for his store, where he could never be overdressed, knowing that a customer might say, "I want something like that," meaning his tie or vest, since men were inarticulate, or at least self-conscious, when talking about new clothes. And Hock enjoyed dressing well; it was a way of armoring himself against the world. He hid himself in beautifully made clothes that were full of distractions—cuff links, tie pin, watch fob, belt buckle. He was reassured by the order, the sense of wearing a uniform. Decades of dressing well.

Now he was naked, or as naked as any man could be in the Lower River. Even the poorest man wore trousers and a shirt—ragged-assed long trousers, a shirt in ribbons. A woman might go bare-breasted—Zizi's aunt's floppy breasts had been uncovered the day Hock had visited Gala. But a man could not bare his chest, and only small boys wore shorts.

Still, he was naked—badly sunburned, and his skin was crusted with dirt. The cuffs of his trousers were in shreds, his sleeves were torn. His hands were clean, because Zizi had brought water in a basin for him to wash before eating, but his clean hands contrasted absurdly with his ragged clothes and dirty face. He was all the more touched that Zizi should care for him in this condition, was almost tearful that she accepted him.

More than that, she brought him soap and a cloth, so that he could go to the stream and bathe. She did not follow him. Such a thing was not allowed in the Lower River, a woman or girl lurking anywhere near a man washing himself. But when he set off for the stream, thinking of her kindness, he remembered his first sight of her at the small lagoon beside the stream, when she had crossed, going deeper, lifting her wrap higher up her legs, and higher to her thighs, until the water brimmed against the secret of her nakedness.

Hock washed himself, soaping his head, splashing like a dog and spewing. Then he wrapped the cloth around his body and walked back to the hut. The heat was so great, he was dry before he'd taken many steps. He rummaged in the bag he'd left behind, found the razor and his spare clothes, which Zizi had washed, and he shaved. After he changed into clean clothes, he sat in the shade, watched by Zizi and the dwarf. He was content for the moment; he had survived his escape attempt. It was better to be here than on the river alone, or in the village of children, or contending with the hostile men at the Agency depot.

Having survived, he was wiser if not stronger. And the order of his life here helped. He wasn't alone. Sitting there, flicking at flies—they were tsetses, small and quick, biting flies that left a pinch on his skin—staring into open space, he tried to work out how long he had been in Malabo. He had believed it to be six weeks. But was it? The arrival week was vivid in its reminders, because it was all he had planned to spend there. The second week was emphatic with disappointment—the ruined school, his pointless labor. After that, an effort to get away. The dance. The visit to Gala and finally his fleeing downriver, now over a week ago. More than six weeks, now into the seventh, maybe two months. He was mocked by this passage of time in which he had accomplished nothing, made more futile by the thought that he was not sure exactly how much time had passed—he who had measured every hour of every day he'd spent at his store in Medford.

He could not find the confidence to think about leaving now. He was physically well, but his mind was too battered to have answers, and it took him a long time to concentrate. He was content to sit, to do nothing, to contemplate his small shady courtyard. He was oddly reassured by the girl Zizi, waiting for him to ask something, and by the dwarf Snowdon, who sat blinking at the flies gathered and hurrying around his eyes.

The next day, Manyenga was back. Hock had seen him crossing the clearing from his cluster of huts, and he could tell from the way Manyenga walked—determined, forcing himself to march—that he had a favor to ask or a demand to make. It was an importuning walk, elbows out, head forward. He wanted something.

"Yes, father," he said, and uttered all the formulaic Sena greetings—that too indicated that he'd be demanding. At last he said, "You instructed me to come back, and myself here I am."

"With your hand out."

Instead of standing, out of respect, or asking Manyenga to sit, he remained on his creaky chair, enjoying the man's discomfort as he rocked on his heels.

"Because you are owing us too much of money."

"Why do I owe you?" Hock said. "I came here many weeks ago to visit you. I was going to leave, but somehow I am still here."

"As our honored guest. As minister. As our friend."

"Is that why I owe you?"

"No, my friend," Manyenga said, and looked fixedly at him. "At the Agency you came away with nothing at all. They didn't respect you—no."

The truth of this was hurtful. He remembered the sneering man, the African servant offering him a drink of warm water, his being threatened and sent away, and his turning and walking into the bush, on a muddy game trail, tramping the leaf litter.

"And myself I rescued you."

The memory of all that was so painful that Hock cut him short, saying, "How much do you want?"

"Petrol, food, transport," Manyenga said, beginning to itemize, his way of nagging.

"Let me go," Hock said. "I'll send you money."

"You never will."

"I promise."

"Just words. How will we know?"

Manyenga wasn't sentimental; he wasn't even pretending to like Hock. He was fierce and toothy, with cold eyes, and he seemed to enjoy reminding Hock that he was a hostage by telling him he was a guest.

"How much?" Hock repeated in a lower voice.

"What is the price of one human life?" Manyenga asked.

What Agency hack had taught him that sentence? Hock had kept some money in his pocket for just such an occasion, so he wouldn't have to rummage for it in Manyenga's presence. He took out some folded-over bills and handed them over.

Manyenga did not close his fingers around the money. He let it rest on his open palm.

"See? We are worth nothing," he said.

As though suspecting that Hock had the advantage, the dwarf crept over to Manyenga and clawed at his trouser leg, setting his head to the side as if he was going to bite him.

Manyenga kicked out at him, and the dwarf tumbled into the dust, honking in protest.

But already Hock was on his feet. He stepped off the veranda and stood so close to Manyenga that his chin was in the man's face. He was at least six inches taller than Manyenga.

"Don't you ever do that again," Hock said, and nudged the man back, bumping him with his chest. At this the dwarf looked up and smiled, showing his broken teeth. "Say sorry."

Manyenga faced him with reddened eyes.

"Say *pepani.*"

Now Snowdon understood and looked pleased.

"*Pepani* to you."

"Now leave us alone," Hock said.

"Not until I say one thing more, father. Remember this. When your rival stands on an anthill, never say 'I have caught you' until you are up there yourself."

With that, he left, the same determination in his stride that he had on his arrival. And Hock remained among the screaming cicadas in the thin hot air and the dusty trees and the gray sun in a sagging spider web of sky, and the dwarf mewling, all of it like aspects of his futility. He was miserable, but there was grim precision to it, and he took comfort in his condition, knowing that it was true, that it was exact, that he was not being fooled in his suffering.

22

H E RESENTED BEING captive in this flattened vegetating place, and he had come to hate the idiot wisdom of the proverbs these ragged people subjected him to. I never want to hear another proverb, he thought, or another opinion from someone so obviously doomed. If there was anything true or lasting in the village, it was in their dancing, but like so much else, this authentic expression of the past had become flat-footed. Instead of grieving for himself, he lamented the village that had disappeared utterly, its school buildings fallen, its well gone dry, its spirit vanished; lamented the evaporated essence of a place that he knew from its bitter residue of dust, like the skid of a footprint of someone who had fled for good. Malabo had become an earlier, whittled-down version of itself, recalling a simpler, crueler time, of fetishes and snake doctors and chicken-blood rituals.

The Lower River he'd dreamed of as a happy refuge for almost forty years; the embankment of beached canoes that had been hewn from ancient fat trees; the shaded village of dried mud, of thick-walled huts with cool interiors, and of smooth swept courtyards of strutting cockerels and plump chickens; the dense foliage of low trees like parasols of green; the narrow footpaths, the half-naked women and the men in neatly patched shirts, the coherence of the tidy weeded gardens of millet and sorghum and pumpkins, and the veiled drapery of strung-up fishing nets; and most of all the welcome, the warm greeting that was without suspicion or threat; something golden in the greenery lighted by the river, the warmth that kept him hopeful for all those years—gone, gone.

What he recalled now on these days of recovery after his thwarted escape was his reluctance to leave, all those years ago, the sadness he felt, not because he was going home to be with his ailing father, but at having to uproot himself from a life he had come to love, the school flourishing, the diligent hopeful students, the self-sufficiency of the people in the village. Back in Medford, among the shelves and glass display cases of expensive clothes, he remembered how in Malabo they mended their shirts, the small picked-out stitches, the sewn-up slashes, the new knees on trousers, the thick thready darns on elbows. Nothing was thrown away, nothing wasted. He had smoked a pipe then. The flat empty tobacco cans of the Player's Navy Cut he bought at Bhagat's were coveted in the village and became utensils, along with his occasional cup-like cans emptied of Springbok cigarettes. He too wore patched clothes. "My grandfather was a tailor," he told the man who worked the treadle-powered Singer sewing machine on the veranda of the Malabo grocery shop. He was proud of his patches. People stood straight, worked hard, and were grateful for the smallest kindness. They asked for nothing.

All that had vanished, and what was worse, not even a memory of it remained. The villagers hadn't been innocent before — there'd been petty thieves in Malabo, and he'd been robbed of a knife, a pen, books, money, an alarm clock, all stolen from his hut or the school. And there had been some bad feeling over his dalliance with Gala, but nothing audible. Now the big trees had been cut down for firewood, and there was no shade in the glary place. The baobab was a stump and a snake nest. The people had seemed unusual to him before, in their gentleness, in the way they had managed the land, their obvious attachment to it. The earth is our mother, a man might say, standing in a furrow with a mattock. They weren't corrupt now; they were changed, disillusioned, shabby, lazy, dependent, blaming, selfish; they were like most people. You didn't have to come all this way to be maddened by them. You could meet them almost anywhere.

He could not tell how this had come about. He hardly asked, he didn't care, and he was disappointed in himself for his indifference. Yet he did not want to care more than they themselves did.

He hated their extracting the trickle of money from him, hated the lies they told him, the lies he was telling them.

And now that he'd traveled partway down the river toward Morrumbala, the humpy, steep-sided rock pile of a mountain, and seen the smaller villages and the settlements on the embankment of the wide river, the strange hideout of children, the free-for-all in the open field, the militaristic depot of the charity, L'Agence Anonyme — after this failed escape, an exposure to the hinterland around Malabo, he was more disillusioned than ever. The flourishing Lower River was gone, its very greenness faded like a plucked leaf. He was trapped in a rotting province that he had once known as promising and self-sufficient and proud. He wanted to forget it all, to leave, but they frustrated every attempt he'd made. No one had hurt him, but their sullen stares suggested to him a greater menace. He simply did not know what to do and where to go. He was broken; he was part of the chaos.

Nothing in his life had prepared him for this. Now he remembered a particular day when Roy Junkins came to the store. Roy was thinner, not pale but sallow, yellowish even, his eyes set deeper in loose ashen sockets, as though he'd been ill and was still recovering. When he smiled, Hock saw missing teeth.

Hock was straightening jackets on a display rack, shaking them to free their sleeves. "Royal — haven't seen you for a while."

"Been away," the man said, and looked sheepish, because it seemed there was no more to say. And there was a gentle laugh he had, of self-deprecation.

"You feeling all right?"

"I'm Kool Moe Dee," Roy said, one of his formulas. "I am back in the world. Heh."

A note in his voice, of relief, suggested that a story of struggle lay behind his sudden good humor.

"You been far?"

"Very far, Ellis." That laugh again. "Concord."

Hock smiled at the absurdity of it — Concord wasn't far. And then it hit him: Concord Prison.

"Why didn't you get in touch?"

"I needed time to think about how I ended up there," Roy said.

"Not a thing you coulda done to help me. My sister visited. But the headline about being inside is, you are on your own."

And then, in a matter-of-fact way, Roy told Hock the details, how from the first he had been picked on in prison, his dinner plate snatched from in front of him, and he'd had to fight to defend himself. He'd been hit in the face by a man ("white dude") swinging a sock with a lump of metal inside, a steel padlock perhaps. "And that's how I lost my grille"—his teeth missing. He'd been intermittently bullied after that, but in time had found a degree of protection with a black faction in the prison. "Imagine—me!"—because Roy had always taken pride in distancing himself from any cause, rejoicing in being a loner. "But the brothers helped me," he said, shaking his head at the memory of it. "They were good."

His stories were of confinement, insecurity, threat, and intimidation. He'd been hurt, he'd been robbed, his cell ransacked. Younger, weaker, fearful inmates were raped.

"You couldn't tell the guards or—what?—the warden?"

"Guards don't run prisons," he said in his growly comic voice. "Prisoners run prisons. They make the rules. And they got some hard rules. If you snitch, you die. And you learn a few other things."

"Like what?"

"Learn to say 'sir.' Heh."

"How long were you inside?"

"Almost a year." Then, rubbing his hands and moving sideways to a display case, he said, in a subject-changing tone, "Show me some shirts, man. Something fine."

He never told Hock what the conviction was for: a year—probably drugs, a small amount. But the details stayed with Hock, the stories of being bullied, the extortion, the threats, his being alone, confined, under siege.

Malabo was a prison now, and the only strength that Hock had was bluff. Why did he not feel self-pity? He grieved for the vanished village, as Gala had done, and he thought of Chicky, but not as the selfish young woman who had demanded her share of his settlement, on the granting of his divorce, saying, "If I don't get it now, I'll never see it."

Chicky at her smallest and sweetest was the face he saw: at

her most unsuspecting, the way she laughed, her chattering in a big chair, her bluish lighted face in front of the TV set, laughing at something silly. And to please him once—because he'd begun to smile—she lip-synched to a reggae song, hunched her shoulders and mouthed the words to "Dem Get Me Mad," and told him the singer was someone called Yellow Man. One day, missing her, he'd leafed through her school notebook and found, in her scrawl, *I want to be cool,* and had to fight back tears. Another time, he watched her through a crack in the door to her room, putting on lipstick—she couldn't have been more than eight or nine. The little neat bundle of bus tickets, held by a rubber band—what urgency in her heart had made her save them? On a walk in the Fells, she was probably twelve, she saw a robin and said, "*Turdus migratorius,*" and blinked and pressed her lips in a kind of mild pedantry. On the same walk, pleased with herself, she took his hand and said, "When I grow up I want to live in a little cottage."

She hadn't been a lonely child. She'd been confident enough. But he'd seen her in the purity and blindness of her innocence. She did not know what was coming, the blight, the cynicism, the disappointment, and then her marriage, which was for him a sorry giveaway; and at last as a young woman she demanded money from him, and that poisoned everything. He needed to remember that she had once been blameless. He grieved for that child.

There was no consolation for him in the thought "Everything happens for the best," because that was general and his misery was particular. Hock did not dare to consider his own plight. The thing was to become strong again. Oppressed by the heat, the bad food, and his futile escape attempt, he was dazed, sensing that he might be dehydrated. He knew the symptoms, and he had them—headaches, lassitude, muscle aches, and sometimes he could barely speak.

Zizi was unchanged. She was like Gala, whom he had known all those years ago: uneducated, but just as strong, like the original women of the Sena. She gave him hope. In his weakened condition, Zizi acted for him, brought him the hot kettle for tea, and filled the basin so he could wash. Since arriving back from his weeklong escape, he'd stopped eating at Manyenga's, or even visiting, as an act of rebellion. Zizi brought him food. Though he offered to share it, she refused. She squatted with the dwarf, watching him eat, waiting for another order. She saw to the washing and ironing of his clothes, and the ironing was something he insisted on, because of the eggs of the putzi flies. He'd been through that before. Zizi was patient, obedient, observing him with large dark eyes, her knees drawn up, her chin resting on them, and wrapped in her purple *chitenje* cloth. While he'd been away, thinking he'd gone for good, she had mourned him in the traditional way, by letting her hair grow—only a week, but it showed. On his return, she shaved her head and held it proudly erect.

A few days after he returned, Hock woke at first light to hear a familiar thumping outside his hut, the *thud-thud* of a pestle dropped into a wooden mortar. He saw that Zizi was crushing maize into flour, standing under the tree, the air heavy with the static heat of morning stillness. She hugged the heavy pestle, lifted it, and let it drop, and as it did, her head jerked from the effort, her whole body falling back. Her face and head gleamed; she was never blacker than when she was sweating. She lifted her shoulders and, taking a deep breath, saw Hock at the window and smiled, then shyly covered her mouth.

Later that day, he saw that Zizi had spread a large mat on the ground in the sunniest part of the courtyard and scattered the newly pounded flour on it, to bleach in the bright light. In Malabo there was an informal competition among the women to make the whitest flour. From the veranda, he saw Zizi on her hands and knees sweeping the flour, turning it on the mat with a paddle, and his heart ached.

He could have said, he knew, "Go into the hut. Take your *chitenje* off. Get into the bed and wait for me." She had obeyed him without a word the morning of his escape, crawling into the bed. He could have summoned her into the hut at any hour of the day or night.

But because of this power and of her obedience, because he could demand and receive anything from her, whatever he wanted, he didn't ask. He only watched: Zizi's bones, her skinny legs, her big feet, her full lips and shining eyes, the glimpses of her small breasts, the way she stood at times like a heron, on one leg. His wish was to see her crossing the stream to bathe, as he'd done on his first day, the way she danced, stepping deeper and deeper into the water, lifting her cloth higher against her legs. He wanted to stand behind the mango tree at the embankment and watch her strip naked, soaping herself, her black skin gleaming with creamy bubbles. But someone would see him.

Go into the hut and wash, he could have said. She would have done it. She would have turned away and allowed him to see her. She was shy, but she was willing—too willing; he couldn't ask.

Yet she always seemed to be obliquely testing him with questions, even asking, "Is there anything else you want?" or in a single word, "*Mbiri?*"—More?

Hock shook his head and wondered if perhaps he was saying no because there was more power in his resisting her, that his rebuffing her gave him greater authority. But it was simpler than that, and obvious. He was a man in his sixties, a very old man for Malabo. He wanted only to be her benefactor, but the Lower River was a district without remedies.

"She respects you, father," Manyenga said when he wandered over one day and saw Hock seated between Zizi kneeling and the dwarf squatting in the shade.

Manyenga knew Hock was being uncooperative. As a pretext for the visit—so it seemed—he had brought an old stumbling man, whom he led by one arm. The man held his face upturned in an attitude of listening. He stroked the air with his free hand.

"He is blind," Manyenga said. "He said he wanted to meet our guest. He has heard about Mister Ellis."

Hock asked the man his name, but it was Manyenga who answered, "He is Wellington Mwali, from an important family. But he cannot see, so he has no big position."

The man mumbled to Manyenga.

"He wants to shake your hand."

Hock reached for the man's inquiring hand, and shook it, but the man did not let go. He spoke again to Manyenga.

"He says that he knows you are a friend to the snakes. He wants to tell you a story about them."

"I'd like to hear it."

"He is a storyteller," Manyenga said. "That is his position."

The man seemed to understand what was being said. He smiled with pride and spoke again in his feeble voice.

"He is tired now. He says some other time. But he is clever"—the old man was still speaking softly in a language or a dialect that Hock could not understand—"he knows there are other people, this little man, and this lovely lady."

"She's just a girl," Hock said.

"Girls are better. You can take her as a wife. You can have any woman in this village. You can have anything."

"No *lobola*," Hock said, meaning bride price, because it was the man who paid the dowry in the Lower River.

"You have plenty."

"I've given most of it to you," Hock said. "And I don't eat children."

But Manyenga wasn't rebuffed. He said, "She is old enough. She can bear you a child. She is making white flour for you!"

Zizi knew she was the subject of this talk. She raised her head, narrowed her eyes, and breathed deeply, and hearing her, the old blind man reached to touch her. She pushed his hand away, and he laughed. He kept laughing softly as Manyenga led him across the clearing.

Zizi still brought news to Hock—talk, the rumors of illness, the whisper that Manyenga's motorbike was broken, or that a dance would be held. Hock asked about Gala. Zizi said she didn't know anything, but later she had a story.

Gala was so sad, maybe disappointed. She had been happy to hear through a rumor that Hock had gotten away on the river, even if her heart was sore. But the news that he had been captured made her sad again. The reason was that she had warned him of dangers. And someone—maybe the laundry woman was to blame—had heard and told Festus Manyenga. They went to her house, some boys. They scolded Gala for warning him. They said they would beat her if she was cheeky again. She must not speak to Hock, ever. That was the story, much as she told it.

"I can talk to her," Hock said. "They can't hurt me."

"But Gala, they can hurt her," Zizi said. "She is very old."

Younger than me, he thought. But he stayed away. And in her role as his protector, Zizi seemed unusually responsive; resourceful, too, revealing an intelligence and subtlety he had not seen before.

A few days after this conversation, she brought him news that a boy had returned to the village from Blantyre, where he lived, one of Manyenga's family, a brother—but everyone was a brother.

"What is he doing in Blantyre?"

"Schooling," Zizi said in English, and again, "Or wucking."

"I want to see him."

Zizi took the message to Manyenga—it would have been against protocol for her to go to the boy directly. And it was an indication of how eager Manyenga was to please Hock that the boy visited within a few hours. It seemed that he was prepared to agree with anything that Hock asked, except the only important one, his release. Let me go, he wanted to say again, but he knew what the answer would be. He would not sit and be defied, or lied to, or jeered at, so he didn't ask. In everything else, he was obeyed. Manyenga had said, *You can have any woman in this village.*

His name was Aubrey, and he was not a boy—twenty or so —but had the thin careworn face of someone even older. Although it was nearing dusk when he arrived at Hock's hut, he wore sunglasses. They were new, and there was something menacing in their stylishness. His short-sleeved shirt was new, not one from the secondhand pile at the market, the castoffs from America they called *salaula,* their word for rummaging. His trousers, too, looked new, and when he saw that Hock was studying them, he offered the information that they were from Europe, a present. He had the slight build and small head and short legs that Hock was used to seeing in the Sena, but he was more confident, somewhat restless, shifting on the stool that Hock offered him, the bamboo one with squeaky legs.

Aubrey had a way of holding his head down at an odd butting angle, with his mouth half open, as though anticipating combat. Just behind his lips, the inside of his mouth was pink. The parted mouth made him seem both hungry and impatient, breathing hard, and for a reason Hock could not explain, the open mouth seemed satirical, too, as if Aubrey was on the point of laughing.

"How old are you?"

"Funny question," Aubrey said.

"Just a normal question."

"Twenty-two," he said, and jerked in his chair, revealing a cell phone in a holster at his belt.

"I want to make a call on your phone," Hock said.

Now the mouth parted a bit more as Aubrey laughed. "No coverage here. This is the boonies."

From the first he seemed to have an American accent, an affected one, something slurring and nasal in his delivery, a deliberate carelessness, a gratuitous rapidity. And *boonies?*

"Where'd you pick that up?"

"My English teacher was an American guy. Malawi's full of Americans. Look at you. What are you doing here?"

"Funny question," Hock said.

"Hey, just a normal question. But I know the answer. Americans like coming to the bush. Even big celebrities and rich people. They're in Monkey Bay, Mzuzu, on the lake. Karonga, and up on the plateau."

"How do you know that?"

"I see them. My job takes me around."

"I thought you were a student."

"I dropped out. It was a waste of time. And it's a laugh what teachers earn here. I'm in community relations for the Agency."

"L'Agence Anonyme, that one?"

"Yeah. The chief got me the job. He was a driver for them."

"But he quit—or was he fired?"

"You have to ask him, bwana."

Aubrey was quick, his English excellent, yet he seemed winded by the back-and-forth. As if from the effort of his replies, he perspired heavily, rare for a Sena man under a tree at dusk.

"How long are you going to be here in Malabo?"

"I'm day-to-day," Aubrey said.

No one spoke English well in Malabo. Manyenga's was generally correct and idiomatic, but his accent made it hard for Hock to understand him at times. This fellow Aubrey spoke English in a way that made him hard to fathom. He was a little too well spoken, evasive, quick to deflect, so fluent as to sound glib.

"Maybe I'll see a bit more of you."

Aubrey said, "Whatever."

"Community relations sounds important."

"Not really. *Mzungus* get afraid in the villages. I run interference," Aubrey said. "Sometimes damage control."

Hock nodded, at first impressed by the deft replies, then put on guard by the casual jargon that had worried him with Manyenga.

"The Agency is mostly Europeans. They think we are dirty and dangerous." Aubrey laughed. "Some of the villages are dirty, but they're not dangerous. They love the food drops."

"What's a food drop?"

"Chopper flies into a prearranged site and unloads."

"On the Lower River?" Hock asked, pretending ignorance.

"All over."

"I'd like to see it sometime."

"It's usually a zoo."

"Why is that?"

"Free food. Hungry people. Do the math." Now Hock began to hate him, but before he could say anything more, Aubrey looked at his watch, which hung loosely, like a roomy bracelet, on his thin wrist, and said, "I gotta go. Maybe catch you later."

23

THE DAYS BURNED BY, and on some smoldering late afternoons of suffocating aimlessness he felt that if he had a gun, he'd march Festus Manyenga to the creek and, in front of the whole gaping village, riddle him with bullets, then kick his bleeding corpse into the water. He sat on his slanting veranda, imagining this horror, sometimes smiling. Even in the times when they were talking—friendly enough, "We are liking you, father," "I'm glad I came back," all that—he wanted to twist a viper around the man's neck and watch the hammer stroke of the fanged mouth against his terrified face.

Hock had, as well, an image of himself holding a cloth bag, like one of the food bags from the Agency that bulged with rice or flour, saying, "Money, take it," and watching Manyenga reach into the bag that held—money, yes, but also a knot of venomous snakes. See how their wrist scars of snake medicine worked then.

He was ashamed of his smile and tried to stifle these thoughts —they were desperate, unworthy of him. But not having the strength to attempt another escape made him feel feeble. And though he tried to consider the villagers indulgently, he didn't trust them. None had helped him; they knew he was helpless, and they were especially cruel to the weak.

Yet Aubrey, fresh from Blantyre, connected to the Agency, was someone from the outer world, moving easily in his new shoes from that world to the village and back; someone who might help him. Manyenga could be enigmatic in his demands—he was superstitious, irrational, excitable, oblique, a villager—but Aubrey, with his smart-guy English and his worldly sarcasm, was different. He was greedy, he was knowable.

"The boy who came yesterday," Hock said to Zizi the next afternoon as she raked the flour into soft, salt-white heaps on the mat.

"With the shoes, with the watch, with the red eyes"—she had seen him clearly.

"Tell him I want to talk to him."

Zizi flashed a twitch of understanding with her eyebrows. Adult and conspiratorial, this time she would not go to the chief first. She was Hock's ally.

"But whisper."

It was another of the English words she knew. "I weespa."

Hock thought, I am going to miss you.

"Tomorrow," she said.

"Better tonight."

"He is not staying at Malabo."

"Yes?"

"But at Lutwe. *Pafoopi.*"

"How near?"

Zizi twisted her lips in vexation, implying *not near,* an inexact immeasurable distance.

"Is this a problem?"

"Night," she said.

Hock stared at her with the suggestion of a smile.

"Night is a problem," she said, using another word for problem, *mabvuto,* serious trouble.

Now Hock was frankly smiling, challenging her.

"Night is dangerous," and she used a more severe word, *kufa,* which meant death.

"Because of"—Hock tried to think of the word for monsters; all he could remember was large beasts. "*Zirombo,*" he said. "*Zirombo zambiri*"—lots of beasts.

Zizi frowned, suspecting she was being teased, but she didn't relent, because she was certain.

"Man," she said, another English word she knew. She made a face and clutched her body. "And boy."

"Beasts with two legs," Hock said in Sena, to lighten the mood.

She seemed so glum, and was probably tired, too, from raking and piling the new flour.

"Men," she said, "wanting women."

"You could take a torch with you. My big torch."

"That is worse," she said in her own language. "With a torch I would be seen."

He was fascinated by her disclosing her fears, she who never hesitated to help him. He was touched by her seriousness, standing before him, shaven-headed, in her flimsy cloth and bare feet. She was actually resisting him for the first time, trying to explain something to him that mattered to her. The instinctive reluctance of Sena people to go out at night was something he'd always known. Animals prowled at night: crocs crept out of the shallows onto the embankments and into the nearby bush, looking for the carcasses of abandoned kills; hippos browsed in the tall grass after dark; hyenas loped along in packs and grunted and dug in the garbage piles at the edge of Malabo, fighting over bones. Some people spoke of snakes at night, though Hock knew that snakes seldom lurked in the dark, never hunted at that time, even the boomslangs remained in tree branches, never dropping at night.

"Hippos. Hyenas."

Zizi clicked her tongue against her teeth, emphatically no.

"*Mfiti.*" Spirits.

Zizi wrinkled her nose in annoyance.

"Just men?"

"Man." She said the word without any lightness, and showed her teeth, as though she was naming a species of vicious animal.

"What do they want?" he asked.

She stared at him, impatient, as though thinking, Why these ignorant questions?

"They want," she said, "what all men want."

But he said, "You can ask the boy in the day. Tell him I want to see him at night."

So it was another day before Zizi set out for Lutwe, going a roundabout way so she would not be seen, to find Aubrey, to whisper to him that the *mzungu* wanted to see him in the dark.

Aubrey returned after nightfall the day that Zizi delivered the message. He arrived suddenly, stepping into Hock's compound with another boy—younger, who didn't appear to speak any English, who knelt before Hock's hut near the dwarf, looking nervous, the dwarf grinning at him, mouthing in spittle his mutter, "Fee-dee-dom."

Aubrey stood aside, just out of the lantern light, scarcely visible.

Two things disturbed Hock about this second visit. One was the way Aubrey sauntered across the clearing, his hands in his pants pockets. He did not observe the customary greeting, calling out, "*Odi, odi,*" and clapping his hands as an announcement, asking permission to enter the compound. This was rude, and uncommon—Manyenga himself usually said "*Odi,*" though often in a satirical tone. Hock was keenly aware of the niceties, wary when they were flouted, like the boys in the village of children who had called him *mzungu* to his face. "Hey, white man" was pure insolence.

The other disturbance was different but just as troubling. Meeting Aubrey for the first time, Hock had taken him to be lean but healthy, certainly healthier and better dressed than anyone else in Malabo. But in the uneven fire of the lantern light Aubrey's skin was gray, his eyes bloodshot, his face gaunt. He was not lean but thin, and with his sleeves rolled up the skin of his arms was dry, crusted with whitened flakes of scurf. Aware that he was being scrutinized, he removed the sunglasses from his pocket and put them on, to cover his reddened eyes.

Or was this all an effect of the slippery light from the smoky orange lantern flame with an untrimmed wick? Hock was uncertain, and suspicious. He had lived too much on his nerves.

"You want to see me?"

Aubrey spoke in a low voice. He knew the meeting was secret. And his direct question was so strange to Hock, who was accustomed to the canny obliqueness of Manyenga and the others.

"Have a seat," Hock said.

Aubrey motioned to Zizi, a two-part hand gesture that indicated "chair"—he pointed to the stool—and "bring it," a beckoning with a stab of his skinny finger.

"No," Hock said when Zizi moved toward the stool.

This surprised Aubrey, and the sudden expression revealed a

slackness in his face to Hock, who saw how a person's health is more obvious when making a physical effort.

"She's not your servant."

Smiling, Aubrey muttered in Sena to the young man who'd accompanied him. Just a few words, and the boy snatched the stool and moved it to a shadowy spot near Hock. As he sat, Aubrey glanced over at Zizi.

"She is proud," he said in a tone of resentment, because Zizi had smiled when Hock had intervened.

"She's got manners."

"Because she works for the *mzungu*."

"I've got a name," Hock said, but before Aubrey could speak again, he said, "You can call me *nduna*."

"Okay, chief."

The boy was quick, in a manner he'd learned from foreigners, as Manyenga had. A sly alertness, not deftness but a slick evasion, and he had the words, too.

"She doesn't work for me."

"Whatever," Aubrey said, tilting his head.

"I'm her guardian."

Aubrey raised his head, facing Hock, but the sunglasses masked his expression. Was he looking at him in mockery?

"And I don't want anyone to touch her."

Aubrey tilted his head again, as though he was silently indicating "Whatever."

"You understand?"

"I hear you."

Hock felt himself growing angry. He had not realized until now how strongly he felt about Zizi's virginity. He was certain she was a virgin—Gala herself had said so.

"I know she is still a girl," Aubrey said. "She has not had her initiation. People call her *kaloka,* the little lock."

Zizi frowned, hearing the word.

"Who's got the key? Maybe you, bwana."

"No one has the key," Hock said with force.

"I hear you," Aubrey said, suddenly contrite. That was his manner—a boast, a wisecrack, and then a retreat when he saw he'd gone too far. "It's special, you know. Most of the girls her age are"—he shrugged—"unlocked. They even have kids. But not her. We say of such a girl that she has all her cattle."

Zizi said something under her breath, hissing at Aubrey.

And after her sharp reaction, Aubrey gave a tight smile, as though he'd just been slapped. He said, "She's being rude to me," and laughed, because the young boy with him had also reacted. "A wet snake, that's what she said."

"Maybe that's what you are."

"In our language it means something else." He became angry again and sat more stiffly, keeping his face out of the light. "Did you want something?"

Hock stared at Aubrey's gray twitching hands before replying. Finally he said, "I've got a job for you."

"Some kind of favor?"

"A job."

"It'll cost you," Aubrey said without hesitating.

But Hock was glad. That's what he wanted, not friendliness, not a favor, which always carried a penalty with it, but a paid-for job. Aubrey, in his crass knowing way, was the man he needed.

Hock said, "Don't worry. I'll take care of you."

The smile on Aubrey's thin face was sly, snake-like, ingratiating. He jerked his head to indicate, "Go on."

"You're going back to Blantyre soon?"

"That depends."

"On what?"

"If you want me to go."

"What if I do?"

Aubrey agitated his fingers, but subtly, touching his fingertips, his city gesture for money.

"I'll give you two payments—one now, the other when you come back."

"Who says I'm coming back?"

"You'll be coming back with my friend, to show him the way."

Now Aubrey smiled, and nodded almost imperceptibly, a tremor of his head, seeing another opportunity.

"You're going to take something to Blantyre for me."

"Like what?"

"A message."

"That's easy," Aubrey said, and as though he'd regretted saying it, he corrected himself. "I can do it. But you'll have to pay me in dollars."

"I'll give you fifty."

Aubrey shrugged. "A couple of hundred at least."

Although Hock had pretended to be relaxed, defying him, Aubrey seemed to understand that Hock was desperate, seemed able to smell it, the hopelessness, the anxiety. And Hock knew that Aubrey could not have seen any other *mzungu* in a hut like this, sitting in ragged clothes, with the skinny girl and the dwarf and the mat of pounded flour in the courtyard.

Tapping his finger on the arm of his chair and leaning close, Hock said, "You get a hundred now and a hundred when you show up with my friend. That's a lot of money."

"I need bus fare. And my small brother"—he indicated the staring boy—"he is needing too."

"You know the American consulate in Blantyre?"

"Everyone knows it," Aubrey said. "There's always a long queue of people wanting visas."

"That's the place. I want you to go tomorrow."

Aubrey said, "What's the hurry?"

"No hurry. If you want to do it, you go tomorrow. That way I know you're serious."

Nodding, Aubrey said, "Okay, bwana." And then, "Where's the message?"

"When you're ready to go, I'll give you the message, and the money."

As they had talked, the moon had risen, a nibbled crescent in a sky of stars, with high thin veils of cloud. Shadows brimmed around them, and they sat in the small pool of light from the lantern. Normally, Zizi would set a row of lanterns along the veranda at this time, because it was too early to sleep, too hot to retreat inside. But tonight, as though understanding the secrecy of the meeting, she merely sat, her knees drawn up, her chin on her folded hands, her cloth wrap gathered for modesty.

Hock could see the whites of her eyes, the dull gleam of her shaved head in the moonlight. He was too moved to speak, because she was pure. The night sky gave him hope, the way it was dusted with streaks of gray and masses of stars, a great flawless capsule of light—hopeful because it represented a bigger world than the small flat shadow of Malabo, like a crater, in lamplight, the moths fluttering around the sooty chimney, bumping it and burning.

In the silence, Hock sensed that Aubrey was eager to help—greedy for money; impatient, too, for the trip to Blantyre. But out of pride, or to keep the upper hand, he didn't show it.

"You were born here, eh?" Hock said.

"Yes, but . . ."

Hock could sense the young man recoil. He said, "But you don't like it here."

"Yes, I don't like."

"What is it about Blantyre you like?"

Taking a deep reflective breath, Aubrey sighed. He did not reply at once. Hock could see that he was trying to formulate an answer. They sat in the shadows thrown by the lamp, and in the silence some talk carried from across the clearing, and smoke from cooking fires filled the night air with buoyant sparks.

Finally Aubrey said, "The lights."

He had to repeat it, he spoke so quickly. But later that night, after Aubrey and the boy had left, and Zizi had gone to her hut, and Snowdon had stowed himself away among the litter and the branches behind Zizi's hut, Hock lay in his cot and said the words to himself, the simplicity, the truth of them, *the lights.*

Aubrey came before dawn, in the dim light of the thin fading moon. He knew the matter was serious, and he knew how to be covert. He had tapped softly on the screen door. Hock was reassured by Aubrey's early arrival, by his obliqueness, and especially by his greed.

Hock had prepared his message—the photocopy of his passport page that he always kept handy, showing his picture, his details, with the message he had printed before going to bed: *I am seriously compromised and possibly in danger. Please help. This man will lead you to me,* and his signature under his printed name.

Folding it small, Hock handed it over with the hundred-dollar bill tucked into it. Aubrey pocketed the pieces of paper, and then he raised his face to Hock's, looking defiant.

"This is going to cost you a little more," he said.

Hock had been in the village long enough to expect that. He had the twenty-dollar bill handy, also folded.

As Aubrey palmed it, Hock said, "Don't let anyone see you."

24

UNTIL NOW HE had not dared to hope, because all he'd found here was failure. He'd known the Sena people before they'd become artful, and he wondered if their plotting against him now was something they'd learned from the *mzungus* at the Agency. Or had they always been artful, and he too beguiled to see it?

He hated to wake each morning in the heat and remember that he was trapped. Yet after all this time the idea of saving himself, being freed from the village, was a mental leap that left him saddened; the very thought made him gloomy, for its futility. In the dust of his confinement the prospect of freedom was so absurd that he seldom left his own courtyard. In the past he had wandered around the village, chatting to people, adding to his word list, looking for signs of snakes. Now he sat under his tree, inhabiting a mirage, blinking away the flies, like other old men in Malabo.

Like the children, too, who never strayed far from their huts and their mothers. In his captivity, his inability to get away from this insignificant village, Hock had become childlike. The feeling had stolen upon him, making him smaller, his avoidance of strangers amounting to a fear he hated to acknowledge. He had come here as a man, with willingness and money, assured of meeting friends and — knowing the people, speaking the language — with a confidence that amounted almost to a sense of superiority. Not racial, it was a complex sympathy, the suave generosity masked as the humility of a passerby pressing a fifty into the hand of a beggar at Christmas, knowing that it would make a difference, and pausing a moment to hear, "Bless you, sir." He had meant well, but that conceit had made him the beggar. He had become reduced; he was a child now, sitting in the shade. And during that time, as he'd become smaller, Zizi had proven herself stronger, almost motherly, someone he trusted and needed, who looked after him, someone older, wiser. He wanted to thank her but could not find the words, and she would have been startled to hear *I would be lost without you*.

He stayed near his hut because lately, when he had taken a walk in the village or out to the road, small children—some skinny and potbellied, others cadaver thin, all wearing castoff T-shirts—had followed him and, laughing, had thrown small stones at him, or darting closer tried to hit him with dried maize cobs or the large blown-open fruit from the sausage tree. He tried not to be angry—anger was not a source of strength here but something that could be dangerous. He cautioned himself to take care.

After Aubrey had left, backing out of the hazy shadows of early-morning darkness, Zizi's mood changed. She became unusually silent, which Hock took to be sullen resentment, seeing Aubrey pocketing the money. Hock approached her and put his arms around her, to comfort her.

"My friend," he said.

She stiffened, her body like a bundle of sticks wrapped in loose cloth.

Instead of saying more, Hock let a day pass. Zizi brought him his meals as usual, with tea; she had her own cooking fire now, and no longer depended on food from Manyenga's compound. She pounded maize, she spread the flour to bleach on the big mat, and by now she had several fat bags of flour she'd made, stored on the veranda of her small hut in the proud manner of Malabo women, visible proof of their hard work and their homemaking.

Seeing that she was unresponsive, Hock said, "That man Aubrey, do you like him?"

Zizi said nothing, but sniffed a little, which he took to mean no. She was holding a bucket of plates in soapy water, from the meal, which she intended to wash.

Assuming she had spoken the word, Hock said, "Why not?"

Zizi made her reluctant face, nibbling her lips, twisting her mouth, then said, "He is not afraid of you."

Burdened by the heavy bucket, taking short steps, her shoulders wagging as she shuffled, she walked away, the plates knocking and gulping in the water. With the bucket bumping against her leg she seemed slow and careworn, like a little old woman—skinny body, big feet. But when she swung the bucket up and hoisted it on top of her head and she straightened, balancing it, she became tall, erect, poised, and Hock desired her again. But it was futile desire. She was the only friend he had; he couldn't risk changing that friendship to anything else, nor did he have the right.

Normally, Snowdon would have chased her and watched her do the dishes. But he sat near Hock with his stumpy forefinger in his mouth, gaping at him, perhaps smiling, perhaps wincing because of the strong glare.

When Zizi returned, Hock said, "Maybe it's true. Maybe he's not afraid of me."

"It is true," she said.

"What about you?"

Zizi folded her arms as if to defy him, and seemed haughty with her head lifted.

"Are you afraid of me?"

She said, "Now I am."

"Why?"

She mumbled some words. He heard the word for rat. He asked her to repeat it. She gave him part of a Sena proverb he recognized: *Koswe wapazala*—the fleeing rat . . .

"The fleeing rat exposes all the others," he said. "That's what you think of him?"

She crouched near the dwarf and made that face again, twisting her mouth like a reluctant child, screwing up one eye.

That was another reason his desire was dampened: she was not a child, but she could seem childlike. She was still whole, as Aubrey had slyly intimated—locked, kept from her initiation. Still innocent: Hock couldn't take that from her. In the village it mattered more than anything. Her virginity was a form of wealth, the value of her bride price, her pride, her only possession.

The day was hot, and the fact that Aubrey had already set off for Blantyre helped raise Hock's hopes. If Aubrey succeeded, he might not be in Malabo much longer, but Hock quickly dismissed this forbidden thought. It was still early. How to give a point to the day was always a problem. The days in Malabo were shapeless and empty, and he felt assaulted by them—the emptiness, the screech of the cicadas, the squealing of bats; the days were idiots.

Toward noon, he said to Zizi, "Help me find some snakes."

She frowned, pretending to sulk, but she got to her feet, gathered the basket, the burlap sack, the forked stick, the collecting equipment. And in the heat of the day, when everyone else was inside or in the shade, they walked across the clearing in the weight of the full overhead sun, to the creek, to look for snakes.

Hock was happy. A hunt for snakes—one of his pleasures from long ago—gave the day a purpose and some meaning, gave the flat and hot and undifferentiated landscape certain subtleties: the sandy patches where the snakes slept, the overhanging limbs that might hold the drooping length of a boomslang, the shallows in the creek where small narrow snakes like the snouted night adder whipped along just below the surface. The presence of snakes gave features to the monotony of the land, and looking for them, he was able to revisit his previous life here and to forget he was a captive.

Walking just ahead of him, the basket on her head, Zizi stirred him, since she was like the embodiment of his other, earlier Africa. Her granny, Gala, had seemed like a new woman then—educated, self-possessed, quick to respond, unexpectedly witty. Yet Zizi had no education, could not read, wore that simple wrap, went barefoot, and shaved her head, and apart from being kept by Gala from her initiation, she observed all the other customs of the Sena people that Hock remembered, even quoting proverbs to make a point. She was restrained in the old way, too, merely frowned at Hock's wristwatch, and had taken no interest in his radio—chuckled when he told her it had been stolen.

The strangest habit she had, and the most endearing, was her singing deep in her throat when she was anxious. The melody was usually a dark, many-angled descant, a growly harmonizing that Hock followed with an aching heart.

She was singing now, the growl growing fainter, as they trod the gravelly hard-packed sand of the worn path at the perimeter of Malabo, through the head-high elephant grass.

Was it fear? It seemed that fear inspired her singing—or, not singing, but a vibrant harmony that rang through her whole slim body as she steadied the basket on her head, the basket in which they'd bring back the snakes.

"What else are you afraid of?" he asked.

Zizi whinnied in reply, a singing in her sinuses.

"Tell me."

"I'm afraid to get married," she said, and that sentence ended with a melody that seemed like an equivocation.

"Yes?" He wanted to encourage her to say more, but he was distracted, searching the hot gravel for snakes.

"But I'm not afraid to die."

As she spoke the words, he saw her dead. It was an amazing pair of pronouncements and made her seem both wise and vulnerable. Virgins were so often martyrs. He thought of Aubrey again, who seemed to mock her for being innocent and yet was intimidated by her. And he remembered his asking her what men wanted, and her replying, *They want what all men want*. He wondered how to tell her that a man can be kind, that marriage can bring children. A husband would protect her and give her status: the Sena pieties that were part of the initiation. But Zizi was wise enough to know that a villager in Malabo chose a wife as he would a field hand, and that the role of a wife came to much the same thing.

But he didn't say anything, because just then he saw a snake and all other thoughts left his head. She saw it too, raising her voice, an alarmed ascending song in her sinuses, and stepped back, reaching to steady the basket on her head.

The puff adder lay on the hot coarse sand but near enough to some dead leaves to seem like part of the trash of twigs and grass nearby, the thick brownish snake as unmoving as vegetable matter, its jaw resting against the sand.

In stepping back, Zizi had braced herself, keeping her knees together and slightly bent. As she murmured her fearful song, now softly slipping it into her throat, Hock could see that her face was beaded with sweat, not from effort or the heat, but wet as though from terror.

So transfixed was she by the sight of the fat snake that she had not noticed that her wrap, the faded *chitenje* cloth that had been hitched under her arms, had slipped its knot and drooped, exposing one neat breast and a swollen nipple, like a pure unsucked fruit at the top of the smooth bulge. She had a body almost devoid of curves, which made her hard muscled bottom and her small breasts so noticeable.

The snake was facing away from them, flicking its tongue, a slitted eye staring from each side of its head. Hock saw what perhaps in her fear Zizi did not see, that the adder had started to swell, slowly thickening. It had seen them. It had not changed its position on the sand, yet it was now almost one-third fatter than a moment ago, when they'd stopped six feet away.

Absent-mindedly, Zizi touched her throat as if registering the vibrato of her song on her skin. Then her hand slipped to her breast, cupping it, her fingertip caressing the nipple. Her mouth was open, the whining melody from it worrying a strand of saliva that was like a lute string vibrant between her parted lips. Her teeth were just visible. She seemed terrified, she'd gone rigid, her eyes glittering as though in ecstasy.

"Pick it up," Hock said.

But she didn't move. Her eyes were fixed on the fattening thing.

Hock had been carrying his forked stick behind his back. Without stepping nearer, he drew the stick forward and jabbed it in the direction of the snake, rousing it. The snake shortened its muscled body and then, uncoiling, chucked itself at the stick. And before it had time to prepare itself for another rush forward, before it was able to draw its body into another explosive knot, Hock clamped the fork of the stick at the back of its wide head. Now, its head pinned, its body whipped against the sand.

"Take it now."

Zizi's mouth gaped, the growly song of fear hovering in her tongue. Her knees were still pressed together.

"Hold it behind its head. Use your fingers to grip it tight."

"I cannot."

"Do it for me," he said.

She removed the basket from atop her head and placed it without a sound on the sand next to her, all the while watching the pinned-down puff adder thrashing its swollen body and pushing at the sand.

"Please," he said. It was a word he tried to avoid saying in the village, a word of the weak, a word of submission.

Zizi hunched her shoulders and knelt, her wrap slipping farther, both breasts exposed, as she reached and gripped the snake where Hock had indicated. As she took hold of it he lifted the stick, so when she stood she had the snake's head and gaping jaws above her skinny fist and the whole body of the snake and its tail encircling her forearm.

The song, a jubilant chant, rose from her throat to her mouth and nose, and it pounded against her sweaty face. The snake's jaws were wide open, not attempting to strike but gasping for air. Zizi's grip was a stranglehold.

"Easy," Hock said.

As if hearing him for the first time, Zizi faced him bare-breasted, holding the snake, the foamy, speckled jaws widened at Hock, its fangs dripping mouth-slime.

Hock was slightly alarmed by the change in Zizi—he had not seen this fierce face nor heard this song before. He reached over and took her wrist and, replacing his grip with hers, picked at the snake's tail, uncoiling its body from her arm, where it had wrapped itself like a tentacle.

"You are strong," he said.

She surrendered the snake, and as Hock took possession of it, she said, "I am not afraid," and her face glowed, her eyes glittered, she was breathless. "Not afraid," she repeated with wonderment, and then was silent, breathing hard, no longer singing.

Back at the hut, they slipped the snake into the basket and fastened the lid. Snowdon saw them and ran to tell the village.

Before going to sleep that night, and the next—because he'd had no word—he followed in his mind Aubrey's progress to the boma, on the bus, to the Chikwawa Road, and to Blantyre; the young man presenting the envelope at the consulate and, as in a movie sequence, its passing from the receptionist to the secretary upstairs and finally to the vice consul.

"'Seriously compromised,'" the vice consul would report to the consul. "We'd better send someone down to check on this." Or the man would go himself, in an official car, Aubrey sitting in the back seat. The matter was urgent; the message was clear.

But even on the third day no one came. No one except Manyenga, who sauntered over, seeming to approach the hut sideways, to see the big snake in the basket, which was news in Malabo. He was impressed, especially when Hock told him that Zizi had caught it; and he was unusually friendly.

"That *naartjie* is for you," he said, handing over a tangerine. The Afrikaans word was used by the Sena people, as was *takkies*, for sneakers. Manyenga often screamed, "*Voetsak!*" when he was telling an underling to go away. Hock felt that someone must have used the word with him.

Snowdon snatched the tangerine from Hock's hand and ran off, waving it.

"Cheeky bugger," Manyenga said, and made a threatening gesture.

"Leave him alone," Hock said, laughing. He could not help seeing Snowdon as anything but a licensed jester, like the fool in a Shakespeare play.

"You are so kind, father," Manyenga said. "That is why you are being our minister. You will be a great chief one day!"

"You don't need me to be a chief."

"Not true, father. You are our elder. You are so wise. You are always doing the right thing for us."

Each of these words—kind, wise, minister, elder—was loaded. All such words, Hock saw, had money value, and could be exchanged for hard currency. It seemed that as Manyenga added each word, the final bill was increased. Hock thought of Aubrey saying smartly, "It'll cost you," when he asked for the favor. In the past, money had not mattered much. Small debts were settled with a chicken or some dried fish wrapped in banana leaves; big debts might cost a cow. Now, with money, every word and deed had a price.

"You are brave, too," Manyenga said, tapping the basket after he had had a glimpse of the snake.

"Brave" was worth a handful of kwacha notes, certainly.

"Zizi caught the snake," Hock said.

And hearing her name, Zizi stared at Manyenga.

"You are making her too proud," Manyenga said.

There was a word for the handmaiden of a chief, a consort, a junior-wife-to-be, and Manyenga used it now, referring to her as "the small woman."

Hock said, "She can handle snakes."

"She can know how to handle anything you ask," Manyenga said, and tapped his head, pleased with himself in his reply.

The next day—no Aubrey—Manyenga brought a bowl of eggs. He was not alone. Walking behind him was the old man whom he had introduced to Hock after they had arrived back from the Agency depot. Hock could not remember the man's name, but as he saw him stumbling after Manyenga, led by a small boy, he was reminded that the man was blind.

"For the big man," Manyenga said, and offered the bowl with both hands.

Eggs were scarce. Why were there so few in a village with so many hens? Only men ate eggs; children were not allowed to touch them. The chickens were not raised systematically; they clucked, and pecked at ants, and laid eggs in the tall grass, in back of huts, in twiggy nests. They were considered a delicacy.

Zizi accepted the bowl of eggs on Hock's behalf.

Tapping the side of his head again for emphasis, Manyenga said, "But none for her, you understand?"

Another Sena belief associated with eggs was that women were made sterile by eating them.

"Because, as you say, if the girl can handle a snake, she is no longer a girl, but a woman."

They were seated, Manyenga and Hock, under the tree, in the creaky chairs. The blind man sat on a stool, holding himself upright.

"I think you are knowing what I mean," Manyenga said.

Snowdon was listening, a gob of drool sliding from the corner of his mouth. Somehow he had gotten hold of an egg. He rolled it back and forth in his stubby hand, like wealth.

Manyenga was still talking in his insinuating way, but all Hock could think about was the nonappearance of Aubrey.

"I remember this man," Hock said. The old man had a kindly face and an intense expression, his eyes dead behind lids that were not quite closed. He leaned on his walking stick, listening.

"He is Wellington Mwali," Manyenga said. He took the man's hand. "This is Mr. Ellis Hock, our friend."

The old man just smiled, murmuring, because he had not understood.

"He has a story," Manyenga said.

And this too will cost money, Hock thought. But he said, "I want to hear it."

Manyenga spoke to the blind man, who hesitated, and smiled again, and then cleared his throat and spoke. He told his story slowly, pausing after every few sentences so that Manyenga could translate. Manyenga spoke with such fluency and feeling it seemed that he was appropriating it as his story.

"You know our black Jesus, the man Mbona, who was killed near here, his head cut off and buried near the boma at Khulubvi?"

"I've heard of him. But I was never allowed to go to the shrine."

"No, no," Manyenga said. "It is a holy place." The old man went on speaking. He took up the story again. "Mbona is a spirit, but sometimes he spends the night with his wife on earth, the woman we call Salima. This is how the great one visits. He makes sure that Salima is fast asleep, otherwise she would become frightened and run away."

The old man's voice dropped to a whisper. Manyenga strained to listen, then spoke again.

"Mbona comes in the form of a python, slipping into the hut beside the mat of Salima. He opens his mouth and licks her body, beginning with her face, so that she believes she is being kissed. All this while he makes the python sound, moaning, and the moans are words, telling her his dreams."

Still speaking, now as if in counterpoint to Manyenga, the old man turned his blind eyes upward, as in a trance state.

Manyenga said, "After he licks her whole body to calm her, he wakes her. And she sees the huge python. But she is not afraid. She sees that it is her husband, Mbona, and she allows him to coil around her body and lick her everywhere, from her head to her feet, telling her his dreams. Meanwhile, he tells her many things in her dreams. The licking makes her sleep again, and his dreams become her dreams. After he goes, she just wakes up. She knows that her husband had been there, and she has all the important information."

"About what?" Hock asked.

The old man nodded, hearing the question.

"About the weather. About storms and rains. About planting. And when his visit is at an end, he returns to his place."

"Where does the python Mbona go?"

"To the pool near the river, which was formed when Mbona's blood turned into water," Manyenga said. "Large flocks of doves drink there, which proves that it is a holy place."

Hock said, "Thanks for the story. Tell the man I said so."

"We are needing you, father," Manyenga said. He saw Zizi squatting, brushing flies from his face. "She needs you. She can make you happy."

The story of the snake encircling the widow and licking her had induced a reverie in Hock, which helped him forget his plight. But as soon as Manyenga stopped translating, he began importuning again, and jarred from his reverie, Hock said abruptly, "How much do you want now?"

"I will tell you in a moment," Manyenga said. "But first the important information. I must know if you are happy."

"I am happy. Thanks for bringing this man to me."

Manyenga leaned closer and licked his lips and said with severity, "And that you will not abandon us again."

His tone was so serious that Hock said quickly, "Don't worry." Then, hearing himself, he added, "Why would I want to leave Malabo?"

"Of course you are safe here," Manyenga said, too engrossed

to hear the irony. "Because we are making you safe." Before Hock could speak, Manyenga said, "Has anyone harmed you here?"

Hock shook his head, unable to put the sadness he felt into words: the terror of the suspense that had crushed his spirit, the dull ache of fear that was like an illness he'd begun to live with. And everything that Manyenga said had had a price.

"How much?" Hock said.

Only then did Manyenga give him the large number, adding that the old man would need some too. He stood and squared his shoulders and waited for the money to be handed over.

25

EVELING HIS GAZE and leaning forward to squint across the clearing into the glare and the heat, in the long days he spent waiting for Aubrey to show up—or would it be some sort of response from the consulate?—he thought only of home. The nest-like comfort of it, his clean bedroom and kitchen, the armchair where he had sat, sorting through his visa application and all the paraphernalia of timetables that had led him back here. Medford now seemed as safe, as reassuring, as mute and indestructible as Malabo had once been in his imaginings. Home was solid, not only because he had nothing to fear, but because it could be trusted. Malabo existed in a web of deceits. Manyenga lied, everyone lied, hardly without pretense. They spoke a shadow language of untruth; every word could be translated into a defiant lie.

Home was iced coffee in a tall glass, crisp lettuce on a china plate, a cold bottle of beer, chilled fruit, the snap of a celery stalk, a clear glass of cool water, a ham sandwich with cheese on newbaked bread, fresh sheets, an oak tree's enveloping shade, his barefoot soles on the polished hardwood floor of his condo, the rattle of white tissue paper in a box of new shirts. The very words. But home was unattainable.

Darkness and cold now seemed to him blessings that sustained life and gave it rest. This heat was like a sickness without a remedy. He went on staring across the clearing, Zizi squatting on his right, Snowdon on his left.

As always, he was muddled in trying to remember what day it was. He guessed that a week had passed since Aubrey had gone, a week of suspense. That meant either that the message had not reached the consulate or that the consulate had shelved it. But surely they would not have ignored such a desperate plea from an American citizen. Hock guessed that Aubrey had taken the money and fled, tossing the message away. So he resolved to give up hoping, and the night of the very day he abandoned hope and tried to think of another plan—he was alone, sitting beside his sooty smoky lantern—a boy in a tattered shirt and torn pants and unlaced sneakers stepped out of the darkness like a cat and knelt and said, "*Mzungu*."

"Don't call me *mzungu*."

"*Bwerani*," the boy said—come with me—no apology. Perhaps he didn't speak English.

Hock followed as the boy had asked, leaving the lantern, walking behind the scuffing boy, through the garden, tramping among the furrowed *dimbas* of pumpkins and corn stalks, so as not to be seen, but traveling in the general direction of the road beyond the village. It was the road that led to Gala's hut, but they were walking in the opposite direction.

Ever since arriving in Malabo, he had been dictated to by the young and the ragged and the insolent. And here I am again, he thought, a big fool, fumbling after a boy on a moonlit path. The seat of the boy's trousers was torn, exposing the muffin of one skinny buttock.

"Come," the boy said again in his language.

Overwhelmed with helplessness, and without any faith, Hock had simply stopped in the cornfield. Hearing that the sounds of brushed and trampled corn stalks had ceased, the boy had turned and seen Hock, his hands on his hips, standing in the field, sighing.

"What's the point?" Hock said, not caring that the boy didn't understand. But when he sighed again and made a move to return home, the boy spoke again.

"Aubrey," he said, but in three syllables, pronouncing it to rhyme with "robbery."

"Where is he?" Hock asked in Sena.

"He has a vehicle," the boy said in Sena. But the word *garimoto* could mean anything with a motor—a car, a bus, a tractor.

Doubting, stepping slowly, he obeyed the boy, and past a row of trees, in the frosty glow of the moon, he saw a van parked at the entrance to a path just off the side road.

Even if the night had been moonless he would have seen the van, a model known as a combi, because it gleamed white, and on a side panel, inside a gold shield, was the large double-A of L'Agence Anonyme. The whole name was picked out on the rear doors. It was the only four-wheeled vehicle Hock had so far seen at Malabo—a novelty, of improbable size, and seemingly new: no dents, perhaps polished, like the powerful instrument of a dramatic rescue.

Inside, one small red light burned, went dim, and brightened again, and on closer inspection Hock could see it was a cigarette that Aubrey was puffing in the front seat.

Seeing Hock, he said, "Get in—hurry up."

The ragged boy who'd led him there stepped beside Hock and pushed at him.

"You give money," he said, his first words in English.

Hock nudged him aside and spoke to Aubrey: "We're going now?"

"Yes, yes. Come inside. We go."

The dimness of the pale moonlight exaggerated the shadows on Aubrey's face, making it skull-like, bonier, more like a mask. The glow on his dark skin and the streaky froth of his sweat on the creases of his neck were greenish.

"I can't leave everything behind." He was thinking of Zizi.

"You have your money?"

Hock had all his money—always had it, because he had ceased to trust—and with it his passport and wallet in a pouch in his fanny pack, the only safe place.

"Some money. Not all," he said, though they probably knew he was lying.

His clothes, some papers, his knife, his stick, his shaving kit, his medicine, his duffel. The snake in the basket. He could leave all of it. But Zizi: once again she was unaware she was being abandoned. Nothing he owned mattered when he realized his life was at stake, and as for Zizi—he'd do something, send her money through Gala, get her to safety, away from the dead end of Malabo.

The ragged boy had pressed himself against Hock's legs, pleading for money. Hock pushed him, and then, in a twitch of superstition, he handed over the Bic lighter he found in his pocket.

"No," the boy objected, and gestured with it, as though to hand it back.

But by then Hock was in the van, in the sudden comfort of a seat with springs, a cushion, a handle he grasped to steady himself. He was momentarily reassured. Aubrey started the engine, slipped the gearshift down, and, rocking the van across some ruts, jounced onto the road.

"Put on your headlights," Hock said.

"No lights."

"You'll drive into the creek."

"Lights are bad. The others will see us."

Aubrey drew his lips back, as if it was an effort to speak. His teeth were long, exposed almost to their roots, the gums shrunken—another revelation of the moonlight. He was nervous and sounded weary, and perhaps it was also the slow bumping progress of the vehicle in the moon-frosted darkness that made it seem that he was driving badly.

Without warning, Aubrey threw his skinny shoulders at the steering wheel and pulled the van to the side of the road. He cut the engine and rolled down his side window and listened.

"What is it?"

Saying nothing, he opened his mouth wider, as though his gaping mouth, his long bony teeth, helped him hear better. And perhaps they did, because, straining to listen, he began to nod.

"The fishermen are just now going out."

A group of young men in Malabo kept a canoe on the embankment at Marka. They sometimes set off in the middle of the night to walk the twenty miles to the riverside village so they could launch their boat before dawn, enter the channel, and be on the mainstream of the river in daylight.

"So what?"

"Moon," Aubrey said, and made a sweeping gesture with his hand.

The ruts on the dusty road had the whiteness of new ashes, and the bushes beside them were blue in the moonlight. The tree branches were iced with the same eerie light, for though the moon was a crusted disk, half in shadow, no clouds obscured it. The sky was clear, and the whole landscape glowed, seeming to lie under a coating of frost.

"They can see," Aubrey said, without moving but still breathing hard.

One of the characteristics of the Sena people that Hock had noticed was their ability to sit without stirring for long periods. It was not repose; it was an almost reptilian trait. They kept alert—watchful, anyway—like bush creatures, snakes in dead leaves, lizards on rocks, blending with their surroundings and only their eyelids flicking. Aubrey seemed to slip into this state of immobility, resting against the steering wheel, his head tilted to the side windows, his eyes on the landscape of cold lunar phosphorescence.

They were near enough to the shallow creek that ran along the right-hand side of the road to hear the gulp of frogs, the odd suck and chirp of insects, and another noise, a rattling like pebbles in a pot, which Hock knew to be the vocalizing of a certain nocturnal heron, with a fish in its throat.

Hock whispered, "Did you give my message to the Americans?"

Aubrey sniffed, an ambiguous reply that in its evasiveness Hock took for no.

"But that's what I paid you to do." Hock was still whispering, but more harshly.

"This is more better."

That was a definite no. "So you read my message," Hock said, louder now. "I gave you something simple to do, but you didn't do it."

"I am helping you," Aubrey said, and he wheezed the words so softly they were scarcely audible.

"Where'd you get this van?"

"The Agency."

Now, parked at the edge of the road, Hock felt only confusion—the uncertainty of night and the seeming indecision of Aubrey. He felt that he was about to be subjected to a greater ordeal, perhaps robbed.

He said, "Listen to me," and moved his head closer to Aubrey's.

As he did so, he got a whiff of dirt—not just sweat on old clothes but illness, the doggy odor of human decay, the stink of rotting lungs. The darkness inside the van seemed to make the odor sharper and inescapable. Hock winced and went on, "I don't have much money."

"No matter."

That answer surprised Hock. He said, "In fact, very little money."

Hock wanted to make sure he wasn't being taken away to be mugged and abandoned. But Aubrey simply nodded, accepting the fact, and faced Hock without blinking. Perhaps Aubrey didn't really care. Perhaps he was resigned to the hundred dollars Hock had given him, and the promise of a hundred more when they got to Blantyre.

"So where are you going?"

"Where you want."

"I want to go to Blantyre," Hock said. And, getting no response, "*Now.*"

"Too much moon," Aubrey said. He hitched himself close to the windshield and twisted his face to look at the sky, making a false smile from the effort, his teeth showing in his narrow face, the shadows of his sharp features turning his face into a mask. "But some clouds are coming."

Hock saw a mass of purple clouds, whitened at their edges by the moon, rising from where the river entered Mozambique, like smoke swelling upward from a bush fire. He watched the clouds advance, broadening, thinning, in the same way as smoke in still air. He found himself silently urging them on, and when the first wisps flickered past the bright moon and veiled it, lifting into shadow, Hock stamped his foot as though on the accelerator.

"Okay, let's go."

Too slowly for Hock's liking, Aubrey cocked his head again, then turned the key and started the engine. He held the wheel awkwardly, gripping it at the top with both hands, hanging on it like a new driver. Then they were moving again, bumping over ruts, brushing the tall grass at the side. Aubrey switched on the fog lights, and they showed the road ahead as bouldery and crusted with mud like a dry streambed.

Aubrey was nervous, he drove badly, and Hock thought, He's going so slow I could jump out here and walk back to Malabo. He knew this bend in the road. They were passing the bank of the shallow creek that lay just past the tall grass, where the village women washed their clothes on the flat rocks and often bathed in the seclusion of the reeds.

Then Aubrey groaned. Hock heard him above the engine that was racing, then slowing, as Aubrey thumped the gas pedal, too hard, then too softly, uncoordinated, the clumsiness of a beginner—or was he as ill as he seemed?

He was moving jerkily, accelerating over each bump, braking as he faltered forward.

"What is it?" Hock said, peering through the windshield. The dirty glass distorted the road.

"You did not give him money!" Aubrey shouted.

Up ahead, in the feeble glow of the fog lights, the ragged boy stood with Manyenga.

Behind this man and boy, spectral in the dim light, a tree lay across the road. Fresh chips that had flown from the stump littered the ground—the tree had just been chopped down—and though it was slender, it was an obstacle. There was no way around it. Manyenga, looking fierce, like an executioner, held the panga he had used on the tree, and the ragged boy from twenty minutes ago, beside him, scowling.

"Back up," Hock said.

"Cannot." Aubrey had slowed the van to a crawl.

"It's not my fault."

"It is being your fault one hundred percent," Aubrey said hoarsely. "You sent the boy away with nothing."

"Why didn't you give him something?"

"You are the *mzungu*."

"So what?"

"You are the money!"

But by then Manyenga was at Hock's side of the van. He snatched the door open. He was in shadow now, but Hock could smell his strong odor—a whiff of anger, the sweaty effort of hacking down the tree, his body reeking of hostility.

Manyenga spoke rapidly in Sena to Aubrey, hissing at him.

It must have been insulting, because it had a physical effect on him: Aubrey slackened his grip on the steering wheel and looked beaten.

"You want to stay with him?" Manyenga said to Hock.

Aubrey had turned his face away from the men.

"You want to die?"

"I want to go to Blantyre. I want to go home," Hock said in a whisper of fury.

Manyenga laughed so hard it brought on a coughing fit. He smacked the panga against his thigh, the big knife slapping at his dirty trousers.

"This is your home, father."

Out of pride, seeing it was hopeless, Hock got out before Manyenga ordered him to, and he walked a few steps from the van, keeping away from the light.

"*Mzungu*," the ragged boy said in two insolent grunts—*zoongoo*. Now Hock understood: because he had not tipped him, the boy had run to Manyenga's to tell him that Hock was fleeing. Malabo was only minutes from the left-hand side of the road. The boy would get something from Manyenga.

On the footpath through the tall grass, Hock picked his way in the half-dark of the cloud glow, parting the moonlit blades of grass.

"Why do you hate me?" Manyenga asked.

Hock said nothing, but Manyenga was aggrieved, or pretending to be, slashing at the grass with his bush knife.

"I have been protecting you!"

Swishing through the grass, Hock said in a small defeated voice, "I want to go."

"You are so ungrateful," Manyenga said. "And you are ignorant, too."

The night was peaceful, not cool, though the heat was softened by the darkness. Hock knew without seeing any huts that they were at the perimeter of the village—he could smell the mud huts, the dead cooking fires, the human odors, old food, dead skin, dusty faces, sour feet, the stink of latrines.

"He was kidnapping you," Manyenga said. "These people are thieves. He is a thief. I know this boy Aubrey. His father is my

262

cousin. They think they are powerful. They work for the Agency. You don't know!"

"How do you know so much?"

"That small boy told me everything. He knows the secrets. He was so angry. He said, 'The *mzungu* gave me nothing.'"

"I should have given him something. Then I'd be free."

"No, bwana. Don't you see what they were going to do with you?"

"What were they going to do with me?"

Manyenga didn't answer. Instead, he said loudly, "You are our chief, dear father."

The talk had woken the roosters, which began to crow, unseen in the darkness. Across the clearing Hock could see a flashlight, and a length of its yellow beam wagging, coming closer, maybe Zizi.

PART V

Ghost Dance

26

ALL DAY LONG in Malabo the heat sank lower, darting its tongue at him, licking at his head, swelling, growing heavier, dropping over him, creeping closer as the day ran on, encircling him. Often there was no sky at all, nothing that matched the word, the sun just a ragged patch of muted light in a threadbare blanket overfolded above him, no blue anywhere, nothing but the fuzzy canopy of gray over the colorless village. The dimmer the sun got, the hotter it was, squeezing his eyelids shut, offering dancing mirages, like sprites flitting across his closed eyes. The heaviness stifled the last of his energy, and he thought, Never mind, and decided to stay in his chair. The heat turned him into someone else, someone he hardly knew, and in a voice he hardly recognized, he called out to Zizi for a drink.

That was probably how everyone here always felt, the reason so little happened. He did not despair at the lack of effort; he was astonished that anything was accomplished at all. Another escape attempt had been a failure, and with each successive failure he became smaller, emptier, narrower, feeling slowly devoured and different. *They will eat your money and then they will eat you.*

You come with money to the poor, and they are so frenzied by hunger that all they see is the money. They never see your face, and so when the money is gone, you are revealed as mere flesh: a surprise. They don't know you. Who can you be?

Manyenga, believing he was a virtuoso, never understanding how barefaced he was, came back again for money. Hock hesitated at first, but gave him some so the man would listen to him.

"I was once a businessman," Hock said.

"That means you are lucky, like an Indian."

"That means I understand the law of diminishing returns," Hock said. "That's the only law that operates here."

Manyenga smiled and cocked his head, as though he'd heard a phrase of music. Then he folded the money into his pocket, saying, "Thank you, father."

He was mocked by the memory of the grateful man he'd been on the first day. And he saw he was changed, a different man, not bitter but sad, and more accepting. He was exhausted by his failed escapes, and the malaria from weeks back had not completely left him. A residue of tainted blood remained in his veins, bringing him down again, with symptoms like the flu: fever and muscle aches and weakness and no appetite. He felt a lassitude from the heat, from his disturbed sleep, from his being continually thwarted. He was unsteady on his feet, and the surprise to him was not that he despaired of his captivity, but that he was often in his smallness absurdly grateful to be waited on.

"Make hot water—tea," he called again to Zizi.

He had always thought of himself as strong for his age, still willing—hadn't this strength taken him back to Africa? But for the first time in his life he had an intimation of old age. These days in Malabo he felt like a fossil, like Norman Fogwill in Blantyre, or like those toothless elders—younger than he was—gabbing under the tree at Marka village by the river. He was weary, with a shaky hand, and he smiled to think of Manyenga's plot to tempt him with a teenage girl. Zizi, his only friend!

Yet he was resentful, and some days after "You are our chief, dear father," he grew sullen, knowing that this flattery was no more than an elaborate insult, Festus Manyenga trapping him with lies. He was in his hut, unable to stand the pressure of the heat on his body and the way the heated air raised the stinks of the village. He lay in his string bed, his mouth half open, breathing slowly. He was dazed, groggy from the heat.

Someone knocked, then he heard two handclaps, and Zizi's voice, her soft singsong inquiry, "*Odi?*"

She entered, padded to the side table. The mirror shook as she set the cup of tea down.

Lying on his side, too tired to move, he was studying her reflection in the mirror. He spoke to the mirror. "I want to see you."

Bewilderment showed on her pinched girl's face for a moment, which gave way to a half-smile, almost womanish, as if she was quietly pleased he was asking something of her.

"Yes, father."

"Take off your *chitenje*."

She drew in her lips and bit down on them, vexed, her face compressed in thought. Hock made a spiraling gesture with his finger that meant "unwrap."

Zizi hesitated, and then, as though remembering, became calmer, turned away, and unknotted her cloth. She draped it over the chair back and faced him again, her hands clasped below her waist for the sake of modesty.

Still watching her in the mirror, Hock said, "Dance."

She didn't move, she simply blinked at the command, *uvina*.

"Dance," he said, pleading.

It was late afternoon, the hottest time of day, the afternoon sun like a gray coal glowing in the glare of a smothering fattened cloud, slanting through the windows of the hut, the heat trapped in the motionless air under the tin roof. Zizi was perspiring, looking confused, hesitating on the uneven boards of the hut floor.

Picking up her cloth, she wrapped it loosely around her hips and left the hut, her feet thumping on the veranda planks and then on the steps as she fled.

I have lost her, Hock thought. He pressed his feverish head, tried to ease his burning eyes by massaging them with his fingers. As soon as he'd made the suggestion, he knew it had been a mistake. She was a girl, devoted to him—but a girl. And it was a great mistake because he had no other friend in Malabo. He rationalized what he'd said by telling himself that he was in despair. He had not embraced the village, but had decided to do just that, wishing to lift his spirits, by asking Zizi to dance for him, the only sweetness that Malabo was capable of offering him. But it was selfish and ill-timed. *I have gone too far.*

He heard the thump of feet on the loose planks of the veranda, the door opening and closing quickly, a gasp of effort, the small crooked bolt shot. Zizi stood in the hut, against the afternoon sun at the window. He could not see her face, only the outline of her long skinny body in silhouette, no features, no face, only darkness defined by the glare from outside.

She turned away and hung her cloth on the window, to serve as a curtain, and when she faced him again, with light on her body, Hock could see that she was white from head to toe, and looking closer, he understood. She was dusted in white flour. She had stepped outside and rolled herself naked on the mat of maize flour that she herself had pounded and spread to bleach in the sun. She had sprinkled the flour on her head, rubbed it on her face, her breasts, her whole body.

Some dancers whitened their faces with flour, some women sprinkled flour on themselves in order to achieve trance states, believing the spirit would come to inhabit this suitably decorated body. But Hock had never seen or heard of any woman this way, coated in white flour, with smooth powdered skin.

Thus arrayed, entirely whitened in flour, she danced for him. Her body was so thin it seemed incomplete, unfinished, yet her nakedness was softened and made sculptural with the dusting of white.

Untwining her fingers, lifting her hands, bending slightly, she parted her legs, then raised one knee and then the other, rolling her head—all the time looking aside, meeting his gaze only in the mirror. She planted her feet lightly, as she'd done at the feast. She had slender arms, spindly legs, and small staring breasts; her eyes gleamed with anxiety. As she danced, humming softly, stepping forward then back, raising her arms, she shook the grains of flour from her body. They dropped to the floor, and stepping in the flour, she left a pattern of dusted footprints.

Lying on his cot, glancing from the mirror to Zizi and back again, without moving, almost unable to breathe, Hock lay watching her whitened form. He ached with desire. He had never known such an agony of pleasure as this simple performance, the slow ghost dance, the powdered legs rising and falling, her head twisting on her long agile neck, the grains of flour sifting to the floor as she danced.

. . .

Someone must have seen. It took only one person to see, for everyone to know. She had been reckless: she'd gone outside and rolled on the mat of flour in front of her hut, near the mortar. She'd taken the risk to please him; in his wildest fantasies he would not have thought of her doing that, and if he had, he would not have dared to ask her. But once she had started, he could not bear the thought of her stopping. And when, after a long while, she found herself dancing in darkness, she giggled a little and snatched her wrap from the window and ran out of the hut.

He had not gone near her, only watched. The flour was a barrier—perhaps she knew that. Dusted that way, she was untouchable.

Soon afterward, the whole village seemed to know what happened. And that incident, an example of his weakness—resentment, boredom, a pang of desperation—had the effect of convincing the village that he meant to stay, that he'd found a way of being happy, that at last Zizi had devised a strategy to satisfy him, perhaps to please him. Was it considered odd in Malabo that Zizi had coated herself in flour to dance for him? Perhaps not. And it was not unknown for a woman to dance with a whitened face. To do so naked was simply taking it to the extreme. It had worked; it had cost nothing; and the *mzungu* was satisfied. They could not have known his true feeling, that he had watched her with inexpressible delight.

But they knew he was beguiled. A man with brown blotches on the whites of his eyes, a cousin to Manyenga (he said brother, but brother was a general term), came to him and said he wanted to buy a motorbike. He did not mention money; that was understood.

"And what will you do for me?" Hock said.

"Zizi will dance for you, sure." The man stared at him, a smile in his spotted eyes, and he said no more.

Hock handed him some money, saying, "But I want a ride on your bike to the boma."

"I will give you, father."

Hock was ashamed. He wondered if money alone was sufficient atonement for his lapse of judgment. But he also knew it was a setup. And he longed for Zizi to perform her ghost dance again, but secretly, so that no one would see.

Manyenga visited after that. Hock told him of the man who claimed to be his brother.

"He will eat the money. He will drink the money," Manyenga said. And then he asked for another loan.

They knew how much he had. They'd stolen some; they could take the rest at any time.

But as a way of jeering at him, Hock said, "Remember the law of diminishing returns?"

The day of Manyenga's visit, Hock set off across the compound with Zizi and Snowdon. He heard the warning whistle, and ignoring it, still walking, the whistle became more insistent, drowning out all other sounds, even the shrillness of the birds. Some of the older boys followed him, keeping just behind him. Hock walked in an almost stately way, holding a basket to his chest. It was the basket in which he kept his money with the snake.

At the creek bank, he stooped and released the snake onto the hot sand, but before the snake could gather itself and slip away, Hock pinned it with a forked stick and let it thrash, whipping a pattern into the swale of sand with its thickened body. The village saw him bearing the empty basket from the creek and across the clearing to his hut, Zizi and the dwarf following him in a shuffling procession. The snake, a puff adder, was not especially venomous, but to Malabo it was deadly. They would know it was safe to steal from him again, and when the money was gone they'd release him.

After that, they didn't whistle in the same way after he left his hut—it wasn't the rising note of urgency that became shriller; it was a softer note, like birdsong, just a signaling tweet. And he knew why.

He walked to the ruined school, looked in on the orphan boys in their lair at the old school office. He went to the clinic and the creek bank, or to the graveyard near the mango tree, where no one ever went because of the *azimu*, the malicious spirits of the dead, that were invisibly twisted in the air there—Zizi and the dwarf hung back, crouching at a distance, as he sat in the shade of the tree, unapproachable, among the tumbled piles of burial stones.

And whenever he returned to his hut, almost without fail some money was missing from the basket where he'd kept the snake.

During this week—the week of the separate raids on his stash of money—he fell ill again. This time it came quickly, wrenching him sideways. It hit him as he was walking back from the ruined school, first a dizziness, then an aching throat and pain behind his eyes, a soreness in his limp muscles, and an urgent thirst.

He wondered whether it was the return of his malaria, or dehydration. He sat down on the bare ground and pressed his eyes. He could not walk any farther. He called for water, though he knew he might be past the point of being able to absorb any liquid.

"Water with salt," he murmured to Zizi, and remembered *mchere*. But she smiled at the word and seemed too bewildered to move. "And sugar."

Women carrying babies in cloth slings on their way home from hoeing weeds in the pumpkin fields stopped and watched him, more out of curiosity than pity, as he clutched his head.

"*Mzungu,*" he heard them whisper. And, "Sick."

What happened to "chief"? They surrounded him as they would have a dog in distress, or any dying creature, and therefore a diversion and not a threat.

Snowdon was near him. Hock saw him from between his numbed fingers, creeping close.

"Water," Hock said, and repeated it in Sena.

The dwarf scuttled away on his wounded feet, and was soon back, approaching Hock with an enamel cup. But leaning over, he stumbled and lost it. The women laughed and clapped, excited by the spectacle, the slumped man, the patch of dampened dust, the dirty cup, the dwarf on his knees.

Snowdon retrieved the cup and gave it to Hock. Even though the cup was empty, the dark dust clinging to its rim, in a lunge of desperation Hock gripped it as if for balance. He held it to his face and licked at it and tasted grit. And the women screeched again.

Encouraged by the laughter, the dwarf snatched the cup from him. The women laughed so loudly that more people came to see—the orphan boys, some men kicking through the dust with their T-shirts hiked up to the top of their heads to keep off the sun.

Hock was surrounded by the whole village, it seemed. But only the dwarf dared to come near him.

"Fee-dee-dom," the dwarf cried out, and the women laughed.

Zizi tried to protect Hock, scolding the dwarf, but the women shouted her down. One woman pushed her aside, and the dwarf poked Hock with his own walking stick. Hock was helpless to resist, and when he looked up the dwarf was drooling through his broken teeth, with a bruised eager face, rushing at him wild-eyed.

Although Hock was enfeebled, struggling to sit upright, the dwarf seemed reluctant to touch him. But he threw pebbles at him, and he mock-charged him. He grunted—he used no language, only low notes bubbling from his snotty nose. But when Hock tumbled into the dust, and a cry went up, the dwarf began kicking him, straining with snuffling grunts, to the rejoicing of the crowd.

Hock's tongue was so swollen when he woke, he could barely breathe. He was still clothed, on his string bed in the hut.

"Chief."

They must have seen his eyes flutter. Without moving, he saw two figures backlit at the window, big and small. One of them was speaking.

"*Mfumu.*" It was Manyenga, murmuring the word for chief.

The smaller figure was Zizi, creeping toward him with the same sort of enamel cup that the dwarf had offered him. Hock raised himself and drank, expecting water, but it was thick and salty—soup—and as he lapped at it he sensed it easing his throat, seeping into his flesh, his body greedy for the salty liquid.

"More," he pleaded when he'd finished.

Manyenga ordered the girl to fetch more soup, and lemon water mixed with sugar and salt. When she was gone, Manyenga spoke again, and though Hock could not tell whether the man was speaking English or Sena, the word "chief" was repeated.

With more of the soup, Zizi kneeling, ready to receive the empty cup, Hock was able to sit up in the string bed, propped against the woven back wall of the hut. Manyenga was standing with his back to the light, but even so, Hock knew that the man was smiling, and something in his posture said that he was relieved to see Hock's strength returning.

But that was just a fleeting moment. After another drink Hock sank back, twisted on the string bed, his mouth open. Just before he slipped into another doze, he heard Manyenga speak again, and became aware from a rustling of voices that a throng of people had gathered outside the hut.

"*Mfumu yayikulu,*" Manyenga was saying in a voice that sounded awestruck and almost fearful. "Great chief."

In the morning Hock sat up with a clearer head and felt well enough to walk, shuffling like an old man. Zizi knelt on the veranda. The dwarf crouched in his usual place, with a torpid smile that showed his cracked teeth.

"Bring me some food," Hock said.

Zizi ran to her hut, fed her smoldering fire, and began to prepare a meal, with a clatter of tin pots.

Hock went to the basket that he'd shoved under his bed. He didn't stoop over—it made him dizzy to move his head. He kicked the basket, and he knew before it tipped over that all the envelopes of money were gone. Seeing the empty basket, he laughed. His laughter must have made an eerie sound, because when he turned toward the doorway, the dwarf rolled sideways through it, then stood and tottered away.

Zizi brought a dish of porridge and some bananas and a cup of milky tea. As she set them down on the table, Hock reached over and held her hand. It was scaly, the skin almost snake-like, slippery, her fingertips hardened from work, the whole hand toughened and yet slender and small. She moved closer, biting her sucked-in lips. He saw mingled pity and gladness in her eyes.

"Dance," he whispered.

Her giggling made him release her. Snowdon clapped his hands against his face, as though mimicking a shocked schoolgirl, scandalized by what he was seeing.

The spell of dehydration had slowed him and made him watchful. For the rest of the day he sat in the shade of his veranda, moving only to slap at flies. As the sun dropped to the level of the trees at the edge of the clearing, he broke a branch from the tree that overhung his hut and made himself a stick.

Followed by Zizi and the dwarf, he walked along the barrier of elephant grass, crossed the clearing, and pushed through the waist-high weeds to the ruined school. In a spirit of visitation, Hock looked in where he knew there were snakes. He poked at the trash piles of dead leaves and roused the black-lipped mamba. Seeing the snake whipping its tail, Zizi stepped back and the dwarf grunted through his nose. Just as darkness was gathering in the clearing, and the orphan boys were kicking a ball, he walked to the decaying baobab stump. He saw the puff adder, though it was almost indistinguishable from the flakes of old bark, thickened inside a widened cleft of the wood.

He was studying the adder when Manyenga appeared, but warily, keeping his distance, because he understood that Hock, staring hard at something he could not see, was probably looking at a snake, and very likely the snake was speaking in its own wicked way to him.

"I've been expecting you," Hock said.

"Chief," Manyenga said with a head-shake of respect.

"The money, it's all gone," Hock said.

"But we are so poor. What can we do?"

"Maybe you'll have to take me to Blantyre so I can get some more."

Now the man was uncertain, clumsy in his excessive politeness, eager to please but confused by Hock's suggestion. He turned and called out in Sena, "Kill a chicken for the chief!"

The orphan boys scattered. And Zizi and the dwarf dropped back too. Manyenga leaned toward Hock and, without pointing, but nodding in a knowing way, whispered, "She is waiting you."

Hock pretended not to hear. Feeling fragile, he squatted near the stump, and as he did the snake stirred. Manyenga stepped back.

"Please, father. Whatever you want."

Although it was dusk, there was enough light from the reddened sky for Hock to see, at the far edge of the clearing, some women holding babies, and some old men, the orphan boys, and girls with firewood on their heads. He was reminded of the crowd that had encouraged the dwarf to mock him when he'd fainted. But this was different. He had not seen them like this since first arriving back in Malabo and being welcomed with apprehension. In his days of illness and being thwarted by them, he had almost forgotten how fearful they'd been. He smiled as he had that first day. Perhaps they were afraid again.

He waited in his hut, the lantern resting on the floor so that the light would be subdued. With his heart pounding, anxious, ashamed, unable to stop himself, he went eagerly to the small window. The suspense of knowing she was coming to him sharpened his pleasure. He saw Zizi hurrying from the courtyard of her small hut. When he heard her bare feet on the wood planks of his veranda he was almost breathless with expectation.

And then she entered, shot the loose bolt, flung up her cloth, and draped it over the window. Her sighing had the earnestness of sensuality. She stood before him, her naked body whitened with the fine dust of flour that adhered to her sweat-dampened skin, like a tall girl drawn in chalk.

Again Hock remembered her reply when he had asked her teasingly what it was that the men in the darkness want.

They want what all men want, she had said, and the memory shamed him. She was wiser than he, and now she looked at him, standing still, the only movement in her body the dark light in her eyes, her eyelashes dusted white.

Then she curtseyed with a formality that moved him, as though beginning not a village dance but a ballet, and this time she was calmer, her dance more graceful and measured than before.

She came to life in the dance, and was transformed, no longer the village girl with the kettle and the bowl of porridge, but a woman the shape of slender, spirit-like scissors, suspended in air, the suggestion of a trance in her whitened face and wild eyes.

The light of the lantern brightened the dusting of flour and gave her a new body, with subtle curves and shadows. After a series of small jumping and turning steps, she stood tall, rising on the balls of her feet, presenting herself to him. She marked out a semicircle on the floor with her whitened pointed foot, then slid her foot along the floor with her front knee bent, performed a full knee bend, with her heels off the floor, and kept her slender arms upraised, and in the course of the soundless dance shook the flour from her body and let the powder sift to the floorboards of the hut, each dance step a white footprint.

27

OCK HAD ONCE tried to imagine a day like this, but hadn't been able to understand how to achieve it. And now the day had arrived: no money in the snake basket, none in his wallet, his pockets empty. He was unburdened. He saw that arriving in Malabo with a bag of money had been his first, and most grievous, mistake; handing the money out, another. Long ago, as a teacher, he'd had nothing, and was invisible for having nothing. He should have come this time with nothing—nothing to steal, nothing to tempt or distract them, as a visiting bystander, detached, on the periphery where foreigners belonged, with only the clothes he stood up in and a ticket home. But he had become involved, entangled, and trapped.

Zizi's dancing, dusted in flour, was his only pleasure, but a chaste one—the powder was like armor. He didn't dare touch her. As for the rest, he was finished, nothing else could happen. The truth was stark, the village inert, encrusted, crumbled under a cloudy sun. Rain never fell. He felt skinny, picked clean, as naked and hungry and poor as anyone in Malabo. Nothing left—he had no money, and most of his spare clothes were gone, including his belt, which he needed now that he'd lost so much weight.

Snowdon lingered, drooled eagerly, and scratched his dirty palm with his stubby fingers, his way of asking for money. For a few coins he bought stalks of sugar cane, which he chewed and spat out, sucking the sweetness from the pith.

"Nothing," Hock said, and was relieved.

Zizi never asked for money, but she represented his one joy, his strength, was his only friend. The village women expected some kwacha notes when they presented him with bananas or pumpkins. One of the women had helped Zizi with his laundry, bringing it in a stack that Zizi scorched to kill the putzi fly eggs embedded in the weave. But there was little laundry these days, because his clothes had been stolen too, and he owned no more than a thickness of threadbare cloth. The sight of it made him sad.

"Father," the laundry woman said, setting down a folded shirt and a tattered T-shirt she'd wheedled from Zizi, in the hope of making money. She held a baby in a sling to her side.

"I have no money," Hock said. He took a wild delight in declaring it.

The woman whined a little and gestured to the baby.

"All gone!" Hock said.

The woman implored him. Flies settled on the baby's face and sucked at the edges of its eyelids and its prim lips.

"Now I'm like you," he said.

Just like them, he was a wisp of diminishing humanity, with nothing in his pockets—hardly had pockets!—and he felt a lightness because of it. With no money he was insubstantial and beneath notice. As soon as everyone knew he had nothing, they would stop asking him for money, would stop talking to him altogether, probably. Yet tugging at this lightness was another sensation, of weight, his poverty like an anchor. He couldn't move or go anywhere; he had no bargaining power. He was anchored by an absence of money, not just immovable but sitting and slipping lower.

More than ever they called him chief and great minister and father. The women were calmer and less competitive than the men. They wanted food for their children, or a tin pot. The men wanted motorbikes, or bus fare, or had a scheme for selling fish or obtaining contraband from Mozambique on the river. They asked for large amounts, and they resented the fact that Hock had no money left. They believed he was lying. And so they kept poking around his house when he was out walking. He encouraged them to do this by taking long conspicuous hikes, leaving his front door ajar.

"They went inside again," Zizi would say.

But he wanted them to know that he had nothing left. And he

hoped they would see that they themselves had had a share in reducing him to this. They had taken all his money, and everything of value. And they were no better off.

They were not diabolical; they were desperate. But desperation made them cruel and casual.

"*Mzungu,*" a man named Gilbert said, to get his attention. Some mischievous men called him "white man" to his face. No one used his name. It was as though when he lost all his money, he lost his name, too.

Gilbert said, "The woman Gala wants to talk to you." And then, becoming even more familiar, the man said, "I am needing a scooter."

Many of them believed he still had money, and some of those people called him *mzungu*, not father. Gala would never have called him that. She might have called him Ellis, since she knew him by that name, but they would have heard it as "Alice."

Zizi walked with him under the mopane trees and through the thorn bushes on the hot path to Gala's hut. He guessed that the old woman had divined that Zizi's relationship with him had changed. Not that it was explicitly sexual: there was something pure and resolute in Zizi's virginal face and her frowning mouth and the way she stood and moved. But Gala would have known—either from village whispers or a guess—that he had seen Zizi naked, dusted with white flour, and had possessed her with his gaze, which was true. It was not a question of his daring to go further with her; he had no right. As for the dancing, there was nothing scandalous in that, since she wasn't truly naked: the flour was her costume, her adornment.

Walking in front of him, Zizi cleared the way, only hesitating at the point where, a month or so before, he had seen the snake rattling through the clutter of dry leaves. He watched her body as she pushed the branches aside, and he thought: Once you have seen someone lovely naked, she is never anything but naked for you, no matter how she is dressed. She was sinuous on the path, her velvety skin glowing, her shaven head beaded with sweat, her neck shining.

Gala was waiting for them. Someone must have seen them on the path and told her they were on their way. Yet she looked impassive, monumental in her bulk, her eyes slanted in her fleshy face.

Hock clapped his hands and called out, "*Odi, odi.*"

The old woman was sitting in the same chair as before, on her veranda, on the planks worn smooth by bare feet, in the same posture as when he had left her—how long ago? And this time, too, she tried to heave herself out of the creaking chair to greet him. To spare her—he could see her effort, the deliberate stages of her hoisting herself, her struggling arms, planting her feet—he mounted the steps quickly and took her hands, and she laughed in helpless apology.

"Come, sit," she said to Hock, and to the woman Zizi had called Auntie, "Bring tea. Go help them, Zizi."

Smiling, patting her great fleshy face with a damp cloth, she shooed the children away.

As with all visits to huts like this, Hock sensed a brimming odor of human sweat, damp clothes, dirty feet, hot bodies; a rippling curtain of stink that was sharpest now in the heat of the day.

"Yes, go help," Gala said to the last of the children, speaking as always in a mixture of Sena and English.

When they were alone, in the shade of the veranda, she lost her smile. It vanished into her plump smooth face and she became darker, heavier, and spoke in a growl.

"You did not heed me."

He smiled at the word. Heed, reckoning, victuals—she was of the generation that used pulpit words.

"Even now you are not attending."

Another of those words. He said, "I am—I always listen to you."

"Ellis, my friend. One month ago I told you my opinion. It was a mistake for you to come here. Of course, I am glad for selfish reasons. Because the man I liked so well—I can even say loved—showed himself to be a righteous person. But you are not listening."

The word "loved" was still glittering in his head.

He said, "Then I'm glad I came."

"It should have been a holiday. But you lingered," Gala said. "Sometimes the tourists and the aid workers visit here. They go to the Mwabvi park at the boma side to look at wild animals. Or they get lost here and ask directions. They spend some minutes and then they go away and we never see them again. That is what you should have done."

"I think you mentioned that."

"Indeed I did. But my words fell on deaf ears. You know we say *muthu ukulu* and so forth—a big head gets a knock."

Her face was leathery, bruised by age and the harsh sun, with freckled cheeks, her eyes staring out of dark sunken skin. He could see her concern, and it alarmed him. Her proverb made her seem obtuse and simple-minded.

"I tried to get away," he said. "I went downriver, almost to Morrumbala, and I was abandoned."

"You fetched up at the children's village."

"The Place of the Thrown-Aways, they called it. How do you know that?"

"We have no secrets here. We know that Festus Manyenga brought you back. We know the Agency rejected you. We know those boys that call themselves 'the brothers.'"

"I didn't like the Agency," Hock said. "I don't trust those people."

"They could have arranged safe passage for you. They have planes. They have vehicles."

"I thought that young man Aubrey might help."

"We know about him. He is sick."

"I thought so. But he doesn't look too bad."

"He is taking the drug, like some others. They get it from the Agency. It is so dear, only a few people have it. It makes them stronger. It makes them dangerous."

He guessed she was talking about the anti-retroviral drug that he had read about, but Gala would not have known those words. He said, "Aubrey said he was taking me to Blantyre. Manyenga had a different story. I don't know what the truth is."

"This looks such a simple place. But no, everyone lies, so you can't know it at all. The truth is absent here."

"Why do people lie?"

"Because they have been taught to lie. It works for them better than the truth. And they're hungry. If you're hungry, you will do anything, you will agree to anything, you will say anything. And they're lazy. This is a terrible place. Why are you smiling?"

Hock said, "When we were both young, you said, 'This is my home. This is my life. This is my country. We can make it better.'"

She laughed, but bitterly, and said, "If I were young again, I would say, 'Take me far away from here.'"

"Where to?"

"Anywhere at all." She saw that Zizi was pouring hot water from the kettle into a teapot. "I worry about her. She is still a *namwali*. Still a maiden."

"Maiden" was another pulpit word, and it suited the thin girl, canted over and delicately filling the teapot. Her posture, so precise and poised, seemed proof of her innocence.

"But she's strong," Hock said.

"I was strong once, but look at me," Gala said. She laughed, and it was true—she looked ruined, puffy-faced, her sad eyes glassy with fatigue, her ankles swollen. "And she is alone."

"She's been looking after me."

"Yes, I know that," Gala said.

What did she know? Perhaps the talk of Zizi dancing naked, and the detail that she rolled herself in flour and bewitched him, ghost-dancing like a priestess. Hock was abashed, felt he ought to explain, but did not know how to begin. He said, "Please don't worry about her."

"I am worried about you. Those people—Festus, Aubrey, the others. They are not to be trusted."

He said, frowning at the absurdity of it, "I have no money left. I have nothing."

"Then you are in greater danger."

"I want to get away," Hock said. "I don't know how."

"You must find a way. Zizi can help." Gala saw Zizi and the other woman approaching the veranda with the tea things on tin trays—a plate of misshapen cakes, the teapot, the chipped cups, the small punctured can of evaporated milk, the sugar bowl. Before they were within earshot, Gala said, "This was a safe place once. Now it is so dangerous." As the women mounted the steps, she said, "Malawi tea. From Mlanje Mountain! Please help yourself, my friend."

They sat drinking tea, talking of the weather, how because the rain had stayed away, the roads had deteriorated. And how to fix them?

"A swing needs to be pushed," Gala said, and tapped Hock's arm to get his attention. "It means you can't do anything alone."

Zizi followed him home, down the path, in silence.

At the hut, she hung her head—politeness, averting her eyes—and said softly in Sena, "Do you want me to dance?"

But the visit to Gala had made him self-conscious, apprehensive, and he said no.

What had Gala heard? Obviously something, because the next day, around noon, a small boy appeared at Hock's hut. Zizi had intercepted him and explained that the boy was carrying a message from Manyenga, who wanted to see him for dinner.

"I'm not hungry," Hock said.

But that was no excuse. Food that was offered had to be accepted, even if the person had already eaten.

"Some boys have come," Zizi said.

"Which boys?"

"They are from the other side," she said, meaning the Mozambique border.

"How do you know?"

"People talk."

People talked, but not to him, and that was the worst of it, that he lived in the village and all the while life continued apart from him. The talk did not reach him, or if it did, he did not understand. He was not only a *mzungu,* but a ghost, an ignorant ghost, existing outside of everything, merely watching, seeing only the surface of things, listening but missing most of what was said, not understanding the shouts or the drumbeats. At other times he was like a pet cringing in the doorway, a creature they kept to be stroked and murmured to, another species, captive and dumb and looking for a smile. He had been reduced to that. And the money was gone, so what was he worth?

Later in the afternoon, nearing Manyenga's compound, he recognized the boys at once—the brothers, in their sunglasses, the one with the cap lettered *Dynamo Dresden.* And as before, he was struck by how American they looked in their T-shirts, sneakers, and shorts, not the castoff clothes distributed by a charity like the Agency, but new clothes that gave the boys a street style Hock recognized from Medford. They were the sweatshop products that had undone his business. Who would wear a button-down shirt and flannel slacks and a blazer if he could get away with a Chinese T-shirt and Chinese sneakers? He looked resentfully at the boys, thinking, China clothes the whole world!

"Father," Manyenga called out, and failing to get his attention, he shouted, "Chief!"

But Hock was still watching the three boys, who sat picking at food on the plates that had been set out on the mat. The boy with the cap was sitting on a chair near Manyenga, the others squatting at the mat's edge.

Another rule was that no one ate until the chief took the first bite, and when the chief appeared, or an elder, the younger members at the meal stood up, turned aside, eyes down, or knelt to show respect.

None of this. They were indifferent, as when Hock had seen them downriver at their makeshift village, as reckless as when they'd led Hock to the football field for the arrival of the Agency helicopter and the celebrities—the food drop. They had all started to eat, they chewed, they licked their fingers, they didn't smile, and when they glanced at Hock it was in an appraising way, as you would look at merchandise in a market stall.

Hock saw that Zizi had not followed him, and guessing that she was back at the hut, he was confused, reluctant to meet these boys again. In their village they had taken no interest in him, even when he'd been starving. He recalled the ease with which they had handled the money he'd given them, fingering it expertly. Now they were in Malabo and talking with Manyenga, who had rescued him from them at the field, amid their scavenging, and had warned him against them. They had seemed like enemies then, and Manyenga a friend to him, but now he couldn't tell the difference. He had no money, he had no friends. What did it matter whether he paid his respects to Manyenga by dining with him and these boys? Life went backward here, and he was more the stranger now than before.

"Eat!" Manyenga cried out, seeing Hock turn and, bent over, limp away. "Eat!"

He spoke as though to an obstinate animal, or a child, or a prisoner, and Hock realized that to them he was all three.

So he returned to his hut, and as an hour or so of daylight remained and it was too hot in the slanting sun to go inside, he lay on a mat on his veranda and shut his eyes and pitied himself for being there, at the mercy of the village, and having to endure the contempt of Manyenga's having a meal with the three boys dressed as rappers. How had they gotten here from that far-off village? Well, he had made it here from there.

Then he slept, the sudden honking, sweating, late-afternoon slumber brought on by heat and despair.

He dreamed of being in a dusty sunlit room, hearing voices. And then he knew he wasn't dreaming—the voices were those of the boys, talking about him to Manyenga, murmuring.

"He is sick."

"Not sick, my friend. He is strong."

"Old, too"—another voice.

"White men can be old and still have heart."

The first words had woken him, but instead of sitting up he remained still, crumpled on the mat, his eyes closed, listening to the mutters.

It was as if they were haggling over him, Manyenga dealing with the boys—he was the salesman, they the reluctant buyers.

"And he can be insolent."

The word was *chipongwe;* it was how he had seen them.

"You are strong. You have connections. You can handle him."

"I think he is listening."

"To what? You are not saying anything."

"He is older than my father."

"Your father is dead."

"That is what I mean."

Some weeks before, when he'd had his fever, he had lain in his hut and heard voices like this. And he had grown sad, unable to move, feeling chills and a skull-cracking headache, and he had been an eavesdropping wraith.

It was like that now, but worse, and the scene that came to

mind was the Somerville woman—what was her name?—lying in her bed with the python beside her. That snake had flattened itself and Hock grew alarmed, knowing that it was preparing to flex its jaws and swallow her.

When they fell silent he opened his eyes and rolled over to face them. He saw them walking away, and Zizi beside him, bug-eyed.

He spoke what he was thinking: "They want to eat me."

"Not eat. But to buy you." Zizi took a long breath. "The big man Festus is wanting money for you."

Exhausted, Hock slept well that night, and was alarmed only when he woke up in daylight and remembered what had happened the evening before, and was appalled.

Zizi was standing beside the bed, looking ghostly against the mosquito net. She said, "They are still here in the village, those boys."

He saw that she was holding a kettle.

"Put the kettle down." She set it down with a clank. "Come here." He parted the mosquito net and she crept in, ducking the curtain of net. She lay on the cot, but held herself compactly, facing away. "Don't worry," he said. "I just want to talk."

28

ANYTHING THAT HAPPENED at night was so muffled and menacing that to the villagers nothing happened at night. In the Lower River, darkness fell in a blinding way, a swift and sudden collapse of light, and in the morning the village was as it had been left at sundown—that overturned bucket moistened with dew, the pucker of footprints so deep in the gray dampened sand they could have been fossils, the scattered and sucked mouthfuls of sugar cane fibers and the bitten stalk, the bunting of torn shirts hanging limp on a line, the blackening stem of bananas twisted on a rusted coathanger on a tree branch, out of the reach of rats and hyenas. Only the Nyau ceremony, a ritual in darkness, was allowable at night, but the last Nyau had been danced long ago, when the presiding image had been Hock's own face—the long nose, the scraps of white rags and plastic—and he had believed that he'd been granted power. But time had shown his power to be no more potent than the rags.

For weeks he believed a miracle might happen. He imagined it this way, as in a movie. On a tray on a desk in the American consulate in Blantyre was an accumulating stack of letters from Roy Junkins, sent from Medford. And a voice: *That's odd. Another one. This guy Ellis Hock doesn't pick up his mail. Maybe we should go down there and see if everything's okay.* The concerned consul would act quickly. Hock extended this scene into a hopeful drama of rescue, the sleek consular vehicle drawing into Malabo and an American in a suit greeting him, then bearing him away.

Hock would halt the vehicle, saying, "There's someone else," and call to Zizi.

He played the scene in his head, to console himself, but it only made him sadder.

He was now so far from that hope he'd begun to think that he might never leave, that he would go on suffering here as he had for more than two months, living on lumpy steamed *nsima*, dried fish, boiled slimy greens, bread and tea, a mango, a wedge of pumpkin, groundnuts seethed in their shells. That nothing would change. Already he knew what it was like to be elderly, to be feeble, to fall ill, to walk with difficulty and hate the sun. He'd lose his teeth like Norman Fogwill. In his recurring mood of bitter pettiness he remembered how in the hour or more that he had spent with Fogwill, the man hadn't stirred or been particularly friendly, and when Hock had risen to leave, Fogwill had remained in his chair.

At one time he might have been strong enough to make a dash to the boma. In the first few weeks he'd felt up to it, but procrastinated in the African way. He might have been lucky. But he had weakened, and declined. He'd come to Malabo a healthy man, active for his age, with the idea of fixing the school and being capable of putting in a day's work at the building. He'd felt optimistic, and he imagined leaving a lump sum with someone like Manyenga for the upkeep of the school, perhaps depositing money in the bank at the boma, the Malabo account.

Too late. His health was gone, and he could tell almost to the day when he'd realized he was too old. Malabo had made him an old man, had tipped him into near senility. He needed those long nights, that silence, that darkness, not just to be restored by sleep but for the illusion that he was free to dream—good dreams, of home and friends and health. He forgave everyone at home, forgave Deena and Chicky. They had not hurt him. Deena had freed him, and Chicky had merely turned her back on him. But when he woke in his hut in Malabo in the monotonous heat of the morning, he was reminded that he was a prisoner.

The boys—the brothers, as they called themselves—did not leave the village, as he assumed they might. They remained, sitting in the shady area of the courtyard at Manyenga's compound, and Hock knew they could do that only with Manyenga's permission. He saw them chatting with Manyenga during the day, as he himself had once done, believing he was a friend. He saw them being brought black kettles of hot water, and in the evening he saw them seated on mats near Manyenga's cooking fire, where he had once sat as an honored guest. They had displaced him, these boys in sunglasses, and he had the sense that they were hovering, waiting—for what?

The tolerance in Malabo for any outsider lasted just a matter of days. Then the guest had to do some work, or leave. Hock saw the boys lingering and, it seemed, running up a debt. Manyenga was too shrewd to endure these boys eating his food and drinking his tea and crowding him, unless something else was happening—a protracted negotiation, Hock guessed, like all the talk over the months it took to arrive at an acceptable bride price.

Strangers in a village usually caused a buzz of activity—speculation, giggling, whispers. But the presence of these boys created a greater silence, a solemn watchfulness; the villagers were more cautious, less talkative, brisker in their walk. And they avoided Hock in the way they avoided anyone with an illness. The days were hotter, the cicadas louder.

"Our friends are still here," he said to Gilbert, who had called him *mzungu* and asked him for money. Gilbert was a fisherman, pushing his bike through the deep sand at the edge of Malabo, setting off for a riverside village near the boma. It would take him the whole day to ride those thirty-odd miles; he'd launch his canoe tomorrow morning.

Gilbert gazed at him with a blank deaf stare. Irony was lost on him. What friends?

"Those boys from the bush," Hock said, "staying with Festus."

"I am not knowing," Gilbert said in English.

When anyone spoke English to him, it was a way of warning him that the conversation would be brief, vague, and probably untruthful.

No one now asked Hock for money, or for anything. Women walked past his hut without looking at him. Only children took an interest, but it was a form of play; nothing frightened them. And when he strolled through the village in the cooler early evening, searching for snakes at the edge of the marsh or in the low-lying *dimbas,* no one, not even children, acknowledged him. He seemed to drift like a ghost, as though he had no substance.

He was real only to Zizi. She brought him food, cleaned what clothing was left, crouched near him on his veranda, and sometimes in secret she danced for him, his only joy. The paradox of a naked girl, entirely dusted with flour, dancing slowly by lantern light in the suffocating hut, his greatest reality and his only hope.

"Why do you dance for me?" he asked.

"I dance because it makes you happy."

Zizi brought him news of the brothers: they still lived at Manyenga's compound. "Still talking." Naturally suspicious, full of warnings at the best of times, she told Hock that they had designs on him.

"Gala told you this?"

"I can see them," she said.

"They pay no attention to me at all."

"That means they are always thinking about you," she said. "They are proud."

He said, "If I could bring a message to the boma—post a letter—my friends in Blantyre would help me."

Zizi stared with widened eyes, swallowed a little, giving herself dimples, then said, "I can do it."

"They'd see you."

"Not at night."

The very word "night" was like a curse. He said, "No one goes out at night. There are animals in the night. It's not safe."

He could see he was worrying her. He'd thought of sending her, but he knew it was too risky; and anyway, she couldn't walk that distance. He told her that.

"*Njinga,*" she said. The jingle of a bicycle bell was the word for bike.

"You don't have a bike."

"But my friend," she said, and swallowed again, "is having."

He was past the point of allowing his hopes to be raised with any scheme. Nothing had worked. He was almost resigned to living here, to decaying here, like Gala. To dying here.

Yet in the long mute smothering hours of the night after that talk with Zizi, he kept himself awake in the dark, lying on his back, composing the letter in his head.

To the American consul, he began, murmuring under his mosquito net. *This is an urgent appeal for your help. I am being held against my will in the village of Malabo on the Lower River, Nsanje District. There is no phone here or I would call. I can't get to the boma. I am sending this message to you with the help of a trusted villager who is at considerable risk, in the hope it will reach you safely.*

I have no money left. It has all been taken from me. I have no possessions to speak of, other than a change of clothes and a few other items. I came here in the belief that I might be useful to these people. That was a mistake.

I have made several attempts to escape, but each time I failed, and this has hardened the villagers against me.

I am not well, having suffered several bouts of fever, and the effects still linger. My health is gone and I am in fear of my life. I have no allies here other than the individual who is posting this letter. My medicine is used up.

The village of Malabo is known to you. I think someone came here from your consulate to deliver school supplies for me and was told I was away. That was a lie. I was seriously ill.

Please come at once. I will pay all expenses. I am absolutely desperate, and I'm afraid that if I am not rescued soon I will be taken from here, perhaps downriver into Mozambique, and kept as a hostage, for ransom. In that case, someone will have to search for me.

I am not sure . . .

But there he stopped, near tears, too sad to continue, fear making him wakeful, his misery keeping him silent.

In the morning he sat and wrote the message on a sheet of paper torn from a copybook, one of the many copybooks he'd bought for the school that had lain unused. He printed in block capitals, taking his time. When he was done, he reread it and began to cry, holding his hand over his mouth to stifle his sobs.

His own letter terrified him, as weeks before, at the Agency compound, he'd seen his face in the polished side of the water tank and been stricken by the sight of the defeated eyes and hollow cheeks of the old man staring back at him.

Until now, he had not put his plight into words, and so he had survived, even managed to convince himself that there was a way out. The days had passed with little to remember except for Zizi's kindnesses. He thought, Something will happen, someone will help. He avoided the mirror in his hut, but his letter was a mirror of his feelings, and the very sight of it frightened him. His cheeks were dirty with tears.

He had not read anything, nor written anything in his journal, for over a month, since heading downriver with Simon and the paddlers. Something about his writing, the order of his sentences, his voice on the page, reminded him of his other life, the world he had left; and seeing his plea, the pressure of his inky pen point, the helpless words, left him in despair.

He folded the letter and sealed it in an envelope, not intending to send it but so that he wouldn't have to look at it. The envelope was dusty, one of several left over from the bank, with melancholy smudges of finger marks on the flap.

Zizi saw the envelope but did not mention mailing the letter. She knew the risks of going out at night alone. Hock could not find a way of phrasing the request, so the question remained unasked.

In the days that followed Zizi hovered around the hut, alerting Hock to the movements of the boys. A week after their arrival they were still at Manyenga's.

"They want money," Hock said.

"Or maybe they are waiting for a vehicle."

Yes, that made sense. They lived a three-day walk away, through the bush, around the marsh, along the riverbank. Even if they left in a canoe from Marka, it was a two-day downriver trip to their village.

"What vehicle?" he asked.

"The Agency helps them. Maybe Aubrey."

Like the others, she gave the name extra syllables, *Obbery*, rhyming it with "robbery."

"He's still around?"

"He is sick."

Hock kept his distance from her until darkness fell, and then he sat near her on the veranda, not lighting the lantern. Finally he crept into the hut, leaving the door ajar so that she could follow. She never spoke. She lifted the mosquito net and slid against him in the cot, lying on her back, her hands clasped at her breast, breathing softly through her nose, and sometimes singing in her throat. She smelled of soap and dust and sweat and blossoms, familiar to him—no one had her odor. He plucked one of her hands and held it—so hard, so skinny, so scaly, like a lizard's. Her whole life was readable in that hand, all her work; it was older than her age, not a child's hand but a woman's, someone who had known hardship, much tougher than his own hand.

"Ask me," she said, as he held her hand.

Her body lay against him, without weight. She did not look at him. Her face was upturned, to the ridgepole of the hut. Hock saw that she was shy, but she was serious in her abrupt question.

In a whisper he could barely hear, needing a moment for him to translate, she said, "I will do anything."

The words, whispered that way, nearly undid him, touched him so deeply he could not speak. It was a crucial moment, one of the few in his life, when an answer was demanded of him, when everything that followed depended on what he replied. He had a choice to make. Once, Deena had said, *It's up to you, Ellis. What do you really want? Make up your mind.* And he had realized it was over, that he'd spend the rest of his life without her. Or Chicky saying, *But what about when you pass? If you remarry, your new family will get it and I won't get diddly. If I don't get it now, I'll never see it.*

He held Zizi's hand, that bony callused little claw, and thought, She is offering herself, I can have her. He had known from the busy way she hovered that she was telling him that. He had shown her that she was safe with him. A Sena woman, even a marriageable one like Zizi, was not looking for sex. Security was what mattered most, the need to be protected, to bear children who would be secure. The man could be old or young, but he needed to be strong for his wife.

Zizi was clothed beside him in the string bed, but what he saw was her dancing naked for him, dusted with white flour, in the seclusion of the room, while he lay before her, the girl lifting her skinny legs and lowering them, shaking the flour from them, her lips pressed together, her soft throat-song seeming to echo a melody in her head.

He said, "I want to send a letter."

"I can take it."

"It needs a stamp."

"I can find one."

"How will you get to the boma?"

"My friend's *njinga*."

"You can do that?"

"I can do more," she said, turning aside and rolling away from him, partly in shyness but also submitting, seeming to present her small hard body. It was a kind of appeal, her posture of compliance, but he was too sad to answer.

"Post the letter," he said. "And when you come back, when we're safe, everything will be ours—whatever you want."

"What you want," she said.

At some point in the early predawn darkness, she left. He woke to find her gone, and the envelope too. He imagined hearing the jingle of a bicycle bell, like laughter.

The activity, the stirring the next day, made him imagine that everything he'd said to Zizi, everything he'd done, lying next to her, had been seen, was known. The boys were up and about, talking louder, ranging more widely in the village. With Zizi gone, he had no ally. Even Snowdon had been lured away from him by the novelty of the three brothers in sunglasses, and the protracted bargaining with Manyenga.

They had to be talking about money. It was now over a week since they'd showed up in Malabo, and they had insinuated themselves into the life of the village, staying in one of Manyenga's many huts in the heat of the day, emerging in the late afternoon when the air was cooler, strolling away from the compound and sauntering through the village, staring at the younger girls, murmuring among themselves, seeming to pay no attention to Hock. Yet it was obvious they were closing in on him.

In defiance, Hock used these afternoon hours to go out and capture snakes. Snakes were his only strength. The adults of the village kept their distance whenever he walked with his bag and his stick. The children followed him, jumping and screeching, daring each other to go nearer.

Hock would find the fattest snake, a sleepy black mamba or a puff adder, and flourish it, allowing it to coil around his arm as he pinched behind its head. And then he returned to his hut, depositing the snake in a basket and fastening the lid.

The day after Zizi vanished with the letter, he went on a conspicuous snake hunt and found a viper. This he carried through the village to his hut, the children following, calling out, "Snake!"

Hock listened for the bicycle bell, but there was nothing, no sign of Zizi. That was the earliest she could have returned. In his heart he did not expect to be rescued; every attempt so far had failed. But he could not imagine remaining in Malabo without Zizi; he could not imagine living without her, as her guardian. Yet she was nowhere to be seen.

Another night, another early morning, another whole day of waiting. Hock walked to the edge of the village superstitiously, to the spot where, on his arrival in Malabo, he had first seen her walking slowly into the creek, lifting the cloth up her thighs as she went deeper, until she was in the water up to her waist.

Hearing rustling behind him, the swish of legs in dry embankment grass, he turned and saw Manyenga. He was smiling—always a sign of concealment for the man. The older, cap-wearing brother approached too, not smiling, looking sullen.

"Time to talk," Manyenga said.

As though not recognizing either of the men, Hock pushed past them and walked down the path and across the clearing toward his hut.

Manyenga called out, "Wait, father."

Hock kept walking, his shadow lengthening.

"You are going with those boys." Manyenga caught up with him, breathless, sucking air. "They will help you."

"How much did they pay you for me?"

"You are making a joke, father."

Hock said, "Never," as he reached his hut. He unhooked the lid of a basket on the veranda and, thrusting his hands inside, snatched two handfuls of dark vipers. Bristling with snakes, he filled his doorway, saying, "We are staying here."

29

HOCK STILL HELD the knots of squirming snakes, which glinted in the last of the daylight—greenish marsh snakes, hissing, contending, their throats widened, their wagging heads flattened in alarm. The villagers in Malabo were terrified of them, and told stories of battling the marsh snake they called *mbovi*, because it was a good swimmer, and often darted at their legs when they were bathing in the creek. But the snakes were small, harmless, they had no fangs, and perhaps that accounted for the scaly drama of their aggression.

Shaking them into their basket, Hock heard a scuffing in the courtyard, and some whining adenoidal clucking. He turned to see Snowdon, who kept his distance because of the snakes, his stubby fingers protecting his face.

"Come," he said. He never used Hock's name, or any name; he hardly ever made an intelligible sound; and so this one uttered gulp of command got Hock's attention.

Snowdon then stumbled and ran, and Hock followed him across the *dimba* of pumpkins and then to the back path. The dwarf labored ahead of him, his snorting audible, pulling his bandy legs along, working his elbows. Stumpily built, he moved as though he was pedaling a tricycle, his head and shoulders bobbing through the low bush. The branches tore at Hock's arms as he tried to part them. Snowdon ducked beneath them, hurrying onward, in the direction of Gala's compound.

The path was a streak of pale powder in the starlight. Hock had once felt daunted, standing under the glittering stars of the night sky of the Lower River. To the villagers his stargazing was proof that he was a sorcerer. None of them knew him, or cared. Malabo, a landmark in his life, had been trifled with, corrupted, then ignored, and finally forgotten, of no use to anyone. That was why, walking fast down this dusty gutter of a path in the bush, he felt he was going nowhere, that he was lost, following the dwarf, who was wheezing and tumbling forward.

Entering the smoke smell of Gala's compound, Hock saw only one lighted window at the front—the door shut, no one on the porch, Gala's chair empty. The lantern light in the room threw the figures into relief, enlarging them, turning them into the silhouettes of three people, hunched over, not moving, not speaking, the shadows as sharp as black paper cutouts.

They were praying. Hock caught some of the words, Gala leading the others in slow imploring moans.

Clapping his hands to announce himself, Hock plucked the slumping door and dragged it open. The praying stopped. The three women he'd seen through the window, looking naked in the echo of their pleading, were ranged around a mat on the floor. The only sound now was from the figure on the mat, unrecognizable, wrapped in a striped towel, lying face-up, sighing softly. The face was bruised, the head enlarged, and one of the women was bathing the raw cut flesh, patting it with a wet cloth. Big winged beetles swung in circles around the lantern light.

"My God," Gala said, dithering at the sight of Hock. She said it again. *Goad*.

But Hock was peering at the figure lying flat. It did not look like Zizi; that was not her face. But who else could it be?

One of the ceremonies mumbled in the dark—forbidden by the missionaries in Hock's time—had been the spilling of chicken blood on the head of a crudely carved foot-high idol—misshapen, foreshortened, the head the size of a coconut. The larger the carving, the more clumsily it was made, with bits of glass inserted in the eye sockets that gave it a blind, half-alive stare. And the blood wrung from the beheaded chicken was so sticky, a fuzz of pin feathers adhered to its wood. This secret fetish had no name that could be uttered aloud because, smeared with the dried blisters of blood, it was an ugly potent thing capable of repelling evil.

The blood gave it subtlety and strength, simplified its hacked angles as if with thick paint, the coated splinters and plastered-on feathers making it more artful, with an aura of power, the gleaming blood lending it the sinewy density of bruised meat.

That was what Hock saw on the floor, a dark swollen head, the scalp split in places, with the chopped-apart raggedness of torn fabric. Puffy eyes, purple lips, the whole skull crusted in darkened drying blood that looked sacrificial.

Only the extreme grief of the women conveyed to Hock that it was not a big stiff fetish doll—that it might be human. The wide helpless hands and feet, their familiar size, the way they lay in repose, told him the bloody thing was Zizi.

"How is she?" He was far too fearful to ask the blunter question, whether she was alive.

"She was beaten," Gala said. "And worse."

Wuss meant everything. And now he heard a groan—she was alive. She opened her eyes, saw Hock in the lantern light, and began as though hiccupping to cry.

Yet her tears made him hopeful. He sensed life in her explosive sobs, a kind of self-awareness, the sobs coming from deep within her, from a part of her that was not broken.

Hearing her cry, Snowdon, peeking at the doorway, began to chuckle, as if the tears from someone in worse shape than he was provoked him to mock.

"Get out!" Gala said, and spat at him, as the dwarf limped to the door and cowered, covering his mouth. She repeated the cry distractedly in Afrikaans, as older people in the Lower River sometimes did, perhaps for its force: "*Voetsak!*"

Zizi was alive, she was murmuring, she shifted on the mat for a better look at Hock. He frowned, thinking that she had never looked younger, more childlike, less sexual; that an injured body aroused no desire in him, inspired only the wish to protect, and an acute fear for its appearing so vulnerable. She had cuts on her hands, and there was blood on the covering cloth and the old towel; the sheet was dotted with blood spatter. The woman who had been bathing her face began to dab her cuts with gentian violet. They wiped it on all the wounds, painting her purple.

"They found her near the boma, two women who are known

to me," Gala said. "They were form-two students here. Thanks be to God, they rescued her."

"How did they bring her here?"

"They didn't have a lift all the way. They were dropped by one of the fish trucks on the road, and they walked, just footing the rest. That is why she is so tired."

This talk reassured Hock. He had not had to ask the dreadful question of whether she would live. She was badly injured, but he gathered from what Gala said that she would make it. And in the short time he'd been in the room, Hock could see that she'd begun to stir.

"Tell me what happened," Hock said.

"Don't trouble her," Gala said in a whisper. "She is hurt. She is weak. And she is ashamed."

It was apparent that she'd been attacked—she looked as though she'd fought off an animal. *She is hutt.* Baboons disturbed in the night would bare their doggy teeth, and bite and scratch. Hyenas were nocturnal and would attack a solitary person if they had the advantage. Worst of all—in the Lower River, anyway—were the packs of wild dogs, which snarled, circled their prey, and closed in, snapping their jaws.

But if it was any of these animals, none of the women said so; and he'd had the suspicion since entering the hut and hearing their sorrowing that it was a peculiar attack that went beyond a beating. They were grieving for her pain, and for something that had been lost: she had been violated.

She is ashamed meant only one thing. Zizi owned nothing, not even shoes, had no money, no ornament; not even the cooking pots were hers. She was a stick figure with no spare flesh, wrapped in a faded purple cloth. But she was a *namwali;* she had the glory of her virginity. She was known in the village for her aloofness, and it was this, in the beginning, that made her a prize for Hock—Manyenga's prize. Her wholeness gave her power, made her desirable, and was perhaps a devious test for Hock. He knew this, which was why he had resisted, for in resisting he had proven himself stronger than them.

Besides, he knew that in her eyes he was hardly human, an old beaky *mzungu* in flapping trousers and a torn shirt. He would see himself with her eyes and be disgusted. All he could offer her was his protection. And he had made a point of keeping her safe, until three days ago, when out of desperation he'd floated the idea of mailing the letter at the boma at night. She'd been afraid, knowing it was the only thing he wanted, yet she'd set off alone. And now she was back from the boma, lying in her own blood. Bloodstains were stiffened in places on her cloth in dark, disc-like patches.

She seemed to rally a little since he'd arrived. She was inert, yet she followed him with her weepy reddened eyes.

"I think she'll be all right," Hock said to Gala, looking for reassurance.

"With God's help," she said, which left the question unanswered.

Hock crouched, about to kneel, when Gala tapped his shoulder, cautioning him, and she turned, making a downward gesture of her hand, paddling the air, urging him away.

The dwarf limped from the door, seeing Gala beckoning Hock onto the veranda. Zizi became fierce, her face set in anger, her lower jaw protruding. He had never seen this expression. She was indignant, refusing to die, clearly insulted — the abuse was apparent in the welts and scratches on her body — but something else showed through: the strength of her anger. She was trying to speak to Hock through her bruised lips.

She muttered a word Hock could not understand.

"Come away, Ellis," Gala said, tugging his shoulder.

Turning from Zizi's pleading, Hock followed Gala to the veranda. In the distance, at the edge of the slant of light thrown by the lantern at the open window, Snowdon knelt, scratching the scabs on his arm and murmuring — Hock guessed — "Fee-dee-dom."

Hock said, "What do you know?"

"Only what the women told me who found her and fetched her here. They knew her. Why are you surprised?"

"Because the boma is so far from Malabo."

"She is *namwali*. She is known. Girls suitable for marriage are well known in the district. I was her guardian until Manyenga took her for you."

"You didn't mind?"

"I knew you would look after her. An elder person is a swamp that stops a fire. But she wandered off."

"You mean to the boma?"

"Yes. And at night. On a bicycle."

Hock wondered whether he should tell Gala the reason for Zizi's journey. He was about to speak when Gala resumed.

"The women could not recognize her at first, her face was so bloody. Her *chitenje* cloth was torn."

Hock said, "Was Zizi going toward the boma or traveling away from it?"

"What difference does it make?" she said.

Then he knew he couldn't tell her about the letter, because it seemed so petty, worrying about a letter when Zizi was lying injured inside the smoky hut. But the question was crucial. If the attack had occurred on her way to the boma, it meant she hadn't mailed the letter, and he would be stalled again, and have to face the brothers.

"It was a blessing that the women were there."

He said, "Why were they there at night?"

"Because of the hunger. You know the harvest will be poor?"

That and the lack of rain were the most common complaints of the villagers who had come to him for money, so common he'd begun to think of it as an excuse, perhaps a lie, because Manyenga always had food.

"There is little rice. There is no millet. Not much flour. We are eating cassava most of the time," Gala said. "The Agency vehicle is making deliveries of bags of flour and rice and beans, taking them to the boma. The women wanted to be early—first in the queue for free rice."

"But it's not safe for them either."

"They are women with small children. They are safe. They have nothing—no money, no valuables."

"Zizi has nothing."

In a reproachful tone, the light flashing on her face, Gala said, "She has what all women want. She is a maiden. She *was* a maiden. Now she is bleeding, because it was taken from her."

Hock said, "That's terrible."

"You don't understand. You are innocent. You don't know anything." The words were contemptuous, but Gala's tone was rueful, softened by her fatalism.

"What don't I know?"

"That such girls are taken by sick men. Men with the AIDS" —she said eddsi. "They take the girls if they can find them. They also take small children."

Hock said, "I've heard of this."

"They believe that sex with a virgin is a cure."

He was too shocked to speak. He groaned, wishing he hadn't heard.

"That is why Zizi was taken—sure."

"She must have fought hard," he said helplessly.

"So hard," Gala said. "They had to beat her, to subdue her, and then they just"—she whipped her hand, the fatalistic village gesture, snapping her fingers. "It's a shame."

"Tell me she'll recover, please."

"With God's help. No bones are broken, but you know what happens with wounds and bruises. They go septic so fast. We must prevent it."

Then Hock remembered. "You said the women were going to the boma to get food from the Agency vehicle?"

"Yes."

"Did they get the food?"

"They found Zizi. They never saw the vehicle."

"Maybe it came and didn't drop the food," he said.

"Why do you say that?" Gala frowned at him. "It makes no sense. The job of the Agency vehicle is to deliver the food."

"I don't know," Hock said. "I think I should go, but I want to say goodbye to Zizi."

"She may be sleeping."

But she was awake, her eyes half closed, her jaw set in the same determined way, as though enduring pain, struggling to stay alive. All her cuts had been painted with the gentian violet, and the patches of purple made her seem like a broken doll.

Putting his face close to hers, Hock said, "Zizi, can you hear me?"

She did not speak, yet she made a characteristic tightening of her face, a slight eyebrow flash, lifting them in recognition.

"Who was it?"

She groaned, her lips were dry and cracked, she could not form a word, though she showed her teeth, beautiful teeth, flecked with blood.

"Was it Aubrey?"

She winced as if pierced with a knife blade.

Hock considered this, and he wondered whether his whisper had been heard by Gala or either of the women, who'd kept their distance, to give him some privacy.

"The letter," Hock said, and let this word, *kalata,* sink in. "What happened?" When she did not react, he said, "Did you post it?"

He waited, but she only rolled her head from side to side, snared by pain, and it seemed she was saying *No* or *I don't know.*

Shortly afterward, when he left, Snowdon led him back through the darkness of the bush, chattering the whole way, perhaps feeling frisky after seeing the broken girl and the blood.

30

THE HEAT OF the Lower River, trapped beneath the white sky, penetrated the dust with the steam of its stillness, driving away all energy, sapping the strength of the people, withering the leaves that dangled limp on the low thorn bush. Malabo had never seemed flatter, quieter, more colorless, the heat baking it to a monochrome, like an old sun-faded photograph of itself.

Or was it their hunger that kept the people idle? Since the news that the upcoming harvest would be meager, Hock had noticed a perceptible slackening, a greater silence. He'd become used to shouts, yelps, the loud teasing of children, the singsong of scolding women. Now there were only murmurs. Something in the screech of the cicadas, like the scrape of a knife being sharpened on a wheel, or the burr and crackle of winged beetles, made the heat seem more intense. In the blinding muted daylight and humid air, in the village of mud huts that were crumbled like stale cake, he heard despair in the whispers, and the small children had stopped running.

He visited Zizi again, tramping through the tangle of bush at midday so he could gather snakes on the way. He plucked one from a swale of drifted sand, another from near a termite mound that rose like a cracked minaret of red dirt. And when he arrived at Gala's, calling "*Odi, odi,*" she looked out from her veranda and saw two weighty flour sacks.

"What have you brought?" she asked, in the expectation of food.

He held the sacks up and swung them. She knew, she laughed, she said, "Snake Man Ellis."

"Some people eat them."

"But the Bible does forbid. Creatures that crawl on the belly are abominable and unclean. It is the law."

"I agree," he said. He knotted the tops of the sacks and slung them in the shade under the veranda. "How's Zizi?"

"A little better."

Zizi lay just inside the hut, propped against a pillow but still on the mat. Flat on the floor, she looked more like a casualty. She raised her hands to her bruised face when she saw him, as though in shame. "*Pepani*," she said. Sorry.

He said, "Don't worry," and sighed at the futility of his words as soon as he spoke them—worse than futility, they represented helpless anxiety.

Behind him, holding a pitcher, Gala said, "I can't offer you anything. Water only. Or tea."

"What are you eating?" He took the plastic tumbler of water. The water was cloudy. He touched the tumbler to his lips but didn't drink.

"Cassava alone. The rice is finished." Gala arranged a bead-fringed doily over the top of the pitcher. "I would like to make scones for you. We have some dried fish. Some few bananas. *Naartjies* too. It is the situation."

Hock lingered, and then went outside and leaned over the rail to look at the flour sacks quivering under the veranda, the squirming snakes inside. The sacks from Malabo were stamped with the shield logo and the words *L'Agence Anonyme*.

"I wish I had something to give you," Hock said when he reentered the hut.

"You have given Malabo everything you had," Gala said. "Your food has been eaten. Your money has been eaten. Your hope, too, all gone. We have eaten you."

That made him remember why he had come. He knelt before Zizi and whispered, "The letter—did you post it?"

Her hands had slipped from her face as she'd watched him talk with Gala, but now with her fingers splayed, she covered her face again and began to cry.

And Hock thought: Why am I even asking? I don't deserve for the letter to have been mailed. I'm responsible for this skinny bruised girl lying here, her cracked lips, her swollen eyes, the scales of dried blood peeling on her ears, and a much worse wound I can't see that will never heal.

When he turned to go, gathering the sacks of snakes from the shade, Gala said, "Snake Man," and nodded. "Behold, I send you forth as sheep in the midst of wolves. Be ye therefore wise as a serpent." He leaned to kiss her, but she hissed into his ear, "The people are hungry. They will do anything."

He wanted to say: Until I saw Zizi, I doubted that. Now I am prepared to believe anything.

But Zizi was better than yesterday, so he was hopeful for tomorrow. Still, given that he had sent her to the boma, he felt he did not deserve to be rescued.

"We are in God's hands," Gala said.

That was like surrender. Any mention of God filled him with despair.

Manyenga was waiting for him at his hut when he returned from Gala's. Odd, the big man standing in the heat, because he seldom left his compound these days. He was someone who had plenty of food, and he guarded it.

"I hope you have something delicious in your gunny sacks," Manyenga said.

"We shall see," Hock said.

"I like the way you say that. Not yes, not no. Like a wise man."

"That's me, Festus."

Manyenga said, "I have arranged a ceremony."

"What ceremony?"

"To make you our chief."

"But I'm already your chief," Hock said in a weary voice, slinging the sacks onto his veranda.

"Of course, but we must have a proper ceremony, with dancers and drummers and music. That old blind man Wellington can play the *mbira* with his fingers. And then the voyage in a canoe. The float on the river."

"And what would be the point of that?" Hock said, playing along. "You are my people."

Manyenga laughed, then just as quickly scowled and became serious. "Yes. You belong to us."

Until Manyenga had said that, Hock had been thinking, Everything this man says is a lie. The remark about "a wise man," the references to the chief, the business about the "proper ceremony"—all lies. And that had been the case since the day he'd arrived. He had forgotten again the length of time he'd been in Malabo—three months now? But it was a guess. Maybe more. He knew the date of his arrival; it was stamped in his passport. But he did not know today's date. No one in Malabo knew it. He was like them in this respect. He'd arrived after the planting, the rains had failed, the maize stalks were tiny, crowded by weeds, the pumpkin vines were withered and whitened with rot. Those were visible facts. The harvest would be poor. Everything else was a lie, every word he'd been told by Manyenga, most of what the others had said. Gala told the truth, but her only message, from the moment he'd seen her, had been: Get out, go home, save yourself.

The way that Manyenga had said, "You belong to us," not with respect but with a growl of menace, reminded Hock that it was the one truth in a world of lies. They had always felt that Hock had been delivered, and his money had been taken. But much more serious than his money, his hope had been stripped from him.

"Festus, I've given you everything I have," he said.

"Not everything. You are still our big man."

"That's me," Hock said, and now, overcome with fatigue, he had to sit. He dropped to the edge of the veranda, near the sacks of snakes, and did not invite Manyenga to join him.

"You are our great chief and father."

"With no money."

"Even without money you are our father." Manyenga, as always, whined the word, making it *maahhnee*.

"I have nothing more to give you."

"But you have much," Manyenga said. "You are a strong man." More lies. "I'm weak. I'm sick."

"You are still so clever. You continue to plot, as a chief plots, whispering to this one and that one, and what and what."

And then Manyenga laughed horribly, showing his good teeth, whinnying, insincere, too loud.

"I'm helpless."

"You have your people. We are knowing."

"What people?" Hock was indignant, straining to shout.

"Us."

"You!"

"Yes, and the old woman. The little man with *mkate*. The girl."

Mkate he knew as leprosy. Snowdon? That was news—or perhaps another lie. He'd thought the dwarf's physical damage was from epilepsy, fits of falling down.

He said, "The girl Zizi was attacked."

"At the boma. At night." Manyenga spoke as though he was reciting the details of a crime she'd committed. "What was this young girl doing at the boma at night?"

"I have no idea," Hock said with a dry mouth.

"As our chief you should know," Manyenga said. "We believe she was sent there."

Hock stared at him. That was another aspect of the darkness—that Manyenga knew everything and still he lied, pretending not to know.

"She was raped," Hock said with all the snarling contempt he could muster.

Manyenga was not moved. "She went alone to the boma, through the bush at midnight." He looked around, saw the dwarf, turned away, and added, "Did she expect something different?"

"She didn't deserve to be raped."

"But why did she go, my friend?" Manyenga said. "Maybe we will never know!" In a different, sterner voice he said, "The ceremony will be tomorrow."

When Manyenga walked off, kicking across the clearing, Hock saw the brothers step from behind the great baobab stump and join him, heads down, conferring.

He knows everything, Hock thought. He has the letter. That was why Zizi was in despair; she believed she had failed him.

And so, in the time remaining before the ceremony the next day, Hock passed the hours in the only way he knew how. He paced the village, and the perimeter of the village, and the banks of the creek where the women were slapping their laundry on the smooth boulders. He carried a flour sack and his forked stick, and he gathered snakes. He found a puff adder sunning itself near the mango tree, a twig snake near the latrine, a nest of yellow-eyed snakes in the leaf trash of a decaying log; he found some more marsh vipers at the creek's edge. They were weapons, they were friends, they were the only creatures in Malabo that had been neutral to him. He had destroyed Zizi, he had disappointed Gala. He had no other friends.

Like the shipwrecked sailor who befriends a vagrant bird with a broken wing, he sought the only creatures he knew would respond to his sympathy. He had nothing else. So they would not fight or eat each other, he separated the snakes into eight sacks.

When he looked for his knife to cut more flour sacks to sew into smaller bags, he saw it was missing. It was a cheap knife he'd bought as an afterthought, with boxes of food, from the market in Blantyre, but it had a sharp serrated blade. At the base of the blade, near the hilt, was a cutout for lifting bottle caps. In his time in Malabo he had not used the bottle opener. The few bottles of soda he'd drunk had been opened by Zizi, grimacing, with her side teeth. There had been no store-bought beer, only the plastic cups of home brew that was like sour porridge. Now the knife was gone and he felt defenseless and incompetent. It was bad that he had no knife; it was worse for him that someone else had it.

He slept badly; he was too hot, too hungry, to sleep well. He lay perspiring on his string bed, the mosquito net confining him, deadening the air.

He suffered the heat; it was something he'd never become accustomed to. He was hotter now than ever, more uncomfortable, because he was dirty and he felt ill, and his weakness made the heat harder to bear. The weight of it against his slimy skin made it no different from a fever.

The drumming pattered in his dream, and then seemed to wake him. He didn't know whether he was still dreaming. He heard dogs barking, the hoarse helpless yapping of village mutts.

Then voices outside told him some people were near, and they tramped on the planks of his veranda, many feet, dry footsoles on splintered boards, and his door rattled and was yanked open, the iron bolt torn off the jamb.

311

He smelled them before he saw them. This is it, he thought. Manyenga's "tomorrow" had meant the dark early morning. Moving figures stirred like upright shadows in his hut, muttering to each other, seeming not to know what to do next. He believed they were intimidated to be in the *mzungu*'s hut. They behaved strangely, unsure in their movements, tentative in their whispers.

"What do you want?"

"You, father."

Hock lifted the ragged mosquito net as though peering from a tent. He recognized two of Manyenga's sons, Yatuta and Aleke, and one of the brothers from the village of children, the one with the baseball cap. Without the other brothers this boy looked very young. The only light was that of a flashlight one of the sons was carrying, whisking the beam around the room, showing Hock how ramshackle the place looked. The beam lingered on the flour sacks that bulged on the floor, then swept across them.

"Why do you want me?"

"For the big dance."

He'd said *gule wamkulu.* Hock knew the dance was secret and strange, not to be observed by an outsider.

It was pointless to ask any more questions. Too weak to resist, Hock swung his legs over and sighed and got up from his creaky bed. He felt the way a condemned man does, rising wearily on death row in the middle of the night to be executed.

One of the smaller boys, Aleke led the way across the clearing to Manyenga's compound. The other two walked on either side of him, as if escorting him, and Hock scuffed along in rubber flip-flops, limping, falling forward.

Manyenga was waiting at the edge of the firelight, near where two drummers thumped and pounded.

"Welcome, chief."

Hock was about to speak, but the walk—the boys moving quickly—had tired him, and he was breathless. He put his hands to his hips and bent over to catch his breath. He was hot, un-shaven, hungry, his gray hair wild. His shirt was dirty—he was out of fresh laundry—his trousers torn, his feet grimy in his flip-flops.

"Chief, please sit. Here is your chair."

The chair had been set up away from the heat of the fire but within the orbit of its light.

One of the brothers approached Manyenga, and Hock noticed that he was carrying a length of coiled rope, cheap yellow nylon braided like sisal.

"No," Manyenga said, waving him away.

But the boy looked anxious, gesturing as though he intended to tie Hock's hands.

Hock said, "What does he want?"

"He is thinking it is necessary to bind your wrists. But I tell him it is not necessary."

"What are you doing to me?"

"We are promoting you," Manyenga said.

"They're taking me." Hock's throat constricted, full of fear, and he gagged again as he said, "This is an abduction. Why are you letting them? You warned me about them. You told me they were dangerous."

"I never said those words." Manyenga's smug bureaucratic smile was one that Hock had seen before. He had assumed this smile whenever he rebuffed him; it would float across his lips, not always a smile, sometimes a sneer of pure contempt. He wore it now, as he said, "They are removing you, with our permission."

"You can't do that."

"We must. We have nothing in the pipeline."

His throat burning, Hock said, "What about my permission?"

"It is not necessary. You belong to us," Manyenga said with the same smile, and he looked upon Hock as a kind of prize, according him the trophy status they reserved for the larger animals whose flesh they ate, whose skins they used as prestige objects. "You are ours. Our great chief."

31

THE TATTERED FLAMES from the stack of snapping branches of their ritual fire lit Manyenga's pitiless smile and reddened his eyes. He was the only muscular man in the village, and his potbelly, and the way he stood, in an assertive pose, made him seem overbearing. He was shorter than Hock, but solid. His shirt, a familiar print, was clean, and his trousers had a crease. His sandals were sturdy, and a good watch slipped on its too large band on his wrist. It was Hock's own watch. Hock recognized the sandals as his, the shirt and trousers, too, and like the watch, these clothes had disappeared from his hut a month or more ago. Until now, he hadn't seen Manyenga wearing the stolen things. By stripping him of his symbols and his wealth, Manyenga had begun to inhabit him.

"Now we must say bye-bye," Manyenga said. "It is so sad for us, father."

Manyenga clapped his hands, summoning the dancers, six or seven skinny girls, and some boys whose faces had been smeared with flour, making them ghostly—they stared from their white faces with dark eyes. A man appeared in a torn jacket, wearing a hawk-nosed helmet mask; shredded reed fibers were bound to his legs and arms, like a scarecrow. He walked stiff-legged and carried a fly whisk. He seemed a more forbidding figure for being so ridiculously dressed, like a dangerous lunatic with nothing to lose. Perhaps he was intended to be costumed as a white man.

The dance, the stamping, the pluckings of the *mbira,* meant nothing to Hock. In the years he'd spent in Malabo, and these months of his captivity, he had not been able to make sense of any of the nighttime dance ceremonies or songs. In his time, all the festivals had been Christian, with Bible readings and sermons. The church had vanished as completely as the school. Yet the secret memory of their drumming and dancing was known to the participants, if not the spectators. Or maybe there was no deeper meaning beyond the syncopation, as in the *Likuba,* like a conga line, the moving bodies in the firelight, the yodeling, the jumping shadows.

Hock sat like a condemned man, awaiting the moment of death, helpless, stunned by the assault of the drumming, the chaotic dancing, the puppet-like jigging of the skinny girls, the yelps of the white-faced boys, and the bawling of the villagers. It pained him to be closely watched by the three brothers, who were seated on the ground, and by Manyenga, smiling, delighted by the drumming and dancing.

"Ah, the vehicle!" Manyenga cried out as the cones of headlights swung into the clearing, the beams lighting the stony ground and the sloppily whitewashed boulders that marked the perimeter of the chief's compound.

The brothers rose and approached the vehicle—a white van that had crushed through the low bushes—and conferred with the driver. Hock could tell by the logo and the name *L'Agence Anonyme* that it was the same van that Aubrey had driven him in his failed escape.

"Back up, turn around," Manyenga called out, first in English and then in Sena, giving explicit commands. And hearing the efficiency of the orders, Hock remembered how Manyenga had told him he'd been a driver for the Agency.

With the arrival of the van, the dancers had ceased their stamping and clapping. The drum rhythms slowed to a scraping patter on the drumheads as the van backed up, jerked forward, then turned and repeated this until the rear of the vehicle was facing the circle of spectators. Pleased with himself, his face gleaming in the firelight, Manyenga marched over and slapped the rear door of the van. "Open!" he called. He yanked the handle, pounded the doors again, and then, frustrated, he roared and the drum patter stopped.

Now a small figure rounded the van from the driver's side. He poked a key into a slot in the door handle, as Manyenga hovered, and swung the doors open.

The dancers and spectators rushed forward and crowded the van, to marvel at the sacks of flour and rice, the cartons of milk powder, the stacked crates with labels that identified them as beans, marmalade, ketchup, salt, baby food, syrup, corned beef, chicken parts, creamed corn, pickles, and more. Some of the boxes were stenciled, others had colorful labels. Hock's first thought was how clean the cardboard was, how well stacked the boxes, the order of them, absurdly framed by the dusty compound and scattered firewood, the hungry people gloating over the load like the jubilant, rewarded faces of a cargo cult.

It was more than food: it represented influence far beyond the village. It was wealth. This penetration of the outer world was something like belief, a concentration of visible power. Small children jumped up and down at the sight of it, others pushed for a better look, and there was a howl of hunger in the laughter.

"We will now unload," Manyenga said, and he directed some of the bigger boys to begin stacking the crates against the wall of his hut.

All the attention was directed at the van, the food, the process of unloading, the interior of the van growing emptier, larger, as the crates and boxes were removed. The very size of the boxes excited interest. *Kitchen Magic Toaster Oven* on one box and *Electro-Mop* on another; but since Malabo had no electricity, these items were no more than random loot.

Hock had turned away and was looking at the one person who seemed indifferent to the spectacle of unloading. It was the driver, that small skinny person who had unlocked the rear doors of the van—Aubrey.

Hock stared at him. Aubrey's face was scratched, welts had been raised on his cheeks in places, and he wore a white bandage on his neck. His arms had been raked, too, and one of his wrists was wrapped in a thickness of gauze. Alerted by Hock's staring,

Aubrey jerked his head away. He blinked, shifted his posture, and touched his face. Then he stepped back, as though cowering.

"You!" Hock called out, and in the confusion of unloading no one heard him, or rather, only Aubrey heard. The shout was enough to make him hesitate.

Hock rose from his chair and took three long strides to where Aubrey was standing. As soon as he had gotten out of the chair he'd felt the strain of the effort, and the thought came to him: I am weak.

Pure fury had carried him forward, and when he reached Aubrey he did not hesitate. He swung and slapped his face with such force the young man lost his balance and fell against the legs of some women who were celebrating the arrival of the food. Aubrey tried to regain his footing, but while he was on his knees, Hock hit him again, slapping him with his sore hand, and Aubrey slumped to the ground. He crouched, whimpering, making himself small.

All Hock's anger, months of frustration, stiffened the muscles in his arm and gave strength to that slap, delivered so hard his hand stung. He hoped that such a slap might flay the skin from the young man's face. Hock stood over him, to assess the pain he'd inflicted, as Aubrey crawled on all fours, away from the firelight and into the shadows near one of Manyenga's huts.

The children who'd been so excited by the sight of the food were distracted by the sudden fight, and they grouped around the groveling Aubrey, kicking out at him, while the women mocked. The attention shifted from the van to the sight of Hock following Aubrey, the screeching children urging Hock to slap him again, crying, "Fight! Fight!"

That was when Manyenga stepped in. He placed himself between Hock and Aubrey. He shouted for silence, he roared again, and when the crowd became quieter he began a speech in English—Hock realized it was for him to hear—and that it was so loud and so pompous, in a language that most did not understand, assured Manyenga of their close attention. Holding his mouth open when he spoke, he affected a gagging British accent.

"This is an auspicious night," Manyenga said. "Never mind that our chief is angry. He has brought us good luck. He was here long ago and he returned to find us wanting and poor. So he did his level best to give us help—"

Hock turned his back on him. He could not bear listening. He walked a little distance and saw that the van was empty now. All the boxes had been piled near one of Manyenga's huts, and a blue plastic tarpaulin was being fitted over the pile and fastened to keep the dust off. Manyenga was taking possession of it all.

"—the *mzungu* is our dear father. Without him we would be lost. We are therefore offering him a promotion."

As he spoke, standing near the fire so that he could be seen, glorying in the uprush of sparks from the flames, Manyenga commanded the attention of the entire crowd. Only Hock was not watching, and hardly listening. He saw a small hunched-over figure bobbing in the shadows behind the van, so small he was hardly visible.

"This is our ceremony of farewell," Manyenga said. "You, find the driver. Make him ready," he added, shoving one of the brothers. "He must stand up. He cannot be intimidated by a little slap in the face. It is time to say goodbye."

The small bobbing figure—was it Snowdon?—moved around the van, efficiently, close to the ground, and then was gone, and when Hock looked again he saw Aubrey emerge from the crowd covered in dust, one side of his face swollen. Hock stepped forward, intending to hit him again. But his arm was snatched and held, his other arm gripped. He was restrained so tightly he couldn't move.

"Shut him in the van," Manyenga said to the two boys holding Hock.

"Festus, wait," Hock said, struggling.

"But we must," Manyenga said.

"You're selling me—I know you're selling me," Hock said. "Why are you doing this?"

In his affected British accent that was like gargling, Manyenga said, "We are doing so because we are hungry."

"And what will they do with me?"

"Those boys will tend to you," Manyenga said. "And one day you will be released to your people."

"I want to be released now." Hock heard the gulp of a whimper in his own voice.

At this, perhaps maddened by the whimper, Manyenga screamed and lost his British accent. "You *mzungu* can go anywhere! You people can do what you like. You are free to just come and go because you have maahhnee! This is a little holiday for you, but this is our whole life, as we are condemned to live on the Lower River forever!"

Hock said simply, "I've given you all my money."

"Because you hate us and demand us to stay here," Manyenga raged, bug-eyed, obstinate in his evasive temper. "You insult us with food, you throw it to us like animals. We are not your monkeys now. Take him away!"

"Help me," Hock said to the women standing near him.

Manyenga laughed, and with a bleak fanatical stare he put his sweaty face against Hock's. "They will do nothing for you. If my people do not obey me, their paramount chief, it will mean a lifelong infamy for them."

Seeing Manyenga's defiance, the women began to jeer at Hock, and the children took up the cry. Hock remembered his fever, the time he'd fallen in the clearing, severely dehydrated. Then, the women had laughed so hard that Snowdon was emboldened to kick him in the face, occasioning more laughter. And oddly, with that memory present in his mind, Hock believed he saw Snowdon hurrying into the darkness with his lopsided gait—the way you might be thinking of a person for no reason and then, coincidentally, the next moment you see him walking down the street.

As he was led to the van—again he felt like a condemned man—Hock heard cursing, a deep serious denunciation, its helpless abuse in great contrast to the hilarity and the speeches and the children's laughter. He heard Manyenga conferring, and Manyenga's consternation.

"You are a devil," Manyenga said, drawing his lips back from his big teeth.

Hock was too weary to react, but if he'd been able to summon the strength, he would have jeered at Manyenga as the villagers had jeered at him.

"Someone has slashed the tires," Manyenga said with venom. "One of your people. It was done with your knife. We have no knife sharp enough."

The cheap knife from Blantyre, with the serrated edge, had been stolen from his hut. Had it been Snowdon, whom he'd almost certainly just seen in the shadows near the van? And now, though it was an effort—he wanted them to know how he felt—Hock did laugh.

"This is bloody stupid," Manyenga said. In his anger, he lost all his guile.

So the ceremony of farewell ended as many of the ceremonies in Malabo ended, in confusion and disorder, and with an air of exhaustion, around a dying fire of black skeletal embers.

As the disappointed villagers vanished into the darkness, Hock returned to his hut. He wasn't saved—he knew that—but he was reprieved for the night. He was being watched: the brothers glared at him as he left. He went to bed and, wearied by fear, slept soundly.

In the morning, nothing had changed. The village was no different from the first morning of his visit months ago—hot, passive, with the burned-toast smell of wood smoke, the thick damp air under the white sky, the sight of scarred mopane trees and dusty leaves and the perimeter of elephant grass, and a sepulchral suggestion of decay from the latrine. Malabo had felt like this forty years before. It was why he had come back. It was why he now waited, hopelessly, to leave. But he had been sold to the brothers. He would probably be transported to the village of children on the riverbank and confined until he was ransomed. He became aware, with alarm, that the only sound he heard was the gasp and catch of his own breathing.

The white Agency van was still parked at the edge of Manyenga's compound, on flat tires. Another day of heat and hunger, another day of his thinking, This is my life now. He knew he was living like a sick man. But nearly everyone in Malabo lived that way, either sitting or lying down, and the tone of every remark, even the lies and the sour hopes, was part of the sickness.

He smiled at the thought that the long Agency van looked like an ambulance or a hearse.

A number of villagers—the women who would have been hoeing the gardens, the men who usually lolled under the mango tree, and many children—gathered at his hut, knowing that he was soon to be taken away. In the foreground, Snowdon squatted, gnawing the fingers of one hand with a befuddled smile, his fool's license. In the other hand he held the knife with the serrated blade.

Standing in his doorway, Hock held up two of the bulging sacks that he'd removed from the veranda to the shadows under his bed. He shook them to prove that they had weight.

"Tell Festus Manyenga that I still have money and food in these sacks in my hut. And there are more," he said. "After I'm gone, he can have them. You can all have them."

He had spoken in Sena, so even the children understood, and some of them ran to inform their chief of this good news.

And when, in the middle of the hot morning, lying in his string bed, he heard an engine straining, he knew the van had been repaired, the tires patched and pumped up. He guessed that Aubrey—the rapist—was at the wheel of this van, which had been paid for by donations from sympathetic people all over the world. The van, emptied of its food, for which he had been traded, food that was now Manyenga's, would carry him away to be kept as a hostage.

The engine sounded querulous as the van maneuvered in the clearing, being put into position so he could be loaded into the cargo hold where the boxes had been. He was a reasonable swap for the food stolen from the Agency; he'd be held and haggled over and sold again. He was no more than a carcass, but he knew they'd have to feed him and keep him alive if they were to sell him. That gave him a flicker of comfort.

Yet in his heart he believed he would die. He had felt that for some time—that he'd returned to Africa to die. In his months in Malabo he'd had intimations of death; in an African village, death was ever present. He had lost the strength to object, and not even his anger could rouse him to resist.

But looking out through the patched screen of his hut window, expecting the van, he saw instead a sleek black Jeep. Accustomed to being subverted, he felt a greater despair at the sight of the newer, more powerful vehicle, probably another from the Agency. This one was a sinister intimidating size, with fat unslashable tires.

Just then, as he faced the Jeep, a quacking American voice was raised across the clearing, a disbelieving voice, harsh in its contradiction, saying, "But we know he's gotta be here somewhere!"

Repeating its complaint, the quacking carried all that distance, from near Manyenga's compound—stern, scolding, full of authority.

Hock stepped out of the hut for a better look, and saw, crossing the stony ground near the baobab stump, a pink-faced man in a shirt and tie. The man caught sight of Hock and walked faster. Then, all business, he turned and called out behind him to his driver.

"Bring up the car!" He wiped the perspiration from his face with a neatly folded white handkerchief. He was near enough to offer a handshake. "You must be Hock—almost didn't recognize you. Quite a letter. Where are your things?"

A kick of hope in his gut made Hock tearful. "I don't have any things."

"Take it easy, sir," the man said. Hock knew him from Blantyre but in his muddle could not think of his name. He was young, dependable, with a good shirt, a silk tie, a linen jacket. "You'll be all right."

Swallowing a sob, Hock said, "There's someone else coming with us."

In the small screen of the rearview mirror skinny arms and small faces were sucked into the distance, jumping children and staring men, pinched by the receding road and the shaken curtains of elephant grass. From the dark water glinting at the end of trampled paths he saw that he was leaving the river behind, surfacing after months of holding his breath.

Now he could breathe. The girl—no longer a girl—sat upright in the speeding Jeep. Even seated she was stately; even wounded, with blood crusts of damage on her face, she was radiant for seeming unafraid; innocent, too, gladdened by the strangeness, smiling at the turbulent grass in the slipstream. She'd never been up this road before. Strengthened by her smile, Hock felt purposeful with her beside him.

The dust rose behind the van, a brown rearing dust-snake. Each time he looked there was more dust, uncoiling in pursuit, but so like a dissolving mirage that he stopped looking back, and lifted his eyes from the mirror to the wider road ahead.

PAUL THEROUX

A DEAD HAND

Jerry Delfont is a travel writer with writer's block. When he receives a letter from an American philanthropist with news of a scandal involving an Indian friend of her son's, he is intrigued. Who is the dead boy found on the floor of a cheap hotel room? How did he die? And why?

As Delfont becomes more and more drawn into these mysteries, he simultaneously becomes increasingly entangled with the seductive philanthropist and her tantric massages. But she is also hiding something and it becomes swiftly apparent that all is not what it seems . . .

'Richly enjoyable, entertaining . . . a satisfyingly tense, almost thrillerish conclusion' *Financial Times*

'Theroux's prose is always a pleasure' *Tatler*

'Original and enlightening' *Daily Telegraph*

PAUL THEROUX

GHOST TRAIN TO THE EASTERN STAR

Thirty years ago Paul Theroux left London and travelled across Asia and back again by train. His account of the journey – *The Great Railway Bazaar* – was a landmark book and made his name as the foremost travel writer of his generation. Now Theroux makes the trip all over again through Eastern Europe, India and Asia to discover the changes that have swept the continents, and also to learn what an old man will make of a young man's journey. *Ghost Train to the Eastern Star* is a brilliant chronicle of change and an exploration of how travel is 'the saddest of pleasures'.

'Funny, informative, lyrical. Theroux is a fabulously good writer. The brilliance lies in his ability to create a broad sweep of many countries' *Guardian*

'A dazzler, giving us the highs and lows of his journey and tenderness and acerbic humour . . . fellow travelling weirdoes, amateur taxi drivers, bar-girls and long-suffering locals are brought vividly to life' *Spectator*

'Relaxed, curious, confident, surprisingly tender. Theroux's writing has an immediate, vivid and cursory quality that gives it a collective strength' *Sunday Times*

PAUL THEROUX

THE GREAT RAILWAY BAZAAR

'I have seldom heard a train go by and not wished I was on it.'

The Orient Express; The Khyber Pass Local; the Delhi Mail from Jaipur; the Golden Arrow of Kuala; the Trans-Siberian Express; these are just some of the trains steaming through Paul Theroux's epic rail journey from London across Europe through India and Asia. This was a trip of discovery made in the mid-seventies, a time before the West had embraced the places, peoples, food, faiths and cultures of the East. For us now, as much as for Theroux then, to visit the lands of *The Great Railway Bazaar* is an encounter with all that is truly foreign and exotic – and with what we have since lost.

'One of the most entertaining books I have read in a long while . . . Superb comic detail' **Angus Wilson**, *Observer*

'He has done our travelling for us brilliantly' **William Golding**

'In the fine old tradition of purposeless travel for fun and adventure' **Graham Greene**

PAUL THEROUX

THE TAO OF TRAVEL

Paul Theroux celebrates fifty years of wandering the globe by collecting the best writing on travel from the books that shaped him, as a reader and a traveller. Part philosophical guide, part miscellany, part reminiscence, *The Tao of Travel* enumerates 'The Contents of Some Travellers' Bags' and exposes 'Writers Who Wrote About Places They Never Visited'; tracks extreme journeys in 'Travel As An Ordeal' and highlights some of 'Travellers' Favourite Places'. Excerpts from the best of Theroux's own work are interspersed with selections from travellers both familiar and unexpected, including Vladimir Nabokov, Henry David Thoreau, Graham Greene, Ernest Hemingway and more.

The Tao of Travel is a unique tribute to the pleasures and pains of travel in its golden age.

'Dazzling . . . like someone panning for gold, Theroux reread hundreds of travel classics and modern works, shaking out the nuggets. A source of inspiration for prospective travelers and a guide to how, in Theroux's view, to travel properly' *San Francisco Chronicle*

'Pure entertainment' *Financial Times*

'One for the armchair traveller and the adventurer who has scaled K2 and swum the Bosphorus. Like a long train journey, once you settle in there's a lot to enjoy. Gripping' *The Times*

PAUL THEROUX

THE ELEPHANTA SUITE

The Elephanta Suite brilliantly explores the shifting stories of those who come to India in search of that elusive something – and of how they react when the country and people they encounter are altogether foreign to their expectations.

Through the eyes of a middle-aged couple, a sharp-suited lawyer and a gap-year traveller, we see illusions and preconceptions unravel, and an extraordinary new India – modern, complicated, uncertain of its coming future – appears before us.

'Theroux has a sharp eye . . . reworking the old colonial themes in light of the country's rapid but uneven development. Theroux hasn't lost any of his insight or power to enthral' *Sunday Telegraph*

'This is India with a human face' *Tatler*

'Beautifully paced, sexy and disturbing' *Washington Post*

'Theroux at his best' *India Today*

PAUL THEROUX

THE LAST TRAIN TO ZONA VERDE

Having travelled down the right-hand side of Africa in *Dark Star Safari*, Paul Theroux sets out this time from Cape Town, heading northwards in a new direction, up the left-hand side, through South Africa and Namibia, to Botswana, then on into Angola, heading for the Congo, in search of the end of the line. Journeying alone through the greenest continent in what he feels will be his last African journey, Theroux encounters a world increasingly removed from both the itineraries of tourists and the hopes of post-colonial independence movements. Leaving the Cape Town townships, traversing the Namibian bush, passing the browsing cattle of the great sunbaked heartland of the savannah, Theroux crosses 'the Red Line' into a different Africa: 'the improvised, slapped-together Africa of tumbled fences and cooking fires, of mud and thatch', of heat and poverty, and of roadblocks, mobs and anarchy.

A final African adventure from the writer whose gimlet eye and effortless prose have brought the world to generations of readers, *The Last Train to Zona Verde* is Paul Theroux's ultimate safari.

'His ability to map new terrain, both interior and exterior, and to report from places that seldom make the news, remains undiminished' *Booklist*

'The dean of travel writers . . . Theroux's prose is as vividly descriptive and atmospheric as ever' *Publishers Weekly*

He just wanted a decent book to read ...

Not too much to ask, is it? It was in 1935 when Allen Lane, Managing Director of Bodley Head Publishers, stood on a platform at Exeter railway station looking for something good to read on his journey back to London. His choice was limited to popular magazines and poor-quality paperbacks – the same choice faced every day by the vast majority of readers, few of whom could afford hardbacks. Lane's disappointment and subsequent anger at the range of books generally available led him to found a company – and change the world.

'We believed in the existence in this country of a vast reading public for intelligent books at a low price, and staked everything on it'
Sir Allen Lane, 1902–1970, founder of Penguin Books

The quality paperback had arrived – and not just in bookshops. Lane was adamant that his Penguins should appear in chain stores and tobacconists, and should cost no more than a packet of cigarettes.

Reading habits (and cigarette prices) have changed since 1935, but Penguin still believes in publishing the best books for everybody to enjoy. We still believe that good design costs no more than bad design, and we still believe that quality books published passionately and responsibly make the world a better place.

So wherever you see the little bird – whether it's on a piece of prize-winning literary fiction or a celebrity autobiography, political tour de force or historical masterpiece, a serial-killer thriller, reference book, world classic or a piece of pure escapism – you can bet that it represents the very best that the genre has to offer.

Whatever you like to read – trust Penguin.